I0770437

Scrooge's Christmas Carol
Releasing the Last Chain

Scrooge's Christmas Carol

Releasing the Last Chain

Written and Illustrated by C Pippin Lowe

Scrooge's Christmas Carol: Releasing the Last Chain
Copyright © 2025 by C Pippin Lowe
All rights reserved.
ISBN 979-8-9906592-4-7

No part of this book may be reproduced in any form without the expressed written consent of the writer, except by a reviewer, who may quote brief passages in connection with a review.

Contact Pippin at: apurto@myyahoo.com **In order to get a reply back the subject line must contain the word Apurto within it. Emails that have an attachment will be deleted rather than opened. I answer emails in accordance to the importance of the communication that was sent, and my availability of time. However, I will try my best to respond.**

Acknowledgements

The first people I want to thank for helping me are the editors Mary Fiala, Susanna Brinnon, Nicole DeVincentis and Laura Wilkinson. The story consultants were also invaluable to the creation of many of the concepts within the plot. These people are Arleen Pippin, Beverly Toll, Chava Schacter, Jenny Acosta and Liz Love. The illustration consultant was Mary Fiala. I also want to give a special thanks to both Su Raymond and my brother Jim.

It has to be noted how important the Internet was to this entire project. Having never been to England, I relied on facts that were researched through dozens of websites. The components for the illustrations were created through the Leonardo and Midjourney websites. Once the various elements of an event were generated, they were then pieced together in Photoshop to create the scene. AI art is a trailblazing tool, but without direct knowledge of what London looks like, I suspect Midjourney's vision of London is faulty. Plus, the idea that AI art should create consistent clothing… well maybe in the next software upgrade.

And finally, I want to recognize the three people who have inspired me to write. When I was in 4th grade, my brother Lawson read a story he had written about a lion to me, and I went through an immediate paradigm shift of understanding. His tale showed me that if he could write stories, so could I. That is the moment I put the task of writing fiction on my 'bucket list'.

The second person was my high school English composition teacher, Mrs. Meyer. I was blessed to have her all three of my high school years. Because she had put herself through college by writing and publishing romance stories, I inhaled her lessons, which created the foundation for my writing.

The credit for those who inspired me would not be complete without wholeheartedly thanking Charles Dickens for creating the best holiday story ever written. I asked the Gemini bot why Dickens used musical terms for his title (A Christmas Carol) and chapters (Stave). Dickens believed that using musical terms brought a whimsical merriment to the story. Considering most of his other writings were closer to melodrama than whimsy, I figured Gemini gave me the correct answer. With that said, I must let you know that there is little that is whimsical about Scrooge's Christmas Carol: Releasing the Last Chain. This book is closer to Dickens's other writings with more drama than laughter. Although there are still a few giggles within the story.

C Pippin Lowe

Table of Contents

Overture

In this introduction, I will clarify the final pages of the book. The first half of the book takes place in both 1854 and 1813 in London, England. This section was researched through various websites, like the British Historic Newgate Prison site. So even though I read over 4,000 web pages to create this half of the book, it was still easier to research than was the afterlife.

The glossary and white paper are invaluable for the clarification of concepts. All words within the glossary are capitalized within the story. This is because each of these terms has been repurposed into a new idea. The List of Main Characters is presented in the order they appear within the book. These two extra documents are somewhat normal within books, but that cannot be said for the Isle of Transmogrify White Paper.

The Isle of Transmogrify White Paper was written for my benefit, to aid me in writing the story. In the past, I have written various articles about science, health, and politics, but have never before written a non-fiction fiction document. I didn't even know that was a thing until I needed it to provide the foundation for the afterlife.

I researched the concepts within the white paper more intensely than those of the Victorian London scenes. I read about every culture and religion's ideas about death and the afterlife. Every idea within this story was a concept I learned about through research. What I did was just fictionalize this knowledge. Also, FYI, anybody that thinks they know what death will bring to "you," is only blowing smoke up their… and trying to get you to inhale the flatulence. *Scrooge's Christmas Carol: Releasing the Last Chain* is only a story. No more, no less.

The book itself stands as a story and does not require the white paper for understanding. However, the plot is out of the ordinary, and I sense the reader may find it valuable to read the white paper before the afterlife section of the story. Just a suggestion.

C Pippin Lowe

Stave One
Marley Returns

SCROOGE STUMBLED FORWARD. Despite his frantic blinking, he still could not see past the darkness. Instinctively searching for support, he thrust his hands outward, but the uneven pathway caught his shoe and dropped him flat. The scorching heat from the floor burned him. Wailing, he scrambled upright.

With sight denied, and touch being dangerous, only smell aided his perceptions. As he inched ahead, the musty stench of sulfur assailed his nostrils.

With each breath in, the odor forced tears out. Through the blur of his tears he detected a faint orange glow beginning to flicker above. With every step forward the brightness intensified.

The cavity, though huge in appearance, seemed absent of walls. Looking up, Scrooge viewed thousands of stalactites, each with a blazing orange tip. The sight created a magnificent spectacle. As he beheld the ceiling's wonder, Scrooge's forward motion stopped, which ceased the illumination. Standing still within the darkness, every movement he made brought the room back into a dim glow. Each step thereafter brightened the stalactites' flame. The color, first a cool orange, quickly changed to red. With each step, all of the appendages grew in heat until the ceiling flamed blue. The radiance brought a sweat to Scrooge's forehead. And then, the entire ceiling erupted into a blinding white inferno.

Within seconds, a massive blaze of spikes lit the cavern so brightly Scrooge's vision was washed away. Scrooge stopped moving, yet it was too late to halt the blaze. As his eyes tried to adjust, he began to identify shapes without details. Where a dirt floor should have been, a sea of fused coins coated the surface of the ground.

Scrooge looked up when a sudden cracking sound echoed throughout the cavern. Each stalactite seemed to be under attack by its own fieriness. The pulsating appendages moved in and out with such a force they appeared to be breathing. Before he could ponder this, white molten coins began to rain down on Scrooge. Upon contact, they changed from coins into chains. The restraints moved like a constrictor wrapping itself around its prey. Scrooge struggled as the squeeze from the bondage took control.

Howling with fright, Scrooge's screams vocalized outside of his dream. He sprang straight up before collapsing back to the mattress. Shivering with anxiety, he moaned under his breath, "Transmogrify". For a while the dream lingered

leaving Scrooge with a foreboding dread until, with time, his thoughts turned to memories.

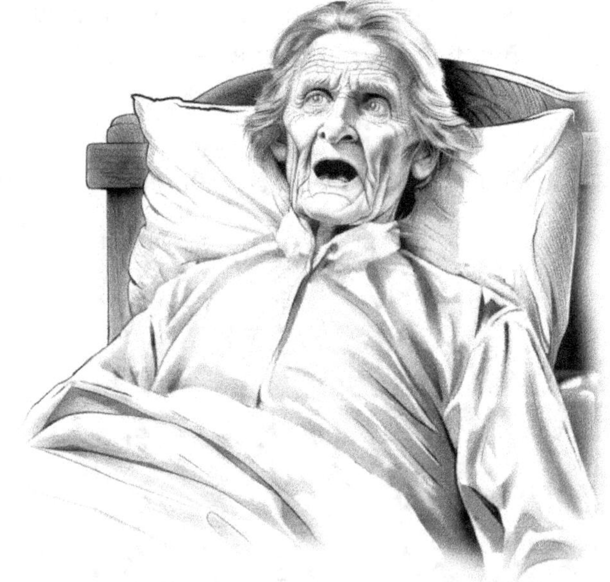

Glancing at the clock above the mantel, Scrooge realized it was still Christmas Eve. He thought about his nightmare and its connection to chains shown to him years ago, on another eve of Christmas.

As he lay in bed, he remembered his encounter with the three spirits. He knew he had changed. For each year, generous and often anonymous gifts found their way from his vault into the pockets of London's needy. The spirits never visited him again, they never needed to. But the ghost, Marley — that was another case. For this would be the year Marley needed Scrooge.

It had been years — eleven to be exact — since that pivotal Christmas Eve in 1843, when the three spirits and his old friend, Jacob Marley, had taken Scrooge on his journey of salvation. And now, the night before another Christmas, he lay alert within his bed thinking of the past.

Scrooge realized he was an old man when the spirits haunted him. Marley may have instigated the saving of his soul, but Scrooge himself understood his life would soon be lost. As he thought about his nearing death, he was at peace and grateful for the life he was given. He regretted nothing, not his years of rejection by a callous father, or his own rejection of the only love in his life, Belle.

For most of his life, Scrooge had dwelled within the passion of greed — he was a glutton for the coin and a scoundrel toward the laborer's condition. Yet, through the benevolence of the specters, Scrooge was lifted above his pettiness and allowed a resurrection of spirit. Throughout the last eleven years, the transformation of Christmas in London had closely followed Scrooge's own metamorphosis. In fact, Scrooge himself was a large part of the holiday's change.

The same year of his abduction into the unseen world the Christmas card brought forth a new tradition. England thrilled over these colorless greetings. With the card, a new industry was sparked for the General Post Office and printers, and thanks largely to Scrooge, for painters. For the first several years, during the month of October, Scrooge hired dozens of poor children to color in the joyous holiday scenes. During November, bundles of six cards were given to all who entered the counting-house. The work itself allowed the children the funds to help their families join a Christmas "Pudding Club", so that their entire clan could enjoy the

foods of the tradition. Nonetheless, within a few years the printers discovered a way to colorize the cards and the children were out of work.

However, Scrooge did not abandon his holiday hiring. Though he himself was not musical, the beautiful voices in a well-orchestrated choir often caused the hairs on the back of his neck to rise. He could feel music as an element transcending all languages, faiths, and traditions. Starting from the day of Stir-up Sunday in late November, Scrooge paid a dozen or more older children to travel the streets of London singing holiday favorites. The carolers were always well-fed by an appreciative public. Many were even able to take sweets home to younger siblings.

Scrooge had begun many personal holiday traditions, for himself and his business. None were as welcomed as his personal Christmas cards. The cherished recipient answered a knock at their door to find a well-tailored young man holding an envelope and asking, "Are you Mr...?" or "Are you Mrs...?" An answer in the affirmative resulted in the envelope being handed over. "Mr. Ebenezer Scrooge sends his respects during this time of holiday spirit." With that, the youth bowed, turned, and walked away. The envelope always contained a card with a picture of one lit candle on it. The printed text in the card always said exactly the words of the carrier, "Mr. Ebenezer Scrooge sends his respects during this time of holiday spirit."

The unique thing about each card was Scrooge's handwritten note. One card might say, "I have become aware of the illness within your family. Please find your debt to Scrooge and Cratchit forgiven." Another could state, "Your daughter has shown extraordinary skills as a healer. Please use the funds provided for her education in this field of study." Often, people carried Scrooge's card with them as a good luck talisman. Many people folded them so they would fit within a pocket.

Scrooge's most cherished tradition is one borrowed by Prince Albert from his country of origin, Germany. In 1848, the prince brought the Christmas tree, and with it, ornaments of apples, popcorn strands, and ribbons to the people of England. Since its appearance, Scrooge has always had a tree at home, and another at work.

Dangling from the boughs of the tree in the office were swinging coin-filled envelopes, each hiding a different amount within its fold. As the children of the employees visited their fathers during the holidays, each thrilled in wonder at those envelopes. For they knew on Boxing Day, while their fathers received the traditional money-filled pouch, they would also be allowed to choose an envelope for their keeping.

Of the five seasons with moneyed ornaments, Scrooge remembered 1851 with the greatest fondness. That Christmas, the tree's jackpot was won by Boz, the youngest son in the Cratchit family. Boz, the unstoppably active boy, won five pounds, four shillings, and a sixpence. The five-year-old took the money to his favorite brother, Tim, and said, "Here Tim, now you can make that leg invention you're always telling me about." With that, he flung the money at his older brother, turned, and darted toward some other holiday adventure. When Scrooge heard Boz instruct Tim to buy his leg apparatus, he decided to take Tim aside and ask him about the invention. Once Scrooge was made aware of the idea, he thought about the plausibility of the concept, deemed it possible, and further funded the creation of the leg straightener.

The straightener worked slowly, but over a few years of steady use, Tim became physically able to rid himself of the crutch. With Tim's freedom of movement came Scrooge's liberty from his past. The shadow from the Ghost of Christmas Yet to Come no longer cast its foreboding darkness on him. It had been replaced with a future cast in light.

The past decade had been Scrooge's best. The business he and Marley started had expanded into a counting-house with a half dozen employees. Thousands used the enterprise yearly. Scrooge's personal generosity had put a focus on the company. People wanted to be associated with the "giver from the commerce district". Each year, the business gained wealth. And each year, Scrooge and Cratchit found new ways to help people stay out of the workhouses.

Eventually, Scrooge realized the day was soon to come when he would be unable to work. In 1847, Scrooge gave Bob Cratchit half of the business as an early inheritance. It took another year for the sign "Scrooge and Cratchit" to be installed.

As Scrooge lay in his bed recovering from the nightmare of the fused-coin entrapment, he gazed at his Yule log flickering light upon the holiday tree in the

corner. Mesmerized by the flame's blaze, he began to remember the afternoon's visit from Fred and the twins. His nephew was the best father he had ever seen. He was neither too conservative nor too liberal with the girls. Yet, he always had a grand time playing their games of High Tea, Pet the Wild Creature, and Nap-Time Dodge. Neither girl was what one would call dainty, but they were sweet.

Fan had the twinkle of an angel in her eye, whereas Ebby... well, her twinkle hadn't quite been determined. She kept her sister engaged in continuous adventures. Ebby had a way of turning a walk in the park into a hunt for the treasure of the Loch Lomond cavern. Trips to the shop often transformed into a quest for Mr. Gaine's Figgy Pudding. Ebby usually dominated people's attention with her curiosity. Scrooge cherished both children, but adored Fan's quiet spirit, for it reminded him of his beloved sister, the child's namesake.

Scrooge smiled as he thought about the twins' earlier antics. While Scrooge and Fred sat near the fire conversing over a hot cup of honey wine, the four-year-olds ran around the room gathering steam. At one point, in an effort to quiet the girls, Scrooge asked Fan to come and sit in his lap. She readily agreed to the request. Gently caressing his wrinkled face, Fan laid her head against Scrooge's chest. As she removed her hand from his weathered features, Scrooge began stroking her feathery blonde hair. Fan closed her eyes and nestled against his warm body. But the quiet was short-lived. Ebby became irritated at the loss of her playmate.

"Fan!"

"Ebby, come and sit with me," Fred requested.

"No! I want to play with Fan," she said, tugging on Fan's arm.

Fan looked at her sister and asked, "Can we play Bah Humbug?"

Fred winked at Scrooge as Ebby replied, "Yes, Bah Humbug."

As Fan jumped down from Scrooge's lap, she told him, "You must play, Uncle."

"And you, Father," Ebby added to Fred.

Both men protested, yet neither child could hear it over their own excitement. After realizing a calm could only be re-established once the children were allowed to play their game, Scrooge asked how Bah Humbug was played. While one child talked over the other, and each completed her sibling's sentences, the rules slowly became clear. Scrooge and Fred

were to play supportive roles, a bit like facilitators. In general, it was an easy game, as one would expect from babies. Fred was to make declarative statements like

"The sky is blue" or "Snow is green". Scrooge would say, "Bah Humbug" when a statement was not true. The first girl to take a step forward when Scrooge said "Bah Humbug" got to keep the location. The other would remain in her original position. The winner would be the child who reached Scrooge first. If either girl stepped forward before Scrooge completed the "Bah Humbug" she would have to step back, and her sister would be allowed to gain the forward step. In the end, the rules were just confusing enough to be challenging.

With the game understood by all, the girls ran to the wall opposite Scrooge's chair. Pressing their backs against the chilly wainscoting, they wiggled around, waiting for their father to broadcast either fact or falsehood.

"Uncle Scrooge, I tell you frogs fly."

Without skipping a beat, Scrooge declared, "Bah Humbug!" Both girls jumped forward.

"Fan, I was quicker."

"You were not."

"Was!"

"I was!"

"Both won... you tied," declared Fred. "Get ready now. Here is the next one. Uncle Scrooge, these girls are both good children."

The sisters giggled as Scrooge looked at them, then, "Ba-a-a-ah..."

Fan stepped forward while Ebby insisted, "We are too good!"

Then Scrooge finished, "Humbug! Uh, ah, huh..." His laughter trailed off and ended in a smile.

Ebby pulled Fan back as she stepped forward, saying, "I won, Fan."

"Uncle Scrooge tricked me," she pouted.

"Now, girls," Fred said. The two quieted down as Fan stepped backwards. "Here goes the next one. I do believe, Uncle Scrooge, these two are both bad girls."

Again, Scrooge hung onto the first word, "Ba-a-a-ah!" The children, antsy with anticipation, bounced from leg to leg. "Humbug!" He quickly finished.

Fan stepped even with her sister before Ebby realized Scrooge had finished.

As the game progressed, each child took the lead position at least twice. The last time they became even with each other, Scrooge was only an arm's length away. Standing there waiting impatiently for their father to proclaim the next assertion, Fan began sliding, inch by inch, in front of Ebby. Once made aware of her sister's movements, Ebby felt obliged to compete in the same manner. Slide, stop, slide, slide, stop — very cunning, yet everyone could see it happening. Fred sat quietly. Scrooge snickered to himself. Fan slipped a bit ahead of Ebby, and then the reverse occurred. The game had gotten a bit tiring as Scrooge's room was rather large, so Fred just let them complete the competition with their sly feet-shuffling routine. Ebby slapped Fan's arm as she inched ahead. Once Fan gained momentum, she, in turn, butted Ebby with her hip. Within a minute, the two converged at Scrooge's knees.

"I won," declared Ebby.

"No, you did not," insisted Fan. "You cheated."

"Alright, girls," admonished Fred.

"But, Father," each said a little out of sync.

"You both won," Scrooge laughed as he threw his arms around both girls.

The twins giggled as they pulled loose of Scrooge. "Can we play again?" asked Ebby.

"Not today," Fred and Scrooge said in unison. Fred continued, "Go play with the toys. Uncle Scrooge and I are going to talk a while longer."

The girls were as good as gold. They quietly entertained each other under the big window facing the street.

The two men had been conversing about things of a forgettable nature when Scrooge brought up a subject paramount to the future. "Fred, you are my only heir. And being such, I feel compelled to ask, for the well-being of my employees, how you plan on handling your inheritance of my half of Scrooge and Cratchit?"

Caught off guard by the seriousness of the matter, Fred exclaimed, "I have not thought about this, Uncle."

"But I do... I must. Will you run the business?"

"Truly, Uncle, I am content as a barrister. A counting-house — it does not quite suit me."

"Yes, I realize that. So, if you sell, try and find a buyer within the company, even if that buyer must pay through installments. And, if you decide to run the business, look to Cratchit for guidance."

"Sound advice. I shall follow it, Uncle Scrooge."

"Then I am content. For I know you will do what is right by me and the business."

Scrooge was not naïve. He realized the business would change once he was gone. He knew his written will could not demand that the future kneel to the words. At best, they would be guidance. Looking to the future, Scrooge surmised that after he died, his name would fade from the city's memory. He could afford to buy himself a memorial to last the life of the city itself, yet resisted the vanity in the concept. The simple headstone afforded to the majority was enough. He hoped a few would think of him from time to time in a favorable way. However, nothing was for sure, so Scrooge made himself all right with that realization.

As the afternoon turned to early evening, Scrooge tired of the company, as did the youth of the visit. Fred bid his uncle a pleasant good night while informing him a coach would arrive at 1:00 p.m. the next day to carry him to the traditional Christmas celebration.

Scrooge had not missed a Christmas at Fred's since that fated day when the Ghost of Christmas Yet to Come had left him pleading for mercy upon his own grave. Though time had passed, the passion of that desperate period never faded

from his memory. And out of love for that moment of grace granted to him, Scrooge looked forward to Fred's Christmases more than all other days. For they were filled with the customs of the holiday — carolers, hot spiced ale, stockings filled with Father Christmas's gifts to the children, and almost everybody's favorite parlor game, Snapdragon. The game, with its dangerous challenge of snatching raisins from a flaming bowl of brandy, thrilled both audience and contestants alike. The spectators applauded as fingers dripping with blue flame tossed burning fruit into an open mouth. Whether it was the sizzle of the mouth's juices extinguishing the blaze that was heard, or the occasional yelp of pain, both brought exuberance from the onlookers. Winning the game was secondary to the excitement of playing. In fact, the winner of the game was given no more than the bragging rights to courage.

Often, the joy of the day lasted a week, starting with St. Thomas's Day on the 21st, and continuing until Boxing Day on the 26th. And even then, many people lingered with Christmas spirit until well after the new year when the charred remains of the Yule log were collected and kept so that they could be used to kindle the holiday log the next year.

Scrooge wished he could shake his nightmare so sleep would return. And though he was physically ready for rest, his mind continued to wander. He was anxious about the next day's activities. He hoped the day would bring forth his best-ever Christmas, for he anticipated this would be his last.

Scrooge lay with his eyes closed while reminiscence kept him awake. Abruptly, without warning, a song from the street below filled his bedroom. A horn and flute played "Greensleeves" with perfection. The sweet English melody brought a tear to the corner of his eye as his thoughts focused on the memory of a child clutching a music box. The song from the street, and the crystal-clear plucking of the same tune on the music box, collided in a flood of remembrances from the previous summer.

The summer had been hot — hotter than other years. Scrooge could recall no year hotter than the recent summer of 1854. He nearly broke a sweat just remembering that heat. The temperature had added to the pain of those events, for it was one more thing to contend with during Soho's struggle.

In rapid fire, September's events inundated his mind. He heard a middle-aged woman ask, "Please, guvnor, could you help me secure medical assistance?" Then the harsh voice of the man standing on the corner of Oxford and Poland, shouting to those who considered him an annoyance, "It is the criminals of Soho who brought God's vengeance." Then Scrooge's thoughts wandered to the riot on Piccadilly, where dozens were injured as they fled from the collapsed man at their feet, all hoping to avoid his fate.

As the flute and horn melody from the street moved beyond his bedroom, Scrooge's thoughts settled on that recent September day in his office where the men could not stop talking about the hundreds, maybe even thousands, lying dead in the street mere blocks from their counting-house. As they talked, young Fingal Wills read aloud a letter from the daily news. "Those who die have themselves to blame for living amongst the filth where cholera is generated. No pity, I say none, should be shown to those that fall from the epidem..."

"Mr. Wills."

"Yes, Mr. Cratchit?"

"Stop your reading. No more lack of compassion shall be uttered, lest it poison our spirits. Please continue your work without delay."

"Yes, sir."

However, the conversation continued among those not silenced. "I wonder what does cause such an epidemic?"

"Why, everyone knows foul vapors are at the root."

"I heard it was an Irish plot to get back at England for contributing to their famine." Fingal raised his head, but only frowned at the comment.

"No, it is a royal plot designed to hold the workers down."

"That is ridiculous. The royals do not need to plot against the commoner. They can have almost anything by merely pronouncing their desire."

"At the chapel this morning, the vicar said fear itself perpetuates the disease."

"Just like the clergy to create such a maligned cycle of circumstance, to which escape would be unattainable."

"The church is the keeper of the truth."

"Indeed, and always looking for a new hell to promote."

"Must I silence you all," said Scrooge.

"Beg your pardon, sir."

For a few minutes, the room fell quiet, yet the thoughts in their minds continued. Finally, it was Fingal Wills who voiced a slightly different topic. "I wonder what will ward off the disease?"

"Don't drink milk."

"Don't drink milk? What kind of advice is that?"

"That is just what I heard. I did not make it up."

"Are you sure?"

"I heard opium stops the disease from progressing."

"In my experience, opium could stop anything from progressing."

"Drinking only beer will keep the disease away."

"And you know this how?"

"In the epidemic of '49, my uncle was the only member of his family to not get cholera. The only thing different about him was that all he would drink was beer."

"Beer, I could do that one."

"Me too."

"I'm sure..." Before the sentence could be completed, the door flew open, interrupting everybody's thoughts. Prior to anyone asking the young woman how she could be helped, she asked the man closest to the door, "Are you Peter Nida?"

"No, Peter is over there," Fingal said, pointing to the man at the desk in the corner.

Holding up a letter, the worried woman ran to Peter's desk. "You must come before it's too late." She thrust the letter into his hand while tugging at his shirt.

"Wait. Stop." Peter removed her hand from his shirt, then pressed a twopence into her palm.

"Hurry, there's no time to waste."

As Peter opened the letter, all of the men in the office gathered around his desk. "What is it, Peter?"

"It's Nancy."

"Your sister?" asked Cratchit.

"She and Elizabeth are ill. I need to go to her."

"Is not Humphry there as well?"

"He is, but there is too much sickness for him to manage," said the girl.

"Peter, you may need help. Allow me to go with you."

"Kindness is truly yours, Mr. Scrooge, but I cannot be responsible for any harm which may come upon you."

"Then those here are now my witnesses. Let it be known, I absolve Peter Nida of any circumstance that may injure me. Now, as this young woman has said, 'there is no time to waste'."

Still apprehensive, Peter seemed to have no choice but to follow his employer into the street. As the two secured a carriage, Peter said, "Little Windmill Street."

"I ain't driving down death's lane. You best get a different ride."

"No, wait. How far will you take us?"

"Oxford and Poland is as far as I'll venture."

"That will do."

Scrooge and Peter entered the cab and soon passed the Royal Exchange, then the Bank of England. On any other workday, these would be the stops for Scrooge, but today, they left the commerce area for the infamous Soho district. By the look of the congestion in the streets, one would never know any part of London was suffering countless deaths at that very moment. Movement along Oxford became so slow that those walking overtook the coach, only to be passed minutes later. Throughout the trip as the carriage constantly shifted between movement and stagnation, the same faces kept passing by the cab's window. The men viewed the unchanging street theatre of two women walking arm-in-arm, talking as though no others existed. Then there was the child running, only to stop for breath, yet soon thereafter could be seen racing again. However the most entertaining was the man continually gawking, either in surprise or awe. What he was so enthralled by could never be determined, but the expressions on his face created smiles on both Scrooge and Nida. All the individuals were in their own worlds. Together, they added the only delight the day would see.

As the carriage stopped at the corner of Oxford and Poland, Scrooge asked, "Where is Gilbert, Nancy's husband?"

"Lieutenant Albright is fighting in Crimea."

"So, she and the children are alone?"

"Yes, but I help them as much as I can."

They stepped from the coach, paid the driver, then began walking south down Poland toward Broad Street. They would be the longest six blocks Scrooge would ever walk within the city. Each step brought sights, sounds, and smells foreign to the London lifestyle. Carts carrying the dead passed them in both directions. The cart entering the area had only one body, whereas the one exiting overflowed with the emaciated remains of souls healthy but hours earlier.

A low, slow groan of sorrow could be heard throughout the parish, with the periodic emphasis of a wail or scream. Tears were on many faces, as was the worry of uncertain times to come. The epidemic had begun a mere 48 hours ago — the toll on lives and grief already greater than myth could imagine.

The closer Scrooge and Peter got to Broad Street, the whiter the street became. Each step lifted a fine powder to the nose, where one could distinctly detect the odor of chloride.

Along with the carts for the dead, the living occupied the streets as well. At the corner of Poland and Broad Street, a calm, uncharacteristic of such trauma, saturated the emotional atmosphere. People, dozens of them, continued to pursue the needs of their lives. And even though the heat of the day oppressed most with a visible sweat, many covered their nose and mouth with a cloth, willing to trade the swelter for the hope of warding off the epidemic. A line of people gathered at the pump to fill buckets with water. Others walked in various directions, each carrying

a suitcase, and within minutes, disappeared from the area. Men put shutters on windows to inform the community of the disease having struck those within the house. And surrounding the entire area, the passion of melancholy overwhelmed.

Near the pump on Broad Street, Peter took a left on Cambridge and continued south. Scrooge followed. Neither man had spoken a word since entering the area. Words seemed inappropriate, almost sacrilege. As they walked together, an onlooker might wonder if either was with thought, or if perhaps obligation had taken control of their actions.

Cambridge is one of those odd little streets that only goes for a block. At the end of the block, though, the street still continues, but the name does not. As one would explain it to a stranger, "The street turns into Little Windmill." Yet, there is no transformation whatsoever, just a new name.

A few buildings from the corner, Peter turned right and knocked on the door. All was quiet. He knocked again, but there was only silence. With frustration, he pounded on the door a third time, yelling, "Nancy, Humphry, come to the door!"

"It's no good," Scrooge said, placing his hand on Peter's forearm. Peter tried the handle and found it unlocked. He entered, but before he could inhale even one breath of air, he was gasping for any air at all. The foul air in the room reeked of sizzling vomit and diarrhea. The combination nearly turned the men's stomachs. For a long while, Scrooge and Peter stood in the doorway, acclimating to the building's contamination. Anxious to investigate the silence, yet dreading the expectation of shock, the two continually called for the inhabitants. "Nancy, are you there? Humphry. Elizabeth. Answer if you hear me." But no sound, not even an echo of their own voices was returned.

Though neither could completely adjust to the odor, a time came when the revulsion no longer tormented them. Together, the men entered in search of the family. From the door of the first bedroom, Peter could see the empty bed was soiled with the various excrements cholera forces from a person. Peter approached the bed and found the side furthest from the door concealed a mat on the floor. On the mat lay Nancy, with her eyes open a fraction. Not certain as to the life within her, Peter knelt beside Nancy and found her gone.

Sitting on the floor, Peter pulled his older sister's upper body into his lap. While stroking her hair, quiet tears began falling from his chin to her cheek.

Scrooge went from room to room in search for the others. After looking through most of the house, he opened a door at the back of the building. Within the room were two small beds, one contained the same dirtiness as had Nancy's bed. In the other, two children lay within each other's arms.

Using a gentle touch Scrooge made himself aware of their conditions. When moved Humphry opened his eyes. However, Elizabeth took no notice of Scrooge's hand upon her forehead.

Humphry said, "We are so ill, sir. Can you help us?"

"Yes, I am with your Uncle Peter."

"Uncle? I heard him in my dream. He called to me, but I was trapped in an oven. Then he left." Looking up at Scrooge, Humphry added, "You are not my uncle."

"He is with your mother."

"Can you help me? I am so thirsty. Do you have a drink?"

"No, but I will fetch some water."

"Not water." Humphry licked his lips as his eyes closed.

Scrooge, numb to the idea of what should be done first, stood as still as a statue, unsure of his next action. Should he attend to the children, fetch water, or alert the authorities of Nancy's passing — all seemed urgent. He finally gave up deciding and just left the children to go get Peter. Rocking on the floor with his sister in his arms, Peter gave no attention to Scrooge as he moved to a position directly behind him.

"Peter, Elizabeth and Humphry need our help."

Peter set free an anguished cry. Startled by the outburst, Scrooge placed his hand on Peter's shoulder to comfort his grieving friend. In a quiet, reassuring voice, Scrooge said, "Come around, the young ones need you. Think of what your sister would want."

Scrooge's words, like a slap to the face, caused Peter to carefully lay Nancy on the floor. As he kissed her forehead, he rose to his feet and said, "We must remove the children from this contamination."

"They seem too ill for movement."

"Yes, yes, I imagine they are." Together, they entered the children's room. Neither child stirred.

Scrooge said, "Does Nancy have clean bedding?"

"I know of extra blankets."

"Fetch them while I remove these soiled linens." Taking care not to touch any of the excrement, Scrooge removed the bedding from the spare bunk. Within moments, a fresh blanket was draped over the bed.

Looking upon the youths, dreading the next step, both men glanced at each other as Scrooge said, "They need to be cleansed before we move them to fresh blankets."

"I have never had such a chore."

"Nor I."

Peter said, "It is the right thing to do."

With water from a bucket in the kitchen, the two cleansed the worst from Elizabeth's body. Because no change of clothing could be found for the child, they dressed her in one of her mother's garments. She never stirred, at least not until she realized she was being separated from Humphry.

As Peter lifted her limp body, her eyes popped open and she screamed with fright, "No! Phry!" Over and over she yelled, "Phry! I want Phry!"

It was alarming to have such a tremendous voice bellow from the frail creature. Peter placed her on the fresh blanket, all the while making an effort to calm her. "Elizabeth, Humphry is still here." But she would have nothing to do with the change. As soon as she was set down, Elizabeth labored to raise herself with the

yearning to return to her brother. Scrooge looked around for anything that might appease her. A doll when offered was pushed away, as was a book with a rabbit on the cover. Desperate to soothe the child, Scrooge latched on to a wooden box from a shelf. Upon opening the lid, the melody "Greensleeves" flowed throughout the room.

Elizabeth looked at the music box, stretched out her arms, and said, "Father." Scrooge placed the opened box beside her. As the song slowed, Elizabeth, through a tenacious struggle, worked to rewind its spring. While she pivoted between relaxing into the music, and then grappling with the turnkey, the men attended to Humphry.

Humphry was able to assist in his own cleansing. With Scrooge's help, the boy rose from the bed, stood against the elderly man, and watched as Peter replaced the bedspread. As soon as Humphry settled upon his bed, Elizabeth vomited on hers. Little was released, yet the men felt compelled to change both the gown and bed covering again. Realizing these ejections could come to require all their time, the men decided to place easily removable cloths under both the children's privates and across their chests.

The ordeal of the day started to wear on Scrooge. He had held up well, but he needed a rest. He sat in a chair between the children's beds. When the music box slowed, he rewound it for Elizabeth. She was silent to Humphry's continual mumbling about being thirsty.

"I am going to Broad Street to fetch water," said Peter.

"They need more than water. They need something to give them strength."

"Without a doubt neither will be able to eat."

"Yes, that is a certainty," said Scrooge. "You are aware of where I live on Sackville?"

"I have been on Sackville but know not your home."

"I live at 15 Sackville. Here, take my key and go fetch the case of canned fruit from under my stairwell. Also, retrieve a hammer and a few nails for opening the cans. They too are under the stairs."

"But, sir, I doubt either child will be able to retain any food."

Annoyed and tired, Scrooge said, "Stop arguing and fetch the items."

Peter immediately started running. Scrooge lived little more than half a dozen blocks from the Little Windmill location, yet it would be over an hour before Peter returned.

Scrooge welcomed the hour of rest. All three, in their own time, descended into sleep. The music box was the last to wind down.

The three awoke simultaneously to a ruckus in the kitchen. Humphry lifted his head, asked if the house was under attack, then pulled a gun from under his bed. Scrooge disarmed the boy while convincing him there was no need to worry. Elizabeth remained silent. Her sunken eyes stared out at nothing and everything at the same time. Scrooge got up and investigated the noise. He entered the kitchen to find Peter standing at the counter with a nail in one hand and a hammer in the other. When he saw Scrooge, he said, "It seems these tins were meant to preserve the food indefinitely. They hardly dent, let alone allow themselves to be punctured."

"Even one hole will be enough for the children to drink the juice through."

"This tin is well indented. I will break through even if the uproar rattles our bones." With that said, Peter hit the nail as hard as he could. The force of the hammer upon the nail caused the can to release a swoosh of air. Peter handed the container to Scrooge and said, "See if either will drink."

As Peter began pounding on the lid of another can, Scrooge took the opened preserves to the children.

Elizabeth appeared to sleep, whereas Humphry followed every movement Scrooge made. "Here, Humphry. Lift your head and drink." Scrooge supported Humphry's neck as he tipped the can to the boy's lips. Humphry took a sip, then another. Within minutes, he had swallowed all the liquid. Not yet having his thirst quenched, he asked for more to drink. Almost within the same stroke of time, Peter handed Scrooge another can.

As the boy slowly consumed the liquid, Peter removed the music box from Elizabeth's bed, then sat down where it had been. He gazed at the small child. Her physical appearance had deteriorated within the short period of time he had been gone. Her bluish lips, sunken eyes, and mouth ajar all gave Peter a feeling of doom. He gently shook the girl awake. Stroking her forehead, he explained how he needed her to drink from the can. She showed little interest and spent no energy assisting him. Through the gap between her lips, Peter poured in a small amount of the sweet liquid. The juice gurgled up and over the corner of her mouth, then flowed down the cheek. Her eyes stared ahead without focus. The only observable movement coming from Elizabeth was the clutching, then releasing of her left hand. Peter took the hand within his, but this only served to irritate her. He continued trying to comfort and feed Elizabeth, yet he was unsuccessful at either.

Scrooge had just finished feeding Humphry when a loud knock was heard at the door. He got up and answered the pounding from the front of the home.

Upon opening the door, both men were so surprised by who they saw on the other side of the threshold they just stared at each other. Finally, Scrooge said, "John, Dr. Snow?"

"So good to see you, Ebenezer. It is a bit unusual to speak with you outside our neighborhood. What brings you here?"

"I assume the same thing that brings you — cholera."

"Indeed, I am on the Cholera Inquiry Committee for the St. James Parish. It is my desire to both help and gather information. Would I be correct in assuming the disease is within the home?"

"It is. We have two children ill. Their mother has already passed."

"May I see the children?"

"Yes, certainly. Follow me."

To accommodate the doctor, a third chair was brought from the living room. It was placed at the foot of the beds, next to the chair where Peter sat. Scrooge sat down in the newly-arrived chair while John positioned himself in the chair between the beds. He examined Humphry first. Smelling a fruitiness, he said, "Have you fed him?"

"We gave him the juice from some canned fruit."

"Canned fruit, quite a luxury."

Scrooge said, "It was a gift."

"Good. But don't give him too much at any one time; maybe a cup every hour. As he gains strength, increase the amount. As soon as his diarrhea stops, begin feeding him soft foods."

Peter said, "So you think he will recover?"

"We will pray it is so. And now to lovely..." Dr. Snow waited for someone to tell him the girl's name.

"Elizabeth."

"Ah, yes, lovely Elizabeth." Dr. Snow began to examine her. Her tiny chest rose slightly with each breath. As he lifted her arm, he took note that her fingernails 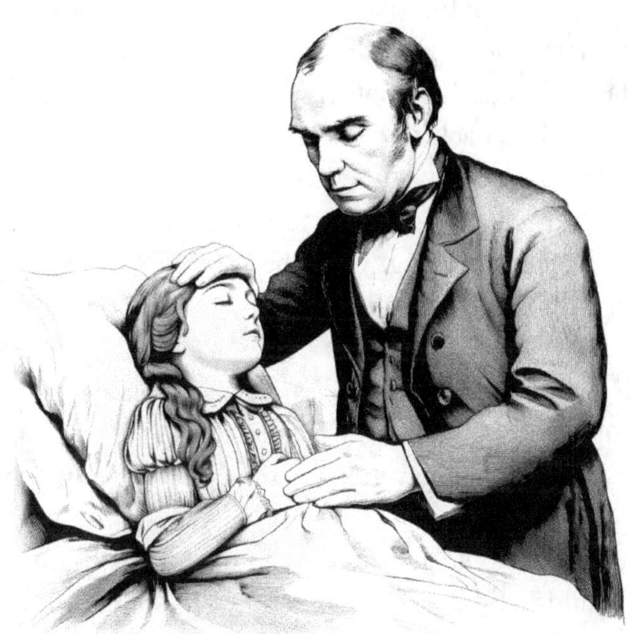 had started turning a bluish color. Pinching the skin on her wrist, he was not surprised when the skin remained a raised lump. Dr. Snow ran his fingers over the lump to flatten the skin. Throughout the entire examination, Elizabeth kept clutching and releasing her left hand.

John Snow asked, "Has this child been able to drink?"

Peter said, "No."

"It is curious that she keeps grasping her hand. I have never seen another person with cholera do such a thing."

For a few minutes, the three of them concentrated on Elizabeth's hand. Peter finally said, "I think she is searching for the music box."

"Well, give it to her if it is a comfort."

With that, Peter rewound the box, then placed it under Elizabeth's hand. As the music began, her hand quieted.

"Will you see me to the door, Ebenezer?"

At the door, Dr. Snow said to Scrooge, "You are doing well by the children. Keep them, and yourself, clean. You should all start drinking boiled water. Furthermore, if either child complains of stomach cramps, place three drops of this under their tongue." With that, he handed Scrooge a small vial of opium, opened the door, and left.

Scrooge pocketed the vial as he entered the children's room. Sitting in the chair between the beds, Peter could be heard sobbing. Scrooge knew why he cried, but waited to hear Peter announce, "She has left us." The music box instantly stopped playing.

Tenderly, Peter picked up Elizabeth. As he began carrying her to Nancy's room, Humphry realized the meaning of the action. Crying, he said, "Not Elizabeth. No. I want her." He lifted his arms to receive his sister.

Scrooge said, "No, Humphry. This is best."

"Let me at least kiss her."

The men visually confirmed an agreement with each other. Peter said, "Yes, kiss Elizabeth." With that, he lowered her to the level of the boy's bed. Humphry caressed the sunken cheeks of his once-playful sister. He opened his mouth to speak, but instead, gently kissed her forehead, then collapsed back to his bed.

After Elizabeth had been placed beside her mother, Peter left the house to retrieve the death cart, some water, and a coach to carry the three to safety in the morning.

Once they had eaten a light dinner, each of the men took their turn watching the boy while the other rested. During the evening, Humphry vomited once, had two episodes of diarrhea, and cried off and on throughout the night. By morning, he had neither gotten better nor worse.

It was mid-morning before Nancy and Elizabeth's cart arrived. The attendant informed the men the burial would take place before late afternoon. Peter was surprised. He expected the normal period of mourning, but the epidemic required the change.

"Sorry, guvnor, we've been instructed to keep present with the burials, lest the dead become burdensome through build-up."

After the cart had begun its journey toward Broad Street, Peter and Scrooge discussed the logistics of the day.

Scrooge said, "I think you should take Humphry to your home. I will attend the burials."

Peter, wanting to be part of both events, thought out all the possibilities before agreeing to the idea. Once the coach arrived, Scrooge helped Peter make it appear as though Humphry had a broken leg. They feared if the driver knew of the boy's true affliction, he would abandon them. This charade did not fool the driver, but he was a brave man with a desire to help this less-fortunate boy.

The coachman drove the three toward Peter's home, by way of the graveyard. At the cemetery, Scrooge stepped out of the carriage, then paid the driver so he could complete the trip to Peter's.

Within the graveyard several men were busy digging deep holes. Two men dug while others, through a pulley system, raised the dirt to the surface. The graves were dug so deep, Scrooge began to fear the men would break through to an underground river, but they never did.

Within an hour, seven caskets on two carts arrived. They stopped next to the only completed grave. On the top of each casket, the name of the person within was printed. The two Allbright caskets were the smallest, with Elizabeth's being little more than half the size of the largest.

The attendants, being numb to the emotions of the day, began lowering caskets into the hole. The first was the largest, a man named Ned Shepherd, then a second and third. Each sat directly on top of the last. Scrooge watched in bewilderment at the stacking of multiple caskets within the single hole. The moment he realized all seven caskets were to be piled within the same grave, he requested Elizabeth be placed directly on top of her mother. And even though the stacking by size would have dictated this to happen anyway, the attendants willingly confirmed they would do as asked.

No fanfare, and only the ceremony of a vicar blessing each casket accompanied the thump of wood on wood. As Nancy's casket was lowered, a tear came to the corner of Scrooge's eye. He fought the tear, but then Elizabeth was lowered upon her mother. The held-back tear dropped, followed by others. Scrooge willingly allowed the tears to flow. As he remembered the girl, he felt a sadness for the tragedy of the situation in general.

Through the blur of tears, Scrooge watched a head, then shoulders, rise from the center of the grave. He wiped the moisture from his eyes to clarify his vision. The head and shoulders not only remained, but continued to rise further from the

grave. His vision was that of aged eyes, lacking the ability of detail. Stepping forward, he realized the rising person had their gaze upon him. Suddenly, Scrooge identified the person as the ghost, Marley. His friend, his benefactor, the mentor of his cleansed spirit — Jacob Marley — stared at him, then breathed the words, "Help me."

The remembrance of Marley's request shocked the now half-sleeping Scrooge to full alertness. As his eyes burst open, he left the tragic memories of the burial ground behind. Lying still within the comfort of his bed, he said, "Eighteen years." Until that moment, he had forgotten that the day was not only the beginning of society's most beloved holiday, but also the anniversary of his friend's death. Scrooge had not thought about Marley once during the day. He was saddened for not having remembered the 18th year of Marley's passing. He said to himself, "Who will grieve for you when I am gone?"

"None need grieve for me, then or now."

"Who said that?"

Scrooge turned his head toward the sound. With minimal light from the fireplace, he could see the outline of a man standing a dozen feet from his bed. Scrooge swung his legs over the side of the bed.

"Jacob, is that you?"

"It is."

"You look different. Your chains... where have they gone?"

"Every wrong we gathered together was released from me when you corrected it."

"What I did affected you?"

"Everything done ripples an effect. No one acts in isolation."

"But how can the living affect the dead?"

"We in the afterworld exist, and all within existence experience movement. Movement is change."

"I understand, yet how does the living change the dead?"

"Any action, or thought directed toward us, can change us. Our progress is less tied to the elements. Therefore, spirits can easily be moved through thought."

"So, by simply thinking of the departed, they somehow become altered?"

"Only if it is the desire of the specter to feel the thought."

"So, your chains are now gone. Why haven't you ascended to heaven?"

"I still have one chain, which I forged before I met you."

"I don't see it."

Opening his shirt, Marley said, "Look deeply." As Scrooge concentrated on Marley's bared chest, the skin became transparent. He could see the heart at its center, and piercing the organ was one gigantic chain link, the weight of which must have been a constant burden.

"It is this that ties you to your purgatory?"

"It does."

"How can you remove such misery?"

"Through your help, if you should choose to assist me."

"I will always lend myself to you, Jacob."

"It is not without its dangers for you, Ebenezer."

"I would walk into death for you."

"The danger is that real. Yet, if successful, so will be the reward."

"I am an old man with little to fear and less to forfeit. So, tell me, Jacob, how I can help."

"Follow me. Stay close at all times, and my energy will become yours."

With that, Marley floated through the wall. Scrooge stood and watched. After a long moment, Marley's head passed back through the wall, "Follow me, Ebenezer."

Closing his eyes, Scrooge followed Marley through the wall.

Stave Two

Betrayal At Work

WATER PARTS WHEN entered, but not brick, or at least it shouldn't. But there was Scrooge once again within a dozen years, floating on the outside of his home, hovering several feet above the ground, with eyes closed and fists clenched. Marley tapped him on the shoulder causing Scrooge's eyes to pop open; then realizing his predicament, he began to fall. Screaming, he plunged toward that which would feel solid if struck, but Marley wrapped his hand around Scrooge's wrist. The coldness of his dead touch chilled deeper than the winter's air, yet Scrooge's descent abruptly stopped.

Slowly the two began to rise above Sackville Street. As they did, Burlington Arcade's skylights began popping off. In quick succession they disappeared. Then the rafters supporting them were gone. As the two friends rose higher and higher, the posh stores of the arcade faded away and the ground on which the building had once stood reverted to grass.

"Jacob, where are we?"

"When are we is the real question."

"Then when are we?"

"At the beginning of our partnership, Ebenezer."

"Is the beginning of our partnership important to your salvation?"

"No, my failing just began the same year."

"1813, then?"

"Yes. Do you remember that year?"

"I remember how sad it was for you."

"So sad," Marley said, thinking about the most regrettable event of his life. Then he added, "Here we are."

Scrooge looked around the dark street. "Where are the gaslights?"

"It's 1813, Ebenezer."

"Um." Scrooge continued to look around then asked, "Why are we at Pressey and Barclay's grocery?"

"Just watch the glass."

Together they stood in front of the darkened window staring into the glass void. Almost without notice, gas lamps within the store grew bright. The ghosts looked on as a man moved toward them. They heard him whistling "God Rest Ye Merry Gentlemen". With a smile on his face, the man stood directly in front of the duo examining the hanging geese. Finally he chose the largest of the birds. Taking it down, he placed the goose on the counter. Looking around the store, Scrooge noticed many of the shelves were bare. He opened his mouth to speak but stopped in thought when he saw a spry Jacob Marley race through the door.

"Noah, Noah, guess what?"

"Well, I swear, little brother, you look like you have seen a ghost." Scrooge and Marley looked at each other; Scrooge smiled while Marley had the look of concern.

"No, no, of course not." Placing the money from his pockets on the counter, he continued, "Lorriane Bignell gave me half a crown as a tip. She said, 'the spirit of the season has overtaken my good senses'." The young Jacob laughed, "I'm just glad it overtook her when I was delivering the groceries."

"Well, Jacob, that will make for an extra fine holiday for you. Were you able to make all your deliveries?"

"Yes, everyone was even home to pay for them."

"Wonderful, Mr. Pressey should be quite happy with the day's receipts. I can not remember a more profitable day."

"That is because there probably never was one."

"Well, it is time to close up and celebrate our own holiday. You sweep out while I count the money and prepare the deposit."

As the two engaged themselves with the end of day chores, the door opened and in stepped an old woman. Her nose was red from the winter's chill. Wind on her face had forced tears to form in the corners of her eyes. Both men looked up to see who had entered. Noah smiled at the woman while Jacob frowned. With walking cane in hand, she slowly made her way to the counter.

"How can I help you, Mrs. Buckner?"

Her voice cracked, "I would like to buy a yam," she said while fumbling with her coin purse.

"We have a couple left."

"Show me your money," Jacob demanded.

"Jacob! Remember the season."

Grumbling, the young Marley went back to his sweeping. Noah rolled the two yams in his hand, closely inspecting both. "Mrs. Buckner, neither of these yams are the best of quality. Would you mind if I let you have both for the price of one?"

"That would be very kind."

"Good, good." He pointed to the goose on the counter and added, "This is the bird I'm going to feed my wife and young Jacob here for Christmas. The thing is, none of us like the wings. They will only go to waste. Would it be all right if I give them to you? Will you eat them?"

"Yes, the wings would be nice. Thank you, Mr. Marley."

Noah smiled at the fragile woman, separated the wings from the breast and, after wrapping the items together, handed her the package. She happily gave Noah her penny, turned, and left.

"Have a wonderful Christmas," yelled Noah after the woman.

After she was gone, Jacob whined, "I like the wings. Why did you do that?"

"Do you not enjoy the thigh as well?"

"I do."

"Do you expect to go home hungry tomorrow?"

"No, of course not, but..."

Putting his hand on Jacob's shoulder, he said, "Jacob, you have much to learn about showing thanks for your good fortune."

Pulling away he replied, "And you, big brother, have much to learn about how the world really works."

"It's Christmas. If we can not be generous now, then when?" Noah paused then added, "Do you even know of Mrs. Buckner's situation?"

"No, but I don't see where that would matter."

"It does, of course it does. Her husband died last winter. Her son, being the heir, turned her out of the home she lived in her entire adult life. She has nothing now."

"That is not my concern."

"Yes, Jacob, the well-being of the community is your concern."

"No, it is not."

Irritated, Noah said, "Just get back to your sweeping."

Scrooge looked at Marley and asked, "You were really that harsh?"

"Be careful of your condemnation, Ebenezer. We were both cut from the same cloth."

"I know. Your brother was a good man, Jacob. I'm sorry about the fate he met."

"He was better than I deserved."

"Jacob, you have become a good soul as well."

"Soon you may not think that."

Scrooge stared curiously at Jacob while the spirit watched his brother count money.

As the two engaged themselves with closing procedures, a riding coach rammed into the curb next to the store. The force caused the wheels to jump before settling at a stop. Both men, as well as the ghosts, looked toward the disturbance.

"Oh, it's Mrs. Swinburne again. Tell her we are closed," Jacob said as Noah walked toward the door.

"No, Jacob, she's a good customer. She wouldn't be here if it wasn't important."

"She's a rich customer, you mean."

"Dear brother, that has nothing to do with it."

"If you say so, dear brother."

As Noah opened the door, the coach driver began wildly ringing his bell.

"Impatient grump," mumbled Jacob.

The open door let in such a gust of chill, Jacob dropped the broom and began rubbing his arms.

When Mrs. Swinburne saw Noah, she cheerfully smiled at him, which showed off both the rosy color of her lip rouge and the gap between her two front teeth.

"Good evening, Mrs. Swinburne. How can I help you?"

"It took you long enough," said the driver.

"That will be enough out of you," admonished Mrs. Swinburne. "Sorry, Noah. I hope you are still open."

"We are in the process of closing, but I am always happy to help you, Mrs. Swinburne."

"Emily, please. I just found out we are going to have unexpected guests. I need a dozen yams and your best bird."

"I'm sorry, we are all out of yams but have some wonderful potatoes left."

"Oh, I was afraid of that. Well, potatoes it will be. Do you have more than a dozen?"

"There should be a couple of dozen."

"I will take them all."

Mrs. Swinburne started to hand Noah a five-pound bank note but then hesitated. She withdrew the bill and wholeheartedly gave it a kiss, leaving the imprint of her lips upon it. As she handed Noah the note, she impishly winked at him. Noah took the money, made sure it had been properly signed, then smiled back at the flirtatious woman. As he turned to go into the store, the driver called to him, "Be quick about it; the cold is paining me."

Noah turned toward the driver, bowed, and said, "Of course, sir." Within minutes he was handing the goods and leftover funds to the woman. As quickly as they arrived, they dashed away, leaving a flurry of snow floating through the air.

It took only a few minutes to finish the closing procedures. The last was Noah extinguishing the half dozen oil lamps. Jacob impatiently stood at the counter, so antsy to leave that, when the door was finally opened, he jammed his shoulder against its edge. He ricocheted off the wood, then began running down the street.

"Jacob. Jacob!"

Jacob slid to a stop on a sheet of ice that had developed from tromping feet compressing snow. With a visible impatience, he turned toward his brother.

"You are coming for Christmas?"

"Noah, I have to meet an important person tomorrow. I don't think I will be able to attend."

"Jacob, what can be so important you have to do it on Christmas?"

"I can't talk about it yet."

"Well, whatever it is, I will not have it end our holiday tradition. Flora is expecting you for dinner. Do you not remember Cromwell's oppression when people gave their lives to preserve Christmas?"

"You know I have not forgotten that, Noah, you will not let me. But I have an appointment."

"I will not have it. Jacob, there may come a day you wished you had family to make merry with."

"And just where are you and Flora going so I won't have family around?"

"We may move. You may move. One never knows."

"Oh, have it your way. I will come." Jacob turned and began running again.

"Dinner at two. Don't be late."

Scrooge looked over at Marley. Marley was staring at his brother. A tear appeared to drop from the ghost's cheek. How was such a thing possible? A spirit is without physical elements. Were then the tears without moisture? Scrooge pondered the thought but said nothing. He only wanted to console his friend, so he put his arm across Marley's shoulders.

Noah began walking in the opposite direction from Jacob. Marley tugged at

Scrooge and said, "Let us follow him." Oxford Street was nearly pitch-black as most of the stores had closed, and the few residences had only dim gas lamps and candles shining through their windows. The sparse lighting made it difficult for Noah to avoid the iced areas. As he walked down the street toward the Bank of London, each breath exhaled flowed around the sides of his face. The people around him were traveling in all directions.

Children were running, Christmas carolers were singing, and the others were on their way to holiday celebrations throughout the city.

Without warning a snowball smashed into the side of Noah's head, which sent him spinning across the cobblestones. Losing his balance, he fell on his backside sending his satchel of money flying through the air. Noah lay sprawled on the ground, breathing heavily while trying to figure out what had just happened. A young man stood over him and asked, "Beg pardon, guvnor, are you hurt?"

Noah looked into the lad's eyes and said, "I think I am fine."

"Here, sir, let me help you up." The youth extended his right hand to Noah.

Once righted, Noah said, "I had a ..." but before he could finish the sentence the boy handed him his money pouch.

Marley and Scrooge watched as Noah thanked the young man, then continued in the direction of the bank.

"I assume Noah has the daily receipts in that bag?" asked Scrooge.

"He put them in there."

"And he is rushing to deposit the money?"

Before Marley could answer his friend, Noah, in an effort to sidestep Christmas carolers, slipped and fell again. This time he slid half-way down Snow Hill before stopping. And again his money pouch went flying through the air. It finally came to rest at the feet of the tallest caroler, Sir Stephen Mackintosh. Sir Stephen picked up the bag, looked inside, then began walking toward Noah. Noah, having had risen to his feet, started searching for the money. A worried look overtook him as he realized the bag could be anywhere within a half block area.

"He looks shifty. He's not going to give the money back, is he?" asked Scrooge.

"A person's honesty is not a physical attribute," Marley replied.

Before Scrooge could comment further, Sir Stephen handed Noah his bag. "You dropped this."

"Thank you. Thank you so much." Noah received the pouch from the lanky fellow.

"Sir Stephen Mackintosh at your service."

"Sir? You are young to have such a distinguished title."

The young man just shrugged his shoulders. Noah again thanked the youth, then continued toward the bank. He arrived at the Bank of London only a minute, maybe two, after the doors had been locked. He turned to go home, and without further incident, arrived safely at his door. After entering, he immediately hid the money pouch under a loose floor board beneath his bed, then promptly began the holiday with his wife, Flora.

Upon seeing Flora, Marley started to weep. As tears dropped from his face, they disappeared before striking the floor.

"Jacob, what is wrong?"

"It's all wrong!" Crying uncontrollably, he exclaimed, "I deserve a damnation beyond Transmogrify. I can not continue this, Ebenezer. I will take you home."

"No, Jacob, no matter what you have done, you do not deserve this never-ending torment."

"My dear friend, you speak without knowledge."

"I am not ignorant of your better side, Jacob."

"And yet you know nothing of this chain. It is my Task."

"Your Task, but why must you suffer indefinitely?"

"Indefinitely? Change for the dead is definite, but only through outreach. By my own energies, I am doomed."

"Humbug! Then where are your bindings from our last encounter?"

"It is you that changed, which altered me."

"Humbug, I tell you. It was your influence that modified me. If anything, we changed each other. So tell me, Jacob, do you still exist? Is it a cloud, a sound, or maybe a mere figment of my imagination I speak to now?"

"No, it is my spirit upon which you speak. As far as to my existence, I am still painfully aware of what I have done."

"As far as your awareness — it seems the desire for change should help to develop reform. Granted it appears transition happens differently for the dead than it does the living, but all can not be lost for you."

"I hunger for your truth, Ebenezer. For if it is otherwise, then this whole mission is past hope."

"On some level you have always known what I speak now is the truth. Remember your first visit to me, some eleven years ago? You told me then that you often sat near me. You called it your penance. Well, what is penance but the acceptance of punishment in an effort to move toward absolution?"

"Dear friend, your enlightened thoughts lift me, but if we are to continue this venture we must go now. There is a meeting to attend."

THE SUN WAS rising without any competition from clouds. As the young Jacob walked briskly through the near empty streets, the crisp morning air chilled his face. Periodically he would slip on an ice patch, but he never lost his footing and seemed to enjoy the surprise of the slide. Within a half hour, he arrived at his destination. Vigorously he knocked at the door.

"I know this place," said Scrooge.

"As you should," replied Marley.

The door opened and in the warmth stood a young Ebenezer Scrooge.

"Come in, Jacob."

Together they entered a room with dual chairs near a blazing fire. Each sat, and while Jacob removed his greatcoat and placed it on the back of his chair, Scrooge cleared his voice. "Uh-um, so you are ready to become my partner?"

"Indeed. I brought the money."

"All of it?" asked Scrooge.

"All of it."

"I thought you had only a hundred pounds. Did you not tell me the last time we met that you would pay the other hundred pounds over a two-year period?"

"I did, but I secured a wealthy backer," said Marley.

"Just as well. Better terms, I assume?"

"Oh yes, much better."

"Good, good business sense," said Scrooge as a faint smile spread across his thin lips.

"Indeed," said Marley.

"Well, I did draw up the papers. However, with the terms having changed, I will have to alter the agreement."

Scrooge took out his quill and ink, crossed out a few lines and added, "paid in full" at the bottom of the contract. It was then that he called for his sister, Fan, to join them. The two men initialed the changes, then made their partnership official. Fan also signed the contract as the witness.

As she left the men to their business, Scrooge said,

"She's getting married in a month. I am not keen on her betrothed, but I am told Father likes him. So for what does my opinion count?" Marley sensed the question to be rhetorical in nature so said nothing. Instead he handed Scrooge a packet of money. After counting the notes, Scrooge said, "Good, we are in business together." Having completed their work, the two then shared a chalice of brandy. Neither were competent at conversation, so each sat quietly, sipping their drink.

Shortly thereafter, Marley bid a farewell and made his way to his brother's home. By the time he arrived, the party had been in progress for over an hour.

"I was about to give up on you," said Noah. "I made grandfather's wassail, come share a toast with us."

Jacob accepted the warm cup. They then entered the living room where Flora greeted them. Her sister Joan rose from a chair. As the four clanked cups, Noah said, "May this holiday bring the joy we all desire."

Flora and Joan cheerfully said, "Wassail." Jacob followed up with his own weak, "Wassail."

"Jacob, I'm so glad you're here. We bought you something special this year. I would have been heartbroken if you had failed to arrive," Flora said.

Jacob lowered his eyes and nervously said, "I wish you had not gotten me anything."

"Why, that is nonsense. I would never let my husband's brother go without an expression of our love. Besides, this year is special; Noah was told a week ago he is going to get a promotion."

"I have not heard of this," Jacob said, looking inquisitively at Noah.

"It's true. Yesterday was the main test. Mr. Pressey said if I was able to handle Christmas Eve without his help, I would be made manager. I think the two of us did well. The store made over a hundred and ten pounds in sales. It seems to have gone off without a hitch. Would you not agree?"

Jacob opened his mouth to speak, but instead just stared at Noah and remained silent.

"Well, it's time to open our gifts, then we eat," said Flora.

Each person received one gift, except Flora, who was given presents from both Noah and Joan. Because Flora had the most presents, she began by opening the gift from Joan. While the others watched, each took a turn opening their gift. A commotion of excitement was made over each gift. To Noah's new pair of glasses, quips were made about his finally being able to see. Joan received perfume, and Jacob's special gift from Flora and Noah ended up being a beaver-skinned top hat. "Now you will look so dapper, the girls will be clinging to your shadow," said Flora.

They were all likable presents, but it was the last gift from Noah to Flora that caused the uproar. Out of the camouflage of the June 7th, 1813 Star newspaper emerged a painted wooden box. The beauty of the box caused Joan's eyes to widen, Flora's lower jaw to drop open, and Jacob to cough while rubbing his forehead.

"Open the lid."

Flora very gently lifted the box's lid; she never knew what to expect from Noah. He was as likely to put something in the box that would pop out to startle her as he was to place an expensive piece of jewelry in the box. Before the lid was even half-way lifted, the song "Greensleeves" burst forth from the box's center. Tears of excitement flowed from Flora, as it was her favorite melody.

After the joy of sharing gifts was complete, the four went to the dining area where they ate a perfectly prepared goose, yams, baked apples with raisins, and the best plum pudding ever consumed.

Jacob ate without tasting the food, and before the others were finished with their pudding, he announced his need to leave.

"Not yet," said Flora.

Noah asked, "Jacob, why must you rush away?"

"I told you yesterday I had an appointment today."

"What is this appointment? You've been on edge all afternoon," said Noah.

"Well, I suppose I can tell you now. I am going to go into business with Ebenezer Scrooge. We are finalizing the agreement today."

"What exciting news," said Flora.

"Why such a secret?" asked Noah.

"I was afraid you would be angry."

"Jacob, I do not expect you to be an errand boy forever. I am happy for you. No, actually, I am proud of you."

"Thank you, Noah, but I do have to leave."

"Well, if you must. Let me send a plate of food home with you."

"No, that is alright. Besides I do not have the time to wait." Without further comment, Jacob rose.

"I will walk you out," said Noah.

Together the two walked down the hall to the front door. "Thanks for coming, Jacob. So, you are leaving the store?"

"Yes. In a week or so."

"Fine. I will see you Monday. Merry Christmas, brother."

"Thank you for everything, Noah."

With that, Jacob left the house and went directly to his apartment.

Scrooge asked, "Why did you lie to your brother?"

"I had troubles on my mind." Then he added, "During that period of time the melancholy gripped me. It still holds me."

"I never guessed your serious nature was anything other than who you are."

"It is what I became. But as boys, Noah and I were always laughing."

"That surprises me," said Scrooge.

"Come, it is a new day," said Marley.

THE MONDAY AFTER Christmas Noah arose early. With excitement, he prepared himself for what he believed would bring him an advancement at work.

He stepped out into the chill of another day and walked toward the bank. He decided he would buy himself a warmer coat as soon as he received the raise he had been promised. Arriving ten minutes before the bank opened, Noah paced in front of the doors. The extra effort of movement did little to keep him warm. As he walked back and forth Bartholomew Pressey, the store's owner, came up behind and tapped him on the shoulder. Noah turned around and with surprise said, "Good morning, sir."

"What are you doing here, Noah?"

"Mrs. Swinburne arrived late, so I was unable to deposit the Christmas Eve funds," said Noah.

"I see, and your Christmas, was it jolly?"

"Oh yes, sir, quite delightful. And your family? Did you enjoy your days off?"

"It was wonderful, especially spending time with Reuben. I hardly get to see him now that he is at Cambridge."

When the bank opened their doors, both men entered the establishment. Noah unlatched his satchel to retrieve the deposit, then stopped mid-step. He forced his arm into the bag, felt around the edges, then brought his hand out empty. Disbelieving his sense of touch, he looked inside, but could find no semblance of the funds.

Seeing the worried look on Noah's face, Pressey asked, "What's wrong?"

"The money. It's gone."

"It's gone; what did you do with it?"

"I put it in the bag."

Both men looked at each other. The distress in Noah's face showed in his quivering lips. Pressey's growing anger revealed itself through narrowing eyes. "Where could it be? Who other than you had access to your satchel?"

"No one. But I did fall twice en route to the bank. However, each time what seemed to be an honorable fellow returned the pouch."

"Honorable humbug; it was Sir Stephen," said Scrooge.

"Careful, Ebenezer," said Marley.

"Who else could it be? He's the one who opened the bag before giving it back."

"Did you actually see him remove the money?"

"No, but..."

"Then take care, Ebenezer, a faulty mindset will cause you harm," insisted Marley.

Pressey said, "Noah, you are responsible for that money."

"I know, and I will own that responsibility. I just do not know what happened," said Noah.

"How could you not know that the money was missing? Did not the lack of weight in the bag give you a clue the money was absent?"

"It would have if I had brought the coins, but because of the late start to the bank I decided to leave them at the store."

"None the less I still have no choice but to place you under arrest," said Pressey.

"Could I not work to pay back the money?"

"I will not have an employee I do not trust. Your unreliability can not be tolerated."

Scrooge looked upon his ghostly friend and found him tugging at his stringy hair. The tugs turned into jerks, then suddenly with a popping sound a pluck of hair freed itself, carrying with it not only a portion of skull but also brain matter. As soon as he liberated one handful, he was repeating the process with the other hand. Oddly the hole created by the hair removal filled in instantaneously, allowing him the ability to repeat the agonizing process again and again.

Noah stood quietly with his eyes focused on the space in front of his feet while Pressey sent for a constable. Noah could have easily run, but every man of honor within the bank would have given chase. Within five minutes, the accused was being led away to Newgate Prison. While en route people stopped to stare at the sight of a thin, well-dressed man being led down the street by the ill-kept, heavy-set constable, only a small boy had the spirit to ask, "Are you going to hang him?"

"Move along."

Newgate, the closest prison to the bank, dominated the area in which it stood. Its massive stone block construction and triple entrance created an atmosphere of both strength and peril.

For the size of the building, the entrance door was tiny. As the constable knocked upon the wood, an image flashed in Noah's mind of an animal trap, which lets victims in but through which none can ever pass back to freedom. A chill of fear ran up his spine. "I do not belong here. I have done nothing wrong."

"Quiet!"

"Please, I promise to find the money."

"You should have thought of that before you stole it."

Noah opened his mouth to speak but stopped when the constable raised his index finger to his lip and said, "You will regret your next word."

Once inside, the smell of urine, rotting corpses, and all matter of foulness drifted throughout Noah's nose, causing him to nearly vomit. The men were led through a short dark hallway to a small room. A well-dressed man in a black suit and broad-brimmed hat unlocked the room's door. Inside the room, a man sat slumped on the floor with his back next to the wall. He made no acknowledgment of the newcomers as Noah was shoved into the room. Without a word, the door was slammed closed and the two trapped men were left in a space without windows, light, or furniture.

The darkness penetrated Noah to his core, causing a chill that direct flame could not have warmed. The seated man stood up, walked to Noah, and with one fist knocked him unconscious. As Noah became aware, he had no idea for how long he had lain in oblivion. The first thing he realized was that he no longer wore shoes or a coat. Disoriented, his body, numb from the room's wintry temperature, trembled. He could not recall where he was, or how he got to be lying upon a stone floor. The only light his eyes grasped was the sliver flowing from under the door. Then, as though that light illuminated his mind, he remembered it all: the missing money, the arrest, the attack. Jumping to his feet he turned in the direction of where he remembered his attacker to be seated and yelled, "Give me back my clothes!"

The quiet of no response echoed throughout Noah's aching head. With less enthusiasm, he repeated himself and received the same silence. Discouraged, Noah just stood in the middle of the room quaking from the cold and his growing fear. He was scared to move or speak for fear he may again fall prey to his attacker. The stillness was broken when the door opened. Only then did Noah realize his assailant had been removed. In the doorway stood a guard holding a young boy by the collar. The turnkey threw the child into the cell. Seventy pounds of youth slammed into Noah's chest, propelling him three feet

backwards. The wall was the only thing that stopped them both from falling. After regaining his balance Noah helped the child to his feet and asked, "Are you alright?"

"Keep your hands off me, bugger."

"Relax, I will not harm you."

"Just stay to yourself."

The only two who could see in the obscure light were Marley and Scrooge. As the youth backed away from Noah, Marley moved in behind his brother. Standing within inches of Noah's back, Marley pushed his hand to the center of his own chest. Located inside the heart's chain spun Fire Twirlers. He relocated all but one of the captured blazes to his shoulder, then directed the remaining Twirler to start spinning the chain piercing his heart. With each flicker from the flame the circular ring of iron rotated faster and faster until it was moving so quickly it appeared to disappear. Marley then bit the end of his index finger off. He placed the finger's exposed bone on to the spinning metal causing sparks to fly from his chest. Upon exiting him, the flickers entered his brother. Noah, not understanding the heat, felt it nonetheless. Slowly he warmed enough to stop his shivering. Marley continued this process until the door opened, at which time he replaced the remaining Fire Twirlers back into his heart chain.

For a few seconds the flood of light caused Noah's eyes to clamp shut. A man pointed to Noah and said, "Come along." Looking through squinting eyes, Noah did as he was told. The turnkey shoved Noah along the narrow corridor through a maze of rights and lefts until they entered an office where a man sat reading at a desk. A fireplace blazed the first true warmth Noah had felt since leaving home.

The man did not stop reading until he had completed the entire document. Raising his head to look at the subject of his reading, he said, "You are either a very brave or stupid man. Which do you suppose you are?"

"I would say unluc..."

"I did not ask you to speak!" screamed the man. "Are you always this boorish?"

Noah said nothing, instead casting his eyes to his shoeless feet. After waiting a few seconds for a response, the man continued, "Well, you must be stupid. You speak when not asked and remain silent when questioned. So what are we going to do with you?"

Again, Noah remained quiet. "Well..." The magistrate looked down at the report, then continued, "Mr. Marley, let me tell you how things work around here." He examined Noah, then asked, "Do you always walk the streets without shoes and a greatcoat?" He paused for the reply, then pounded his fist on the desk and bellowed, "Answer me, Mr. Marley!"

Stunned by the magistrate's demand, Noah quickly responded, "They were stolen by the man in the waiting cell."

The magistrate smiled, then said, "It seems you get stolen from a lot. Why do you suppose that is?" He paused for an answer, but when none was offered, he continued, "You have just learned the law of Newgate. Protect yourself or you will lose everything. You will not be pampered by me, or any of the turnkeys. There are a lot of law-abiding people who do not have a bed, warmth, much to eat or even clean water to drink. So why should you have it better than them?" This was a question he knew would not get a reply, nor did he want one, so he continued without pausing. "Being magistrate for London is my occupation, as it is the same for the turnkeys. We are not here to do good for you, or even society. We are here to make a living. Everything you will receive will personally cost me money. So you will be given only the pound of bread and water the law demands. Anything else will have to be purchased, or someone on the outside will have to bring it to you. Expect nothing from me, and we will both remain happy. Do I make myself clear?"

Noah nodded his head to affirm the words were heard.

"You are a quiet one. That just may work to your advantage, but I doubt it. You look like a dead man to me. If you do not replace your clothing, I wager you will be dead within three days. Get him out of here." The magistrate chuckled as he enjoyed the thought of just having intimidated another newcomer.

After being pushed through a maze of corridors, Noah was forced into a large room holding mostly men. Two women and a young boy huddled together in the corner furthest from the fireplace. A dark-skinned woman was scrubbing the boy's neck while the second woman held a cup of whisky from which the swab was moistened. All but four men sat around a long table near the blazing fire. Six were playing cards, five drank beer, and the last three clustered together whispering amongst themselves. Of the four not at the table, three were rolling dice, and the last was urinating in a metal pot near the women and boy. Only a couple of men drinking beer looked up to watch the newcomer enter.

Noah turned toward the gate as the guard secured the entrance. He stood cold, confused and incarcerated among those he never would have looked at twice on the streets. The closure to the gateway opened a floodgate of emotion. Without warning, an explosive anger overwhelmed him. He ran at the door as though it were open. He flung against the wood with such a force that the sound was heard throughout the room, and then every face turned toward him. The dice rolled into the fireplace, cards fell out of hands, beer splashed on facial hair, the women stepped closer to Noah as the boy stepped away, the three deep in conversation hesitated, then continued, and the man urinating missed the pot.

Dazed, Noah turned toward the table. Studying each man, he quickly found the one he was trying to locate. The next moment, he began running at the scoundrel,

yelling, "Give me my coat back!" He grabbed the collar of the man wearing his coat and yanked him so hard it pulled him off the bench and out of the garment. The two began battling over it. "You stole my coat."

"I bought it," said the man as he struggled to his feet.

Each matched blow-for-blow with the other. The fighting only ended when the man who had actually stolen the coat spun Noah around and landed a fist to his jaw. For the second time in as many hours, Noah dropped to the floor unconscious.

As he came back to awareness, Noah realized both women, and a young boy were standing over him. While regaining his senses, the black woman said, "Quiet now, honey. You ain't gonna get nuthin' in here by makin' enemies."

Noah looked at the woman as though she were from a different planet. Then a young man within the group sensed his confusion and explained, "She's from

America. Escaped from the land of the free to freedom. Just let her take care of you. She's good, she's helped me with these nasty bug bites."

"Guvnor, you stay clear of that James Maxey. He poisoned his wife and daughter. And he'll work against you too," said the second woman.

Sitting up, Noah rubbed his jaw and asked, "Who's James Maxey?"

"Why, he's the one wearing your coat. Bought it from Nathan Simons, the one who knocked you unconscious."

"I'm going to get that rotter."

"No, you ain't. I's taking care of you now. And you's staying clear of him too." The black woman paused to feel Noah's jaw, then continued, "I'm Dinah Smith. Don't rightly know my real last name. It stayed in Africa. You can just call me Dee. Everythang's short with me. Don't think anythang's broke on ya."

"What are you here for?" asked the boy.

"A misunderstanding," Noah mumbled.

"Bloody, didn't know that was against the law. I may never get out if there is a heavy penalty for that. But let me introduce myself. I'm Joseph Freeman, Swell Gang member. Have you heard of the gang?"

"No, don't believe so."

"Just as well, easier to make your way through a crowded theatre if they think you're one of them. Never got wealth, but them rich blokes, well, they're rich." Joseph paused to look at the bump on Noah's face before adding, "I'm the best dipper in the gang. At least I was until they nabbed me. Probably going to get hanged now. My best mate met the rope a while back. Can't expect no different for me." The well-dressed youth shook Noah's hand, then added, "This wonderful ladybird is Martha Hart, and I'd give her my heart any day."

"Please to meet ya, mister..." she paused, waiting for a response from Noah.

"Marley. Call me Noah."

"Mister Marley, you are a pleasant-looking fellow, and I have pleasant experiences to sell. Course kind of hard to do in here, but not impossible." She winked, then added, "I believe your shoes are walking around with Levi over there." Martha pointed to a man standing next to the fireplace, then added, "We can get them back for you. He's a Jew, and no one will help him. The coat, it's gone. You best keep close to the flame during the day."

Noah looked over at Levi, then confirmed the shoes were his. The four huddled together plotting their strategy for regaining the stolen footwear.

Walking toward Maxey, Marley said, "Maybe they can't do anything about that cowardly killer, but I can."

Scrooge called after his friend. "Jacob, Jacob, what are you doing?"

"Making life uncomfortable for him."

Marley stood in front of Maxey, and with his fingernails he began to flake the skin on his forearm into a powder. After he had shredded the skin, Marley continued by scraping the ghostly tissues below the epidermis. Within a few minutes his entire forearm, to the bone, was a pile of dust. He inhaled until his

chest grew to twice its normal size, then, while retaining the ghostly air, he held the tattered arm in front of Maxey. With one quick release, he blew the mound of ethereal flesh into his face. Instantly Maxey started to sneeze in quick succession, then frantically began rubbing his skin.

"I'll do it again, or something worse if I have to," Marley said as the wholeness of his arm reappeared. While he rejoined Scrooge he quipped, "He won't get over that anytime soon."

"Can I do that kind of stuff?"

"No, Ebenezer, if you were to tear up your arm you would retain some of the injury back in the flesh. With the luck of an angel you will never have to do this kind of thing in death."

"With the luck of an angel," echoed Scrooge.

Maxey continued sneezing and coughing to such an extent that everyone near him backed away.

The door to the cell flung open. Occupying nearly the entire entrance space stood an enormous turnkey. In a deep bellowing voice he yelled, "Alright you bitches and curs, it's time for the yard. Some of you dogs have got people waiting. Hurry up, I've no time to waste."

Every person, except Noah, raced toward the door. Being the last person in line, the gatekeeper stopped Noah and said, "Last out pays the toll, that will be a penny."

Infuriated, Noah asked, "And what if I decide not to pay?"

"Then you don't get to talk to a young man who looks just like you at the cage. The family resemblance is twin-like. Wouldn't you agree?"

Noah took a coin from the toe of his sock and tossed it at the extortionist. "Here is your bloody penny." Without haste he side-stepped the husky turnkey and followed Joseph, who had waited for him. Together they made their way to the narrow yard. The extreme chill of winter penetrated his skin like the fangs of a rabid dog, without malice, yet nonetheless inflicting great harm. Noah hurried to the iron barred enclosure facing the street. Waiting on the street side was Jacob. Before Noah had even touched the bars leading to the free side, he ordered his brother to give up his coat and shoes to him.

"Where are yours?"

"Never mind that. Just give me yours, now!" Jacob did as instructed. As he handed the coat through the bars, a metal spur snagged his arm creating a cut over two inches in length. Jacob jumped back while shouting, "Bloody! What was that?"

Together the two inspected the iron rod and saw that someone had taken a knife and cut into the metal, causing a portion of the iron to curl away from its host. The barb created a sharp point, which would snag anything that passed near it. Upon closer inspection they realized someone had made a sport of cutting the bars. Several had various lengths and thicknesses of metal projections protruding from them. Carefully Jacob handed Noah his shoes. Putting on Jacob's clothes, the leftover warmth caused Noah's toes to tingle. As his feet started to regain feeling, the thought of reclaiming his shoes from Levi left him. Noah groaned more from the pleasure of the heat than the pain of the numbness. Immediately, Jacob began hopping from foot-to-foot in an effort to repel the chill.

"Mr. Pressey fired me," said Jacob.

"You were quitting anyway. I need you to help me."

"I came as soon as I heard."

"Thanks for coming. I want you to bring me the warmest clothes I've got. Bring everything from underwear, to boots, and a hat."

"I'll bring them tomorrow."

"Bring money, at least a few pennies each day. And food, plus water. I'm counting on you, Jacob. Do you think you can do this for me?"

"Yes, of course, Noah."

"You're a good brother. Does Flora know?"

"I don't think so, but then you know how news travels."

"Go to her as soon as you leave me. Tell her, but don't let her come here."

"How can I stop her?"

"I don't know. I just can't have her seeing me like this. I'm counting on you, Jacob, to keep her away from this wretched place."

"I will do my best."

"Mr. Pressey told you what happened?"

"Yes, he had to when he fired me."

"I did not steal that money. You believe me, don't you?"

"Yes, of course I do."

"Oh, thank you, brother. You don't know how important it is to me that you trust me."

"I know you wouldn't steal money, even if you had none."

"Well, I don't know if I would go that far."

They smiled at each other, but the situation was too serious to laugh.

"I need you to try and figure out what happened to the money."

"How do I do that?"

"Try and find the note Mrs. Swinburne paid with. Before handing it to me, she marked it with a kiss. Look for the imprint of her lips."

"She probably does that to most of her notes. She flirts with all the pants and even some of the skirts."

"Yes, yes, but this one was different."

"In what way?"

"As she handed the bill to me, her hand smudged the rouge which left a fingerprint at the top of the lip image." Scrooge looked at Marley as Noah continued, "In the end, her lip print created a pattern which looked more like a mother hushing her child, than a seductress in search of a mate."

The young Jacob's eyes widened as Scrooge looked upon Marley. "I know that bill, Jacob," said Scrooge.

"It does not surprise me you remember."

"How could you do this to your own brother?"

"How could I do it to anybody, Ebenezer? Why would I do it to anybody?" He paused, then answered his own question. "The opportunity just presented itself — and I took it."

"Yes, but stealing the money with which we became partners?"

"My spirit has lived with the burden of having stolen that money for nearly half a century. And now, my heart has a shackle that time alone will never dissolve."

"Your suffering is nothing compared to Noah's."

"True, though, that is, all suffering pains." Marley howls with anguish as he rips the chain from his heart. A ghostly spray of blood and dust gushes from the wound. Within a moment, the heart self-repairs and the chain, larger than before, grips it with an intensified torment.

"I don't know if I can continue helping you."

"Then I should take you home."

Stave Three
Caught Then Controlled

BEFORE SCROOGE COULD deliver a word, Marley snatched him from 1813. Scrooge sighed a faint protest, yet allowed his distressed friend to pull him from the

prison. The fierce speed of Marley's departure caused Scrooge to brace against his friend's thrust of motion. As Marley rushed toward the future, an outburst of activity accelerated London's change. Burlington Arcade reappeared between blinks. The rapid change of buildings rising while others fell gave London the illusion of breathing.

Marley only slowed when smoke swamped the sky. He was unaffected by the billowing cinders, yet Scrooge, while tearing up from the smoke, nearly suffocated from the ash. Hacking every syllable, he asked, "Jacob, what is happening?"

"Covent Garden Theatre is burning!"

"Burning?! That happened 50 years ago."

Abruptly Marley stopped. Suspended over London, they each looked at the other. Scrooge continued to cough, then without warning Jacob grabbed Ebenezer's arm and shot the two of them straight up out of the toxic cloud.

Scrooge cleared his throat, then asked, "Have you taken us further in the past?"

Marley searched every direction in hopes of discovering a landmark that would identify the time period, while Scrooge watched silently. Then, without warning, Marley shouted, "Over there." He pointed across the Thames. "The Crystal Palace has already been moved to Sydenham Hill."

"So we must be in the present," said Scrooge. "The Palace — why it was only moved a couple of years ago."

"It looks like the building has been there several years."

"No, how can that be?"

"Look around the building, Ebenezer. The trees have grown quite tall. That doesn't happen in a couple of years."

Scrooge studied the building's grounds, then said, "I think you may be right."

"I overshot the time period," said Marley, more to himself than to Scrooge.

"We can get back, right?"

"This is not supposed to happen."

"But we can get back — right?"

Marley did not answer. Instead, his thoughts focused on trying to understand their predicament. Could he actually have propelled them past 1854?

"We can find the date on a newspaper," suggested Scrooge.

Again Marley did not answer. He remained a quarter mile above the city, closed his eyes, then fixated on his inner place of contemplation. As if a hatch had opened, Scrooge plunged toward gravity's pull. "Ma-a-ar-ley-y-y!"

Marley stiffened,  causing Scrooge to plummet. Though he continued screaming, Scrooge knew Marley was caught in his own silent world. His race downward gathered speed, until he heard his mother's voice say, "Finally, I will be able to hold my baby boy." The words drained his fear. As he dropped the city's sounds became noticeable. Though he would not look down, he felt the earth's frozen fingers reaching up. Oddly, he was ready to finally be caressed by the parent he knew loved him. One

who gave her life for him, yet still remained devoted in spirit. So Ebenezer closed his eyes for the inevitable.

Expecting his flesh — no, his actual life — would soon lie pulverized upon London's cobblestones, Scrooge calmed all his muscles. As his spirit succumbed to relaxation, a force beyond him grabbed his arm. Startled, he looked skyward for identification. Swaying in the breeze was a black cape. As the cloth continued to flap, Ebenezer identified the bones of a skeleton beneath the cloak. And he screamed.

Dangling at the mercy of the Ghost of Christmas Yet to Come, Scrooge asked, "Am I dead?" The specter only began moving upward. Terrorized, Scrooge started twisting. Though he hoped for freedom from the apparition, the specter only gripped his coat tighter.

Once even with Marley, the Ghost of Christmas Yet to Come hurled Scrooge into his friend's rigid spirit. Marley barely flinched. As Scrooge drew his next breath the specter again pushed him into Marley. Repeatedly the black-cloaked ghost forced the living into the dead. Scrooge protested, but it did no good. The specter propelled them together so often, and so forcefully, that Marley finally became alert.

The fog within Marley quickly moved from confusion toward panic. "This phantom will destroy you," he warned Ebenezer. "Don't let his bones touch your skin." The specter kept thrusting the two together. The abuse was continuous, yet neither man understood the spook's motivation. Finally Scrooge grabbed hold of Marley's sleeve and yelled, "Stop him, Jacob!" Instantly the specter whisked the pair back to 1854.

Then — Scrooge again surrendered to gravity, dropping several feet. Upon impact, his knees buckled to the ground. Marley put his arms under Scrooge's shoulders and lifted him to his feet. " Is there any injury?" he asked.

"I think I was destined to lie upon the cobblestones today."

Marley looked at his friend with a questioning eye, but only said, "The Ghost of Christmas Yet to Come has spared us."

"Again," replied Scrooge.

Marley had no idea what his friend

meant, but assumed it was not important, so he continued his task of taking Ebenezer home.

As they neared Scrooge's door, Marley's chest began to glow orange, grow hot and heave outward. Beneath the ghost's iridescent skin, Scrooge witnessed his friend's single chain pulsate with each pumping of his heart. Each beat from the dead muscle brought a thrust of molten metal to the surface of the chain. "I'm on fire!" screamed Marley. "I am burning up!" As steam escaped his forehead, new shackles began to form around the heart's chain.

Together they watched as a second and third link attached itself to the metal ring, but it wasn't until the fourth link pierced Marley's skin that Scrooge yelled, "Jacob, we must return. You... you are under attack!"

"The risk is too great!"

"Our bravery will be powerful," Ebenezer insisted. "We must — for I fear for your..." As his voice floated away, he focused on Marley's face. The agony of the new chains caused Marley to wince as he agreed. Slowly they began moving to the past.

1844 passed, then 1834, and when 1829 moved to 28 the newest of Marley's chains disappeared. Once they settled into 1813, the third chain disappeared. As they neared the prison, only two links remained attached to Marley's heart. Though they did create an added drag, Marley quickly adapted to the burden.

The day, December 28th, had the thickest fog in London's blurry history. Newgate Prison was nearly hidden by a soupy mixture of mist and fireplace exhaust. As the two approached Noah's cell, they watched as a stagecoach hit a wagon full of firewood. Throughout the city the sound of crashes, slides and abrupt stops filled the air while often the visuals were unavailable to the travelers.

As they entered the room of prisoners, a murkiness lingered in the air. Even

with the haze Marley and Scrooge could see the trouble overwhelming the room, and Noah was in the middle of it. Most of the inmates watched from the edges, as did the turnkey, while Simons manhandled a young boy not yet a dozen years of age.

"You owe me this," said Simons as he grabbed the hat from the boy's head.

"It's mine!" cried Henry. He put up quite a struggle, but was no match for the thug. That is until Noah came to the boy's aid.

"This boy is my property," said Noah.

"You can't own a person."

"And yet I do," insisted Noah. "Now release my property!" Henry looked at Noah and opened his mouth to speak, but Noah quieted him with a fierce look.

"Sure, I will release him, but the hat is mine."

"No, it ain't," said Dee, the dark-skinned woman, as she clobbered the thief with a piece of firewood.

At her feet lay the good-for-nothing, out cold. Henry picked up his hat and bowed to both Noah and Dee. "Thank you, guvnor. I owe you both."

In unison both adults welcomed the boy, "You stay with us until your parents claim you."

"Then I will be with you forever," Henry commented.

Noah looked at the orphan and asked, "Do you think forever is long enough?"

The three smiled, then moved away from Simons' unconscious body. While the criminal lay helpless, others pilfered his possessions. By the time Simons regained consciousness, barely his underclothes were left. He stormed with indignation. Vowing revenge, he moved toward the heat of the open fire, and there he stayed.

At the opposite side of the room, Noah gathered with Dee, Henry and two other friends, Martha and Joseph. "Why are you here?" Noah asked Henry.

"Joseph knows," he said, looking at the gangly boy towering above him.

"He's my apprentice," said Joseph.

"It appears he has missed a few of your lessons." Noah smiled at his sarcasm, but then realized prison had already changed his mindset, for he never would have made such a flippant comment about criminality a mere two days earlier.

The rest of the day passed without incident. As sleep is never readily available in prison, that evening Noah surprised even himself, when he released his fear of being attacked by the killers near him and dropped into a long-overdue rest.

WITH THE LIGHT of dawn, the day as usual brought the men from the sleeping dungeon to the day room. The only difference was the lack of women. Noah figured they were just late, but they never arrived that day. When asked, the turnkey just said, "It is none of your business." Without them, the room cast an aggressive gloom over the day. Petty fights sprang up throughout the cycle of hours. Noah kept the boys, and himself, out of the fray.

The only other men quiet that day were the three that had been huddling together since Noah's arrival. Their self-imposed isolation seemed normal. No one had ever been curious about them, so once again they silently clung to their own aloof world.

On that Wednesday, Noah expected no visitors. He had almost decided to forego the trip to the exercise yard where family and friends were allowed to contact inmates. However, the desire to clear the sorrow of his arrest sent Noah into the day's frozen air. He hoped the crispy breeze would lift his spirits, but had no idea just how profoundly his desire would materialize.

Cold air assaulted his face. The shock of the wind's force brought tears to the corners of his eyes. As he compelled himself to face the weather, his thoughts turned to analyzing the events of his demise. Yet Noah would never come to the correct conclusion. His mind was not capable of imagining that Jacob caused his tragedy. It would take the collapse of Noah's character for him to even approach the truth. Nonetheless, as he circled the yard, his tension began to ease. At least until his visitor arrived.

As Noah rounded the circle inmates walked for exercise, his stride ceased upon the discovery of Flora standing at the visitor's cage. She stood there, in silence, watching him. Internally Noah fumed that Flora had gone against his wishes. Externally he was thrilled at the sight of her.

"Why are you here?" he demanded.

"Because you are my husband."

"You should not have to suffer this matter."

"And yet I do. Willingly." She then added, "I bring you news."

"Good news?"

"No, just news. Your trial has been scheduled for two weeks from today."

"Has Jacob found a barrister for me?"

"All of them want a large deposit. I am determined to find the funds."

Noah looked at her with tenderness. It was at that moment that Noah realized representation at his trial would probably not be available, so he brought forth his favorite subject — his wife.

"I wish you had not come." Looking away he added, "I did not want you to see me this way."

"You can not shelter me from this."

"Though I wish I could," he mumbled to himself, then spoke to Flora. "Your smile lifts me."

"I miss you starting the morning fire, while I lay toasty beneath the covers," she teased.

"And I miss being able to slide between those same sheets, after you have warmed them before bed."

Though the boundary of bars interrupted their full embrace, each reached through to the other's hand. Interweaving fingers grasped a passionate squeeze. As they lingered in each other's hold, Noah began to feel a solid object in his grip.

Looking into Flora's eyes Noah acknowledged the presence of the mass. Rolling their hands together, both felt the item pivoting between them. Flora tugged at his grasp, but he resisted. For him, the feel of her soothed his sorrow, so he would allow no substance of matter to break her touch.

It was only at the urging of the turnkey's "too close" policy that Noah released his clutch. Only then did he identify the quartz crystal her grandfather had brought her from Switzerland. It was his last gift to her before his passing, so the shock of it now being in his possession caused him concern.

"What is this?" He looked at the glass-like gemstone. He, of course, had seen the stone every day of their marriage resting atop Flora's dresser. This stone was special, even in the world of quartz, for at its center stood the phantom of a younger crystal. Covering the inner point of the crystal blanketed a black powdery mineral.

"We are this crystal, two in one," she explained.

"I can not take your grandfather's..."

"This is my crystal, Noah. Besides, when Grampa gave this to me, he said the day would come when I would feel an obligation to pass the stone to 'a loved one in

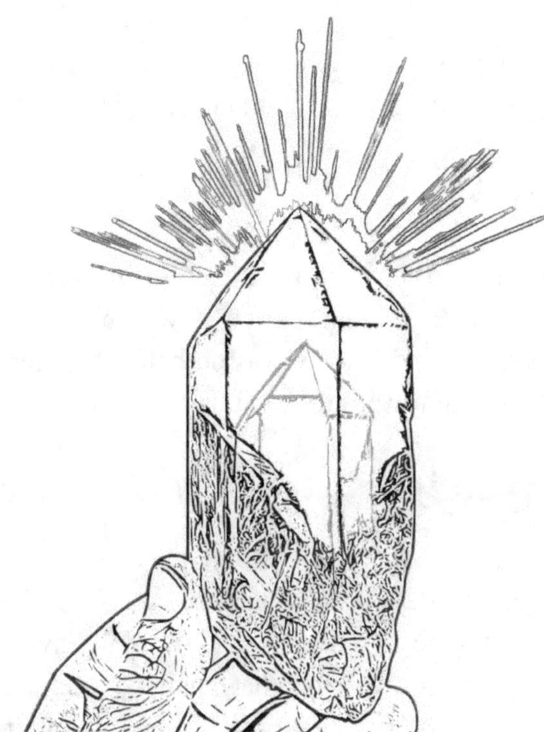

need'. He told me the love of two is contained within this one stone."

"Should I do anything special with it?" he asked.

"With this stone, my strength is yours to use whenever it is needed."

"My dear sweet Flora. Thank you."

"Ebenezer, come take a good look at this thing," requested Marley. As each stood on either side of Noah, they admired the stone's qualities.

"Well, that is amazing. It appears that a scattering of chimney soot settled on the tip about half way through its growth," said Scrooge.

"Yes, and it's perfectly formed too."

Even though the turnkey had continued to watch Noah and Flora for the violation of "extreme affection", they stayed within each other's touch. After a fair amount of time, the turnkey yelled the demand that all inmates return to the day room. Noah ignored the cry out from the jailer.

Instead, Noah lifted Flora's hand to his lips. As he kissed the back of her fingers, a hawk began to circle just a few feet above their heads. Surprised by the bird's willingness to suffer the cold, Noah looked up, then told Flora, "We will soar again."

The guard grabbed Noah by the shoulder and yanked him from Flora's touch. Angrily he said, "Listen to me, convict. When I talk — you react. Do not ever ignore me again! Now move." With that Noah began walking toward the building. The rage of the turnkey was a minor price to pay for his brightened spirit. He did not look back at Flora. The fear of sobs forced his eyes forward. That day, Noah willingly paid the penny to the jailer for being the last inside.

"Tell me something, Jacob," said Scrooge.

"What is your request?"

"Do you already know everything that has or is about to happen?"

"No, I only have the knowledge of my living experiences."

"So you did not know about the crystal?"

"That is right. Truth be known, I did not even know that Flora had visited Noah," explained Marley.

Ebenezer asked, "So we are here to change the outcome of the trial?"

"No, that is not possible. We are here to get a full understanding of the tragedy."

"What are we going to eventually change?"

"Noah's misery."

That left Scrooge speechless. He paused in thought, then cautiously asked, "I had actually figured that out. But how...?" Scrooge did not know how to phrase the question so more information could be gained, and Marley was no help. His friend just looked away from him, then started moving toward the next day.

THE WINTRY MIX of cold and fog began the day of Noah's arrest. And now, five days later, the weather had turned to the extreme. London was not used to days of below-zero temperatures. Inside Newgate, the only thing that changed from the bitter cold to the ferociously frigid was that the inmates pushed the community table as close to the fire as possible. Most of the inmates sat around the fire that day; they had to, to survive. Getting along was another issue.

Everybody in the room knew to avoid both Maxey and Simons. On that Thursday, actions to avoid any one person proved to be ambitious. All were trapped. Noah and his group clustered at the table, as did most everyone else. The three reclusive men sat at the fire's edge. They continued to evade the other inmates. However the shunning was mutual, as the rumor had traveled around the room that these three were spies against the other prisoners.

The day brought nothing of worth to the room. Each prisoner suffered their own personal agony. Attempts to lighten the mood through humor, or stories, did little to lessen the collective torment.

"Why is that man lying on the floor?" asked Henry.

"Stay away from him. He's been bitten by a rat," explained Noah.

"Does he have rabies?"

"Maxey or Simons would have murdered him by now," replied Martha.

"So what is wrong with him?"

"Gaol-fever. He is a dead man, just ain't stopped breathing yet," said Dee.

"Why is no one helping him?"

"Henry, you are a curious one," said Joseph.

"It may not be as contagious as rabies, but Gaol-fever still kills those it infects," said Noah.

"I want to help him."

"Look Henry, no one wants you to get sick. Also, he is different from us."

"He looks the same. Besides, Dee is different too; she is both a woman and black. So what is different about Levi?"

"His religion," said Martha.

"Oh." Henry nodded with understanding, and not another word on the subject was spoken.

"So, Martha — what is your story?"

"Some luck, some misfortune, but mostly just working the streets."

"That sounds like a tragedy."

"The hardship is I am getting released soon, and you are all staying."

An uncomfortable pause caused Noah to change the subject.

"So tell me, Henry, where is your family?" asked Noah.

"Joseph is my..."

In rapid response the group chimed in:

"Instructor."

"Master."

"Owner."

"No, he is my cousin," explained Joseph.

"And about becoming a pickpocket?"

"Necessity. We lost most of our family in a boating accident. Gotta eat." Joseph added, "Besides, Henry tricked me."

"I did not. It is not my fault I am a better lifter than you," bragged Henry.

"What are you talking about?" Dee asked.

"Last year, after the funerals, I was training Henry in the art of grabbing-the-gold when the little fiend handed me my wallet after the lesson."

The other three laughed, slapped the table with approval, and then declared Henry the smarter of the two. They chatted throughout the afternoon. All forms of topics were raised as each told their story, but one subject stood out — slavery.

"Dee, tell me how an American black woman made it to England?" Joseph inquired.

"I had help from my slave owner."

"What did they do? Put you on the ship?"

"They did, but without the goal of my escaping once in Great Britain."

"So you are a runaway?"

"I am free!"

"I want to go to America, do you miss it?" queried Joseph.

"The sin of bondage may never be washed from that land. It holds no benefit for me."

"What happens if Old Bailey sends you back?"

"The courts own me now, so they can have their will. But let me tell you this, I will always escape the master's chains."

"Blessed be," replied Martha.

"Blessed be," repeated Scrooge.

THOUGH THE END of daylight usually brings a night of dreading the sleeping dungeon, this evening brought a peaceful rest, at least until the hint of light. As a shadowy dawn lingered, several turnkeys stormed the dungeon.

"All of you bums stand in a row!"

Stunned by the intensity of the demand, every prisoner looked at the guards, yet waited to act. Each of the jailers held as many sets of leg-irons as they could carry.

"You will get up, NOW!" screamed the guard.

"You have a minute. Anyone not in line stays in the sleeping room," roared another. All of the men scrambled to their feet. That minute passed in seconds as every convict rushed to obey.

"Stand with your feet apart," instructed a turnkey.

The men did the unavoidable; each allowed a prison guard to lock their legs together.

With the weight of shackles clanking, Henry asked his cousin, "Why is this happening?"

"Bloody quiet!" shouted the overseer.

It was Martha in the day room who informed the men the reason all were wearing leg cuffs. The three elusive spies turned out to be jail-breakers.

"They were quiet about it, but I heard them break through the roof."

"How did you hear that, when your sleeping room is also in the dungeon?"

"See that bloke," Martha pointed to the heaviest of the two guards. "I fixed the bulge in his pants last night."

All but Henry understood. "Why would you fix his pants?" he asked.

Martha just ignored the question and continued, "I even helped the three."

"How?" asked Joseph.

"As that creep stumbled through pokes at me, I turned him so he faced away from the window. Then I watched the three drop a makeshift rope between the prison and College of Physicians."

"And the guard had no idea?"

"He was a little busy at the time," quipped Martha.

"Why does a woman betray herself?" asked Scrooge.

"No, Ebenezer, the laws forsake women," replied Marley.

"There is nothing forcing Martha," insisted Scrooge.

"How about the desire for release from Newgate?"

"Why is that important?"

"Ebenezer — nobody wants to be in prison! The only reason Martha has not already been released is because she does not have the twopence to pay her liberation fee," explained Marley.

"Is there no other way to get the money?"

"Not for her. You tell me, Ebenezer, what right to ownership, or even to a modest living, does she have?"

Marley waited for a reply, but the answer was understood, so Ebenezer remained silent.

RIGHT AROUND DUSK, the day room's massive door swung open. At the threshold stood two of the turnkeys carrying a limp man. A hangman's bag covered his drooping head while leg and wrist-irons prevented resistance. Without ceremony, the guards threw the man to the floor, then left.

Few of the other prisoners showed any interest in the unconscious man. However, Henry insisted on helping. With care, he approached the fellow. In order to prevent injury to Henry, his four companions stood near him as he lifted the bag from the senseless man's head. Although Henry showed surprise at the individual's unmasking, the others did not. Heaped on the floor was one of the three prison-breakers.

As soon as Martha, Dee and Noah identified the man, they returned to the community table. Joseph stayed to assist Henry in the needs of the escapee. The man's entire head was swollen. Henry hoped the man would not regain his mind until the bruising in his eyes decreased. Together, the two boys dragged the jail-breaker to the fireplace. They placed him near the dying Levi. Slowly, the man started to groan.

Once the boys joined the community table, Dee told them, "I would give ya all a grog, if I had it."

"Yeah, I be celebrating big today," agreed Martha. "And not just with grog. New Year's Day deserves the good stuff. But I bet there is not a pence among us, right?"

As Martha half waited for an answer, Noah began to realize the truth that 1814 had arrived. Christmas was in the rear but one week, and yet, a lifetime of frights had occurred within those seven days.

The others remained in conversation while Noah drifted into reflection. The upending of his fate created confusion. He wondered why a loving God would do such a thing to not only him, but to any person. What loving purpose could there be

in such treachery? And yet, he prayed with all of his heart that Jesus would protect Flora, and he believed God's son could. He did not want to feel sorry for himself, so when anger pierced his thoughts, he pushed away from the table and walked to the double-grated window.

Dazed by the opening's chill, Noah immediately retreated to the heat. Standing alone, he struggled to contain his rage, and then when he realized his future could no longer be shaped by his plans — he released tears. Sorrow and anger merged into one.

Marley waved Scrooge off as he stood next to his brother. From across the room Scrooge heard Marley howl as he openly grieved for Noah's hardship. Only Levi among the living heard the yowls from the spirit. As Levi began to shake from the noise, Marley said, "Wish I could change this for you." Looking into Noah's reddened eyes, Marley continued. "I pledge this to you Noah — I will help your soul recover from the pain of this life spirit, or my own spirit and soul will I surrender in replacement of yours." The guilt coming from Marley had the opposite effect on Noah, for tears turned into sobs.

As Noah jerked his body in an effort to control the weeping, Marley put his arm across his brother's shoulder. "Noah, remember gran-mama's story about the caterpillar?" He paused to give Noah the normal response time after a question, then continued. "The caterpillar is born with one goal — to crawl around the plant-world eating as much of it as is possible before the worm's end." Marley breathed in the frosty air, then said, "Oddly the caterpillar is not even aware of its true purpose — it just transforms. To the worm within this creature, life is over after its massive devouring. The caterpillar is saddened by its coming end, for eating is its life. Yet the creator knows the beast's true purpose. The transformation always planned for the animal is the creature's destination."

Marley paused, planned his next words carefully, then said, "Your soul knows of your coming transformation. I can tell you to be calm, and yet, I know not when you will be delivered from this horror. As the worm has no idea it will become the most beautiful example of nature, so we as humans have no idea of our perfect essence either. We just become fully functional through our spirit's plan." Pausing, Marley finished, "Most humans are not aware of their journey's objective, and yet even through the unknowing, we often do great things. Noah, you should know that though your life has ended, your future is moving forward."

As Noah, along with the other males, returned to the sleeping dungeon, Joseph asked, "Can I help?" Noah swiped his eyes with his sleeve as he continued in silence. Light left the day, and then in the darkness of sleep, Noah's torment finally dwindled.

That evening, as the turnkey closed the door to the day room, he made note of the need to remove Levi.

WITH ANOTHER DAY came another prisoner return. The day was a Sunday, so the prison's only organized event was church, and all were required to attend. The Ordinary barked a fierce service at the captive audience. Passages of hell for all in attendance seemed to be the theme of the sermon. As the ceremony ended, Noah promptly forgot every word spoken.

Back in the day room, the returning prisoners were greeted with the groans of a man lying at the center of the room. As the prisoners shuffled their chained feet past the disoriented heap, the previously returned prisoner recognized the form on the floor and attacked.

It all happened quickly, and not one being had the instinct to stop the assault. They just watched in alarm as the first prisoner assailed the second.

"You turncoat!" yelled the first prisoner.

"I had to..." complained the newly returned man. The first man stopped the second from completing his thought. Instead he wrapped the chains of his wrist shackles around the seated man's neck and pulled up as hard as he could. Lifting the man several inches off the floor, the entire room heard the cracking of the bones in his neck. With a hard thump the attacker set the prey back on the floor where he just remained, unmoving.

As the room looked on in bewilderment, they realized the man was dead. It all could not have happened faster. Even a bullet would not have been as abrupt. All of the children and many of the women in the room began to scream. The murdered man sat frozen with the weight of his head being pulled downward by his ruined

neck. Oddly he looked like a turtle with bulging eyes, drooping mouth, and a large pointy nose. No one cared that the man was lifeless. The room of prisoners only feared the punishment that was likely to be administered to them.

Before the men in the group could confront the killer, two turnkeys entered the room swinging batons. "All right, swine, back away," said one of the guards to the room of people.

Pushing through to the corpse, the officer placed his hand on the deceased man's shoulder. Promptly he fell over. The turnkeys demanded the group send forth the killer. Wishing to keep themselves safe from retaliation, every person, even Noah, pointed to the perpetrator.

As the guards secured the murderer, two new turnkeys entered the room and carried the corpse away. None of the turnkeys desired to discipline the others, so the crisis went the way of the day and faded with the light.

MARLEY'S SPIRIT WONDERED if the young Jacob had missed his calling in life. He had always been masterful at the business of business. However, the counting house was never his passion. It was just his livelihood. And now as Marley watched the attention his younger self delivered to his horses he knew —

knew he would have been more useful to society as a stable hand than a moneygrubber. Yet that was in the past, and he was here for the future.

Scrooge and Marley watched as young Jacob brushed, fed and loved the horses. Pampering his beasts comforted the guilt of his betrayal of Noah. As his brother suffered in a cage, he played horseman with his twins, Smoke and Shadow. He had always owned the pair of Thoroughbred horses, for he had given the muscle of his youth to the stables. Originally the deal made was that Jacob worked without pay until his foal was born. At that time he would own the horse, yet continue to work for the animal's food and housing. This arrangement turned out to be a first-rate transaction for Jacob, for when the twins were born, the stable owner gave the ambitious boy both colts.

After grooming the pair, Jacob put his forehead to Smoke's brow and said, "I have dishonored myself beyond repair. You, my friends, are my only hope of regaining a righteous path." Stroking each horse equally he added, "Let's play with what little time we have left." In the next breath, Jacob mounted one of the steeds, then began galloping through the open field. He darted in and out as the horse made every effort to oblige his direction.

The painful weather conditions led to the shortening of their ride. 'Could it get colder?' Jacob wondered as he put away the riding equipment. After giving both colts their normal feed, he presented each with half a frozen apple. As they chomped the fruit into mush, Jacob made his way to Newgate.

While he walked, Jacob figured out a method for liberating Noah. He should have acted immediately upon his brother's arrest, but the fear for his own safety caused him to cower. It would have been simple to return the money within a day. Noah himself had provided an explanation with his spills on the ice. Even the most suspicious constable could see the rationale in a story that the "money fell out of the bag". However, that is not what he did. Instead, Jacob allowed the situation to fester into a nightmare.

Smoke and Shadow were Jacob's only assets. The decision to sell the horses labored in Jacob's mind for days. He resented the idea of having to suffer any personal loss. Yet he realized the situation would only improve if he surrendered his cherished colts. Jacob knew that selling one horse would bring enough money to pay back both Pressey and the jail costs.

He contemplated keeping Shadow, but that was not fixed in thought. Both horses had provided the same playfulness and friendship to him. Smoke was ornery with his ability to open up gates. Shadow on the other hand had a passion for running under branches in the hopes of throwing the rider.

But it was the event of both horses working together to save Jacob's life that made the final impression on his decision. He remembered the day the horses kept him in the center while three coyotes circled them. The first coyote moved left,

then Shadow moved left for the block. A second pushed right as Smoke countered the move with a head fake to the right while delivering a kick to the gut of the third coyote moving in on Jacob. The dance of circling and kicking at the beasts lasted for several minutes.

In the end, Shadow suffered a bite to his thigh, Smoke had scratches on his neck, yet Jacob remained unharmed. As the coyotes disappeared into the forest, Jacob made note of the trail of blood covering their path.

Nearing the prison, Jacob resolved to sell Smoke and Shadow together. The twins had never been apart and he knew his selfish desire to keep one would hurt both, so he determined to do the right thing and let them stay together.

AS SCROOGE AND the ghost waited for Jacob to arrive, Marley asked his friend, "Ebenezer, do you have any idea what awaits you upon your passing?"

"Jacob, why do I feel your question is setting me up for trouble?"

The two looked at each other, then smiled, "You are right. I have no honest reason for meddling," said Marley.

"No — no, I do not mind such a conversation. I just did not want to be shocked by the delivery of bad news," replied Scrooge.

Marley began the conversation, "You know when I died, I opened my eyes from what I thought was a 'good night's sleep', then went about my day of getting dressed, going to work and things of that nature."

"Why would you do that?"

"It just seemed like a normal day. However, that did not last long. Soon things got very bizarre. I became aware of my chains, then I realized my skin was translucent."

"Is that when you realized you had perished?" asked Scrooge.

"No, that became obvious when I was standing before Teint and Apurto."

"Who?"

"You will meet them soon."

"I still don't know who they are."

"Teint tracks those that enter and leave the Isle of Transmogrify," said Marley.

"There's that word again."

"What — Teint?"

"No, Transmogrify. I think I have been there," answered Scrooge.

"That is not possible; you still live."

"And yet, I'm sure I was there this very evening."

"You are still alive, right Ebenezer?"

"Last time I checked."

Marley then repeated his original question, "Ebenezer, do you have any idea what awaits you upon your passing?"

"My best guess is — everything you went through, but more...?"

The young Jacob stood at the prison waiting for Noah to arrive. Jacob had willingly become Noah's lifeline. Most days he brought the money and food that Noah needed to survive. On what felt like the coldest day in London's history, Noah finally arrived at the visitor's cage. His face showed signs of exhaustion.

"What have you done?" asked Jacob.

As Noah shuffled his shackled feet, he replied, "I watched a man get murdered. And what have you done, little brother?"

"I just mean — why are you wearing leg-irons?"

"Because there has been a prison break. The turnkeys will do anything to make a pence."

"I do not understand," said Jacob.

"Let me just say this prison is a moneymaking business, and every guard is on the take."

"So how much money do you need today?" asked Jacob.

"All the pence you have got."

"Seriously?"

"They will not take these shackles off until I pay for their release," explained Noah.

"Seriously?"

"Stop saying that! Do you think I am misleading you?"

"No, of course not," replied Jacob. With that he gave his brother all of his pennies — 13 pence total.

"This is good, Jacob. Thank you." Noah then asked, "Have you found Sir Stephen Mackintosh yet?"

"No, but I will. I am going to get you released from this prison, Noah." Jacob continued, "My spirit will not be calm until I do."

Noah looked at his brother out of the corner of his eye, then cautiously said, "I appreciate that," then added, "I do not understand your passion, but I am grateful for your devotion."

The brothers spent as little time in the weather as was required for the exchange of funds and information. Once both had been transferred, they quickly moved toward their respective heated areas.

JANUARY 4TH STARTED like the previous day — foggy and cold, but improved throughout the period. By the end of light the fog had lifted, the cold lessened and the third prisoner was returned to the day room.

With the arrival of the last escaped prisoner, the remaining inmates began to pound the table and shout, "Remove the chains!" Throughout the building, prisoners screamed to be released from their ankle bondages. At first, in hopes of quieting the mob, the turnkeys yelled threats of torture. Eventually when nothing silenced the group, the warden decided to remove the shackles from the prisoners who could pay the liberation fee.

Noah offered to help his friends pay their fees. Offended by the suggestion, Henry stormed, "I have my own money." Both Joseph and Martha acted like they wanted Noah's money, but neither took it. Dee, being without a penny, took him up on the offer.

Once freed from their chains, Dee began to rub her healing ointment on the abrasions the shackles had created. All five of the friends cooed as her soothing touch alleviated their pain. As for Dee, her sigh of relief was so loud it drew the entire room's focus.

Near the end of the day most prisoners began to feel feisty. Usually the group just bought grog, and then got drunk. However, both Maxey and Simons relieved their pent up energy by relieving their bladders out the window. As they later explained to the turnkey, they were conducting an experiment as to  whether their pee would freeze before it hit the street. It did, but the man being subjected to the frozen urine still howled as he passed beneath the falling ice. Though it was a disgusting thing to do, neither man experienced any punishment.

The next morning Noah as usual shuffled into the day room, one prisoner behind another. Over time he had hardened to the institution's method. Days began to run into each other as the acclimation toughened into perseverance. Each day Jacob brought coins. Most days Flora brought love. Between the two, Noah survived.

ON FRIDAY THE 7th, Jacob arrived at the visitor's cage with good news. "I have found the money," he announced.

Wide-eyed, Noah replied, "That is outstanding!" He then promised Jacob, "I will build you a stable if you can resolve this loss for me."

Jacob rejected the thought. "No, I do not want a reward. If I can free you from this abuse, my reward will be your freedom."

Noah was overcome with emotion, "How do I deserve such a brother?" Jacob just grinned. For the remainder of the day Noah flaunted a smile, yet the next morning would bring him a new panic.

The morning introduced the day with a change to the routine. Martha was already waiting in the day room. As the men entered, each noticed her standing next to the open fire, but thought little of it. Only Maxey understood the reason for her early appearance, and he attacked her for it. "You may think you are going to be released, but not before I first get mine."

Shoving her against the fireplace he said, "I am not going to pay for a leftover seducer."

"I do not perform for free," she said attempting to slip beneath his hold.

"We will see about that," Marley growled as he intensified his attack.

Noah, though alarmed by the assault, expressed nothing that would display his newcomer status. "Leave her," he yelled.

Without flinching, Maxey grabbed Martha's breast, then forced a kiss on her. Noah, in the same moment, wrapped his arms around Maxey's chest, then pulled with such a force that Maxey dropped to the floor. Instinctively, Martha kicked her

assailant in the head, which stunned the criminal, but did not stop him. However, Maxey was no longer interested in Martha. Slowly he rose to his feet, turned toward Noah, and then with tremendous strength slammed a seven-inch sliver of wood into the would-be hero's side.

As Maxey withdrew his hand, the room watched as Noah spurted blood. He was fortunate, for his greatcoat stopped the fragmented piece of wood from causing serious injury.

As Maxey exited the area he whispered to Noah, "I am going to make sure the hangman uses a short rope on you."

With the help of his friends, Noah was promptly repaired. Dee, who had just entered the room, used another of her ointments to protect the wound while Martha ripped her petticoat into strips for bandages.

Toward the end of the day, Martha gained her release from Newgate. Before she left the prison, she hugged all of her new friends. As Martha embraced Noah, she whispered into his ear, "Do not tell your wife about this. It will only worry her without resolution." Then, without warning, she kissed Noah with such intensity it pushed him off balance. As he stumbled to regain his footing, she left.

THE NEXT MORNING both Noah and Jacob arrived early at the visitor's cage. Once they completed their daily exchange, Jacob immediately left. Noah continued to walk circles around the courtyard. Thoughts of the summer's sun filled Noah's mind as his body made every effort to control its shivers. As he moved toward the prison's entrance, a voice could be heard calling his name. Turning around, he noticed Flora waiting at the visitor's cage. Noah burst into a huge grin as he ran toward her.

Upon arrival Flora showed half a smile to Noah. He studied her face, then asked, "What is wrong?"

She looked down as she replied, "I'm all right."

"Look at me, love." He lifted her chin so her eyes peered into his. "What is wrong?"

"It's just me."

She turned to walk away, but Noah stopped her movement. "If you leave me now, I will suffer worry all day over you."

She looked Noah straight in the eyes, then whispered, "I think I am with child."

Marley immediately fell to his knees and cried, "No, no — this truth is too difficult!"

"Jacob, why is this such a concern?" asks Scrooge.

"Ebenezer, you know the same as I of this tragedy. And yet, I had no idea that Noah was ever told about the baby. One more victim. How can I ever redeem myself?" The question was more than rhetorical for Marley. He now feared that nothing he did would ever right his wrong. The loss of so many blameless spirits, and now a child. Bloody hell, Marley hated himself.

For a long moment Noah stood motionless. He wondered what his response should be. Joy overpowered his fear when he reassured Flora, "This is going to be all right. Jacob has found the lost money. Hopefully he can repair the situation before the trial. If he does, we will be stronger after this."

Flora recoiled from Noah's tenderness. "Wishes will not make reality, Noah." Tears began to flow down her cheeks. As they reached her chin, Noah used his hand to wipe them dry.

For what seemed to be an eternity, Noah stood silent. Words of encouragement faded, yet a story from the past sprang forth. "Do you remember the day we met?" he asked.

"Yes, of course I do," she said.

"You did not like me, did you?"

"I thought you might be — simple." Her smile increased Noah's desire to continue.

He said, "Well, I was simple. Simply captivated by your charm."

Flora's smile widened as she remembered the incident. "You certainly made a fool of yourself."

"You would not give me a glance. I had to do something," Noah replied.

"So you acted like a clown on purpose?"

"Have you not realized by now — I am a clown."

Flora laughed. She knew Noah's silliness seldom appeared, but when it did, it was a joy. Together they retold the story. "It was such a shock when you swept your hat across the pathway in that grand gesture of chivalry."

"I was trying to be impressive."

"So the shower of grain was planned?" she asked.

"I had no idea that when I made the 'grand gesture' the vast amount of wheat that would fly," Noah explained.

"It went everywhere, but mostly on you."

"That I planned too," he admitted.

"So let me get this straight, you wanted to impress me so much that you put a handful of wheat in your greatcoat's arm cuff." Noah nodded his head in agreement as Flora continued, "I could hardly believe it when you signaled for me to pass in front of you, and then the grain scattered everywhere."

Together they laughed. "You know, Flora, I am excited about the baby."

"It is just a possibility. I will know for sure in a few weeks."

As Flora handed Noah a couple of pennies, Simons attacked. "You stole my clothes!" he yelled, slamming Noah's head into the fence. As Simons pressed Noah's face between the bars, one of the homemade barbs, cut from the metal, scratched Noah's cheek. Flora screamed.

Simons grabbed the pennies from Noah, then muttered, "I don't know which of your pals knocked me out, but I'm going to punish you." The odor from the criminal's body filled the area. His breath alone caused Noah to cough. "I have a feeling you are going to die today."

"No!" Flora shouted. She reached through the bars, grabbed the thug's hair, then pulled with such a force most of the strands were liberated from the scalp. Simons hardly felt any discomfort. Flora's attack only resulted in him pressing Noah into the barbs of the cage with a savage anger. The pressure from the piercing spurs caused blood to flow over Noah's face.

"Get ready for God's hell," he said, pushing on Noah's head with all the power he possessed.

"NO!" howled Marley. The ghost reached into Simons' chest, grabbed his heart, then compressed the flesh. As the muscle of Simons' organ conformed to the shape of Marley's bones, Noah reached behind himself and grabbed Simons' hair. In an effort to free himself he yanked the felon's head backward. The counter-attack infuriated Simons to such an extent he intensified his assault. Marley squeezed until his grip closed tight upon the heart.

As the three men struggled for control, Simons began to loosen his clutch, then with his free hand he grabbed his chest. Crazed with madness, he cried out, "What are you doing to me?"

Noah pulled free of Simons, but Marley did not release his seizure of the heart. As the would-be murderer staggered from the visitor's cage Marley followed. "Jacob, release him," commanded Scrooge.

Confused, Marley replied, "I don't think I can."

"Just pull away."

Simons lurched to and fro in an effort to gain freedom from his pain. "Help me, Ebenezer," cried Marley.

Scrooge grabbed Marley and pulled, yet his energy went without reward. "My hand is clamped too tight," shouted Marley. Frantic, the two made every effort to separate from Simons, but the criminal's heart itself clung tight to Marley's grip.

"He is going to die," said Flora.

Without warning, Simons dropped to the ground. The fall pulled Marley's arm from his shoulder. Lying in the corridor, still attached to the heart, the individual bones of Marley's hand began to twitch, then they all disappeared. As his arm replaced itself, he said, "I think I killed him."

"You know Noah is going to be blamed for this," replied Scrooge.

The guard, now aware of the fallen villain, raced to his aid. "What have you done?" growled the turnkey.

Noah turned to the guard, with blood flowing from the gash in his cheek he said, "Simons attacked me."

"He said he was going to kill Noah," said Flora. Showing the jailer the clump of hair still in her hand she added, "Nothing was going to stop him, not even pain."

"Well, it looks like something painful did stop him." The guard kneeled at Simons' side, then reported, "He's still breathing." As he got to his feet he said, "So if pulled hair would not end an attack, I wonder what did?"

"He grabbed his chest — then just fell."

The turnkey looked at the couple. "I have been watching you," he told Noah. The guard then added, "You are worthy of respect. This one..." he paused, looking at Simons still motionless on the ground, "...he deserves..." and without warning the man kicked Simons in the head. The guard untied the bandana from around his neck, then handed it to Noah. "Here, my neck can suffer the cold today. Clean yourself up."

Noah and Flora just stood there shocked. "Are you daft? You are bleeding all over yourself. Clean yourself up!" The guard grabbed Noah's hand, then placed the cloth within it.

Noah accepted the handkerchief as Flora said, "Your kindness will be rewarded."

The turnkey looked at Flora, shook his head in disagreement, then said to Noah, "Do you know my name?"

"No, sir."

"Keep it that way." With that, the turnkey picked up the dropped pennies Simons had stolen from Noah, then left the three to settle their disagreement.

Within a few minutes Simons began to recover. While moaning, the dazed criminal grabbed his head with one hand, then rubbed the area of his heart with the other. Slowly he recuperated to the point where he could rise to his feet. He stared at Noah and Flora as they watched him. Neither knew if the other would continue the assault. However, with caution, both sides retreated.

Simons lined up in front of Noah for the return indoors. As the door opened Noah grabbed Simons' collar, then stepped in front of him. "Get your pence ready. Never again will I be last when you are available for payment of the toll." Simons just sighed, then accepted his new position.

Once indoors, Dee administered several of her ointments to Noah's injury. "This stops the bleeding," she said showing the contents to the group. "This one causes the skin to stitch together without a scar. And this one quiets the pain."

"Are you a doctor?" asked Henry.

"No, darlin'. I only have my salves. I leave doctoring to the men with knives," answered Dee.

"Well, Jacob, you seem to have the luck of an angel today," said Scrooge.

"So it seems. Someday I will learn to control my anger."

"No, no you will not. Your anger was honorable. Control would have only resulted in Noah's demise," assured Scrooge.

Marley's face showed no emotion, but he knew that lived history could not be changed. Noah was not going to die that day.

Stave Four

Hard Justice

THE END OF the day brought a new strength to Noah. Before the men left the day room for the sleeping dungeon, he pledged to never allow another person the opening for attack.

Tuesday launched a period of mundane and dull events in the prison. The crowd of inmates amused themselves within their own private groups. At midday, the turnkey entered the day room to announce, "The following people will go on trial at Old Bailey tomorrow." Everyone in the room heard their name called.

No one was surprised, but the notification did have the effect of muting conversation. Each prisoner spent the remainder of the day thinking about their fate. Most would probably be judged guilty, so fear for their future created a situation where all retreated into silence.

Young Jacob was the only Marley with a task that day. Twice he had attempted the sale of Smoke and Shadow only to hear the same thing from each buyer, "I only need one horse." Though Jacob explained the special relationship between the twins, neither man was persuaded, so both sales were lost. As he ran toward his old place of employment, he decided to sell the two horses at a discount, since his manager, Mathew Pepin, would require such an enticement.

Inside the stable doors, Jacob found Mathew attending the horses. Refreshing the bedding, replenishing the food, and removing the manure were his duties. As Jacob entered the stable, Mathew could be heard whistling. The tune was unclear yet pleasant to the ear. Approaching the busy man, Jacob said, "Mathew, you old French vagrant."

"Well, well, if it isn't the young errand boy," Mathew said resting his pitchfork against the wall. "Good day to you, Jacob. What brings you to your old haunt?"

"Do you remember last year when you wanted to buy Smoke and Shadow?"

"Of course. The offer is still open," answered Mathew.

"I was hoping that would be so," Jacob responded.

"So 300 pounds for the two?"

"You are getting an exceptional deal," said Jacob.

"Obviously it is enough, because you are here willing to sell. Is that correct?"

"Yes." Regrettably, Jacob finished the transaction. After he bid Smoke and Shadow a final farewell by giving each an apple and a hug, Jacob then raced to the Old Bailey Courthouse to try and secure Noah's freedom.

Upon entering the courthouse's front entrance, Jacob was immediately asked, "Can I help you?" The lad that posed the question seemed too young to be working at such a famed organization.

Without a pause in thought Jacob requested, "I am here to see Honorable William Domville."

"He is working at his home office today. Can any other person help?"

"Is he the presiding judge for tomorrow's trials?"

"Yes," answered the youth.

"I have important business to discuss with him today. Can I have the address of his home office?" requested Jacob.

"No."

Somewhat surprised, Jacob tried to explain, "He needs to know what I have discovered about an upcoming trial."

"You will have to present your evidence at trial," insisted the helper.

"But if I can talk to him today, there will be no trial."

"I understand, and I wish I could help you. However, if I release the judge's location, he will release me from this job, and I need the work."

Jacob realized the undertaking to clear Noah would not be as easy as he first hoped. He bid the pleasant but unhelpful boy farewell, then immediately rushed to the post office. As the office workers were in the middle of closing for the day, Jacob requested to view the London Post Office Directory. After an unpleasant look from the attendant, he finally agreed to allow Jacob two minutes with the book. With time to spare, Jacob placed the judge's address in memory, thanked the custodian, then made haste for the location, but the building was dark. Jacob stood outside the judge's door, defeated.

MARLEY AND SCROOGE arrived early at the courtroom. Sitting in the "family and friends" section of Old Bailey, the two invisibles from the future waited for the proceedings to begin. As they peered down upon the court area, Scrooge inquired from Marley, "You asked me if I knew what would happen after I pass — of course I can never know such a thing until presented with the possibilities. But to that same issue, tell me what you have become now that you are not of flesh?"

"I am working toward becoming a Mogrified Spirit," answered Marley.

"Are you in damnation right now?"

"This spirit — my future is in transition. And to your question, no one is ever condemned. Some end up lost, but it is through their own action or request."

This made little sense to Scrooge. "Of course, people that murder and rob others must be doomed."

"No, their spirit is of value once cleansed of the deed. In fact, the knowledge of such an event is used to help new worlds avoid such errors."

"So murder is only an error," quipped Scrooge.

"It depends on the intention of the murderer."

"So someone in battle, or an executioner, is not punished, whereas a drunk who accidentally runs over a pedestrian is punished?"

"None are punished," answered Marley, then seeing Scrooge's probing look added, "that is not the purpose of the Infinite Consciousness."

"But how could a murderer ever be made clean enough for the...?"

"Infinite Consciousness," Marley said finishing Scrooge's question.

"Yes, I guess that is what I am asking."

"Every spirit that lives has some quality the Infinite Consciousness wants to incorporate into its greater being. That is not always achieved, but it is the goal."

"Is not the Infinite Consciousness fearful of contamination from impure actions?" ask Scrooge.

"No. It is not possible to contaminate the soul of the Infinite Consciousness. The human spirit is the container of corruption. Once it sheds its wrongdoing, it is then transformed."

"Are not the spirit and soul the same?"

"Of course not," replied Marley as he watched prisoners flow into the room. While each inmate shuffled their leg-irons toward the convict's enclosure, the general public continued to fill in the upper area where the two invisibles dwelled. Within minutes all types of clerks, lawyers, and paid onlookers entered the courtroom.

It was only after the room had been filled that the bailiff announced the judges. "All rise. The Court of Old Bailey is now in session, the Honorable Judge William Domville presiding." Judge Domville, along with a second judge, entered the room, then made their way to the center seats behind the bench. With that, a deafening buzz could be heard throughout the room as the various workers scurried in an effort to prepare the details of each convict's circumstances.

Other than the balcony, where Scrooge and Marley perched at the rail, the judges sat above the other working groups within the room. The clerks and court reporters sat around a half-circle table just below the judge's bench. To the left of the judges and below the general public area sat the twelve men on the jury. The prisoners settled into an enclosure located a half dozen feet behind the clerk's table. Within the prisoner's pen the twenty that would go on trial that day stirred little and said nothing as the courtroom commotion settled into a disquieting wait.

"Bailiff, call the first defendant," ordered Judge Domville.

"Joseph Freeman, rise and face your accuser," demanded the bailiff. Noah watched as his friend walked to the defendant's box. Standing within the holding pen, Joseph followed the movements of the judges as the bailiff continued. "You are being indicted for feloniously stealing a watch from Ephraim Weedon on December 11th at the Theatre Royal. How do you plead?"

"Not guilty."

With that Ephraim Weedon took his place in the witness box that was little more than a raised platform positioned within the space in front of the clerk's table. A black-suited man entered the witness holding pen located on the opposite side of the room near the jury box. With all players in place, Judge Domville asked Weedon, "What is the value of your watch?"

"Twelve pounds."

"And did you get the watch back in the same shape as it left you?"

"Yes." He pointed to the man in the witness holding area, then said, "The constable William Taylor returned the watch."

"Good. Please explain how this all came about," requested the judge.

With that Weedon told of exiting the play *As You Like It*, then of how Joseph brushed up against him as he lifted the watch. Instantly Weedon realized the crime being committed, then yelled for help, "Stop him, thief..."

After the prosecutor's testimony, William Taylor spoke of the same event with only slight variations. Joseph had no defense except to say he was sorry for the harm he caused.

"Sure, everybody is sorry, once they get caught," replied the unnamed judge behind the bench. Joseph's story was one the two authorities heard multiple times during every session at Old Bailey. The boy knew he was going to be punished; he just hoped little physical injury would come to him. Without much thought, the jury found him guilty, and Judge Domville sentenced him to seven years of transportation to Australia. He was not as displeased as most would be with the sentence, for he desired adventure.

The judges and jury made short work of most trials presented that day. Nineteen of the twenty defendants were charged with feloniously stealing. Only James Maxey had committed a violent crime. While in jail, the felon acted like he would bite the head off a viper, in reality he had no more courage than to poison his wife and stepdaughter. But to the courts murder is murder. So within fifteen minutes the jury found Maxey guilty and the judge gave him the recommended punishment — death.

As wrist shackles were being added to Maxey, the bailiff called the next defendant, "Dinah Smith, rise and face your accuser." Dee pushed up from the inmate's bench, then entered the defendant's box where the mirror dangling above the area reflected the sun's light directly into her eyes. As she sneezed twice in quick succession, her body made all efforts to dodge the light.

"Steady yourself," demanded the judge.

Dee settled into a spot where the light caused the least discomfort. Then the bailiff continued, "You are being indicted for feloniously stealing a greatcoat from Hannah Denhous on December 23th. How do you plead?"

"Guilty."

"You do realize I will have no choice in sentencing if you submit such a plea?" inquired the judge.

"Within truth I have no choice either. I did take the coat so I could get warm, and I'd do it again," Dee proudly admitted.

The jury looked on as Judge Domville pronounced both the sentence required by law, yet included his own bias in the decree and lessened the severity of the punishment. "Dinah Smith, I sentence you to be 'whipped indoors' a total of 10 lashes." Even with the reduction of lashes, all of the women within the courtroom groaned at the idea of a bare-chested beating.

After Dee's trial, Noah began to merge the remaining cases into one story. In each crime, though different in the details of the who, what and where of the misdeed, the outcomes for the most part were the same. Something was stolen, someone stopped the thief, and now someone was going to punish the criminal.

The most interesting trial occurred just before Simons', and it provided the entire room, except the prosecutor in the case, with a much-needed break from the stories of evil and misfortune.

On December 27th three young friends — Katharine Fitzgerald, Ruby Ann Marr and Mary Egdurb — entered Bluck's Boutique. All three bought and paid for ribbon within a minute of each other. The owner, Benjamin Bluck, flirted with

Katharine by telling her she was pretty enough to marry. Katharine rolled her eyes at her friends as the three giggled at the idea of marriage to such a letch.

Ruby then paid for her ribbon, and Bluck said, "If you ever need a place to sleep, I can find one for you."

"Aren't you kind?" she sarcastically replied while winking at her friends. All this was going on like a game of 'humor the Casanova' until Mary paid for her ribbon, then Bluck turned mean.

As Bluck was handing Mary her change, he grabbed her hand, then yelled, "Why are you girls stealing from me?"

"Release me, old man! You are delusional."

With that, Bluck began to scream like a banshee. "No, none of you have paid me for the ribbon."

"Stop that! You are a scoundrel!"

Before any of the women could make their escape from the store, Davis, the constable, stopped their exit. After Davis had quieted the four, he then listened to their stories. Even though the three women told the same story, and the store owner had the reputation of lustfulness, the officer believed the store owner's story, because — well, because the others were girls.

So off to Newgate they went, where the magistrate had no pity for the three. For some reason, the turnkey put them in their own cell at Newgate and never allowed them into the 'day room'. Their trial was unique in that Judge Domville was knowledgeable of Bluck. The judge had past experiences with Bluck's false accusations, and he was not going to allow his court to be deceived again. He instructed the jury to find the women not guilty, and when the jury did as told, he ordered them to be freed.

As a last ruling in the case, the judge sentenced Bluck to pay all court costs, the costs for housing the women at Newgate, and a sizable fine for lying. The women received nothing but their freedom.

As the three women left the courtroom, Simons was called forth to give an account of his crime. His act of lawlessness showed him to be both stupid and brutal. The prosecutor, Franklin Paxton, explained finding his only black sheep butchered among a field of white sheep. The savagery of the kill played on the minds of every person listening.

Paxton detailed the finding of legs, guts and other parts spread throughout the pasture. He then followed the blood drippings to Simons' yard where he found the sheep's head spiked atop a stake. The gruesome sight made it obvious to the farmer who had committed the crime, the blood-stained man standing within feet of him. Confronting Simons, the farmer shouted, "That is my sheep's head."

"Do you want it back?"

"No, I want your head on that stake," he said tackling Simons to the ground.

After several minutes of fisticuffs, and more time of wiping blood from their faces, Constable Hugh Petherick stopped their brawling by arresting them both. Once in the magistrate's office, the criminal was jailed, and Paxton was sent home.

The only difference between Simons' larceny, and all but one other theft being judged that day, was the sentence. Without any misgiving, Judge Domville announced death to be Simons' justice.

As clouds shaded the afternoon sun, the mirror above the defendant's box no longer reflected light upon the inmate's face. This was the only thing that went easy on Henry that day. When the bailiff called his name, he just remained seated.

"I said — Henry Freeman, rise and face your accuser," yelled the bailiff. Joseph pushed his cousin forward. Slowly Henry entered the defendant's box. He focused his eyes on Joseph sitting below him in the convict's enclosure. "You are being indicted for feloniously stealing a watch from Laurence Brand on December 28th at the Theatre Royal. How do you plead?"

Henry remained silent.

"How do you plead?" demanded the bailiff. Still silent, Henry began to shake at being the focus of attention.

"You must plead," said Judge Domville.

Henry opened his mouth, but nothing came out. "Are you able to speak?" asked the judge.

Henry sounded a squeak, but not a word was voiced. Irritated, the judge continued, "You will not be reprieved from your crime through silence." He waited for a response from Henry, but the only thing that materialized was a puddle of urine at the youth's feet.

"This is your last chance, boy, speak or be found guilty!"

The courtroom fell into a silence that roared with tension. Finally Judge Domville said, "You have left me no choice. Henry Freeman, I find you guilty of the crime of feloniously stealing. I sentence you to death." With this proclamation, Henry immediately fainted, so Joseph ran to his cousin's side. Helping the boy to his feet, the elder Freeman asked, "Your Honor, may I be heard?"

"You may if you can clarify a reason for not upholding my verdict."

"I can, your Honor."

"Then speak."

"Henry is my cousin. It is fear that has gagged his tongue. We are born from country fishermen. A year ago, our parents, along with several brothers and sisters, lost their lives in a boating accident."

"How does this tragedy speak to the present?"

"I would have died in that accident if Henry had not saved me." He paused to wait for any response from the judge, but there was none, so Joseph continued. "As the boat sank, I hit my head on something, which forced me into unconsciousness." Again a pause and again silence. "I'm not sure how Henry was able to pull me to safety, but he did. Sir, if it weren't for Henry, I would be with the Creator, and Henry never would have become a pickpocket — for it was me that taught him that skill."

"Your honesty is refreshing. So to the remaining Freeman clan, what shall I do with you?"

Joseph perceived a need to remain quiet as the judge pondered their situation. The question itself was rhetorical, for Judge Domville knew exactly what he wanted to do. "You are both guilty, but with your circumstances your punishment should allow you the ability to reform." He then paused and posed a question, "Do you have the ability to improve yourself?"

"Yes, sir, we do."

"And will you work at becoming honest citizens?"

"Your Honor, I promise to repair our past deeds."

"How?"

"Well, you are already transporting me. If we are both transported together, I will take it upon myself to raise Henry in an ethical way. We will work hard for England at building the new world in Australia."

"My mistrust of convicts has me wondering if I can have confidence in your word."

"How can I assure you?" asked Joseph.

"I do not think you can, for only your future actions will show me the truth of your words."

"Maybe past actions can help you decide."

"Explain yourself," demanded the judge.

"When Henry was a toddler, he learned to walk backwards first. Why, no one knows, but for over a year he moved, for the most part, through the world in reverse. The family had actually gotten used to him doing this when one day, on a walk, he suddenly shoved both myself and his sister Emily to the ground. As I hit the dirt, I heard a crashing sound all around us. Turning toward Henry, I watched as a huge tree branch came to rest mere inches from his feet. Henry saved us that day. Plus, he never spent much time walking backwards after that incident."

"It seems you have to have Henry with you, just to stay alive," the judge commented as the courtroom giggled.

"That is probably true, sir. If you sentence Henry to death, please do the same for me."

The judge stared at Joseph, determining his seriousness. He knew this statement was lunacy, but did not blame Joseph for the telling, or chivalry, within the concept. "On any other day I probably would do just that, but today Australia needs workers, so I sentence you both to transportation for life. If either of you ever return to England, you will be hanged. Do I make myself understood?"

"Yes, your Honor, thank you," Joseph said.

"You can thank me by upholding your word."

"Yes, of course, sir." With that the two boys returned to their seats.

"Do you see your younger self anywhere?" asked Scrooge.

"No, but I remember being kept in a separate witness's room. However, I never did give any testimony," replied Marley.

"Why?"

"I sat waiting in that cold, musty room for hours. All day, in fact. When the sun began to go down, I left, because I figured the trials were finished for the day," explained Marley.

"Why did you not ask?"

"I could find no one to ask."

"And even if you would have testified," Scrooge paused, then continued, "you probably would have lied, right?"

Marley sighed long and slow, then replied, "Probably."

Scrooge motioned toward Flora who was sitting near them in the public gallery. "Unfortunately, she will not be allowed to give witness," he said.

"She does not have any knowledgeable facts of the case anyway."

The activity within the courtroom scurried with motion as the various clerks, lawyers and judges caught up with the needed documentation from the multiple verdicts rendered throughout the day. Once updated, Judge Domville said, "Bailiff, call the next defendant."

"Noah Marley, rise and face your accuser," shouted the bailiff. Without hesitation, Noah walked to the defendant's box.

As he stood motionless, the bailiff continued, "You are being indicted for feloniously stealing 112 pounds from Pressey and Barclay's grocery store on December 24th. How do you plead?"

"Not guilty."

Noah watched as his old boss, Bartholomew Pressey, entered the witness box. A rotund man dressed in a black robe and cape approached Pressey. With each step the lawyer's belly jiggled from side to side, his long white wig flopping forward with each step. The man's sway gave one the impression that a gorilla was loose in the courtroom. "Are you the owner of Pressey and Barclay's grocery?" asked the barrister.

"I am."

"And is Barclay within this courtroom?"

"No, he has retired."

"So being the sole owner of the grocery store, please tell the court about the theft that occurred at your business."

"Noah had been working for me for four years, and I thought it was time to trust him with the Christmas Eve's activities," began Pressey.

"Why did you trust him?" asked the lawyer.

"He seemed like the perfect worker — always on time, good with people, and I thought honest."

"He is honest!" yelled the ghost Marley.

Scrooge looked at Marley, then said, "This is going to be hard for you. You can not change anything, so for your own sake, calm yourself."

Marley looked upon Scrooge with anger, then without a sound moved next to Noah in the defendant's box. Scrooge was surprised that Marley had left him but understood his need to be near his brother.

Mr. Pressey continued the tale of encountering Noah at the bank, discovering the money missing, and then having his clerk arrested. There was little more to the story than that. "It breaks my heart to have Noah turn on me this way. Before this happened, I looked at him as almost a third son," he said ending his telling of the event.

At that point Pressey's lawyer asked Noah, "Is there anything that you can say that will change the facts of the event?"

"I did not take the money. It must have fallen out of the bag as I made my way to the bank after closing."

"Now let me figure this out — the money 'fell out of the bag'. How?"

"The ground was icy and twice I fell en route."

"Did you have the intelligence to look inside the bag after each fall?"

"No."

"Then what makes you think the money fell from the bag?"

"Because it was not there when I went to deposit it."

"And there is the problem. You want us to believe you are telling the truth, but you are lying are you not? It is you that stole the money, and not some phantom pedestrian. Is that not the facts?"

"No, I stole the money," Marley the ghost roared with such a force that it caused the lawyer's wig to move off his forehead.

As the lawyer adjusted his hair piece, he asked, "Well, Mr. Marley, did or did you not steal the money?"

As Noah shook his head 'no' his invisible brother spoke the word, "Yes."

"Speak up," instructed the judge.

"Yes, yes, yes, I did it," cried the specter.

A hot steam of anger rushed from the ghost's body as Noah said, "I would not have done that to Mr. Pressey. He told me he was going to make me his manager, and I would not have injured that possibility."

"So you not only spoiled your raise, but you destroyed it. Is that not correct?"

"No, you pompous jackass." Marley looked at Scrooge, then added, "How can I change this for Noah?"

"Jacob, you know that nothing you do will change what happened in the past," Scrooge called to Marley.

The rest of the trial continued as expected with Noah being found guilty. His sentence was somewhat surprising, but in truth expected by any person knowledgeable of court procedures. "You are sentenced to death," announced Judge Domville. From the balcony Flora could be heard weeping.

Wrist shackles were immediately put on Noah. As he walked to the prisoner's bench, Henry stood up, then moved next to him. The boy hugged Noah with such emotion that Judge Domville interrupted their moment. "There will be time for that back at Newgate. All prisoners are to remain seated." As Henry took his seat next to Noah, Noah extended his arm over the boy's shoulders.

While the remaining trial got under way, a commotion erupted in the jury box. It seemed as though most of the twelve men were itching to be finished with the session. The entire day had passed from morning to evening without even one moment of rest. The men complained of being tired and hungry. Nonetheless what they mostly wanted was time in the lavatory.

Judge Domville quieted the twelve by telling them everyone was in the same situation, and then he continued the final trial. The jury almost instantaneously found the man guilty of feloniously stealing, and the judge announced transportation as the punishment. With that, the session was ended and all but Scrooge and Marley left the room.

"Now what?" asked Scrooge.

"The tragedy unfolds," replied Marley.

"So we are going into a hardship greater than this?" Scrooge said, gesturing to a now empty courtroom.

"This is a church compared to our ultimate destination."

With that mental thought, Scrooge quieted, then followed Marley to the next day.

As inmates shuffled into the day room, a general melancholy controlled the area. Friends clustered together so as to console each other over their sentences. Joseph was the only outlier. Cheerfully he spoke to Henry about the great adventure they would experience.

Henry exploded, "I would rather be hanged than go on another boat!" The outburst hushed the room.

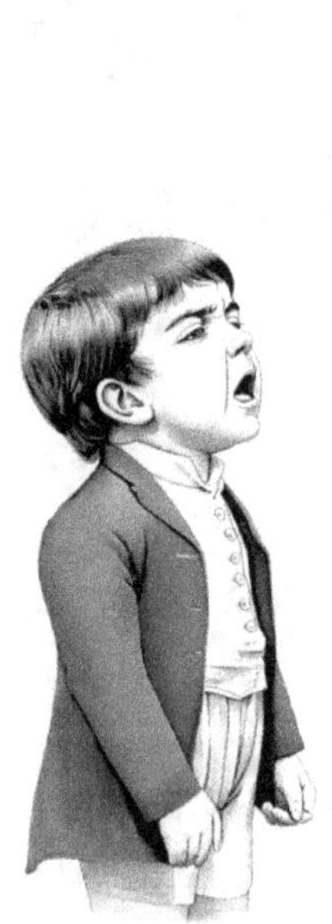

A tear set upon the corner of Joseph's eye as he said, "I also fear the water, Henry. Nothing scares me more."

"I'm not going with you, Joseph."

"What will you do?"

"Well..."

"Are you going to escape?"

Without hesitation, Henry proclaimed, "Yes, I am young. I can escape as we are walking to the ship, and no one will know I am not a regular boy."

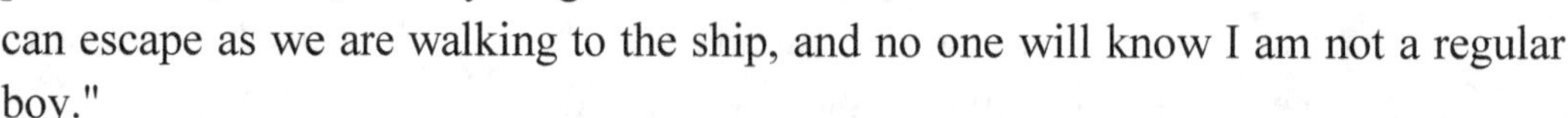

"Henry, everyone is going to know, because you will be wearing both leg and wrist-irons," said Joseph.

"Bloody crap!"

"Look, Henry, you are braver than anybody I know. We can do this, together," Joseph said as he squatted to be at Henry's eye level. "Look at me."

Henry reluctantly lifted his eyes to his cousin's, then whispered, "I'm afraid."

"I am too. I just act like I have valor, but you, you have courage I will never equal."

"Yes, Henry, you are the exceptional one here," stated Dee. "My dear cherub, listen to me — you have the power of flight. You just need to learn how to move your wings."

As Henry looked upon the weathered-face of the African woman from America, the door to the day room swung open. The turnkey announced, "Dinah Smith."

"Yes," Dee replied.

"Follow me."

Without a pause, Dee followed the man out of the room. As they made their way through the dank corridors of the prison, Dee began to inhale calming breaths. By the time the whipping room door was opened enough to receive her, she had placed her mental focus into a prayerful state.

Once inside the whipping room a hooded man secured Dee to the manacles on the wall, removed her shirt, then said, "You have been sentenced to a total of ten lashings." Looking directly into her face he continued, "For what I will bestow

upon you within this room today, you will not speak of to another. You must use silence to protect yourself, me and those brought to this room in the future. Do you understand?"

Dee was without a doubt bewildered yet shook her head in the affirmative as she answered, "I will keep the secret of this room until my death."

Pleased, the hooded man said, "Then prepare yourself for the strap." He counted each of his steps as he walked to a spot directly behind Dee. Before she realized it the man snapped the whip. The rawhide made a distinct double crack as it contacted Dee's flesh. She remained motionless as the movement of blood began to trickle from the fresh wounds.

In quick succession the man cracked the whip four more times, then paused. Dee wondered why the man seemed to be merely brushing her back with the lash. With each crack of the whip she felt a rush of air on her back, but not the deep sting of contact. After the first five lashes, the man then started popping the whip in the open space near Dee. Once the count of five additional air lashes were sounded he stopped, walked over to Dee and said, "When are you going to talk of this?"

"At death."

With that, the man walked Dee to the counter who tallied the marks on her back. After the required number of open wounds were counted, Dee was allowed to put on her shirt. She hoped she would be returned to the day room, so she could bid the others farewell, but the turnkey walked her to the front entrance.

As Dee left the prison, she wondered how five lashes delivered ten cuts. She did not dwell on the bewilderment, for the promise of silence until death caused her to just let the whole flogging dissolve from thought. Instead she smiled at the realization that freedom was hers again.

Noah was waiting at the visitor's pen for his brother when Dee passed by him. "Dee, Dee," he called to her.

She stopped mid-step and walked to Noah. "Good, I wanted to bid you farewell," she said.

"Were you punished?"

"Yes," she stumbled through the rest of her response. "Ten lashes. That ain't too much."

"So what will you do now?"

"Ain't no answer to that."

"Here, take this." He handed her the last of his pence.

"No, today all I need is my liberty." With that, she handed Noah his money back, gently brushed her hand against his cheek, then began putting distance between herself and the prison.

In an effort to stay warm, Noah bounced from foot to foot. Finally, after thirty minutes, Jacob arrived. As Noah watched his younger brother approach the prison, his anger grew into a storm. "Why did you not testify at my trial?"

"I was there all day, but..."

"I don't care about your excuses. Your indifference has gotten me killed."

Jacob was shocked by his brother's statement. He feared his crime had been uncovered and nearly succumbed to his inner pressure of guilt. As he opened his mouth to confess, Noah interjected by saying, "You have got to fix this. I should not have to die for something I did not do."

"The Home Secretary is scheduled to review your death sentence tomorrow, and I will be there," assured Jacob.

"I need you more now than I have ever needed anybody since birth."

"I will convince him you should be given leniency."

"I know you will try. When is this review scheduled?"

"In the afternoon. It starts at three," said Jacob.

"Before you go, I would like you to bring me extra food and a bottle of rum tomorrow."

"Are you planning a party?"

"Yes, and I have to have those things tomorrow. Can you bring them?" Noah asked.

"I will be here by noon, is that soon enough?" answered Jacob.

"Yes."

After Noah returned to the day room, Henry asked, "Have you seen Dee? I have been waiting for her, but she has not come back." The high pitch in his tone highlighted the worry in his face.

"She has been released. I watched her leave," assured Noah.

"Was she bloody?"

"No, no, the crown is not filled with savages."

"I will miss her."

"I know you will."

Henry then whispered into Noah's ear, "She reminds me of Joseph's mum. I think I miss Auntie Arleen more than anyone."

"In this world, Henry, people can do great things if only one person believes in them. You have two people who believe in every step you will make."

"Really, who?"

"Joseph and — me." Henry wrapped his arms around Noah's waist, then for a moment laid his head against his friend's chest.

"Break it up over there," yelled the turnkey.

As the darkness overtook the prison, all but the transport and condemned prisoners had been punished, then released. The day room felt abandoned.

Friday morning left Noah depressed. As he waited in the visitor's pen for his brother, he reflected upon the various events since Christmas. It was beyond him to wonder the why of his situation. Instead his mind moved toward the future by focusing on protecting Flora. In prison he could do little to help her. Keeping her secure worried him more than death, and personal extinction did frighten him. He knew he could not promise

her safety, so he did what those without hope do — he prayed.

"Sorry I am late — had some trouble getting the extra food for you," Jacob said.

Noah finished his prayer then opened his eyes. Standing before him were two arms holding a bag. "You did not have any problem buying the rum?"

Jacob peeked around the bag, then said, "Rum is running in the streets. Drinking is all people are doing these days. The weather has everyone hibernating with liquor." As Jacob handed the various foods to Noah he added, "I have been told that Honorable Addington is a fair Home Secretary."

"Is he fair enough to give me a pardon?"

"That I do not know, but if he can be convinced, I will persuade."

"If you sway him, come back and tell me," Noah requested.

"You will be the first to know." The brothers turned to leave, then in an afterthought, Noah turned back and called to Jacob, "I love you." Jacob just acted as if he had not heard his brother's words. Within an hour, the younger Marley entered the Home Secretary's office.

Jacob quietly waited at the head of Honorable Addington's desk as the Home Secretary continued to write. Finally Jacob cleared his throat. "Yes, yes, I know you are there," said the nobleman. After he finished his thought, Home Secretary Addington placed his quill pen back into the inkwell stand, then raised his head to view the lad standing before him. "Can I help you?"

"I am here to plead for leniency in my brother's case."

"And your brother is?" asked the official.

"Noah Marley. He was convicted of theft, but he did not commit the crime."

The Home Secretary looked back at the paper he was writing, then said, "I have heard that every day from men I am more inclined to believe than you." With that, he picked up his pen and started to once again write.

"I found the money and have brought it. I want to give it back to Pressey and Barclay's grocery store. Then you can let my brother go."

"Wait, wait, wait — justice doesn't work that way."

"Why not?" asked Jacob.

"Because a crime has been committed, and judgment was made. You can not right the wrong by simply repaying the money," said Honorable Addington.

"Why not? The crime was the taking of money, so why won't repayment clear the wrongdoing?"

"Because, my dear fellow, other costs have occurred since the crime."

"Then I will pay those costs too."

"Why did you not come forth before the trial?"

"As soon as I found the money I went to see Judge Domville, the day before the trial, but I was unable to find him available."

"And at the trial, why were you silent then?"

Jacob answered every question the Home Secretary had as to the reason for his delay in action. "All right, let me examine the court's records." With that both men fell silent as the nobleman read the report on Noah's case. Finally, Honorable Addington looked at Jacob and said, "I am not inclined to release your brother. His crime warrants punishment."

"But he told the truth. The money did fall from his bag when he fell. I retrieved the money from the boy who found it on the ground."

The Home Secretary studied Jacob, then said, "I do not believe you. You would have never gotten that money back from a saint, let alone a commoner."

"You have to let Noah go."

"Why?"

"His wife is having a baby."

"That is still no reason to overturn his verdict."

Scrooge looked at the ghost Marley, then said, "I thought you did not know that Flora was with child."

"I did not know at that time. I just said that in hopes it would influence him," said the ghost.

"I will pay you anything you want," said the young Marley.

Addington rebuked Jacob's offer by threatening his freedom. "Do you want to join your brother?"

"If that will get him released, then yes, take me to jail instead."

"There is more to this than you are saying. Why are you willing to take your brother's place?"

"He saved my life. I owe him," replied the young Jacob.

"That is another lie, is it not?" asked Scrooge.

The ghost sighed, then admitted, "I would have told any lie to get Noah released."

"And yet, telling the truth was not an option?" Scrooge waited for Marley's response, but he knew none would come.

"I will give you every shilling I own, plus take Noah's place in prison, if you will free him," petitioned the young Marley as he handed the money to the Home Secretary.

"Well, hanging is too harsh of a punishment for your brother, so I will decrease his sentence." Quickly the man wrote some numbers on a sheet of paper, then counted the exact amount of money needed to pay Noah's debt. "I will release your brother for time served. I only need enough money to make Pressey whole, and to cover the costs of Noah's incarceration." Addington then returned the remainder of the funds to Jacob and warned him, "If you ever try and bribe me again, I will jail you for a year."

"As you should," said Jacob.

Honorable Addington groaned at Jacob's over praise, took up his quill in one hand, then waved Jacob away with the other hand. "You have done what you came to do, so be gone."

With enthusiasm Jacob raced from the building, then ran the several blocks to the prison. It did not surprise him that visiting hours had passed, but he was so excited he stood there until darkness forced him to leave.

As Jacob whistled his way home, Noah placed the party bag on the table, then said, "Get out your cups, boys." As he put the bottle of rum on the counter-top he added, "Tonight we party, for tomorrow brings our parting."

Joseph looked at the bottle and said, "Your brother must like you; this is the good stuff."

"I assume he does," replied Noah placing a loaf of bread and a brick of cheese in front of the bottle. Henry licked his lips at the sight of the food. "Ready for a banquet?" Noah asked, patting the seat next to him.

Henry sat down, then asked, "Do I get as much as you?"

"No..." answered Noah.

Henry frowned, then said, "That's all right, I'm smaller than you. I don't eat as much."

"You didn't wait for me to finish, Henry. I'm going to give you more than me. You are going to need the extra energy for the walk to the ship." With that, Noah ripped the bread into three fairly equal sizes. The process was repeated with the cheese, except the pieces were not at all equal in size. Noah handed Henry the biggest pieces of both. The boy giggled with delight as he bit down hard on the cheese.

"Here's yours, Joseph," he said handing the lad his share. Joseph placed his cup on the table as he sat across from his friends. Noah then poured each half a cup of rum.

Henry was too busy devouring the cheese to even look at the cup in front of him. Joseph guzzled the drink. After finishing he held out the cup and asked, "Please, sir, can I have some more?"

"You have got to pace yourself," Noah said as he poured another half cup.

"Sure. How's the cheese, Henry?"

"Ummm," was all that could be heard from the boy.

The three gorged themselves until all the cheese was consumed and only fragments of bread remained. Henry placed his sliver of bread in front of Noah and said, "Look at my belly." He lifted his shirt, rubbed his stomach then added, "It has never been this full before."

"I'm glad I could give you a first. Are you ready for a toast?"

"Do you have a toasting fork?" asked Henry.

"Not that kind of toast, but this kind of a toast," Noah said, raising his cup. Joseph followed Noah's lead and lifted his drink. Together they looked at Henry, who nearly inhaled the last of his food, then clanked his cup against the others. "You two have made this experience bearable for me, and I will miss you. So let's drink to Australia."

"All right, may Australia move to Germany," said Henry.

"I will not toast to that. It makes no sense," sneered Joseph.

"That's probably why it's a good toast, Joseph. The way you are enjoying that rum you aren't going to remember any toast at all in a half hour," said Noah as he forced his cup toward the others.

"Fine, may Germany move to Australia." Without a pause Joseph clanked his cups with the others, then drank.

"No, no, stop. That is not the toast. I want Australia to move to Germany."

"Henry, you haven't figured this out. If Australia moves to Germany, where is Germany going to go?"

"Oh yes, I guess Germany has to move to Australia."

"That's it, same toast," said Joseph, clicking his cup against the others.

Together they drank, and Henry immediately started coughing. "Oh my, this stuff is horrible."

"With rum, you have to drink until you like it," said Joseph.

"That's not going to happen," Henry said as he poured the remainder of his liquid into Joseph's cup. He then went and filled his cup with water.

Returning to the table, Noah asked, "So tomorrow is the big day?"

"I hears it, tomorrow. Yes, tomorrow," responded Joseph.

"I'm telling you, Joseph, you are not going to be able to move, let alone trek five miles to Woolwich tomorrow, if you do not slow down."

"Noah, I know you are right, but I do not care. When again will I be able to party in this lovely prison?" he asked.

Together they made a toast to nearly everything. The food was gone, but the boys stayed full with drink. "I toast Noah," Joseph said. Not waiting for the clanking of cups he drank his empty, then belched. Henry giggled as he let out his own nearly silent burp to which Joseph let go another gush of sound. Then Henry, a little louder than his first time, emitted a true belch.

This exchange of stomach roars continued between the cousins until Noah breathed deep and then sounded a belch the entire room heard. Henry giggled as Joseph looked upon Noah with envy. They all became silent, stared at each other, then erupted with laughter. Fighting off tears of humor, Noah asked, "Have you two always been so competitive?"

"Only when we're competing," replied Joseph.

Noah laughed so hard he fell off the bench. The shock in Henry's face caused Joseph to act. He went to Noah and helped him to his feet, "Are you hurt?"

"Joseph, you are a pleasure to drink with," said Noah.

"And you thought I was drinking too much."

As they again took their places at the table, Noah commented, "I guess gravity is more powerful when drunk, who knew?" After regaining his composure, he added, "So tell me, what is the most competitive thing you two have ever done?"

Silence overtook the three as the cousins looked at each other in search of a response. Then a smile overcame Joseph as he said, "Well that has to be the day Henry and I were fishing on the River Adur."

Noah smiled as Joseph prepared to elaborate. "No, don't tell him about that," cried Henry.

"Here, take a sip of my drink. It will soothe your bashfulness," offered Joseph. Henry grabbed his cup and took a swig. Coughing, he said, "Maybe I could get used to that crap."

"Well, bloody Henry, get rid of that earth juice, and join the men," said Noah.

Henry finished the water, then Noah poured him a small amount of rum as Joseph told the story. "We both threw out our lines at the same time, and instantly I felt a powerful tug. I cried out, 'Henry, I got one'. And he yelled back at me, 'So have I.'" Joseph took another gulp of drink, then continued. "We struggled over our catches. First I thought I was pulling mine toward the boat when all of a sudden the fish pulled hard against my line. Then Henry squealed, 'I think I have almost got it.'"

"I did not squeal," protested Henry.

"Bloody if you weren't excited. Anyway, this went on for several minutes where we both declared success over our catch, only to have the fight continue."

"So did you eat well that night?" asked Noah.

"Well, I did," replied Joseph.

"I ate too. You shared with me," commented Henry.

"Well, that was the least I could do."

"So what happened to Henry's fish?" Noah asked.

"We pulled and pulled without much success. Then I decided I was either going to haul in the fish or break my pole. I yanked so hard that Henry took a dive into the river."

"What did you do, rock the boat or something?" Noah wondered.

"It's the something. When I finally hauled in the fish, I saw my hook was attached to the beast's tail, yet a second hook, Henry's hook, remained in its mouth."

Noah shook his head, then laughed, "Did you have any idea that was happening?"

"Why would I? Who hooks a fish in the tail?"

"Obviously you," replied Henry, a little irritated.

"So, Henry, your cousin here has totally humiliated you. Can you best his story?" asked Noah.

"I got an even better one," replied Henry. Without hesitation he jumped into his tale. "About two years ago we were fishing, but it was a lake — I don't remember which one."

"You boys do a lot of fishing," said Noah.

"Well, we are from Brighthelmston. What else can we do there?" said Joseph.

"I'm talking," complained Henry. He waited for silence, then continued, "Jimmy..."

"Who's Jimmy?" asked Noah.

"That was my older brother," answered Henry as he again waited for silence to proceed. "We had been fishing all day, and Jimmy hadn't caught even one fish. He kept saying the waters were bad, but Joseph and I were pulling them in like a siphon."

"Ah, Jimmy — there's a lad that hated to lose at anything he considered a competition," added Joseph.

"Anyway, Jimmy wanted to move, but we didn't. So he flung his line out as far as it would go, only to have it get tangled in a tree branch across the lake."

Already Noah was smiling when he mentioned, "Small lake?"

Henry nodded, then continued, "We did not want to lose the line, so we followed the string to the tree limb. All the while Jimmy was tugging on the line,

hoping it would turn free. It didn't, so now we are under this huge tree trying to figure out exactly which branch had caught the hook," Henry paused as he waited for comments, but none came, so he continued. "Finally, Joseph tracked its location and began to jump up in hopes of grabbing the branch, and he did. So there he is, swinging a foot off the boat, trying to loosen the string, when a snake dropped onto his back."

"Was it an adder?" asked Noah.

"I thought it was," answered Joseph.

"Joseph, you would not be here if it was," insisted Henry.

"And yet I am, so it must have been a smooth snake," said Joseph.

"I doubt it. They are both rare, and cautious," asserted Noah.

"I don't know," said Henry. "It was just a snake. Anyway, Joseph screamed like a baby..."

"I did not."

"Before we knew it, he dropped from the branch into the lake. The snake made an exit as Joseph kept yelling, 'It's going to kill me, it's going to kill me...'"

"It almost did."

"I don't think so." Henry paused, then finished his story. "Joseph popped to the surface holding up a twig, yelling, 'I got it.' Jimmy just shook his head, then asked, 'Do you always have poor vision?'"

"I had water in my eyes," complained Joseph.

As the three tapped mugs in a toast to good fish stories, Noah asked, "Where is Jimmy now?"

Joseph looked at Henry, and as tears began to form in his eyes, he answered, "He died with the rest of our family."

"I've seen him once since then," said Henry.

"No, Henry, you just saw someone who looked like him. You wanted to see him."

"Joseph, don't tell me what I saw! Besides, it was a dream, and Jimmy came to me."

"It's all right. I believe you, Henry. What did your brother do in the dream?" asked Noah.

"The sky was a different color, no blues like ours. It was kind of orange and green."

"That makes brown," said Joseph.

"It was not brown. It was like swirling oranges and greens. Why don't you believe me?" he asked Joseph.

"I believe you, Henry," answered Noah.

"But my own cousin doesn't," he said, glaring at Joseph.

"He is just drunk. He knows you are telling the truth. Did Jimmy say anything to you?" asked Noah in an effort to move the conversation along.

"No, but I understood him. The light rays on the horizon put a halo around him. His hair was ablaze of color, as if from another world. He looked at me, then turned toward the setting sun. Jimmy wanted to walk into the sunset."

"Was something stopping him?" asked Noah.

"Me — I felt his worry for me." A tear dropped from Noah's chin as Henry continued. "I waved to him. He turned and started to run into the orange glow. I could see him slipping away, and I cried, but I was no longer afraid to be without him."

"That was beautiful," said Joseph as he swigged his drink, then immediately dropped his head on the table.

"Looks like he is gone," said Noah, motioning his head toward Joseph.

"He lives in the world of the gone," replied Henry. He took a sip from his cup, swallowed hard, then said, "This stuff is all right, I guess. Noah, what is your fishing story?"

"Well, I never had the pleasure of living near a good fishing hole, but I do have a water yarn." He paused for a moment, then continued, "When I was about twelve and Jacob was nine, we were swimming. Actually, we were just trying to cool ourselves from the hot sun. Anyway, we came across this large set of flat rocks that were about an inch below the water's surface. The group of three or four rocks lined up perfectly together so one continued the other. Together they created a slight incline." Noah took a deep breath, then resumed the tale. "Jacob sat down, still totally clothed, at the high end of the stone formation and pushed off. He slid all the way down the rock."

"That sounds fun."

"It was, and that was also the problem."

"How can fun be a problem?"

"We both slid down the rock for over an hour. When we tired of the activity, we headed for home. That is when I noticed Jacob had worn out the seat of his pants. I could see his butt cheeks from a block away," laughed Noah.

Scrooge looked to Marley's backside, then asked, "Looks like you recovered. Did you get scratched?"

"A little, but mostly I could hardly walk for a week," replied the ghost.

"That sounds painful," said Scrooge.

"That was the most enjoyable day of my life," said Marley.

"Did you tell your brother?" asked Henry.

"The damage was done. I didn't see any reason to point out his bareness. Of course, mum noticed the moment he walked into the house, but she thought it was entertaining too," replied Noah.

The two looked at each other, then simultaneously howled with laughter. "Uhhh," moaned Joseph, barely lifting his head, then dropping it to the table again.

"We won't be hearing from him again today," said Noah. He placed his arm across Henry's shoulder, then asked, "Can I talk to you about something important?"

Henry took a big swallow of rum, placed his mug atop the table, then said, "All right, I'm drunk. Now what are we talking about?"

"Joseph thinks he is going on a grand adventure, but England will put you both to work. There will be troubles."

"Will there be nothing good about Australia?"

"Of course there will be. You'll be with Joseph, and I'm sure there will be some good fishing holes."

"Noah?" Henry rose from the bench, cupped his hands around Noah's ear, then whispered, "I'm not going to Australia."

"You do realize you will be in irons tomorrow?"

"Yes, but I have figured it out. Watch me." With that, Henry inhaled as much air as his body would hold, and his stomach puffed as he waited for a count of thirty. With a gush, he released the breath. "When the turnkey puts the irons on, I'm going to make my wrists and ankles huge by holding my breath. This will make them loosen when I just breathe normally. I can slip out of the irons later."

"I have to give you this, Henry, your mind is a thinking instrument. However, there is one problem — the turnkey isn't going to be shackling your stomach."

"I know that."

"You can try that, and I hope it works, but..."

"I know — I know the hands and feet don't hold air," said Henry.

"That's an odd fact of biology, Henry. Is the reason you don't want to go because of how your family died?"

"I think so, and it is so cold. Why are they doing this now?"

"I can't tell you for sure, but it is a long trip. Maybe the season works for them later."

"I'm still going to escape, if I can."

"Go where your heart directs, but you seem to be a thoughtful person. So tell me, how do you strengthen yourself?"

Henry did not quickly reply. Instead he said, "I do not think I understand your question."

"Well, think of yourself going into battle against England's greatest enemy..."

"France," interrupted Henry.

"Yes, yes, France. So how would you prepare for a battle with Napoleon? Would you pray, or sharpen a weapon, maybe even practice sword work? How do you find the strength within yourself to face troubles?"

Without hesitation, Henry answered, "I sing."

Noah looked into the boy's face, then commented, "Why am I not surprised? That sounds wonderful — at least in my world it does. So, do you sing songs I would know?"

"Sometimes. But mostly I make up songs."

"Sing me something."

Henry paused before he broke into a round of "The Beggars Chorus". He sang the uplifting melody with the sweet voice of a girl. Noah looked upon him with awe as the boy hit every note with perfection. After he had finished, Noah said, "That is excellent. You have a talent, Henry, and I have an idea."

"Will I still have to go to Australia?"

"If you can get away, do it, but if England catches you, they will hang you."

"So I just have to be scared for months?"

"Whenever you are afraid, start singing. As you are walking to the boat, sing whatever will give you strength in battle, for Henry, you are going to war with your greatest fear — the ocean. So you will need your most powerful weapon — your voice."

"What if someone doesn't want me to sing?"

"Do it anyway. You won't be hurting anyone."

"But everyone is bigger than me. They might hurt me."

"That might be true. There are evil folks around," he said, motioning his head toward Maxey. "In that case, stop, or maybe make up a flattering song about the man that wants your silence."

"Flattering?"

"You know, sing about how the man is smart or good looking, but do not make fun of him. He is bound to toss you over the side of the ship if you do."

"That is what I'm afraid of."

"You can do this, Henry, you are the strong one. Someday Joseph is going to be following you, so you need to learn how to control your fears and strengths now."

"You think Joseph is going to follow me?"

"He already does, but don't ever control another, guide them." Noah paused, then with conviction added, "You are the Sampson of song. Be fearless with every verse, and your strength will only grow."

"I didn't know music was that powerful."

"Music has always been one of humanity's soothers of spirit. You have been empowered with the ability to use it."

"Thank you, Noah, I am going to get on that boat — I think."

"Just keep singing, even if it is just to yourself."

With that, Henry hugged Noah and said, "I wish you could come."

"My love for you has grown as well."

The door to the day room swung open as the turnkey bellowed, "All right, it's time for your sleep lockdown."

"What, huh," moaned Joseph.

"It is good to know you are still breathing," said Noah as he stepped behind Joseph and helped him to his feet. "Henry, you grab his other arm," he said, flopping Joseph's left arm over his shoulders.

Together the three walked toward the door, but when Noah went left at the room's center post, and Henry went right, Joseph went head-first into the pole. "Excuse me, sir, but you should watch where you are going," Joseph said to the pole.

"He is probably going to feel this tomorrow."

Stave Five

Shrouds Of Sorrow

THE MORNING CAME too quick for the three still dizzy with drink. As they entered the day room, turnkeys immediately began separating those to be transported from the others. Joseph slapped Noah on the shoulder as he made his way to the side of the transporters. Henry hugged Noah, looked up into his face, then said, "I will remember our talk."

As the turnkey pulled the boy from Noah, he jerked free from the brute, began to hum a tune, then walked to the turnkey shackling Joseph. There he waited for his irons to be secured. Once all were fixed for travel, the turnkey ordered the group to follow each other in single file. Joseph and Henry left the room without turning to see Noah's farewell wave. Within minutes the clear tone from a high voice could be heard from the street, singing.

As the music faded, new turnkeys entered the day room. They marched the remaining prisoners to the Newgate Chapel. This was the Sunday routine, yet Noah was horrified when the guard forced him to sit at a table that held a coffin atop it. All sentenced to death were placed around the morbid display. Simons never lifted his head off the table, while Maxey never took his hands off his crotch. Among bad company, Noah just stared at the villains across the casket as the ordinary began shouting about the terrors of hell. "Repent, repent before it is too late."

As the chaplain continued to belittle the prisoners, Maxey began spitting at Noah. Globs of drool hit Noah's clothing with regularity. Noah sank as low as he could on the bench, then kicked with the entire strength of his leg at Maxey, but he only accomplished the thumping of the table with such a force the coffin bounced. Immediately a turnkey slapped Noah's left  ear, then noticed the spittle stuck to Noah's shirt, and without a thought, whacked Maxey with his stick hard enough to cause blood to spurt from his mouth, followed in quick succession by a tooth.

The two-hour event continued without further commotion from the condemned pew. The same could not be said of the regular prisoners, for they grew restless with each shout of disapproval from the preacher. One prisoner cried out for the ordinary to kiss a viper, another wanted the chaplain to suck on arsenic, and a third just peed in the corner of the room.

After the service, those seated at the condemned pew were each taken to their own rooms where they spent their last day in solitude. Abandoned to his own thoughts, Noah spent his time in reflection. The realization of his coming death first created a confusing calm, then a disturbing terror caused him to tremble. Alone with his impressions, Noah kept returning to musings of Flora. If only he could be held in her love one last time. As he lingered in her remembrances, the ordinary from the service entered his room.

Noah gave the man no more than a glance, while the parson sat at the other end of the bench. "I am here to hear your confession."

"Don't you mean sell his tragedy?" cried Marley as he watched his brother remain still. Scrooge looked at his friend, but he, too, kept his silence.

"Tell me, Noah, how did you come to this end?" asked the ordinary. Noah took no notice of the man's question. Instead he looked straight at where Marley and Scrooge stood, pointed to their blank space, then said, "Ask them."

The preacher looked to the void, then asked, "Who?" He waited for a reply, but none followed, so he continued, "I am here to relieve you of the burden of your crime." Again he paused before he stepped next to Noah. Putting his hand on Noah's shoulder, he said, "Tell me your story, so you can be free to leave it behind."

Finally Noah looked up at the clergy, then said, "I will tell you everything if you will get me to see my wife tomorrow before I am hanged."

"That is not how this works."

"Then leave."

The man put his hand on Noah's forearm, then pleaded, "Let me help you before it is too late."

"Tell the turnkey he must take me to the visitor's area at dawn tomorrow. That is the only way my story will be yours to sell." With that he pulled his arm from the man's grasp.

The ordinary stood, then walked to the door and asked the man standing guard, "Will you be here to present this prisoner to the executioner?"

"I will," replied the turnkey.

"Would it be possible to allow him into the visitor's area before the event?"

The guard took a deep look at the parson, then said, "Only if you give me 30 percent of your take from his story."

The ordinary's cold eyes looked through the guard as he whispered, "A week from today I will settle up with you."

"Then at first light I will let him go anywhere, but free."

With that the preacher returned to Noah to get his story. Noah obliged with the biggest lie of his life. He kept it within the realm of the theft, but elaborated with a tale of plotting to undermine Pressey so he could not only steal the money but abscond with the store itself.

Pleased he had a moneymaker, the ordinary left Noah to his fate.

YOUNG JACOB ROSE before the sun, and with the excitement of good news was hardly dressed before he began racing toward the prison. The frigid air burned his lungs, yet he pushed the feeling aside. He would be seen as Noah's hero. He liked that thought, but mostly just wanted his brother released so this nightmare could end.

As he periodically paused to catch his breath, the smile on his face deepened. It would not surprise him if the Home Secretary had Noah already released. In his mind he envisioned Noah waiting for him on the free side of the visitor's pen. His sprint toward the fence slowed as he heard the sound of a howl, then stopped all together as he tried to identify the location of the commotion. His ears honed in on the pitch of screams that could only be female, and once again he quickened his pace.

Scrooge and Marley looked on as the prison came into view for young Jacob. From a distance Jacob saw an unidentifiable mass of figures crouched near the ground. The cries of terror filled every inch of sound in the area. Jacob focused on the scene, realized the horror before him, then rushed to Flora's side.

Huddled in a heap sat Flora covered in Noah's blood. As she clamored to hold her lifeless husband, the spread of his blood covered all parts of her clothing. Jacob stopped short of physical contact. With disbelief, he took in the scene before him. Noah slumped to the ground, yet still had his left wrist attached to a sharp barb on one of the prison bars. As his arm dangled, the weight of his body caused the hook to deepen its cut. Blood spurted from the wound with every movement Flora made.

Finally Jacob placed his hand on Flora's back and said, "We need to get help."

"No, it's too...," Tears replaced the end of her sentence.

"Guard, guard," yelled Jacob.

As the turnkey ran toward the confusion, Jacob tried to lift Flora to her feet, but she resisted. Slumped in Noah's blood, Flora remained inconsolable. The turnkey felt Noah for life, which all present could see had left him. The guard then attempted to free his wrist, but the barb held tight. With a strong pull, the turnkey ripped Noah's arm free from the prison fence. Noah immediately fell into the yard where his blood continued to pool.

Without recognizing any other Marleys were present, the turnkey began dragging Noah toward the door.

"No, wait. Where are you taking him?" asked Jacob.

"He is ours," claimed the jailer.

"How do we get him back for burial?"

"Bury him with your thoughts." With that, Noah was dragged inside the prison.

"What does that mean?" yelled Jacob. But no more was to be explained to either grieving relative.

Jacob just stood there, not knowing his next action. Before him wept his distraught sister-in-law, and within him seared a pain he had never felt before. How in the hell could he have let this happen? Slowly he got Flora to her feet, then helped her take every step needed to get home.

Once Flora was indoors, away from the prying eyes on the street, Jacob sent for her sister, Joan. As he waited for her arrival, calming his sister-in-law became Jacob's task, but he failed. Even when Joan arrived tears continued to dominate her sister. Joan did nothing to halt Flora's sorrow. Instead she focused on getting Flora cleaned up. The dress she wore was immediately burned. With fresh clothing came an unpleasant quiet from Flora; she still cried, yet in silence with a whimper.

As soon as he could, Jacob left Flora to her sister's care, then ran back to the prison. He was now bloody, but he did not care, for he needed to retrieve Noah's body for burial. He tried the main entrance into Newgate, but it was locked, so he knocked as hard as he could. Eventually a turnkey opened the door, looked at the bloodied man, and then said, "We are not St. Bartholomew's hospital. We are a prison. Go there for help."

As the man started to close the door, Jacob shoved his leg through the opening, pushed the door wide then said, "I am here to retrieve my brother's body."

"And your brother is?"

"Noah Marley."

"Oh, the suicide. Come with me." The man walked Jacob to the magistrate's office.

Writing in a journal, the warden did not even glance up at Jacob as he said, "What do you want?"

"My brother died today, and I want his body for burial."

With that, the magistrate put his pen in the inkwell, looked up at Jacob and asked, "Your brother is...?"

"Noah Marley."

The magistrate shuffled some papers on his desk, then grabbed the one pertaining to Noah's death. "It says here he committed suicide. You can not have him. Now I'm busy. Be on your way."

"Why can I not take him for burial?"

"All prisoners marked for hanging become the property of the College of Physicians. I assume your brother is being dissected as we speak."

"But no one gave permission for this," said Jacob.

With that the warden let out a laugh that echoed throughout the entire area. "Permission, permission — well, I am so sorry we overlooked your wishes. Your brother was sentenced to hang." He paused, shuffled some papers on his desk, then read from one. "'Noah Marley's sentence of death has been revoked. He is to be immediately released.' Signed by Home Secretary, Honorable Henry Addington." The magistrate looked up from the paper and said, "I guess I just did not get time to put this order out."

Jacob wanted to ask how long the order had been lying on his desk, but thought better of it. However, he demanded, "I want my brother."

"And I want to put you in jail. So who do you think is going to get their wish first?"

"When can I get his remains from the College?"

"Be assured, you do not want them. Remember your brother in the best light you can. Hold your funeral if you want, but there will be no body."

"This is not justice," yelled Jacob.

"No, no, it is the law. Again, Mr. Marley, if you want to keep your freedom, leave now. I will not tell you again."

Jacob took the warden at his word and exited the prison. As the turnkey latched the prison door behind Jacob, his attention was forced, by the roar of a cheering crowd, to watch as both James Maxey and Nathan Simons dropped to their fate.

For hours he wandered without direction through London's snow-covered streets. People stared at his blood-covered suit, but none made an attempt to understand his situation. When he finally arrived home, the only thing he did before collapsing into bed was to burn his clothing.

The next morning brought to Jacob the dread of having to tell Flora that Noah would not be returning for burial. He stamped his feet as he walked from his bedroom to the kitchen. He pounded his fist on the counter as he made himself a meager breakfast. And then, he slammed the door as hard as he could when he left his home. His anger slightly diminished with each step he took toward Flora's.

Joan answered the door before Jacob had time to knock. She put her finger to her lips, then whispered, "Flora is still sleeping."

Jacob entered the hallway, then said, "I have news to tell her."

"Not today. She had a sleepless night..."

"This can not wait — unless you would like to tell her that Noah will not be returned to us because..."

"No, no, you should tell her that." They walked to Flora's door, knocked, then opened the door just enough so Joan could tell her sister that Jacob needed to speak with her.

Flora put her robe on, wiped the tears from her cheeks, then entered the hallway where Jacob waited. She just stared with vacant eyes as Jacob coldly blurted what he thought was a comforting lie, "Noah has already been buried. Our service will have to be performed without his body."

Flora collapsed to the floor, causing both Joan and Jacob to rush to her limp body. Together they lifted her upright. Jacob, in an effort to support her, put his arm around her middle, then said, "We will get through this together."

"Together. Together? Where were you at the trial? You let him be convicted."

"No, I was there, they never called..."

"Stop lying. You were never there."

Jacob said nothing, because, in truth, it was like he had never been at the trial, for he left without giving witness. As he watched this compassionate woman be crushed by the events of his making, Jacob for the first time understood the totality of his crime. His theft destroyed his family.

"I want you to leave."

"Is there no way I can help you?"

"Jacob, you are self-serving and cold. Begone before you freeze my house."

With that Joan escorted Jacob to the door. He asked her if she would be returning to her own home. "Yes, both Flora and I will be going to my house off French Alley."

"Your encouragement will provide comfort. Consider me obligated to help."
As Jacob left, he called to Flora, "I will check up on you tomorrow."

Jacob walked to the nearest tavern, sat in the corner, then drank from day to night.

THE TEMPERATURE FROZE Flora's eyelashes as tears erupted without control. With each blink, her eyes struggled to pull the lashes apart. Ahead of her turned the wheels of an empty hearse. She followed the wagon alone, for no one shared in this

ritual. As the hearse began its climb to the cemetery, it picked up speed. Flora quickened her pace. Struggling to keep up with the hearse's momentum, she cried, "No, no, stop!" The death carriage disappeared from her sight.

"Flora, Flora — wake up, Flora," said Joan as she shook her sister.

"Uh? What..." A look of bewilderment took over Flora's face.

"You had a nightmare," said Joan.

"Are we, then, going to bury Noah?"

"No, he's gone, sweetie."

"Then it wasn't a nightmare, it was reality," Flora fell back to her pillow where she slept for the entire day.

Jacob did check up on Flora every day, and every day Joan turned him away. "She's still sleeping. It will take her some time to recover. Give her time."

With the same event of daily rejection, Jacob walked to the same tavern, sat in the same corner and drank until drunk.

"Is that all you did while on furlough from the counting house — drink?" Scrooge asked, scowling at his friend.

"Mostly."

After three days of the same awkward event playing out, Scrooge asked Marley, "Why do we linger here?"

"Because there is one more series of events you do not even know ever happened."

"Why is it such a secret?"

"I was too ashamed to tell you," said Marley.

"So why now?"

"Because it may be more important than Noah's demise."

"Did you do something to Flora?" asked Scrooge.

"I killed her husband."

"But that has already happened. Again I ask, why do we linger here? Why aren't we helping Noah?"

"I'm trying to tell you, Flora is Noah's story. What happens to her can not be subtracted from Noah."

"Their situations are combined, like out of two comes one?" asked Scrooge.

"Exactly, there is only one mission here. Be patient. I will put your life in danger soon enough," Marley said with a dastardly yet playful smile.

More days passed as Scrooge and Marley watched young Jacob drink himself numb. Scrooge began to form questions with which a conversation could better pass the time.

"What were you thinking, all alone in the corner there?" Scrooge asked Marley as he motioned to young Jacob.

"Who said I was thinking?"

Scrooge paused, then carried the conversation in a different direction. "Jacob, I know you do not always like to answer my questions — but I would like you to answer a question I already asked you once."

"And I didn't answer it?" asked Marley.

"You were blunt in your vagueness," replied Scrooge.

"I will try and answer any question you have, if I can."

"Why aren't the spirit and soul the same?" asked Scrooge.

"Oh, that question again. Well — it is a question worth answering, if I can." Marley paused to choose his words carefully, then said, "The spirit and soul are different, as the spirit never exists without the soul."

"So the soul is more important than the spirit?"

"Well, not in the strictest sense," answered Marley.

"All right, then tell me what the soul is," requested Scrooge.

"The soul is directly connected to the creator — the Infinite Consciousness."

"Infinite Consciousness, what is that?"

"For people, it is the creator of existence, but it mostly just provides love," answered Marley.

"Love, that is just a feeling, an abstraction," said Scrooge.

"No, love is the physical energy contained in Acceptance."

"Acceptance?"

"Acceptance is achieved only after the spirit has transformed its harmful earthly actions. That is what I am working toward right now," said Marley.

"So our connection to the soul, or the Infinite Consciousness, is through love?"

"The Infinite Consciousness is associated with every thought judged to be both good and bad. However, you are correct in thinking love is the energy shared between the soul and spirit."

"So if the soul is love, then what is the spirit?" asked Scrooge.

"Our spirits are the forces that drive each of us through our days on earth. Spirits are the holders of both the strengths and weaknesses we each carry."

"Jacob, the term 'Infinite Consciousness' sounds like an awkward name for God."

"Ebenezer, if you think of God as an old man on a throne who judges the worth of dead people, then no — the soul is so much more than that. Judging dead people is not the work of the Infinite Consciousness."

Scrooge thought about this for a moment, then asked, "Who does judge the dead?"

"At death each person knows their worth. The only judgment comes from the spirit to the spirit."

"Jacob, I am more confused than before the start of this conversation. Do people have both a soul and a spirit?"

"You have spirits, Ebenezer. The Infinite Consciousness carries the soul." Marley hesitated, then added, "Every baby is born with a spirit attached to it that comes from the Infinite Consciousness. That spirit is love without conditions."

"So the soul is love?"

"The soul is everything — love, laughter, invention, and even destruction, but mostly for the Mogrified Spirit it is Acceptance."

"You make it sound like a person can touch and hold Acceptance."

"It is tangible. I have been showered in it, as have most who spend the start of their immortality within the Isle of Transmogrify."

"So what does the Infinite Consciousness get out of its relationship with people?"

"Love," answered Marley.

"What? If the Infinite Consciousness is love, in and of itself, why does it need our love?"

"To accomplish its work," replied Marley.

"Its work of..."

"Provenance."

"Oh, do explain that," requested Scrooge.

"Provenance is easy. It is simply the creation of new universes."

"And the human is needed how?" asked Scrooge.

"The soul is always expanding its cosmos. That makes new worlds in need of our experiences. Of course, the creator gives to all of its creations the breath of its love, but it can not give it the toils the human must overcome to survive. When human love is returned to the Infinite Consciousness through the process of Transmogrification, that love, or Acceptance, holds the lessons learned during the individual's life. These human adventures are given to new societies. Our earthly struggles are needed by the soul. For our memories strengthen new worlds by way of bringing forth experiences lived."

"Well, I wasn't expecting that thought," said Scrooge. Then added, "So it's all about human-learned knowledge?"

"An awkward way to say that, however collecting knowledge learned through participation, that seems to be the worth of us."

"Do people get anything other than a short life out of this arrangement?"

"A Mogrified Spirit gets an everlasting existence. Is that not enough?"

"I'm not judging. I'm just asking," answered Scrooge, then asked, "Will I remember my human experiences after Acceptance?"

"Yes, without your memories your humanity can not be accessed. All cleansed spirits continue forever," replied Marley, then asked, "So again, is existence not enough?"

"Sure, a happy existence, even a bland existence. But an existence like Noah's last weeks — no, no, that is not enough," insisted Scrooge.

"Noah's last three weeks were not the total of his life. And yet, I understand your grievance."

"So what makes up for such pain?" asked Scrooge.

Marley stepped next to Scrooge, raised his hand to his friend's chest and then said, "I have not been given approval to show you this, but I am going to do it anyway. Stand still."

"Wait, what are you going to..."

Before another thought could be expressed, Marley reached into Scrooge's breast, gently placed his palm on his heart, then started to glow. As the yellowish light intensified, Scrooge

closed his eyes to the force from Marley's touch. "Only the smallest quantity can I give you," said Marley as he pulled his hand from Scrooge's chest.

Like the strings of an inactive marionette, Scrooge went limp. Marley attempted to support him as he regained his composure. "Why did you stop? I have never felt joy that caused my heart to tremble with frenzy. Do that again."

"I wasn't given permission to do it the first time."

"Jacob, what was that?" asked Scrooge.

"My spirit of greed's Acceptance."

"Will you get in trouble for giving me some?" Then added, "Tell me, Jacob, how did you learn to do that?"

"No, I am in no danger. The soul's joy is felt by every newborn at birth. Both of us have always had the ability to feel the soul's power. The love essence is one of the spirits each baby receives from the Infinite Consciousness."

"One of the spirits. How many spirits does a person have?"

"There are at least three at birth," replied Marley.

"Other than the soul's spirit, what other spirits does a person have?" asked Scrooge.

"Their mother's and father's. That is what makes up the basic infant."

"You mean there are basic or beginner babies," said Scrooge, then asked, "Are there also advanced babies?"

"It isn't judged that way, but most babies are born with other spirits."

"Like what?"

"Timothy Cratchit's leg handicap was a spirit that entered him at birth. Other people receive spirits of genius. There are all kinds of spirits. Some we would call good and others bad, but each helps to create the individual's personality. In essence, spirits combine within a person to create their self-power."

"How many spirits do I have?" asked Scrooge.

"Now or when you were born?"

"Is there a difference?"

"Most certainly. Every person adds spirits as they gain new focuses. They also drop spirits when they are no longer being used. However, the three basic spirits can never be removed from the person," explained Marley.

"People who do horrible things never lose the Infinite Consciousness's spirit of love?"

"Never."

"I don't believe that. I think there have been people that have no spiritual connection to love at all."

"The connection can be frayed, but never broken, unless of course the individual itself breaks the connection," said Marley. "The Infinite Consciousness never breaks the relationship," he added.

"Do people often break away from the Infinite Consciousness?"

"Yes, but even then, all is not lost. However, it becomes extremely difficult to overcome such a Spirit Breakage."

"Do many succeed?" asked Scrooge.

"Most do — eventually," replied Marley.

"Why does a person have to have permission to use the soul's love?"

"As far as permission, that was the wrong word. But Acceptance is too strong to be placed upon a living person for long. The energy has to be filtered, so it will not initiate the process of Instant Transmogrification, which would be a tragedy if I started that."

"Would it kill me?"

"Most certainly."

"So what is Instant Transmogrification?"

"Ebenezer, I tire of explaining. We will see the Crater soon."

"All right, but just one more question," Scrooge paused, then continued. "Jacob, are all of your spirits with you now, or do I speak with only one of your spirits? Also, you never answered the question about how many spirits I have."

"That is two questions." Marley paused for emphasis, then continued. "As for the question I overlooked, you have five spirits, Ebenezer. Now as to the spirit you see before you, I am from the Abyss of Final Transmogrify. All of my other spirits have evolved into Acceptance and are now residing with the Infinite Consciousness. Only the spirit you see before you is still working toward that goal."

As Scrooge pondered Marley's reality, young Jacob rose from his table and stumbled toward home. Scrooge inquired, "How many more days of this do we have to watch you drink yourself stupid?"

"Tomorrow is the last day. After that, events will finish within days," said Marley.

"Why did we wait anyway? Why not just jump to the day?" asked Scrooge.

"That did not work out so well when I took you back to 1854. I overshot that year. It rendered me unconscious. I would have never stirred if I hadn't felt you being shoved into me."

"Yes, that was unpleasant, for if the Ghost of Christmas Yet to Come had not saved me — well, I'd be upon the cobblestones of London," said Scrooge.

For an instant, Marley puzzled over Ebenezer's statement, then said his next thought, "Prepare yourself, Ebenezer. Flora's story is not going to be pleasant."

"When has any of this been pleasant?" asked Scrooge.

The next day began as had the last several days — young Jacob was turned away by Flora, then went to the same tavern, sat at the same table, and drank until drunk.

"This is for sure our last day of watching your younger self wallow in self-pity?" asked Scrooge.

"Yes, tomorrow things change again."

"So, Jacob, I have been wondering about something personal."

Marley looked at his friend, then replied, "Of course you have. What else is there to do right now, but wonder?" He paused, then asked, "So, old friend, what is on your mind today?"

"Is there a specific reason for your needing me to help you with this task?"

"I thought you knew already. I need you to help me save Noah."

"Yes, I do know that, but why me?"

"You make me fearless, Ebenezer. Without your living connection to the Infinite Consciousness, my spiritual connection does not have the strength to free Noah. Believe me, I have tried. It is my Task Of Outreach. Acceptance will be out of my grasp until Noah achieves it first."

"That does not explain why you need me."

"Because I have no one else, Ebenezer. You became my brother after Noah's death. I do not want to put you in danger — and yet I need your help."

"You keep telling me I will be in danger, but I do not understand why I will be in greater trouble than you," said Scrooge.

"You will be vulnerable to every vicious heart that would love to murder a breathing human again."

"And if I get killed?"

"Then you will be dead," answered Marley.

"Will I have no protection?"

"I know of none. But we have not stepped into Transmogrify yet, and the choice is yours to reject this hazard."

"I have survived all of the pitfalls placed in my life. I will not shy from Transmogrify if it leaves you without help, brother."

"I will always protect you, Ebenezer, with the very existence of my spirit, if need be."

"Then the two brothers will save the third," said Scrooge.

"Whether we are successful or not, you have already saved me," said Marley.

With a surprised look, Scrooge watched his friend. "When did I save you?"

"It is you that repaired most of my incidents of greed. I would have eventually been freed through my Task Of Outreach, but you hastened my release to the soul, where it now dwells within Acceptance. You saved me, Ebenezer, by changing the focus of our business."

The two spoke of many subjects that day. As dusk over-took the light, young Jacob stumbled home, and then passed out just inside his door. There he remained until morning.

The next day was a struggled to begin; groans caused by a hangover slowed his walk to Flora's. He was late arriving that day, for he thought it hardly worth going anymore. However, the surprise in Flora's voice stunned him out of his drunkenness. "They are going to take everything away from me," she sobbed.

Confused, Jacob replied, "That can not be. What exactly has happened to give you this idea?"

"A man from the court came yesterday. He said that on Monday they will be holding a hearing to determine the sanity of Noah at the time of his suicide."

"I've heard of that before. That is normal," said young Jacob.

"Is it normal to leave a person's family without any means?" asked Flora.

"I will go with you. Together we will stop this."

"Will we?"

"Yes, I will be there for you this time," assured Jacob.

Flora studied Jacob's eyes. As she stared into their blueness, she hoped to recognize Noah's passion for defending her. That image never appeared, but soon she realized her husband's brother was all that was left to her for protection. "Be here Monday morning by eight. We will go together to the hearing."

"I will be here early," said young Jacob.

Jacob left Flora for his bar. He purchased his drink, went to his table in the corner, placed the drink on the table, then just glared at the empty chair. There he stood frozen in idleness, as his mind wandered through various plans of how to protect Flora. He took a long look at his beverage, then turned and left the tavern.

The only blessed event of the day was that the temperature finally broke above freezing. As Jacob wandered the streets of London, he was brought to a quick stop when his horses, Shadow and Smoke, pulled a cart past him. He just watched as his past companions left his view. He was curious as to why such an expensive pedigree was being used for draft animals. However he did not dwell on the thought, for their future was no longer his.

As young Jacob roamed the streets, Marley and Scrooge followed close behind. "Well, at least we do not have to watch your younger self inebriate every ounce of your being today," commented Scrooge.

"But we still have to get through tomorrow, so who knows what I will do with a new day."

"Well, you know, Jacob. Do you not remember that Sunday?" asked Scrooge.

"I do remember. I just wished I could forget this entire period," admitted Marley.

"Then let us see what happens." With that they moved to the next day and watched as Jacob was once again turned away by Flora. The two specters followed the young Marley as he sidestepped the tavern.

As young Jacob aimlessly wandered through the ice-crusted streets, Scrooge asked a question. "Why is love stronger than hate?"

Marley scrutinized Scrooge's face for any sign as to why he asked this question. Finally he answered the inquiry. "It is not hate, but fear that is love's near equal."

"So which is stronger, love or fear?"

"Ultimately love is stronger, because it holds the force of compassion," replied Marley.

"And yet does not fear also hold passion?"

"Yes, passion, but not compassion."

"So fear is without worth?" asked Scrooge.

"No, society works through both love and fear — as do most people — and yet, there are people who develop their spirit in only one way," answered Marley.

"How is this applied?"

"Well, Ebenezer, such people always act with compassion if their spirits are of love, and others only create chaos when fear is in control."

"In a sense, things appear to be equal — love and fear, that is. Only difference is in the usage?"

"They are not equal. They both have power, yes, but humans can not exist without love. They fade away. Whereas fear is only beneficial when running from a wolf. Fear may save a person, but it will never improve them."

Scrooge took in the concept, then replied, "To me, staying alive seems paramount for existence. Who needs improvement when life itself is being challenged?"

"That is a valid point, yet..." Marley paused before he said, "I may be dead, but I still exist. Fear could be essential when in danger, but think about it Ebenezer, when was the last time you were threatened?"

Scrooge did ponder this, yet said nothing, for his greatest fear had been that of loss and lack, not danger. After a moment Marley continued, "And then, again, can there be a greater challenge than one that binds the heart, so that advancement becomes probable?"

"I feel we are thinking in two different ways. You, with an abstract desire for social progression, and me, with a more practical vision about how society actually works."

"No, it is all one vision, but this conversation is simplistic, in that the duality of fear and love are the legs humanity stands on. And yet, to the Infinite Consciousness, both mindsets are the same. There is no relative duality within the creator," explained Marley.

"So the Infinite Consciousness is without options? Does that not show a lack of creativity for the creator?"

"Again, when you are the creator of everything, all options exist, because you made them, and as for 'creativity', there is no greater work that the Infinite Consciousness does than create new worlds. This demands an intense focus of imagination, yet only cleansed love is helpful in the stabilization of new planets. The fact that Earth's society has developed the most debilitating form of Spirit Breakage makes those apparitions who complete the climb out of the Crater the most valued love within the universe. Coss Acceptance that comes from the Crater is more in demand than is gold."

"What exactly is the Spirit Breakage that makes the earth so special?" asked Scrooge.

"If I were to just tell you, you would not clearly understand. However, we will be going past the Crater of Severed Spirits, where you will see why the Coss are of such importance to the Infinite Consciousness."

Scrooge continued his questioning, "So humanity has to go through difficulties in order to be of value to the soul?"

"Exactly."

"That is just malicious, Jacob."

"Ebenezer, it is the essence of our value. And it goes to the mechanics of the universe." Marley paused to allow his friend a moment to respond. He then continued, "A pure human spirit at death is of little use to the soul. Fortunately it is not possible to escape the earth's tether without imperfections. Even babies die with failings."

"Are there other planets where love is collected?"

"Yes, like I said, this is the inner workings of all planets, and the way of the creator. However, the Infinite Consciousness also collects: wise thoughts, inventiveness, socially helpful methods, and much, much more. But that is collected through planets that have perfected such qualities. Earth has only one quality that is of value to the soul."

"So Earth ends up having the best love, because it has the worst habits?" asked Ebenezer.

"That does sound like an oxymoron, but it is truth. However, just to give you a better picture, there is another planet where murder dominates society. No person over the age of five dies without having first become a murderer, yet Earth's worst transgression is more harmful."

"How can anything be more harmful than murder?" asked Scrooge.

"Because humans purposely separate themselves from the Infinite Consciousness. Such an estrangement leaves the individual without any help from the soul. Their Transmogrification process — it is difficult."

"Separation? Estrangement? So the person is discarded?"

"The individual has not been abandoned but has freely separated itself through its earthly actions. This Spirit Breakage makes it more difficult to be cleansed because of the isolation. They get no help from anybody." Marley watched for a response from Scrooge, then said, "Well, I guess Apruto collects them at times."

This did get a reply. "So they do get help?"

"No, they are still on their own, but even then most spirits in the Crater end up in Acceptance," explained Marley.

"So an earthly Spirit Breakage is worse than murder?"

"Those whose action put them in the Crater are, but not those in the Pool."

Scrooge had dozens of questions, but Marley cut him off as dusk overcame the day. Young Jacob walked into his house without having resolved any of his troubles. An uneasy night of slumber found him nonetheless anxious to defend Flora. He arrived a half hour early at her home. As he waited for Flora to put on her coat, Jacob asked her sister, "So you will be moving to your home tomorrow?"

"Yes, after this hearing we will make the move."

"Even if she is left Noah's property?"

"Yes, she will need a permanent residence no matter today's outcome," answered Joan.

Flora came into the entrance hallway, looked at Jacob, then asked, "Will they let me keep anything?"

"Your body."

As tears flowed down Flora's cheek, Jacob realized the lack of hope his response offered. Not wanting to sabotage her day, Jacob tried to correct his statement. "I will do everything in my power to make it so you can keep everything, even the money you and Noah put away to buy a home."

"Without a living, that money will not last. Beyond our savings I have no method of survival." A strained smile crossed her lips as the two of them made their way to Old Bailey. The courtroom they entered was smaller than the one that held Noah's trial. Sitting above the civilians were five judges. For Flora's hearing, these five men would also act as the jury.

The judge in the center seat did most of the talking. "Call the first defendant."

"Flora Marley, please make your presence known." With that, both Flora and Jacob entered the witness box. Pointing to Jacob, the judge asked, "Who are you?"

"I am Noah Marley's brother."

"Is your property in question?"

"No. I am here to help my sister-in-law."

"Then let's continue." The judge took a deep breath before stating, "We are here today to determine the sanity of Noah Marley, who on January 17th took his own life not an hour before he was scheduled to be hanged." He looked at the witness box to make sure there was no protest, then resumed his verdict. "Because Noah Marley committed suicide in order to forego the shame of being hanged, the court has no option but to declare a verdict of felo de se."

"NO! Do we not get to speak?" screamed young Jacob.

A bit shocked by the outburst, the judge quieted Jacob by simply saying, "Let me finish!" All became quiet within the room. The magistrate looked to the other judges before continuing, "This verdict has been determined and is the right one. For to kill yourself in order to escape the sentence of death requires a judgment of felo de se. You are hereby required to forfeit all of Noah Marley's property to the Crown."

"NO!" Jacob and Flora screamed in unison.

The judge's look penetrated the defendants, "What is it that you know that changes this fact?"

Jacob looked at Flora, then answered, "Flora is with child. Are you willing to impoverish a baby?"

"You seem to bring that lie out whenever it is convenient," said Scrooge.

"It works," was all that Marley said in response.

The five judges deliberated in silence before the main magistrate spoke, "That is important news. Because we do not punish those without blame, we have changed our verdict to non compos mentis. You will be allowed to keep Noah Marley's assets." With that, the hearing moved on to the next defendant as Flora and Jacob left the room.

Once Flora was away from the commotion of the courtroom she turned to Jacob, hugged him, then said, "Thank you, but how did you know?"

"Know what?"

"That I am going to have a baby."

Shocked by the news, the younger Jacob just stared at her. First at her belly, then her face, and then a penetrating glare into her middle again. The biggest of grins overtook young Jacob as he said, "I will help you from beginning to end, Flora. Your child will want for nothing."

"Just a father," she replied. The last day of January was as cold as any other during the month, but neither of them noticed the weather's extreme any longer. They walked home in silence.

THE NEXT DAY Flora opened the door to a breathless Jacob. With excitement, he blurted out, "There is a Frost Fair on the Thames, do you want to go?"

"Not today."

Jacob looked at her, then, concerned for her physical well-being, asked, "Is the baby troubling you?"

"It's no trouble, Jacob, it is just the process."

"How can I help?"

"Just leave me to my sickness; maybe we can go tomorrow."

With that Jacob left, but when he returned the next day, Flora's condition had not improved. He dropped by a doctor who had once set a broken arm for him. Jacob asked if there was any treatment for pregnancy sickness.

"We now call it morning sickness."

"Can it be helped?"

"Soothing foods, ginger tea is helpful for many. For most a walk in fresh air helps."

After thanking the doctor, he spent the day wondering where he could buy ginger without having to enter Pressey and Barclay's grocery store. Eventually he found the Honey Lane Market where he was able to purchase ginger.

As he walked home, the thought of becoming an uncle brought a smile to his face. It would be one of his last expressions of happiness.

THE NEXT DAY Jacob brought Flora the ginger and told her of the other remedies for her illness, but she was still too ill to attempt the travel to the Frost Fair. As Jacob left, he decided that if Flora did not go the next day, he would go alone. He had not seen a Frost Fair since he was a child and did not want to miss the event.

Scrooge and Marley watched as young Jacob roamed the cold streets. "I wish we didn't have to wait during the days when nothing is happening," said Scrooge.

"Most are better at leaping time than I am. It won't hurt us to wait again, Ebenezer."

"Can I ask you a question?"

"I expect no less from you," replied Marley. He then added, "Ebenezer, you never again need to request if you can ask a question. Just state your query, and I will try not to be too blunt or vague with my answer."

"I don't want you to get into trouble and say something you should not."

"Do not worry about that. A question can always be answered, even if the response is not understood."

"So no subject is prohibited?" asked Scrooge.

"None. That does not mean I have an answer to every question, but you can ask."

"Then I have a great curiosity about the one you call the Infinite Consciousness."

"There is not a living human that doesn't ponder about the creator," said Marley.

"But why does it have such an awkward name?"

"The Infinite Consciousness is not a name, but more of an identification of its purpose."

"But why not call it by a name instead?" wondered Scrooge.

"Humans are not born with the ability to perceive its name." As Scrooge's face exhibited a bewildered look, Marley continued, "We just do not have the ear that can decipher the syllables."

"Who does have the physical ability to hear the Infinite Consciousness's name?"

"That is developed through an evolution into peace. Societies that move beyond the trials of day-to-day activities eventually give birth to those with more perceptive senses." Marley paused, then asked, "Besides, Ebenezer, how would knowing a name add benefit to the human condition?"

"It just seems aloof and standoffish to not be given the ability to know the soul's name. Do you not agree?"

"No, I do not agree. Is it standoffish to not provide legs to a fish? Is it aloof to require birds to only walk? We are who we are for this moment, and it is a blessing with or without any words, titles or names."

"Jacob, you are getting a bit vague again."

"If, at this time, the truth can not be known — well, it is because it is vague."

"Does the Infinite Consciousness want people to be bad, so it can collect better experiences?" asked Scrooge.

"Well, from a human perspective it may seem that way. However, the experiences we encounter are mostly the product of our social surroundings. Our society is never interfered with directly by the Infinite Consciousness. Instead, influence is made upon the individuals themselves."

"So the answer is...?"

"No. The Infinite Consciousness has one goal for humanity, and it has to do with people becoming their most benevolent self. The creator would gain no benefit by encouraging the individual's malicious identities. It is solutions that new worlds need from humanity, not contentiousness."

"Jacob, have you ever met the Infinite Consciousness?"

"No."

"Will you ever meet the Infinite Consciousness?"

"Not directly."

"Does anyone ever meet the Infinite Consciousness directly?"

"I know of no one."

"So, if no one ever meets the Infinite Consciousness, then how do you know for sure it exists?"

"I can only say that I have benefited from its showers of Acceptance over the Pool."

"So the Infinite Consciousness is but a shower?"

"Within Transmogrify maybe. Yet the creator is more mysterious than Acceptance."

"So you have never met this mysterious creator, but you think you know it — how?"

"As I said before, I have met its influence — as have you, Ebenezer." Marley then took control of the day, "The morning is coming. It is time to go."

NOT ONLY DID the morning bring a break in the weather, but it also brought an expectation of pleasure for Jacob. As he rounded the corner near Joan's home, he hoped Flora would be well enough to join him at the Frost Fair. He did not expect her attendance, but believed she would enjoy the outing, so while knocking on the door, he planned a counter argument if she refused his offer.

Joan answered the knock, and without seeing who was on the other side of the door said, "Come on in, Jacob. Flora is waiting for you."

As Jacob entered the foyer, Flora could be seen shoving a large box into her canvass bag. He put  his hand on Flora's shoulder, then asked, "What are you doing?"

"I'm going to sell this at the Frost Fair," she said showing Jacob the contents of the bag.

"But that is the music box Noah gave you."

"Yes, but the baby will need the money more than the music."

"Don't do this. I was with Noah when he bought your present. It lit him up with excitement when he thought about your joy."

"But I am not happy, and just the thought I should be cheerful... it brings me grief."

"Is there nothing I can say?" asked Jacob.

"You can say anything, but I have decided." She paused, then requested, "Jacob, could you help me with my coat?"

He grabbed her coat, held it out so Flora could easily place her arms into the sleeves, then said, "It has not been this warm in a month, but you might want gloves and a hat, just so you won't have to worry about the cold." Flora agreed, and soon they were both dressed for the day's events.

As they walked toward Blackfriars bridge, the silence between the two filled the void with sounds of others hustling through their normal Thursday morning tasks.

Marley watched while his younger self guided Flora around Snow Hill, then onto New Bridge Street. The two passed the covered shops at the Fleet Market before one word was spoken between them. As the street opened up into a wide lane, Jacob told Flora, "I will support you and the baby."

"That is the least you can do," mumbled Scrooge.

Marley knew he deserved that comment. Yet, no remark was uttered as he continued to watch.

"Jacob, you are not responsible for me," said Flora.

"Yes — yes I think I am. I could have done more to free Noah, yet I was afraid."

"Afraid? Afraid of what?"

Jacob did not answer the question, but instead restated his plan. "I will provide for you. That is why you need not sell the music box."

"I may not accept your help."

Jacob was shocked, for never had it occurred to him that money would be rejected. "I do not want anything in return. I will not control you or the child, but I know if I ever wish to consider myself an honorable person, I must help you."

"Again, Jacob, this seems all about you."

"It may seem that way, and maybe it is to some extent, but truly it is you I am most concerned about."

Flora looked at Jacob, grinned a cautious smile, then watched as the sights from the fair came into view. Standing atop the bridge the two observed the commotion beneath them. All manner of ice chunks created a barrier of stagnation between the London and Blackfriars bridges. A couple dozen tents housed various enterprises. Everything from bare-chested women captivating the men, to young boys playing Skittles in an attempt to charm their favorite girl filled the day's activities. Laughter, drinks, and the smell of roasting flesh permeated the entire fair.

Jacob and Flora began their descent down the curved staircase to the landing dock. About half way down the steps, a waterman required a fee to be paid to which Jacob asked, "What do you mean? I have to pay you a twopence in order to pass?"

"That's reasonable. I'm in charge of this dock. I still need to make a living, even if I can't ferry you across right now."

"No work, no money," insisted Jacob.

"Over there." The boatman pointed to the other side of the Thames, then continued, "You will pay twice the amount."

"A pence, or a pound, I'm not paying you anything," Jacob said as he took Flora's hand. The two of them continued walking toward the landing, as the waterman followed them, determined to get his payment.

"If you do not pay me, I will tell the others, and you will not have a moment of peace here."

Jacob looked into the face of the ferryman, then relented. "Here, take it," he said, shoving a twopence into the man's hand.

"There are two of you."

"Don't press this," replied Jacob as anger overcame him. Realizing he had gained as much as he could, the man let them pass without further interference.

As they stepped onto the ice, the bells from St. Paul's Cathedral began to chime the hour. The sound of each strike echoed throughout the area. As Jacob took a second step onto the ice, a blindfolded youth ran into him. The force of his push caused Flora to slip, but she only dropped the bag carrying the music box before she was able to regain her balance. Other children playing the game teased the blindfolded boy as they dodged his grasp. No one paid any attention to either

Jacob or Flora. The group of children quickly moved away from the new arrivals. Jacob just shook his head with disapproval. He opened his mouth to criticize them, but stopped mid-speech.

As the two moved into the crowd, a small girl riding a sheep raced past them.

Jugglers, sword swallowers, and magicians practiced their talents as the crowd of enthusiastic watchers cheered every amazement. Flora began pulling Jacob in the direction of two tents that were selling general merchandise. "Maybe these people will buy my music box," she said. Entering the smoke-filled room, they were informed by the owner that he was only selling and not buying.

Not discouraged, Flora pulled Jacob to the second tent of enterprise, where the owner kindly remarked about the extraordinary craftsmanship in her music box. However, there was no sale there either.

As Flora exited the merchant's tent, she came nose to trunk with a lumbering elephant. The beast swayed from side-to-side as its owner led it over the ice. A crowd of youths followed the huge creature while it made its way along the Blackfriars bridge.

As the procession trampled over the snow, a scream suddenly could be heard throughout the area. "It's cracking the ice!" With that, the scattering of feet away from the brute left the area void of all others but the elephant. Even the owner temporarily jumped away. However, no elephant plunged through the ice that day. As the elephant finally exited the fair the thrill from the danger soon subsided.

Jacob led Flora past the various tents of alcohol and food until they came to a huge fire roasting a sheep. A young man cried out to the crowd, "Warm yourself by the flames, smell the delights of the cooking meat, prepare yourself for the best tasting mutton, and all for only sixpence."

Jacob asked the fellow, "Does a sixpence get you a portion of the meat?"

"No, that will cost an extra twopence."

"Um, it's surprising people are willing to pay to only watch."

The man shook his head in agreement, but only repeated his cry to the attendees. "Warm yourself by the flames..."

Jacob and Flora moved on. Within a step, Flora explained the reason for paying the sixpence. "Jacob, can you not see that they are paying for the party, not the meat?"

Jacob thought about it, then agreed. "That makes some sense, but by the vendor's words it sounded like an anticipation of the meat."

"Well that, too, but the day of cooking may not fall within every person's time limitation. Many may wish to spend only the time needed to warm up."

"But still I would want a bite of the meat for that price."

"It would be nice," agreed Flora.

While walking down the center of the Thames, they passed several printing presses making personalized cards of the event. Over the shoulder of one customer, Flora read the text of a recently purchased card. "This was printed on the RIVER THAMES, on Thursday, February 3, 1814, opposite Queenhithe stairs." She wondered how many of these cards would actually make it into the next generation's hands.

Jacob cared not a bit about the cards and quickly moved Flora beyond the presses until he came to two human-powered swings, the Sky Lark and High Flyer. Both had seats that would accommodate four, but the High Flyer was more than a foot taller than the other, so that is the one Jacob paid to ride on.

At first Flora was unwilling to take the ride as she feared it would cause her to become sick, but Jacob talked the swing pusher into stopping at the first notice of Flora's discomfort. With the assurance of a quick exit, she entered the swing and soon felt its sway. The two moved higher and higher until Flora called out, "slow down" to which the man obliged. This caused Jacob to say, "We will have to give him a good tip."

Flora smiled at her brother-in-law, then said, "You do remind me of Noah sometimes. I am glad to have you, Jacob."

"Such a good woman," Marley whispered, as the young Jacob just looked away in silence.

"What were you thinking about when she said that?" asked Scrooge.

"Thinking — I was crying inside. Those words brought home the truth that I would never see Noah again."

"It always seems to come back to you, Jacob," replied Scrooge.

"Of course it does, Ebenezer, for who else can I speak for?"

As Flora and Jacob departed the swing, a Skittle's ball rolled over Jacob's foot. He picked up the wooden ball, tossed it back to the player, then said, "Maybe your next throw will actually hit a pin or two." Flora giggled at this, for she, too, thought the inebriated man needed some practice. But before the competitor could respond, the area burst forth with an outcry from a man chasing a child. "Stop him, he stole my wallet!"

As the two raced passed them a large man put his huge foot out into the path of the fleeing youngster. The boy fell hard upon the ice as the one following leaped upon him. Neither Flora nor Jacob stayed around to view the outcome, but both assumed the wallet was retrieved.

As they made their way along the center of the Thames, they were approached by a man carrying arrows. "Win a half a crown if you can shoot a bulls eye. Just a twopence per arrow."

Jacob looked at Flora and said, "I used to be a really good shot."

"Yes, but are you still?" asked Flora.

Jacob shook his head in the affirmative as he gave the man a sixpence for three arrows. Flora watched as he took aim, then shot the arrow toward the bale of hay that had a target attached. Luckily he hit the target, but none of its circles. "You can still do it," said the man selling the arrows.

As Jacob steadied himself for the next shot, a man tapped Flora on the shoulder. Upon turning, Flora instantly recognized the man from the general mercantile tent who had admired her music box. She smiled at him, as he did to her. Pointing to the tall gentleman behind them, he said, "This fellow is looking for a nice present to give to his newborn son." He paused as Flora and the man acknowledged  each other. The shopkeeper then continued, "I was thinking your music box is the nicest item I have seen today. Are you still interested in selling?"

Without hesitation, Flora replied, "Yes, if I can get even half of what it is worth." With that, she opened the box, and the pins on the wheel began playing the old English melody.

"Oh, that is delightful," said Edward, the man standing behind the merchant.

The merchant exclaimed, "Just as I said. Well, let me leave you to the deal." With that, he turned toward his business, but before he could leave, the man shook his hand, using the gesture to deposit a quid into his palm.

Turning his attention to Flora, Edward said, "My name is Edward Albright. What would you want for the box?"

"I'm sure it would be worth seventy-five quid new."

"Possibly. Is your price, then, thirty-five quid?"

Flora could hardly speak. Memories stirred with emotions as she turned slightly from him. Lowering her head to avoid showing her tears, she wept until moisture began to drop off her chin.

Edward waited for her response, then asked, "Do you really want to sell?" Slowly she nodded her head in the affirmative, but before she could voice the acceptance of the offer, Edward made a new offer. "I will give you forty-five quid.

Surely this box is worth ninety quid to begin with, do you agree?" With that he stepped forward to offer the money, but instead slipped into foot traffic. Flora quickly turned her head toward Edward, flinging the last tear from her cheek. Grabbing his arm, she made every effort to help him resist the force of the crowd's flow. As the two steadied themselves, they began to slowly move with the crowd. Finally Edward repeated himself, "Do you really want to sell?"

"Yes, thank you. I am sure your son will love the music."

"I have a drawing of him. Would you like to see it?"

"That would be delightful."

They slowly began to move with the crowd down the center of the Thames. Edward removed the image from his wallet, then held it out to Flora. She took the paper from the man and was greeted with a smiling infant only months old. "He is cheerful. It's a nice drawing too."

"I am the artist."

Flora smiled at the man, then said, "Well, it is still a good drawing." With that she asked, "What is your son's name?"

"Gilbert, Gilbert Jacob Albright."

"I have my own, Jacob, he is right here." She turned to show him the archery competition, but they were now too far away to view the event. "Oh, we have wandered off. I must get back to him," said Flora.

"Of course." With that, the two finished their transaction and parted directions. As Flora returned to the archery competition, she realized Jacob could not be found. New men were shooting the bale. The only familiar face was that of the arrow seller. She approached him and asked about Jacob.

"He left, five minutes ago. Look around. I doubt he has gone far." As Flora turned to leave, the man added, "Worst shot all day. He had more chance of winning in his sleep."

Flora did search the area, yet Jacob was gone. She wondered if his desire for the drink had pulled him into one of the many tents of liquor. After half an hour, she gave up the search and began walking toward home.

"Where were you?" asked Scrooge.

"Where do you think I was?"

"I know not your mysteries."

"I was looking for Flora. I went over to the music and dancing boat. It occurred to me that she might have gone there to sell her music box," replied Marley.

"Why would you think she would go there?"

"Because they are music lovers." Marley then pointed to Flora walking toward the Blackfriars bridge and said, "We have to follow her."

"But we have been following your younger self."

"Not today. My eye has always been on her." With that, Marley began moving toward Flora, and Scrooge shadowed his friend.

As Flora neared the Copper Plate Printing Press, she slipped on a patch of ice and fell backwards. Her back met the ground with such a force the life within her moved. Grabbing her belly, she slowly rose. Lifting her bag, Flora looked upon the forty-five quid lying loose within

the pouch. Reminders of her life with Noah combined every emotion into an overwhelming devastation. As tears began to blur Flora's vision, sorrows rang out.

Aimlessly trudging through fresh snow, she paused at the "Danger! Thin Ice!" sign, then with the speed of a fox, raced toward crisis. Her anguish controlled every thought as she yelled, "I want to die!" Before any need of self-preservation could engage, the baby kicked as the ice gave way to her ruinous desire.

Off in the distance Jacob's muffled voice could be heard yelling, "Flora, Flora, where are you?"

"We have to save her," cried Scrooge.

"If only we could," replied Marley.

"Why did you not tell me of this when it happened?"

"My sorrow could not face my guilt." Marley hung his head as he said, "We now have to go back to 1854."

"Wait, I thought we were going to help Noah."

"Time travel and the Isle Of Transmogrify are not on the same path, Ebenezer. Navigation to the afterlife requires that the Consciousness Relocation occurs in the present." With that said, Marley slowly started moving them back to 1854. They arrived at 15 Sackville within moments of when they had first departed. Scrooge realized it was still Christmas Eve, for the streets were filled with carolers. As with Scrooge's first venture into the past, over a decade ago, this newest journey had also been experienced from outside of time's forward motion.

Stave Six

Entering The Afterlife

STANDING NEXT TO Scrooge's now extinguished fireplace, Marley said, "I know I have already told you about the danger of Transmogrify, but this will be your last opportunity to forego moving in that direction." He took a deep breath, then asked, "Do you want to continue?"

"Yes, I do have some fear, but — well, let us just be on our way."

Marley detached a vial stored between the chains of his heart. He handed his friend the container of liquid, then instructed, "You will need to drink this potion."

Scrooge removed the cork and drank the elixir. Immediately he began coughing. "What is this?"

"Poison," said Marley, then quickly added, "Only the dead can enter Transmogrify."

"Jacob, when you were talking about me being in danger, I had no idea you were going to be the dangerous one." With that, Scrooge made every effort to vomit the contents of the fluid, but the potion worked with a speed that could not be stopped.

As Scrooge collapsed into his chair, Marley tried to reassure him, "Trust me." Tapping his chest, he said, "I have the antidote, Ebenezer, you will not die." With Scrooge nearing death, Marley whisked his friend off to the Isle Of Transmogrify.

Slumped at the entrance, Scrooge's vitality dwindled to barely noticeable. In a panic, Jacob made every effort to pluck from between his heart's chains the bottle containing the poison's antidote. Try as he did, Fire Twirlers kept the vial secured within its restraints. Only with perseverance did the vessel finally drop from the chain, then directly passed through Marley's palm. The bottle hit the collapsed Ebenezer on the back of the head. Marley grabbed at the vial before it could strike the ground, yet the container proved difficult to control. Each time Marley thought he had a grasp on the bottle, it would start to slip through his featherlike body.

"Why has this dead not begun Entanglement?" asked Teint.

Marley made no effort to face Transmogrify's guards. Instead he hurried himself with Scrooge. "I'm having a bit of trouble here." It had never occurred to Marley that Scrooge would not be able to help himself drink the antidote. As Scrooge began to gasp for air, Marley attempted to deliver the life-saving liquid to his friend's lips. Scrooge just clamped his mouth tighter, which intensified his struggle for breath.

Desperate to keep Scrooge alive, Marley bit off the tip of every one of his left-handed fingers. With the finger bones extending beyond the skin, Marley cupped his five digits together so they would form a small platform. Balancing the vial on the flat surface of his combined finger bones, Marley hoped the bottle would not fall through his hand before he could get the medicine into Scrooge. With his teeth, he removed the cork from the antidote.

As feared, the vial began to pass through Marley's fingers. Struggling, he finally was able to twist the protruding bones in such a way it slowed the bottle just enough, so it did not complete its fall through his hand. Realizing his grasp on the bottle would be short-lived, Marley reached into Scrooge's chest and directly dropped the liquid into his stomach.

Teint and Apurto's platform had lowered to within five feet of the Londoners' when Scrooge began to stir. "Why has this dead not begun Entanglement?" repeated Teint.

Scrooge opened his eyes to the glare of a floodlight blinding his vision. Next to him stood Marley's faded form. Before them, a platform hung suspended from what appeared to be nothing. On top of the stage stood two colorless forms. Teint, the angel whose beacon of light had the ability to both penetrate the heart's emotions while dimming the eye's vision, stood before Marley and Scrooge in radiant command.

"Jacob Marley, why has this dead not begun Entanglement?" demanded Teint. Marley again ignored the light being's question. Instead he helped Scrooge to his feet.

Next to Teint stood an animal roughly the size and shape of a dog. Yet, its markings were closer to that of a tiger. The creature's short brownish fur highlighted its black stripes. As the dog-like animal coiled around and through Teint's light, the markings on his hind end began to absorb the radiance.

When the beast's stripes began to glow,  Teint slapped his own chest then commanded, "Apurto, here, now." With that the animal raised himself onto his hind feet, steadied himself with his tail, then rubbed the top of his head against his companion's cheek. Dropping back to his feet, Apurto joined Teint in his concern for the two in front of them.

"Jacob Marley, you have brought a living person. Why?" inquired Teint.

"I need Ebenezer's help in freeing Noah Marley."

"I can not allow this. You know he could be harmed. He can not save your brother if he loses his own life."

"I will protect him," assured Marley.

"How?"

"We will walk the Road Of Phantoms and never ascend to the Corridor. For added safety, we will not step from the Road. I will offer myself up for Instant Transmogrification if Ebenezer is injured," said Marley.

"Instant Transmogrification is not something you can bargain with. At any time you can choose to complete your Transmogrification, but you can not manipulate its use. So, do you want to go through Instant Transmogrification now?" asked Teint.

"No, no!" Marley shouted. "I just want to agree to any punishment required if I fail to protect Ebenezer."

"A punishment? There is no penalty great enough to cure any injury that may be inflicted upon a living one. Wanting punishment after a preventable injury will not be allowed. No, he must go back."

"My life is nearly over anyway. I am not afraid of the end," said Scrooge. After a short pause, he added, "I want to help Jacob. I am here at my own desire."

Both Teint and Apurto turned their attention to Scrooge. Teint's glare felt like a challenge to Scrooge as the gatekeeper voiced, "Prove to me you welcome nonexistence."

"After my death will I not be here in Transmogrify?" asked Scrooge.

"No, Ebenezer Scrooge, if you die in Transmogrify you will never have existed."

Shocked, Scrooge asked, "What will happen to me?"

"Earth time will adjust to accommodate your deletion from time's record," explained Teint.

"Deletion?"

"All aspects of you will be expunged."

After a silence where only the sounds of Transmogrify could be heard, Scrooge finally broke the conversational quiet, "I wish to help Jacob."

Apurto, the caretaker of Transmogrify, jumped off the platform. After approaching the would-be invader, Apurto sniffed every inch of Scrooge. In the end, the beast only yawned. The sight of sharp teeth spooked Scrooge. Never had he experienced a creature whose jaw was hinged behind the ear. The idea that Apurto could bite him in half caused Scrooge to recoil from the mouth.

Teint again slapped his chest and commanded, "Apurto, here, now." After observing Scrooge's encounter with his pet, Teint said, "Your bravery has failed you. Your earthly fears will betray you in Transmogrify." As Apurto returned to the platform, Teint continued, "Transmogrify has no great need for your help. You must ret..."

"Wait, the Transmogrification of a Condemned Innocent is at stake," cried Marley.

Teint stopped the motion that would have returned Scrooge to the living and asked, "Condemned Innocent? Is there no chance of Transmogrification without the help of this earth-bound?"

"Within a millennium, maybe."

"Your statement is exaggerated. None carry on in Transmogrify for that length of time. Why do you believe Noah Marley's Condemned Innocent spirit will not become a Mogrified Spirit?" asked Teint.

"He was punished for a crime he did not perpetrate. Plus, he committed suicide," answered Marley.

"Why do you think he committed suicide? He has never dwelled within the Pool."

"The warden at Newgate said he committed suicide."

"Ah, yes, the warden. He now dwells within the Fields Of Destructive Compulsions for his laziness. The truth was known among the turnkeys that Noah was murdered."

The shock of Noah's true death silenced Marley. Teint lifted his arm, and next to their raised platform, an image appeared. As he lowered his arm, the scene of Noah's last moments on earth began to be revealed. Within the screen of moving images, Marley and Scrooge watched as Noah walked to Newgate's visitor fence. While he waited for Flora to arrive, James Maxey could be seen giving the turnkey the remainder of his funds. As the guard pocketed the money, he then turned and walked indoors.

Maxey approached Noah undetected. Once behind him he thrust Noah's head into the metal picket fence. The force from the shove knocked Noah unconscious. While Noah lay next to the fence, Maxey raised his prey's arm, and then dragged it the full length of its measure over one of the sharpest barbs. As Maxey murdered Noah, he whispered into his ear, "Little fish get eaten by big fish." Stepping free of the spurting blood, the killer left Noah dangling by his wrist. Entering the prison, Maxey smiled, for he knew Noah would die before he did.

"So you think this event created a Condemned Innocent in Noah?" asked Teint.

"Maybe even two," replied Marley.

"That would only happen if Noah were responsible for multiple deaths. He is not even guilty of his own death."

"His wife, Flora, died a few weeks after him. Her death may be on Noah's spirit as well," said Marley.

"In truth, the responsibility of both of their deaths is on you, Jacob Marley. It is Flora who dwells within the Pool, not Noah. Your reality has been a lie." Marley lowered his eyes as Teint explained, "Noah Marley did generate a Condemned Innocent spirit, but seems to be progressing as expected, for he recently passed from the Pit Of Anger into the Abyss. He will finish his Transmogrification on his own. But Flora, she sleeps too long."

Surprised by Flora's stagnation within Transmogrify, Marley asked, "You mean she still sleeps in the Pool?"

"Yes, Flora sleeps even though she has been sprayed with Coss Acceptance." Teint then added, "She still resists the awakening."

"Is not Coss Acceptance the guarantee for triggering Entanglement?"

"For most, but some can not be stirred until other aspects of their death have been put right," said Teint.

Marley assumed Flora's hibernation within the Pool Of Broken Spirits was his fault. The only thing he knew for sure was that Noah would never complete Transmogrification without Flora. He then offered, "We will save Flora as well as Noah."

"We will?" inquired Scrooge.

"I thought Noah was your focus," said Teint.

"I thought the same," agreed Scrooge.

"Noah is my Task Of Outreach," replied Marley. He then added, "Flora may be more worthy of our help than Noah."

"All spirits are worthy of help, even those who have cut ties to the Infinite Consciousness are helped by the mechanics of their Mog," said Teint.

"Teint, please show me the answer you need," requested a timid Marley.

"Clever, Jacob. I can not solve this problem; the dangers are many. Possibly every minute will bring a trouble that could end Ebenezer."

"If I can not offer myself up for Instant Transmogrification upon failure, or avoid dangerous spirits by traveling the Road only, or even camouflaging Scrooge with my own spirit when needed, then I do not think I can protect him."

"Camouflage... camouflage," Teint muttered as he cloaked the remainder of his thought in silence.

"I've become skilled at..." and within the next moment, Marley changed his appearance into that of Scrooge's.

Teint smiled as he looked upon the double images of Scrooge standing before him. The angel then spoke of a truth Marley had not taken into account. "It may be best if you take on the appearance of an entity that spirits fear, and not change into the one they wish to prey upon."

Marley pondered this reality for a few moments before he, too, grinned. However, his frustration with the inability to find a solution for protecting Scrooge controlled his thoughts. As possible answers crossed paths in his mind, he was instantly forced to refocus his attention on the remaining chains binding his heart to his ordeal. Without warning, the chains began spewing sparks.

"Jacob Marley, why have you removed a Fire Twirler from Transmogrify?" demanded Teint.

Removing a nearly spent Fire Twirler from between the inner space of a chain, he held it out to Teint and said, "I can make this perform any action desired." Marley looked at the barely spinning fire ball, then added, "Not this one. It burned itself out before I could use it, but I have four more."

"Why have you removed any Fire Twirlers?"

"Because they add a physicality to everything they are directed toward." He then waited for a response from the angel, but Teint remained quiet, so Marley continued. "I have already used one to help warm Noah while in jail. My four remaining Fire Twirlers will be used to defend Ebenezer from harm." He paused again to hear only a silence that caused him concern. "I will only use them in the aid of Ebenezer." Still Teint just glared at Marley. "I can return them to the Fields Of Destructive Compulsions when we pass it, if you would prefer."

Teint finally said, "You have slowed the progress of a spirit by capturing their Fire Twirler."

"No, no, I only catch them when they have passed into the Road Of Phantoms. They can not survive that trespass. I am doing them a favor by using them as an energy source."

"No, that is not a Fire Twirler's purpose. You are slowing down an individual's Transmogrification when you trap their energy. Fire Twirlers are not to be used by other spirits." Irritated by Marley's lack of responsibility, Teint asked, "You are aware that Fire Twirlers are what compulsive spirits create so they can release their destructive habits?"

"To some extent," replied Marley.

"Well, let me broaden your knowledge," Teint said with a hint of sarcasm. "When a Fire Twirler is trapped, the spirit who created it goes into a standby mode until it is either returned or consumed. Jacob, you have slowed the progress of spirits."

"But all spirits capture Fire Twirlers."

"Do not say 'all' when it is but a few who manipulate Fire Twirlers."

"These Fire Twirlers are the only way I can assure Ebenezer's safety." Marley then added, "With Fire Twirlers, I will be able to ward off any attack."

Teint considered all aspects of Marley's scheme before he said, "I will allow you to enter with Ebenezer, but only if you stay on the Road away from other spirits and save the Fire Twirlers to be used when Ebenezer, not yourself, is in a life-threatening situation."

"Ebenezer will be my only concern." Marley then whispered to Scrooge, "Let's go before he changes his mind."

As they stepped behind Teint's platform, a curtain of illumination lit up the scene being played out in Transmogrify. Changing from black to cobalt blue, the sky above Marley and Scrooge instantly made visible hundreds of spirits traveling to and from Transmogrify. Marley pointed to the group, then said, "The Task Of Outreach keeps us all busy."

As spirits passed over them, Scrooge asked, "Why are they above us?"

"The Road is too dangerous for spirits, especially near the Crater Of Severed Spirits. Most phantoms travel the Corridor, but you and I, Ebenezer, must keep to the Road. That is our agreement with Teint."

As they entered the deeply blue area, Apurto growled at them. Upon their first step inside Transmogrify the sky lightened, but only a bit. Before them could be heard the sounds of spirits at work. The five upper Mogs' activities could be heard but, from the entrance, not seen. As Marley took his first step inside of Transmogrify, the second chain attached to his heart disappeared, and with it dropped a Fire Twirler. As it spun free of its abductor, Marley said, "You better stay safe, Ebenezer, I only have three of those remaining." Waving for Scrooge to follow, Marley added, "Maybe you will be safe without a fourth."

Scrooge took his second step into Transmogrify, the gravity of the afterlife pressed down on him. "JACOB, I can't breathe."

"I was afraid..."

"I'm burning up, what is this place?"

"I was not expecting..."

"Do something!" Scrooge demanded.

As Scrooge pulled himself into a fetal position, Marley crouched next to his backside. Wrapping himself around his gasping friend, he hugged him so deeply that his ghostliness combined with Scrooge's flesh. As the two beings became indistinguishable, Scrooge began to take shallow breaths, sweat filling every pore of his structure. Rising to his knees Scrooge said, "If I don't cool, I will ignite."

Marley removed one of the Fire Twirlers from between his heart's chain. The little energy blaze spun with such a speed that flames sprayed off in every direction. With the vision of a glacier in his mind, Marley held the Fire Twirler next to his skeleton. With this mental image in control of the Fire Twirler, Marley's structure turned to ice. The chill decreased his mobility. Though stiff, Marley flung himself over Scrooge. Slowly Scrooge revived from the dual attack of Transmogrify's gravity and heat.

"We will have to stay within a short distance of each other, or gravity will again crush you. The heat you will learn to manage."

"Why is there such an intense pressure here?" asked Scrooge.

"After death, the ability to physically feel becomes almost absent. However, the need to perceive our senses is required for our work toward Acceptance. Without an intensified gravity, no spirit would be able to complete Transmogrification."

"And the heat, why is it so hot?"

"I did not expect that. Heat just does not affect most spirits, so I did not know to make plans for it. Why I didn't think of it, I don't know, because it makes sense that Transmogrify would be hot. Every area has its own energy source, which of course creates heat. Once we crest the hill over there, the sparks will become obvious." Marley pointed to the top of the hill before them.

Scrooge regained his footing just in time to greet the chaos of a floating head biting his neck. "What bedlam is this?" exclaimed Scrooge as he grabbed the injured area. But before any explanation could be offered, another head attacked Scrooge.

With urgency, Marley raced past Scrooge while shouting, "Fast, follow me, Ebenezer." Without thinking, Marley shot so far ahead that Scrooge found himself released from their shared gravity field.

As Scrooge dropped to his knees, he clutched his chest. Wheezing, he whispered the word, "Stop."

Marley paid no attention to his friend's utterance. Instead he focused on knocking away the approaching heads.

"Help me," cried Scrooge as he surrendered to the forces attacking him.

Marley turned to view his friend lying upon the Road, motionless. Racing back to him, Scrooge began to revive as soon as Marley reentered their shared gravity field. Attached to Scrooge's neck were the teeth from a spirit's head. The head itself did not appear to be available for reassembly. So Marley carefully grabbed both sides of the teeth, then pulled them apart just enough to effect Scrooge's release. Helping Scrooge to his feet, he ordered, "Follow me." Marley began running toward the center of Transmogrify. "Run, Ebenezer, and this time keep up with me."

"Why are we running toward the heads?" yelled Scrooge.

"It's the only way to escape."

The only escape Scrooge figured they were involved in was the abandonment of their good senses. Frantic, the two raced toward the hilltop. With each step, the dismembered heads continued to assault Scrooge's flesh. As they neared the crest of the hill, the Road gained several feet of distance. When twenty feet became thirty, Scrooge replaced his fear with frustration. Grabbing the head currently in attack, he threw it to the ground with such a force it bounced, not once, but repeatedly. The unfortunate cranium reached new heights with each rebound. Scrooge raced past the deflected skull in pursuit of Marley's gravity.

At the top of the hill, Marley abruptly stopped. Scrooge ran right through him as several of the heads flew over the top of the hill. Realizing he would soon be out of Marley's gravity, Scrooge turned toward his friend, leaned over and said, "I have never moved so fast in my entire life." Heaving air in and out of his lungs, he asked, "Why have we stopped?"

"Is it not obvious?"

Scrooge pondered the question, then replied, "Not to me."

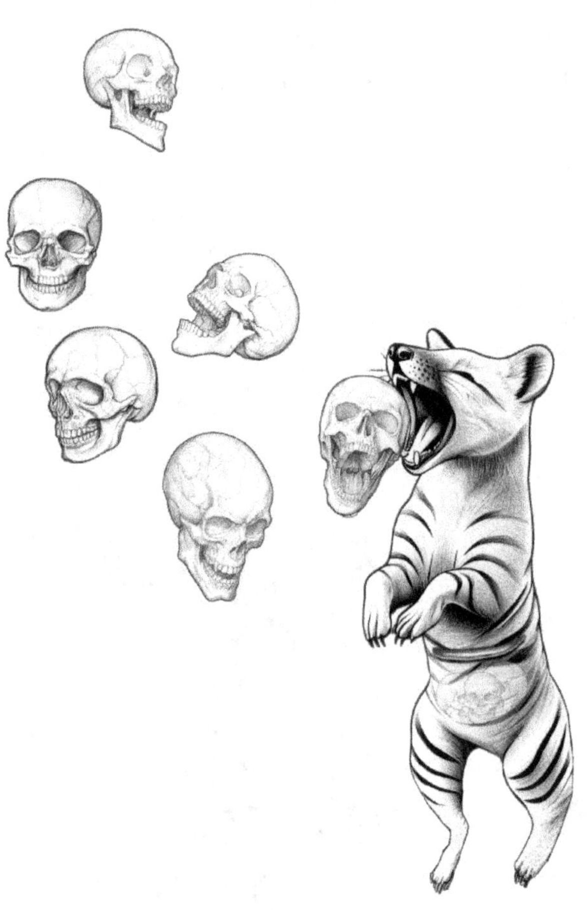

"The heads, look," he said pointing upward, "they no longer care about you, Ebenezer."

Scrooge watched as a couple of heads flew mere feet above his eyes. Gaining his breath, he pointed over Marley's shoulder, then asked, "What is Apurto doing?"

Marley turned to face the front gate. Together the two friends watched as Apurto used his tail to power his ability for bouncing twice his height. At his apex, Apurto snatched one of the spirit's heads, then gently placed it into his marsupial pouch. As Apurto filled his pouch with dismembered skulls, Marley explained, "Those fierce biters were never after you, Ebenezer."

"You could have fooled me."

"They only had the desire to escape Transmogrify. Apurto is capturing them, because it's his job."

"I don't understand. How do such skulls even exist?" asked Scrooge.

"They are what is produced whenever there is a Coss Acceptance release."

"Why?"

"None within the Crater are allowed any help, from either the Infinite Consciousness or other spirits," said Marley.

"I still do not understand why the Infinite Consciousness abandons those in the Crater."

"Ebenezer, it is just the opposite. Those within the Crater abandoned the Infinite Consciousness."

Apurto grabbed another head as Scrooge asked, "So what Apurto is doing helps?"

"Yes, Apurto is trying to save those spirits. Whenever a group of Coss achieves Acceptance, the force of their release pulls apart the spirits closest to them. Apurto is just returning the parts so the spirits can be made whole again."

Scrooge is shocked by this reality. "The salvation of some creates the destruction of others?"

"It is the mechanics of the Crater."

"It seems brutal."

"The difficulty of existing without the Infinite Consciousness's influence is not cruel, it is excruciating." Scrooge winced at the thought as Marley pointed toward the entrance, then said, "Soon Apurto is going to return the heads to the Crater. Most of them will reassemble with their other limbs."

"Most of them?"

"Some will be lost when their head or backbone is not recovered. Otherwise, even limbless Coss will eventually achieve Transmogrification."

"Look!" Scrooge yelled as he pointed to Apurto. "He just swallowed a head!"

"His pouch is out of space," explained Marley.

"So..."

"Well, he can't let them escape Transmogrify, can he?"

"So he eats them?"

"That's better than a bunch of roaming heads traveling the universe."

"Not to the individual heads."

"Ebenezer, each spirit creates their own agony. They had a choice in life, yet all within the Crater willingly appropriated authorities that only belong to the Infinite Consciousness."

As Apurto lowered himself to the ground, his pouch settled upon the Road's surface. Dragging his belly, the custodian of Transmogrify began moving toward them, the mass of a dozen heads within his pouch slowed his travel. As he passed them in pursuit of returning the skulls, Scrooge and Marley finally surmounted the hill overlooking Transmogrify.

Marley watched for Scrooge's response. The roar of Transmogrify could be heard from the entrance, but the glare, that had been undetectable. As they crested the hill a blast of bluish light confronted them. Scrooge stopped in midstride as his mouth dropped open. Directly before them stood hundreds of trees surrounding the

three pits of the Plains Of Violence. Extending out from the entrance of each pit were countless one-room boxes. Each contained a spirit, sometimes two, depending on the progress of the spirit being housed within the Contemplation Chamber. Surrounding the three pits was the Forest Of Burning Trees. Though forest fires are mostly unheard of in London, Scrooge instantly realized this eruption of flames was outside of his known reality. He watched as every tree burned only from inside the center of their trunk, and all of the leaves, branches and bark remained pristine. Scrooge pointed to the Plains. He doubted his vision, yet only expressed his bewilderment with one word, "Why...?"

Sensing his confusion, Marley offered, "The Forest of Burning Trees powers the Pits."

"The flames seem to be consuming no wood?"

"The Infinite Consciousness provides the fuel. The forest is just the method of power transfer, but not the actual energy itself."

"Why...?" asked the confused Scrooge.

"My best guess, and it is only a guess, is that those that occupy a Chamber need all of their personal energy to complete their Transmogrification."

"Why?"

"There are some bad characters in there, Ebenezer," Marley said, then continued. "Violent acts do not resolve themselves through time, they fester. I have a feeling the Task Of Outreach was created just to help those in the Plains. The

Chambers look calm and organized, but one thing I know from personal experience is that the Chambers are hard work."

"If the Infinite Consciousness powers the Plains, who powers that area?" Scrooge asked, pointing to the Cycle Of Greed.

"Most Mogs are set up so the spirits themselves generate the power needed for the area."

"Why does there need to be any kind of energy force at all?" wondered Scrooge.

"I can only think of two reasons. First, it seems there is a lot of energy spent on keeping the gravity we need within Transmogrify."

"This is so spirits can experience themselves as physical beings again?"

"Yes, just enough to perceive their own life's actions."

"And the second reason?" asked Scrooge.

"Each spirit is provided with the conditions they will need in order to form their Tasks Of Outreach, so they can eventually become a Mogrified Spirit. Transformation into Acceptance takes a massive amount of energy."

"Most Mogs generate their own energy? How do they do that?"

"Each has its own way. Even in the Pool Of Broken Spirits those that sleep still generate the area's power through the tears they shed. However, within the Plains Of Violence, and in the Abyss, the Infinite Consciousness provides all the energy."

"Why doesn't the Infinite Consciousness provide all the energy to everything?" asked Scrooge.

"It can't," Marley replied as he began walking toward the Plains Of Violence.

Quickening his pace, Scrooge asked, "I thought the Infinite Consciousness could do anything."

"Not when the tie has been cut."

"I do not understand."

"Ebenezer, what do you do when a person betrays you?" Scrooge had no immediate answer, so Marley continued. "It is difficult for an individual to cut their connection to the Infinite Consciousness. Nonetheless, those who maim others while deceiving themselves into thinking they have the Infinite Consciousness's power behind their act end up condemning their own spirit to the Crater. Again he paused, then finished his thought with, "Those in the Crater suffer the most within Transmogrify."

"The Crater — where the biting heads are from?"

"The heads would never exist if the Infinite Consciousness could directly help those with a Spirit Breakage," answered Marley.

"Are those in the Crater the only ones that cut their own Infinite Consciousness connection?"

"You mean a Spirit Breakage?"

"Yes, that seems to be what you are calling it," replied Scrooge.

"Those who take their own life also cut their tie to the Infinite Consciousness. I guess it is a slap in the face to reject the Infinite Consciousness's most precious gift — life."

"But they don't suffer as much as those in the Crater?" asked Scrooge.

"They are asleep, and only connect up with their suffering once they awaken."

"Definitely sounds like something I am going to have to see to believe."

"That is the way of Transmogrify, Ebenezer."

As Scrooge gained the focus of the entire area, he realized there were environments of commotion as far as he could see. To the left were the Plains Of Violence with their flaming trees, but across the Road the grinding sound and sparks of metal upon stone dominated the scene. The bone-crushing noise created a ferocious tension as spirits endlessly plodded around an iron disk. As the metal scraped over the flint, sparks flamed in every direction. Yet no matter the commotion, the toiling spirits focused only on the object at the center of their platform — the Golden Crown Of Greed.

Marley pointed to the turning wheel, then said, "That is where my spirit of greed transformed."

"Will I have to shuffle around that circle?" asked Scrooge.

"Not unless you change your ways again." Marley then said to Scrooge, "We are not concerned with the greedy. We need to make sure Noah has been transported to the Abyss Of Final Transmogrify. Follow me." Marley quickened his pace to the Pit of Anger, where Noah's spirit had originally been sent.

Though Jacob Marley had died long after his brother, his transformation from the Plain's Pit Of Dishonesty had occurred before Noah could resolve the issues of having been both falsely accused of theft, and then viciously murdered. Noah's Condemned Innocent spirit struggled with the pain and anger caused by both actions.

"I hope Teint was correct when he said Noah was in the Abyss."

"I assume Teint would know," said Scrooge.

"Of course you are correct, but we are going by the Pit, so I want to just make sure."

"Trust but verify?"

"That pins the need."

With the overpowering roar of grinding at the Cycle, the contrast of a deafening silence coming from the Plains Of Violence created a foreboding despair within Scrooge. Even the muted sounds from the Forest Of Burning Trees added to the sensation of hardship.

Of the three Pits, Noah's was first on the Road. The two watched as the Contemplation Chamber's door closest to the Pit Of Anger opened. Out stepped a spirit. The spirit's next stride was made directly into the Pit, from which it then instantly disappeared from view.

"Where has the spirit gone?" asked Scrooge.

"It is already in the Abyss." Seeing Ebenezer's confusion, Marley then added, "The Pit is little more than the gateway. The work occurs in the Contemplation Chambers," Marley said, pointing to the now empty Chamber. "Watch."

They observed the Contemplation Chamber as it vanished. The box just disappeared. The next Chamber in line shifted to the Pit Of Anger's entrance. Without a wasted moment, the spirit from that Chamber entered the Pit, then evaporated from view as it arrived in the Abyss.

The process of spirits leaving their isolation Chamber only to be transported to an area ominously called the Abyss repeated continuously. While Marley and Scrooge watched the flow of spirits pass through the Mog, one Chamber seemed to get stuck when no spirit exited the door. All action halted in the Pit Of Anger until the entire Chamber began to lift upward, then floated away.

"Where is it going?" asked Scrooge.

"The spirit within that Chamber did not complete its Task Of Outreach before it arrived to the Pit."

"So where is it going?" asked Scrooge again.

"To the back of the line."

"That does not seem fair, that it has to start all over."

"The Contemplation Chamber's purpose can not be denied. Without a Task, no spirit within Transmogrify is ever allowed into the Abyss. Except..."

"Jacob, do not go silent now."

"This is almost too much information for you, but the Coss go directly to Acceptance. They do not spend any time in the Abyss."

"Yes, my friend, that means nothing to me," replied Scrooge.

"My words could never explain such a visual as the Crater to you, Ebenezer." At this point Marley realized Noah was absent from the Plains, he added. "Teint was right; time to trek toward the Abyss."

"How long will that take?"

"Maybe months."

Shocked, Scrooge tried to form a question, but none presented itself, so he just stared at Marley with hopes he would pick up on his confusion. "Don't worry, Ebenezer. It depends on Transmogrify's population as to the length of time it will take us to travel the Road."

"Population?"

"Sure, Transmogrify has been shrinking ever since the Crusades ended."

"Shrinking?"

"Most Mogs have a constant flow of spirits, maybe just a little growth as the Earth's population expands."

"Then why is there ever any change in size within Transmogrify?"

"The Crater and the Pit Of Physical Harm have an unnatural influence on Transmogrify's dimensions."

"Jacob, that does not explain a thing."

"Answer me this, Ebenezer, does war produce more dead in a quicker period of time than would be created without it?"

"Logic would dictate so."

"In my mind, Ebenezer, there are only two reasons for war. One to expand the territory, and two to conform the mind-set."

"So the Crater is where warriors go?"

"Warriors more often spend their afterlife in a Chamber. But it depends on their motives. The Crater is where humans are sent who kill others while thinking the Infinite Consciousness wants them to do that. That poor Crater, it just expands and contracts as humans harm through spiritual ignorance. Every holy war brings a size change to Transmogrify," explained Marley.

"Holy wars, there has not been one of them in a long while."

"But we did just get over the witch trials. A number of officials and faggot carriers were added to the Crater during that period of time."

"So it's not just holy wars?"

"Do you think one person would have been burned if not for the church?" Marley asked but did not wait for an answer. "No, Ebenezer, the only reason a spirit spends their time in the Crater Of Severed Spirits is because they harmed others while thinking they were doing the Infinite Consciousness's work." Marley paused to wait for a response, but when none came forth, he continued, "And, that error of conflicting passions will end up destroying a portion of them." Marley took in a deep breath, then ended with, "So who ultimately is more harmed in the end — the victim or the perpetrator?"

Scrooge realized Marley was being rhetorical and wanted no response, so he just continued to follow his friend. As the two passed the Pit Of Physical Harm, Marley glimpsed a view of James Maxey. The killer sat in the fifth Chamber from the entrance. Within his Contemplation Chamber, Maxey prepared for the Pit in silence. His expression had lost the harsh features of his earthly face. Yet Marley recognized the criminal's characteristics. Reaching into his chest Marley grabbed a Fire Twirler, brought it forward and announced, "I'm going to send him to the back of the line."

"Wait, Jacob, we only have two left, and you promised Teint..."

"Maxey is not going to achieve Transmogrification before Noah."

"But Noah is already ahead of Maxey. Is he not already in the Abyss?" asked Scrooge.

"Yes."

"So leave it be, Jacob. Maxey is not going to achieve Transmogrification first."

"And I was so looking forward to adding thirty years to his miserable wait," Marley said, placing the Fire Twirler back between his chains.

"Do you think Teint would have stopped you?"

"No, it is more likely I would have been sent back to the Pit Of Anger." He paused, then added, "Thank you for speaking with reason, Ebenezer."

Scrooge smiled, then in an effort to comfort Marley, passed his hand through the spirit's shoulder.

As the two passed the Cycle Of Greed, Scrooge was glad he would not have to spend any time walking the circle. He wondered which Mogs he would be in once his Entanglement was achieved — that is if he can escape Transmogrify's annihilation of living visitors. While in the process of passing the Cycle, Scrooge watched as one of the spirits turned its head from the golden crown at the center, then instantly disappeared. "Did you see that?"

"What?" asked Marley.

Excited, Scrooge pointed to the circle as he said, "A person just perished from the Cycle."

"They aren't people anymore, nor are they gone. They just proceeded to the Abyss Of Final Transmogrify. Don't worry, Ebenezer, they are fine."

While they passed the silent Pits on their left, and the Cycle was grinding away to their right, Scrooge felt the splash of water on his clothing. Just beyond the Plains Of Violence stood a narrow but lengthy area of torrential rain. Approaching the source of the moisture, Marley instructed Scrooge, "Stay away from the Rains Of Darkness."

"Why?"

"No one knows what the Rains are for, but that water will incinerate you."

"Incinerate? How can rain burn?"

"I don't know, Ebenezer. All I know is that spirits are in terror of it. The rumor is that the Rains are used to keep Fire Twirlers out of the Plains Of Violence."

Scrooge wiped away the liquid that had fallen onto his clothing, then said, "It just seems like water to me."

"Don't touch it anymore!"

"Jacob, I have never seen you so animated."

"All I know is that stuff destroys. Leave it alone."

They passed the Rains Of Darkness on the left without harm. The two continued to walk as they watched new spirits arrive at the Cycle of Greed. While a half-dozen arrivals settled into their new reality, sparks, like a dragon's roar, flared across the Road. Shocked by the offense, Scrooge instinctively jumped from the flames. His attempt to avoid the burn only resulted in him slipping off the Road. Instantly engulfed in the Greed's flares, Scrooge cried out, "Jacob..." But before he could express his need, he dropped.

Marley grabbed Scrooge's fiery clothes. The collapsed human remained still as the sparks entered Marley rather than Scrooge, and the flow of fire surrounded the two. As Marley absorbed the flames into himself, Scrooge began to cool. With a force nearly human, Marley pulled Scrooge back on to the Road where they both collapsed.

Scrooge moaned as he lay nearly paralyzed from the scorching heat. Recovery from the thrashing of sparks remained elusive for the two. Marley, even though less affected by the flames, rolled around in his attempt to recover. Huffing and puffing,

Scrooge lay flat on his back. Lying motionless, he watched the spirits above him move along the Corridor Of Phantoms.

The flow through the Corridor was constant as spirits moved to and from Transmogrify, each on its own mission. As Scrooge observed those travelling above him, it suddenly occurred to him that none were wrapped in chains. Scrooge pondered this reality, so as he pointed upward, he asked, "Why are none of those spirits encased in the chains of their actions?"

"Chains tether spirits to Transmogrify when out of the area. They are never needed within the Mogs."

"Oh, look at that spirit," Scrooge said pointing to a spirit without legs. Before Marley could warn Scrooge against calling attention to himself, the legless spirit turned its focus to the two lying upon the Road.

"Now you have done it," said Marley.

Within the next instance the spirit positioned itself directly above Scrooge. Scrambling to his feet, the spirit demanded from him, "Who are you, and why do you live?"

Scrooge quickly gave his name but had no answer to the second question. Marley tried to be the go-between for Scrooge, but the legless spirit would have nothing to do with Marley. The specter remained fixated on Scrooge. "Can not a spirit have a place of its own without your kind invading?"

"I wish you no harm. I am here at the request of my friend, Jacob." Scrooge pointed to Marley and then added, "Teint has approved of my entry."

"Teint would never make such an approval," insisted the spirit.

"True, but Ebenezer is here to help save my brother, Noah, who is a Condemned Innocent," Marley explained.

The handicapped spirit quieted as his stare focused on Scrooge. His anger turned to concern as he confessed, "I'm a Condemned Innocent too. Difficult..." His thoughts of human trespass dropped away as he remembered the crisis in which his Condemned Innocent spirit was formed. A tear developed as he thought about the pain of having both of his legs cut off. The revisited terror of being left to die in a pool of his blood softened the spirit's demeanor toward Scrooge. "You are here to help a Condemned Innocent?"

"Yes," replied Marley.

"Then I approve. You can continue." With that the spirit drifted back to the Corridor.

"That was odd," commented Scrooge.

"You are fortunate you weren't forced from Transmogrify. Any spirit can require that of you, so don't look up again," commanded Marley.

"Why did that spirit have body parts missing?"

"Spirits are allowed to use the physical form they think they will need in order to become a Mogrified Spirit."

"But why would any choose to go without legs?" asked Scrooge.

"Ebenezer, sometimes you ask impossible questions."

"Well...?"

"You really think I know the answer to that question? The reason is personal for that spirit, so of course I have no knowledge of their rationale. Your question can not be answered — at least not by me." Marley paused, then instructed, "Now if you have recovered from the sparks, let us continue."

Less than a dozen steps past the Rains Of Darkness, Marley pointed to a pathway that was comprised entirely of spirits' limbs. "Let's cross the Dam."

Scrooge stared at the tangled pathway, observing the interactions between the detached legs and arms of spirits. As the hand of one spirit grasped the leg of another, together with thousands of others doing the same, they formed a pathway of moving but stable limbs.

"My better judgment..."

"No reason to bring that in. Just follow me, Ebenezer."

"But the Road — Teint said..."

"Every chance I get, I bypass the Crater Of Severed Spirits. We all do. So just follow me."

"But I have been hearing so much about the Crater. I don't want to bypass it."

"Trust me, you do."

"Such a disappointment."

"We are not on holiday here. Come on, Ebenezer, before more Coss Acceptance is released along with a flurry of new heads."

Scrooge stood at the entrance of the Dam Of Disconnected Parts, fixated on the thousands of clasping hands. The clutching and release of so many fists created

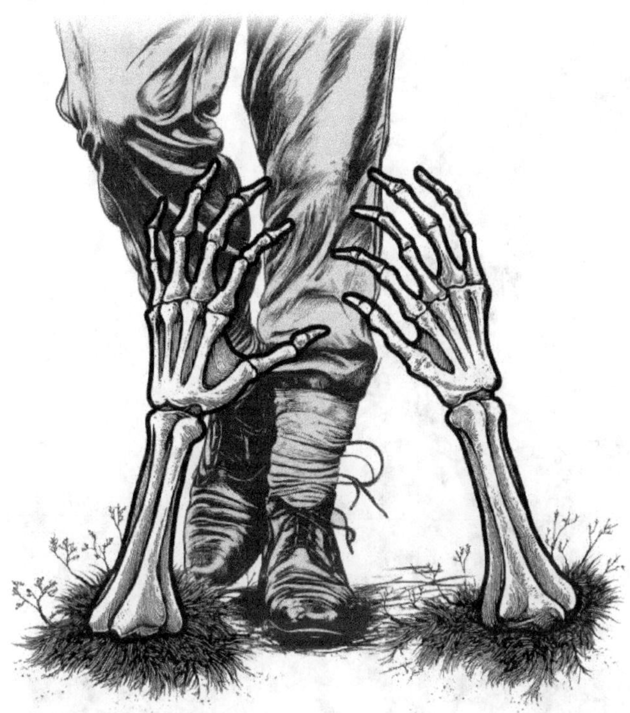

a visual dance of fingers. As appendages constantly shifted, Marley took a step onto the Dam. Tentacles of confused claws grabbed for his skin, yet he continued unharmed. "See, they are powerless," Marley assured Scrooge.

Comforted by his friend's confidence, Scrooge followed Marley onto the Dam. The first step was oddly solid for Scrooge. With the second step, a hand reached up and grabbed for the flesh of his leg. Scrooge felt a tingling sensation next to his bones, but the skeleton passed through him. Each step brought new hands grasping, then passing through Scrooge. He was nearly halfway across the Dam when two hands simultaneously grabbed him from each side of his leg. The two claws met in the middle of Scrooge's leg, joining fingers around his tibia, and trapping him to the location. "Jacob, Jacob, they have me!"

Surprised, Marley grabbed one of the hands. The two skeletons had encircled Scrooge with such a captivating hold the spirit's bones did not need to defend against Marley's prying pressure, for they had formed into one solid bone around Scrooge's ankle. As the two toiled to achieve Scrooge's freedom, another pair of hands reached into his other leg, trapping it likewise to the Dam. Flailing like a tree in the wind, Scrooge screamed in terror. As Marley twisted, tilted and made every effort to disengage the spirit's appendages, Scrooge began to be pulled downward.

Just as his knees disappeared into the mesh of bones, Apurto appeared. Without warning the beast shredded the hand pulling the hardest on Scrooge. Freeing the tension of its descending pull caused the remaining limbs to loosen their grip on him. As Apurto's jaws clamped tight upon each offending hand, the spirit's hold upon Scrooge was reduced to naught. After freeing the human, Apurto grabbed the seat of Scrooge's pants, then pulled him back to the Road.

Once safe, both Scrooge and Marley faced the beast and said, "Thank you."

Apurto just growled, "Yhaah-ae. Yhaah-aee!"

"I don't think he likes you," said Scrooge.

"I doubt that he likes either of us," replied Marley.

As the caretaker raced toward the Crater Of Severed Spirits to deposit the collected limbs, Marley and Scrooge slowly followed. They passed acres of spirit appendages within the Dam Of Disconnected Parts. Most were constantly shifting in an effort to grab onto anything. Being five times wider than long, the

Dam provided hours of gawking for the pair as they continued to walk toward the Crater.

Uncertain of what the Road would bring next, Scrooge purposely decided to trail behind Marley. Sensing his uneasiness, Marley tried to reassure his friend. "I will protect you, Ebenezer." He then added, "Just remember, those on the inside can not harm any that travel the Road."

"On the inside — inside of what? Jacob, I would be buried among fingers and toes right now if it were not for Apurto rescuing me. Why did you put me in that danger?"

Marley just shrugged his shoulders and said, "I will do better by you, Ebenezer." He waited for a reaction, but none was given, so Marley changed the subject. "Soon you will see the apex of the Crater."

"Jacob, with a nickname like the Crater why would there be an apex to such a place?"

"Ebenezer, this is not a conversation of importance."

"Why not?"

"Because it will reveal itself soon. Just be patient," assured Marley.

"So is Acceptance important enough to talk about?"

"Acceptance is what this place is all about — so what is on your mind?" Marley paused, then waited for a response.

"On earth, love has no physical properties, but you say Acceptance is physical. And Acceptance is love, right?

"Acceptance combines both the cleansed human experience and love energy."

"Neither of those things have a bit of material substance to them. So my question stands, how can Acceptance possess any physical properties?" asked Scrooge.

"As you already know, Transmogrify has a gravity that compresses everything. That even applies to the love energy of Acceptance."

"So outside of Transmogrify..."

"It spreads out so its physical properties are no longer detectable. However, all words and concepts have energy contained within them," said Marley.

"Energy can not be seen or touched. It is not physical," insisted Scrooge.

"And yet it does physical work. So, Ebenezer, how can something that is not physical perform physically?"

Scrooge contemplated in silence as they continued toward the mounting white glow on the horizon. Suddenly he asked, "Jacob, is there any place where Acceptance actually becomes a solid substance?"

"Ebenezer, I don't even have the ability to hear, or understand, the Infinite Consciousness's name, how could I ever know that?" He quickly thought about the idea, then added, "It is an interesting notion — imagine sitting on a rock of love — I assume even the hardest of individuals would soften at such contact."

"Do you think it would solve the world's problems?"

"You mean instead of England's bloody code it would just become the bloodstained code?"

Ebenezer laughed at the thought. "It does seem our culture is rooted in violence."

"Forced conformity without empathy is society's principal injury toward the individual."

"So a brick of love might not change a thing?" asked Scrooge.

"Sure it would, for the people in contact with it. But for the mob who moves only along the path controlled by the social order, then unfortunately change only happens when forceful people press for adjustments." Marley paused, then continued. "Change is not always beneficial, Ebenezer. Depending on the individual doing the pressuring, change can make things worse within society."

Scrooge pointed toward the skyline, then exclaimed, "The white glow is turning orange!"

"Damn!" Marley yelled, jumping on top of Scrooge. As the two collapsed upon the Road, a swoosh of motion passed over Marley. While a surge of warm air rushed beyond them, the clattering of spirit bones crashing together could be heard overhead. As the limbs fell into the Dam Of Disconnected Parts, skulls forced their way toward the entrance. All the while, Marley protected Scrooge from the swarm of biting heads.

Once the motion of the wind could no longer be felt, Marley allowed Scrooge to stand. Before he was completely vertical, Scrooge lifted his nose upward, took in a flood of air, then asked, "Is that roses I smell?"

Marley looked at Scrooge like he was a lunatic, then answered, "No, Coss Acceptance always has the faint odor of fresh baking bread."

"That's not food I smell, that's a flower," insisted Scrooge.

"I tell you, you are daft. Coss Acceptance has the best smell I have experienced."

"Yes — roses."

The two looked at each other, snorted in disagreement, then dropped the subject. "I think I can now see more than just the top of the Crater," said Scrooge, pointing to the apex's motion of iridescent fluid and fluttering wings. Marley just quickened his pace.

After a couple of hours, without any warning, the Crater Of Severed Spirits just appeared to Scrooge. Like a fog lifting, the Crater's motion became visible. Marley had been watching the Crater's commotion since the Dam. However, Scrooge, lacking any known references, had to wait until his mind caught up with the visuals before his understanding became possible.

Scrooge felt the heat of the Crater long before he could see the furor of spirits struggling within it. He came to a standstill as the bubble that contained the Crater exaggerated every spirit's climb up the quartz and lodestone walls. The impenetrable texture of the Crater's containment wall appeared similar to water in that it was in constant motion, yet had a slight magnification, and though dynamic in action remained transparent.

As Scrooge's vision focused upon the shimmering membrane containing the Crater, a rising Coss vomited Baabel all over the side of the covering sheath. Scrooge jumped back as the fluid dripped into the Crater.

"Nothing but Coss Acceptance can penetrate the Crater's wall." Marley paused, pointed to a glob of Baabel clinging to the barrier, then added, "You should just be happy you do not have to smell that stuff."

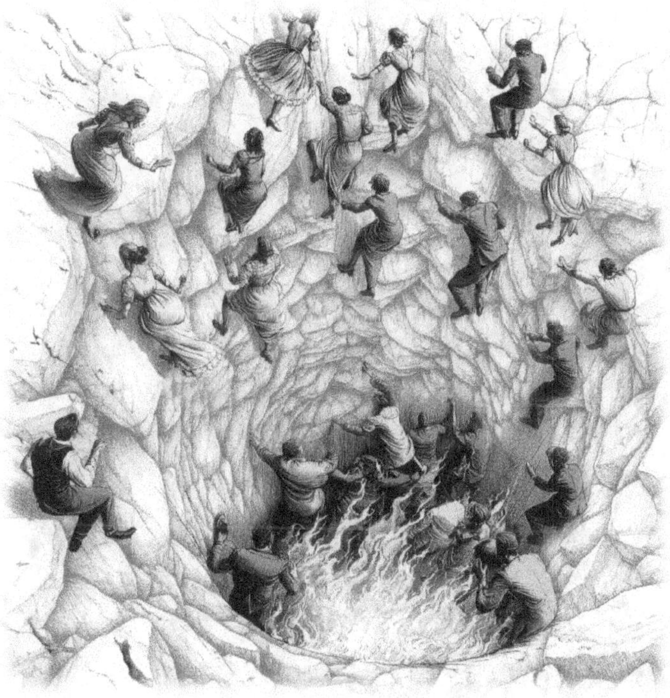

"I thought it smelled like roses," commented Scrooge.

"You are confusing Baabel with Coss Acceptance." Marley pointed to the collection of Coss gathered near the top of the enclosure, then said, "Baabel released from the more mature Coss at the top has a pleasant odor, yet that young Coss just christened us with something closer to dung than perfume."

Confused, Scrooge asked, "Why do they spew anything?"

"Ebenezer, can you see to the bottom of the Crater?"

Scrooge squinted as he peered into the depths of the Crater. The various motions of activity slowed his perception of the chasm. As his vision moved past the thousands of spirits climbing the walls beneath him, he fixated on the deepest point at the center of the Crater. Newly arriving spirits collapsing into the flames dominated his view. "It's an inferno down there."

"Without the smelly Baabel, the entire Crater would be a mass of flames," explained Marley. He then added, "In general, fire does not affect a spirit, but down there," he said pointing to the blaze, "it might hurt."

"Why do you think that?" asked Scrooge.

Marley, lost in thought, only said, "We need to move past this place quickly. Stop staring and keep walking."

Scrooge slowed down. With each step his infatuation with new impressions stalled his legs. Among the flames at the Crater's trench struggled spirits attempting to move past each other, each climbing over the top of others. The Lake Of Flames

circling the bottom of the Crater only lessened its fire and siphoning motion upon the release of Baabel. For in that instant, the swirling blaze would be temporarily smothered. Only briefly, though, for as the spirits continued their climb over the quartz and lodestone covering the Crater, sparks again set fire to the pool of degrading Baabel.

Once a newly arrived spirit had moved beyond the Lake Of Flames and was climbing the side of the Crater, their experience became one of toiling toward the ledge where transformation into a Coss occurred. While the journey up the Crater's sides held both terrors and awakenings for each spirit, the goal was to acknowledge, then transform their idea that they were themselves the Infinite Consciousness into a desire to be in alliance with the Infinite Consciousness's actual plan of Provenance.

Being bombarded with the chaotic movement of spirits within the Crater caused Scrooge to lose focus. The confusion of unfamiliar activities dazed him into a standstill. Marley concentrating elsewhere, failed to realize Scrooge had stopped walking. Upon hearing his friend's scream, he twisted around only to find Scrooge once again crumpled on the Road. Returning to him, he deliberately explained, "Ebenezer — you — have to — keep close — to me!"

Pushing himself to his knees, Scrooge replied, "Then don't move so fast."

"We have a lot of territory to travel, Ebenezer. If you think the Crater is huge, and it is," Marley said, swinging his arm over the vastness of the place, "then the Fields Of Destructive Compulsions is going to shock you." He grinned, then slyly added, "That Mog could be bigger than the whole of earth."

"No, it is not, Jacob," Scrooge said, half smiling.

Marley clasped his fingers around Scrooge's upper arms, and then with a quick jerk, helped him to his feet.

"What is all of this I am seeing?" asked Scrooge, as he performed the same arm swing over the Crater that Marley had just completed.

Marley grasped the truth that Scrooge had been captivated. Watching him watch the chaos of the Crater made him realize he would not be able to move his friend along the Road until he allowed Ebenezer a good old-fashioned gawking at the Crater.

Scrooge observed in silence as Marley watched the emotions on his friend's face change with each new set of actions playing out. Before the friends, struggled a spirit not more than a dozen feet from them. Scrooge became mesmerized by the angst within the spirit trying to gain a position atop the ledge. The spirit toiled as did thousands of others trying to accomplish the task of mounting the ridge where their transformation into a Coss would occur.

Finally, standing with its back to the riveted pair of watchers, the spirit slowly raised their arms perpendicular to their body. Motion stopped as the specter's arms developed into multiple wings, each covered with black feathers. Scrooge's mouth, already being in a gaping state, dropped wide open when each wing's attachment to the body blinked open. From each of the eyes flowed a cascade of light.

The metamorphosis from spirit to Coss reached completion when a massive amount of Baabel flew out from the beak of the bird-like creature now standing in front of them. The transforming individual continued to vomit the greasy Baabel. With each ejection, the Coss rose higher into the Crater's center. Eventually a fluttering of wings began to carry the creature to the amassed collection of Coss gathered at the crown of the enclosed Crater.

"Look, Jacob," Scrooge shouted while pointing at a malformed Coss. The creature spun in circles as it battled to create an upward lift. The beast's rotating contortions caused Scrooge to close his eyes in an effort to prevent a queasiness from overpowering his stomach.

"You should cheer for that Coss."

"Why?"

"They have already survived one Coss release — and by the looks of them not all of their limbs returned to the Crater."

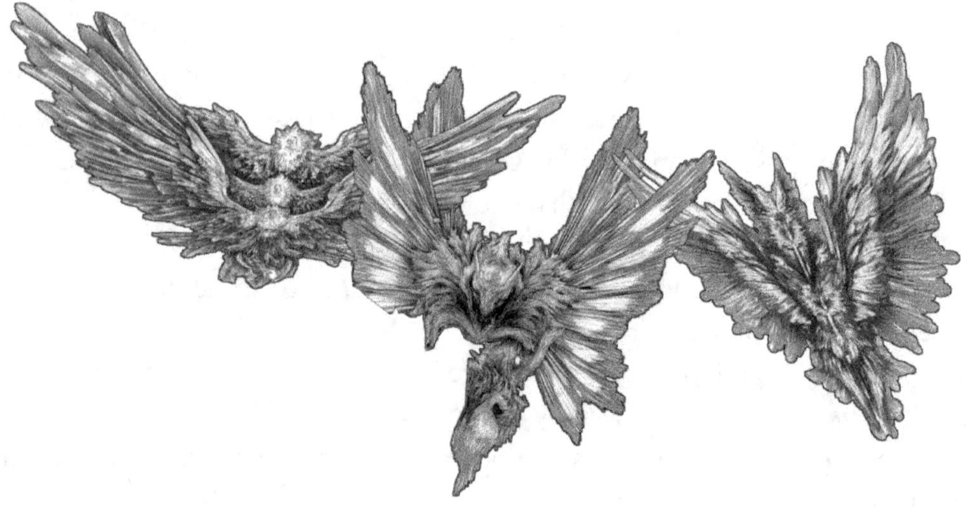

"Do you think that is one of the heads that bit me?"

"No. Skulls are returned to the Lake Of Flames. Their climb to the ledge starts anew, but only after enough of their bones have reconnected. The heads that attacked you are still joining up with body parts."

"That just isn't fair," complained Scrooge.

"Ebenezer, you know the Crater is not about fairness. It was created so a spirit could evolve without any outside help."

"It seems to be an excessive burden that for some who are nearly finished with the Transmogrification process, they end up ripped apart by other escaping Coss."

Marley swung his arm over the vastness of the Crater, then said, "Nothing in there was created with malicious intentions."

Scrooge moaned as he pointed to the still floundering creature, then asked, "Is that Coss going to be all right?"

"It will probably end up being the happiest Coss Acceptance to come from that group," Marley said, pointing to the group of connected Coss at the apex.

They watched as hundreds of black-winged creatures pushed their way into the rising crowd of gathered Coss. The flutter of motion mesmerized the pair, yet Scrooge only focused upon the wounded one.

With deliberate care, the disabled Coss neared the intertwined mass of feathers and eyes. Each push upward by the crippled one was countered by a more powerful group thrust downward. The clumped mesh of spirits moved as with one breath. Twirling beneath the multitudes, the newly transformed Coss persisted.

"That Coss is going to drop from exhaustion," Scrooge worried.

"Just watch," instructed Marley. The two followed the dance of the awkward one trying to fit in, however, only Marley was prepared for what came next. For as Scrooge had predicted, the Coss did without warning start to fall back toward the Lake Of Flames.

"No!" screamed Scrooge. "We have to..." But before the next word cried out, two Coss detached from the collective, then plummeted to the level of their descending companion. As they slowed their fall to a near stop, the two locked feathers with the anguished creature. Together the three climbed back into the accumulated heap of Coss at the Crater's apex.

The flow of new Coss into the horde captivated Scrooge as the churning of blacks, grays and whites transformed the mass into a swirling storm. All the while Baabel rained down upon the struggling spirits climbing the walls. "I assume that two of the arms that trapped you in the Dam came from that crippled Coss," Marley said, trying to hide his grin.

"That thought crossed my mind as well." Scrooge smiled back.

Together they observed Baabel splashing over the climbing spirits. Scrooge wondered why some spirits seemed to be repulsed by the fluid while others purposely rubbed it all over themselves. For those spirits, it appeared to be a tonic in which the ointment energized the climber.

"Why are there such opposite reactions to Baabel?"

"It's the smell and purpose of the fluid."

"Purpose... it looks like it just helps the Coss to stay in flight," said Scrooge.

"It keeps the Crater self-sufficient."

"I thought it was the lodestones and quartz that do that."

"No, those power the Crater, which in turn is electrified when the climbing spirits create the sparks that maintain their confined area." Marley pointed to those clambering up the sides of the enclosure, then said, "Those poor spirits have lost their love connection. Climbing while thinking about their crimes, they then accept responsibility for their actions, not in their head — which is easy — but in their heart. That is their only path toward Acceptance. They are not given the privilege of working a Task Of Outreach, so past actions can be repaired. All transformation happens in that hole," he said, again swinging his arm over the Crater.

"Yes, but that Baabel is still a mystery," Scrooge said, pointing to the downpour before him. "Why do some spirits like Baabel, while others are repulsed by it?"

"I already told you, it is the smell, Ebenezer."

"It smells like roses, why would any ever dislike that?"

"In truth, a newly formed Coss produces Baabel that is closer to the smell of actual vomit than roses, Ebenezer." Scrooge just scratched his head as Marley continued. "Can you see the Coss at the top of the apex?"

Scrooge strained to focus on the swirling assemblage of spirits. "At the very top?"

"Yes, tell me what you see," instructed Marley.

Straining for visual clarification, Scrooge finally stated with confidence, "There is only a white light up there."

"Look closer — do you see any feathers?"

Scrooge studied the iridescent flow. "Feathers? No, no feathers, yet that white light appears to be comprised of every color."

"And still it remains white," said Marley.

Scrooge asked his friend, "What color should it be?"

"All colors, when combined, create a murky grey, not white, Ebenezer."

"I'm not following your point. Should I be seeing grey?"

Slowly Marley explained, "The magic of that iridescence is not in its color, but in its light. However, it is Baabel that keeps the Crater sane."

"You mean the stuff that smells like roses?"

Marley pointed to the churning glob of radiant glow, then explained, "Baabel is a dynamic substance." Scrooge just watched as Marley waved his arm back and forth to emphasize his words, "The black-feathered Coss eject an oily horrible liquid, but as they rise and start to compress into the group, their color, feathers and Baabel change into Coss Acceptance. In the end, those at the top end up regurgitating themselves."

Scrooge's eyes widened as he shook his head in bewilderment. "They retch themselves?" he asked, staring at the constant rain of Baabel.

"Well, it ends up being more like a steady drip of their essence." Marley pointed to the apex and continued. "Those Coss have already transformed into Acceptance. Soon they will dissolve the Crater's ceiling, and then the lot of them will fly to the Abyss Of Final Transmogrify where Coss Acceptance is collected."

"Even the black-feathered ones?"

"When the top is breached, all are converted."

"That is when the heads attack?" asked Scrooge.

"Yes, that is the unfortunate mechanics of having to survive and change without help. Although no harm was purposely designed into the Crater, Ebenezer, this is the only Mog where not all spirits will become Acceptance. Some will be lost."

Marley paused to watch Scrooge's reaction, then pointed deep into the Crater as he shouted, "Look, Ebenezer! Is that not Queen Catherine de' Medici?" Toiling below them was a rather homely woman, dressed in a full-length gown which covered all but her hands and face. With each thrust upwards, the sparks she created lit her dress on fire, only to be doused by the fresh flow of Baabel being released by the black-feathered Coss.

"I would not know her. The French are of little interest for me, Jacob."

"Me either, but — I know that is her," Marley exclaimed, then asked, "Did you ever meet Matthew Pepin, the owner of the stables I worked for as a child?"

"I never had the honor."

"Every August 23rd he dug out this filthy image of her, put it on the wall, and all day long would fling horse manure at her picture."

"I guess the French did hold an interest for Matthew."

"He's French," said Marley.

"Kind of extreme for him to be so against the French queen, then."

"No, that is not it. He was always reliving the St. Bartholomew's Day Massacre where she," he said, pointing to the struggling woman beneath them, "murdered his family during the Protestant Huguenot purge. Only the families that fled to England and America survived. If Matthew has a say, it will take her a long while to free herself from the Crater — if she ever does."

"Speaking of Matthews, is not that Matthew Hopkins, the Witchfinder General?" asked Scrooge, pointing to another laboring within the Crater.

"So it is. England's own woman torturer."

"That was sure a period of time where lies controlled the world's actions," said Scrooge.

"I hope Apurto someday swallows his head."

"Do those kind of statements bring harm to you, Jacob?" asked Scrooge.

"You mean wishing another ill will?"

"Will you be punished for that thought?"

"Punishment — that is such a human reaction to disapproval, Ebenezer." Marley quieted himself, then said, "Have you seen enough? Can we make our way to the Chute now?"

"I am not sure I am ready for that, but let us travel the Road." With that said, the two once again moved toward more danger.

Stave Seven

So Many Dangers

AS THE TWO shuffled toward the Chute, Marley asked, "Would you like to see why you drop to the ground every time I leave your side?"

"You aren't going to do that again, are you?"

"Only if I have to."

Scrooge pondered his friend's words. He knew Marley gave him the correct answer, but still, he was not happy with it. The idea of being pushed to the ground by an invisible force caused him to shy away from Marley's inquiry. "Jacob, I do not think learning more about Transmogrify would be beneficial."

"Nor would it be harmful."

With a penetrating look, Scrooge studied Marley's expression in the hope of discovering the tease within his statement. Marley for his part remained stoic and serious. "Honestly, Ebenezer, if you do not trust me, why are you here?"

"No, Jacob, that is not my caution. You must admit you do not always know my limitations."

"It is hard to remember all your frailties. I only want to show you something fascinating."

"And it will not harm me?"

"Not even a little."

Scrooge stared into Marley's eyes, still looking for a sign of deception, but soon realized that such an expression would be vague and difficult to identify, so he asked, "Will it harm me not to know this?"

Marley studied Scrooge in hopes of understanding his fear. While observing the scowl upon Scrooge's face, he immediately grasped the dread. Annihilation within Transmogrify threatened the existence of Scrooge, and he, Marley, had been careless. Dangers were present, and yet they were not his dangers — but only Scrooge's.

With a more complete awareness of Scrooge's anxiety, Marley resolved to be vigilant in his protection of him. "There is no reason to trust me. I have been a thief, a liar, and a coward. It is only through my death that I was given this grace for improvement. And yet, your truth at this moment is not mine, for yours is one of not belonging here. I have been negligent in my ability to comprehend your risks, Ebenezer." Marley paused as he formed the promise he would make. "If at any moment I sense you are going to be destroyed, I will call out for my Instant Transmogrification, which will consume me, and send you home."

"Teint said that could not be part of my entering Transmogrify."

"No, Teint said that if you were killed, I could not save you by asking for Instant Transmogrification as a punishment. But I can ask for it just before you are harmed, which should save you."

Scrooge did not know if such a maneuver would work, but he felt the emotion in Marley's voice and gave way to his confidence. "Then show me your fascination."

"It is easy to do." Marley pointed to the Crater, then said, "Put your finger on the wall, but for only one second."

Still cautious, Scrooge approached the wall, stared into the storm of activity within the Crater, then quickly

pressed the tip of his right index finger to the membrane. Spontaneously he began to giggle. As laughter overcame him, Marley yanked Scrooge's arm from the wall, "I said one second."

Howling with laughter, Scrooge doubled over as he made the effort to regain his composure. "Only one second of this delight — Jacob, you are still a cantankerous miser."

"Now look what you have done," Marley said pointing to the track left by Scrooge's finger.

Rising up, Scrooge marveled at the multiple horizontal lines now displayed within the membrane. To himself he counted their number, then asked, "Did I leave all seven of those lines?"

"And they will take a while to fill in too. Why you are giggling escapes me, but do you see what you have done? Do you understand the meaning behind the lines you created?"

Scrooge quieted his laughter in an effort to solve the question, but finally he just said, "No."

"Can you tell that the Crater is spinning faster than the eyes can track?"

"Faster than I can see?"

Scrooge puzzled over the concept as Marley explained. "The Crater revolves at such a high speed that suction is created within the Lake Of Flames." Marley paused to allow Scrooge a chance to reply. When no response was given, he continued. "The circular motion intensifies Transmogrify's gravity."

"Why does Transmogrify need a stronger gravity?"

"I already told you why — it is so spirits can have the ability to feel again. In the Abyss, spirits experience an intense physical sensation," replied Marley.

"Jacob, can you feel right now?"

"Feel what?"

"Anything."

Marley pondered this question before he suddenly clapped his hands together, then said, "I did feel that. It is different, though. Instead of feeling the pressure of my palms striking each other, I felt the bones in my hands move past one another. It feels more like brushing against something, than a slap."

"So you need more gravity to feel anything?"

"I do, and I assume so do other spirits."

"I thought gravity was the same everywhere," said Scrooge.

"To the best of my knowledge gravity is just — pressure. But let me ask you this, would there be any gravity if there were no atoms? I mean, stuff falls; if there was no stuff, would there still be gravity?"

"That is a little beyond my schooling, Jacob. However, the question appears to be similar in nature to the chicken and the egg paradox."

"Yes, a paradox indeed."

The two continued in silence until Scrooge asked, "What makes the Crater spin?"

Marley looked toward the Crater's apex, then, as he pointed to the Coss, said, "They do."

Scrooge studied the massive form at the top of the Crater but could not detect any movement other than that of Baabel being vomited. "I see no spinning."

"Yes, I know. When spirits traveled the Road, they could not see the rotation. That all changed once the Corridor Of Phantoms was created. From that view point," Marley pointed to the Corridor with its multitudes of traveling spirits, then explained, "One can not help but see the spinning apex. Coss Acceptance swirls with colors that glisten."

"You mentioned that the Corridor was created. Who 'created' the Corridor?"

"Spirits did, of course." Marley paused, then clarified his answer. "In truth, we just stopped using the Road."

"Why would you do that?"

"The word is that Apurto needed the break from having to constantly pull spirits from the Crater." Marley smiled his sly grin, then said, "I personally think it was more self-serving. Before the Corridor, we all had the experience of a new arrival pushing us from the Chute as they entered the Crater."

"So the Infinite Consciousness just let spirits change Transmogrify?"

"We do not become mindless creatures at death. The Infinite Consciousness allows us the free will to control our situation."

"Why doesn't the Infinite Consciousness just redesign the Chute?"

"I think it is because human challenges are of value. The Infinite Consciousness has no indication of what a person's actions will be, and that quality of life is irreplaceable."

"That would mean the Infinite Consciousness has no idea as to whether I will be destroyed in Transmogrify, or returned to London," said Scrooge.

"It knows all the possibilities, but not the actual event."

"So it only knows the past and present, but not the future?"

"The future is easy to view, but impossible to solidify before it happens," answered Marley.

Scrooge remembered his own change of heart from years earlier; it had allowed him the time needed to scrub the date from his own headstone. He felt the truth of Marley's words, yet wondered out loud, "How can a person view the future without having experienced it?"

As Marley stopped, he instructed his friend to turn around.

With this command, Scrooge halted his forward motion, but only stared at Marley instead of following his order. "Let me show you." Slowly, Scrooge turned to face the direction from which they came. "Now walk forward." Instantly, Scrooge started to walk back along the Road. "No, that is going backward — walk forward while facing backward."

As Scrooge pursued Marley's request, he cried out, "I am going to stumble."

"Exactly, yet you are traveling the favored method of day-to-day life for most people. With difficulty they walk forward, while constantly looking backward."

"And predicting the future?"

"Now turn around, Ebenezer." Scrooge did as instructed while Marley continued. "Stop, look down, and then close your eyes." As Scrooge started to breathe deeply, Marley said, "Good, relax with each breath." Scrooge focused on

his breathing as Marley resumed his guidance. "Now think on a subject for which you have a question about the future."

"I do wonder about my own death."

"That is most people's number one issue. Continue your breathing. With each breath, feel the essence of your desire for knowing the future."

"Essence of desire?"

"Stop thinking, Ebenezer, start feeling." As the two stood silent in the middle of the Road, Marley quietly supervised. "As you feel ready, keep your eyes closed until directed, yet raise your head toward the horizon." Scrooge did as instructed. "Now slowly open your eyes, Ebenezer, and tell me what you see."

"Fanny?" Scrooge then added, "She looks healthy — and beckons me." In the next moment he cried out, "She is fading."

"Are you comforted?"

"I want to follow her."

"Is your future reassuring to you?"

"How can it be? I do not understand it."

"Your vision, Ebenezer, is the most likely view of the future. All events are only potential in nature, for no future vision can ever be experienced the way it is seen. Instead it just becomes the present." Marley hesitated, then finished with, "For the most part, the future is just a maintained habit."

"What happens when something unpredictable occurs?"

Without pausing to reflect upon his knowledge, Marley said, "Nothing unpredictable can happen."

"Jacob, that feels like a lie."

"When it comes to prognostication we live in a paradox — an unsolvable puzzle where all possibilities eventually collapse into the moment." Marley looked into the depths of Scrooge's eyes before continuing. "Even though every circumstance exists before an event, the only constant for all is change. The option that ends up becoming the future adjusts the least. For, most often, it is the path already being followed. Because of this it only has the requirement of solidifying the past and future into the present."

"So in other words, everything is attainable until... it... isn't?"

"And because of that contradiction of possibilities colliding with actualities, the mix up between the two gives every person the ability to create their own destiny."

Scrooge thought about Marley's confusing concept, but rather than question it, instead switched his question. "If travel to the future is not possible, then what happened when I found out about your crime against Noah, and you took me back to London?"

"The Ghost of Christmas Yet to Come nearly killed you."

"No, it did not — it saved me."

Marley's eyes widened with shock as he stammered through his explanation. "I — I was not aware."

"You were not aware of anything. Why was that?"

"You know how you raised your head to view the future on the horizon?"

"Of course I do. We just did that."

"We did the same thing in London, except instead of looking at the horizon, we jumped to it." Marley paused to gather his understanding, then continued. "In a way, we stretched into the future, but where we ended up could never have been the final destiny for that moment. The future always needs to pass into the present before it is crystalized."

"It is confusing," whispered Scrooge to himself.

"The truth often is," Marley whispered back.

As they continued along the Road Of Phantoms, a distant roar could be heard which intensified with each step until it was more deafening than that of the Earth's tallest waterfall. Screaming, Marley told Scrooge, "I have been pondering the method of getting you over the Chute."

"And your solution?" yelled Scrooge.

Marley behaved as if he never heard the question, but instead assured Scrooge, "We have not come this far to be turned away by the Chute."

"So how many potential outcomes are roaming around in your head, Jacob?"

"Too many."

The explosion of sound escalated. Together they approached the Chute with the same respect all spirits gave to the Crater's danger. As Marley and Scrooge neared the deafening gust, both friends watched as a new spirit launched into the

depths of the Crater. A second spirit followed the first into the Lake Of Flames. As the friends neared the edge of the Chute, a third spirit nearly collided with Scrooge as it also joined the others at the bottom.

They watched the three spirits struggle within their new surroundings. Thrashing as though the flames hurt, and drinking in the Baabel as if by drowning they could end their misery, the three eventually slipped below the surface of flames. As they disappeared, more established spirits replaced them. All were competing for freedom out of the fire. None would achieve it before the next release of Coss Acceptance.

Scrooge just shook his head while asking, "How are we going to pass through this blast?" Without thinking, Scrooge put his hand into the wind. His thrust into the roar spun him around, then threw him, now very confused, to the Road.

"Ebenezer!" After Marley assured himself that Scrooge suffered no harm, a scolding ensued. "Ebenezer, how can I keep you safe if you are jumping into danger?"

"I wasn't thinking."

Marley shook his head with disappointment as he continued. "Put your head back on your shoulders."

"It's not my head that hurts, but my wrist," he said shaking it.

"I need to get you over this chasm, so stop making it difficult."

"You have done an enormous amount of harm, Jacob, and you are calling me difficult?"

Marley silenced his frustration, then asked, "How would you get past the Chute, Ebenezer?"

"With your plan?"

"I don't think it will work, but I can't think of anything better. So let's try it."

"Try what?"

"You are going to jump across the Chute."

"No, I am not!"

"It is only four feet, and I will help."

"Can you jump the last three feet for me?"

"Your stride is longer than that, Ebenezer." Marley hesitated, then instructed, "Let me see you jump as far as you can."

"Across that force?" he said, pointing to the Chute.

"No, no, no! Step away from the Chute, then show me what you can do. Do not jump into the Chute."

"As a fact — I was not going to jump into the Chute — no matter what you told me to do."

"Well, alright, we have that figured out at least. So go ahead and show me how far you can jump."

Without warning, Scrooge thrust himself forward. "Hmm, two feet." Marley shook his head as he rhetorically asked, "What are we going to do with that?"

"Jacob, why are you just thinking about this now?"

"Ebenezer, I have been worrying about this since..." Marley's voice faded away as he turned to thought. Silence overcame them until Marley abruptly stuck his arms straight in the air, then shouted, "I've got it! Hand me your greatcoat, Ebenezer."

As Scrooge removed his coat, an instant relief from the heat overtook him, "Oh my, I should have thrown this thing away days ago."

"Days ago?" Marley repeated, then said, "We just entered Transmogrify less than an hour ago."

"You are being a deceiver again, Jacob."

Startled by the accusation, Jacob explained, "Oh, time — I keep failing with the thought that you still experience a second-by-second existence. In here the clock is replaced with just — motion. Transmogrify is more of an experience-to-experience continuance than the constant ticking of a clock."

"All of this leaves me vulnerable, Jacob, and you keep forgetting about my limitations."

"I have pledged my survival for yours. If it comes to that, Ebenezer, I will, with solace, fade to nothing so as to save you."

As Scrooge handed Marley his greatcoat, he confirmed the oath. "I accept your assurance, and hope it never is required."

Marley grabbed for Scrooge's coat, but it passed through his hand, then fell to the Road. "I think you are going to have to tie one of the arms around my wrist, so it can grip itself."

Scrooge did as he was instructed and, although the coat started to pass through Marley, when the knot met the bone, enough substance was shared between them to halt gravity.

"Do not worry, Ebenezer." With that, Marley flew straight upward as Scrooge collapsed downward. Within the next instant, Marley stood on the other side of the Chute. As Scrooge hoisted himself to his feet, Marley instructed, "I am going to toss you the coat, yet keep it bound to my wrist. Grab it, then I will pull you across."

Before Scrooge could reject the idea, Marley threw the coat over the ravine, but it just flew back at him. Try as Marley did, the greatcoat was never by itself going to hurdle the Chute. "What are we going to do?" yelled Scrooge.

Without explaining himself, Marley reached into his chest, then yanked out two of his ribs. As he hunched forward to lessen the pressure of having lost part of his structure, Marley attached the bones to the bottom of the greatcoat. Throwing the coat across the violent wind did not end the rebound upon Marley. Instead, it hit with a force that caused a yelp from the phantom. Not deterred by the pain of the slap back, Marley kept trying until finally Scrooge caught the covering.

The explosion of wind upon the coat propelled Marley to the edge of the Chute. Grinding his heels into the Road, he struggled to stay upright. As his location kept shifting, Scrooge yanked the coat. The force heaved Marley upward. Leaving the security of the Road, Marley yelled, "Ebenezer, do not let go," then added, "stop pulling me."

Scrooge eased the pressure. Marley resisted the Chute's force, yet had little strength to thrust himself back to the Road. As he endured the windstorm, Scrooge yelled, "I'm going to whip you back to the ground."

Before Marley could respond, Scrooge raised his arm, then pulled with his entire force downward. With a thump, Marley hit the Road. As he regained his footing, he called out, "It is me that has to pull you across, Ebenezer, not the other way around."

The two steadied themselves against the blowing violence, and collected the last of their energy. Without warning, Marley yanked Scrooge halfway into the Chute. While in midair Scrooge pulled back on Marley's effort. As he fell back to his side of the Road, the reversed momentum propelled Marley, along with Scrooge's coat, into the Crater. Hearing his friend scream all the way into the Lake Of Flames, Scrooge lost his companion's gravity. Tumbling to the Road, he lay helpless.

The windblast flung Scrooge toward the opening. Curled into a ball, he slammed against the Crater's wall. The force of the circulating barrier behind him propelled his body toward the mouth of the gorge. Surrounded by the gust, Scrooge lifted off the ground and was propelled toward the Chute. Instinctively he grabbed for anything solid. As fingers slid across the Road's surface he struggled to secure himself. The threat of flying into the violent hole heightened Scrooge's terror. With a thrust he wedged his fingers into the corner where the wall and Road met the Crater's entrance.

Consumed by an intense focus, Scrooge gained control over his fingers, then his hand, and then two hands. Progress back to the Road slowed, as the windstorm kept Scrooge swinging in a horizontal position across the Chute. The constant gust, though all powerful against a spirit, could not by itself dislodge the weight of Scrooge. Even at that, he struggled to maintain his grip. More than the wind, he

worried over his own sweat. As he felt the beads of lubricant loosening his grasp, his breathing began to labor. Every muscle in his body worked to sustain the situation. Yet the slippage was not controllable. First the second hand gave way, and then — Apurto grabbed his one clinging wrist.

Seeing only the teeth surrounding his hand, Scrooge howled. Apurto, undisturbed by the human's panic, bit down harder, breaking the flesh. As blood trickled down the beast's chin, a newly arriving spirit slammed through Scrooge. The thrust nearly ripped Scrooge free from the creature's grip. As the spray of blood continued Apurto's bite intensified. And then, as a second spirit shot through the Chute, Apurto yanked Scrooge back to the security of the Road.

Grabbing his wrist in hopes of controlling the flow of blood, Scrooge moaned as Apurto jumped into the Crater. It could have been a second, or a year, but within time Apurto could be heard dragging Marley out of the Crater. With each thrust upward, out of the Lake Of Flames' suction, Marley lost the extra weight created within the spinning enclosure. Apurto snarled at the two of them as he deposited Marley back onto the Road.

Standing on the opposite side of the Chute from Scrooge, an appalling smell began to permeate from Marley. As Scrooge regained his balance, Marley asked Apurto to help Scrooge across the crevice. Apurto seemed to grin, then just ran away. Marley yelled after him, "You miserable cur! Come back and help!"

"You stink like a — well, you tell me Jacob — what is that smell?"

"It's Baabel, and unimportant."

"You must have lost your sense of smell at death."

Screaming, Marley cried out as loudly as his voice would penetrate, "How are we going to get you across, Ebenezer?" Stomping his feet through every word, he added, "There — is — no — reason — why — that four-legged beast — could not assist — us!"

"There is always a reason," floated a voice several feet above them.

Looking upward, the two watched as a familiar spirit fluttered between the Corridor and the Road. Without legs the spirit had a grace of movement more agile than did either Marley or Scrooge. "What is all the trouble down here?" asked the ghost.

"Ebenezer is too old to jump the Chute."

"I would rather be 'old' than dead, Jacob," rebutted Scrooge.

"Can you not lift him over it?" asked the spirit.

"That idea does not even make sense," said Marley.

The floating spirit smiled, then offered help. "I think I can get him over the Chute."

"Really, you without legs can lift him?"

"Did I say that?"

Marley paused, then apologetically said, "Any help will be welcomed."

"I will need some Corridor mates to create the barrier." With that, the spirit shot back into the flow of entities above the Road.

Only an instant passed before the handicapped spirit returned with a dozen or more associates. All hovered a safe distance from the Chute as Scrooge watched the parade above him occupy his visual space. Without consensus, the legless spirit began giving directions. "I want all the tall spirits at the top of the bridge. The shorter ones will create the Road's anchors."

"You are going to build a bridge of spirits that rises above the Chute?" asked Marley.

"No, that would be too unstable. It would only take one weak spirit to topple such a construction."

"So what do you mean by 'bridge'?" asked Scrooge.

"Our bridge is going to use the Chute's own force to strengthen itself."

"Sounds like magic."

"It is better to watch than for me to explain," answered the spirit as it turned to direct the others. "Grab your companion's heart chain to maintain your grip." As a collection of ghosts lined either side of the Chute, the handicapped one continued. "Catherine, you are too tall to be the Road's anchor. Cora, you will anchor Catherine."

Catherine, with her extra tall stature, lay on her side facing the Chute's force. With only the top half of her body feeling the gust, a second spirit moved next to her. Also lying on its side, the spirit faced Catherine. She grabbed its heart chain, which created a linked structure. Offset by only a foot, the chest of the spirit was forced hard next to Catherine's head.

From both sides of the Chute, spirits began to build the connecting structure. Each new spirit crawled up the back of the previously linked ghost. Even facing the

Chute's blast at a forty-five-degree angle could not halt the blustering force. As the two sides of the bridge moved closer together, the most exposed spirits fluttered in the wind. Their only survival from the Chute was the grip seized by another of their heart chain. That all changed once the last spirit connected the two sides together. Instantly the Chute's force pushed hard on the structure, strengthening its arch.

Hovering next to Scrooge, the handicapped spirit instructed, "Quick now, move behind the platform."

Scrooge walked up to the edge of the Chute, looked down upon the gaping hole, sighed with dread, then very calmly said, "I still can not jump that far."

Shocked, the leader spirit smiled, then reassessed their needs. After no more than a pause, it briefed the remaining spirits, "Fergus, Bess, Paul, we still need your help."

"I can help too," said Marley.

"Jacob, you can make the platform that connects both sides of the Chute. Just float into place behind the bridge. Lie on your side, then grip both sides of the Chute. We will pin you in place."

"Ebenezer is flesh. He is going to pass right through me."

"That is why he does not belong here," grumbled the legless spirit.

"We have already been through that. We need a more substantial platform than just — me," complained Marley.

"I know that. Fergus and Bess will hold you down. Paul can be your reinforced double."

With the plan conveyed, the spirits moved into place. Although Marley was tall enough to span the Chute, Paul was not. As he trembled in an effort to stay attached, the handicapped spirit moved in to fill the gap. With all the ghosts now occupied within the structure, Scrooge dropped to his knees. As he began to crawl upon the formation, the soft bumpiness of the spirits caused Scrooge to slip.

"Do not fall," ordered the legless spirit.

With each motion forward, Scrooge sank into the squishy spirits holding him up. Only constant movement held him above the ghosts. As he completed the crossing, the entire structure gave way to the Chute's explosive force.

While ghosts flung off in every direction, the legless spirit was cast into the Crater. The wailing sound of dread trailed the visual of the disappearing helper.

Without thinking, Marley grabbed the last of his Fire Twirlers, then launched both of them at the handicapped spirit. As one missed the ghost the other Fire Twirler set the spirit aflame. Scrooge screamed in horror. Marley, through thought, pulled hard on the Fire Twirlers. The spirit was dragged back to the Road, basically unharmed.

The entire group, as they began to go their separate ways, thanked each other, but none was as grateful as was Marley. "Your courage shames me. Can I have the honor of knowing your name?"

"No, you will not be able to forget it," answered the handicapped ghost.

"I hardly remember a thing anyway. So why does forgetting your name matter?" asked Marley.

"My name holds the power of freedom." With that said, all but Marley and Scrooge returned to the Corridor.

"I like freedom," Marley yelled after the spirit.

"Everybody likes freedom, Jacob," said Scrooge. Then he asked, "Why do you suppose that spirit helped us?"

"My guess is because it is his Task Of Outreach to help within Transmogrify." Marley took in a deep breath, then said, "Some spirits never return to Earth, they just work the Mogs and the Corridor until they achieve Acceptance."

"Do you think he will help us over the Chute when we return?"

"Who said we are going to return by way of the Crater?"

"So we will not return by this path?"

Marley laughed out loud with a maniacal cackle before saying, "We will let the Fire Twirlers help us."

"Why did we not use them this time?"

"My heart chain did not hold enough of them for that." Marley smiled, then without pause, cried out, "You are dripping blood, Ebenezer!"

"This...," Scrooge said, displaying his wrist to Marley. "Apurto had to bite me to save me."

"Only in Transmogrify..." sneered Marley.

Scrooge shook his head back and forth as he explained, "Apurto pulled me from the Chute just as I was ready to lose my grip." Looking at his blood-soaked hand, he continued, "It does not actually hurt."

"Yet it could become your death. Quickly we need to reach the location of the next Coss Drenching." With that, Marley began to accelerate his gait into a slow run.

As Scrooge struggled to keep up, he cried out, "Jacob, why is this needed? My wrist does not bother me."

"There is a dissolving solution in your body — run if you can."

As the old man and the spirit scrambled toward the Drenching, the Crater's activity continued to churn like a machine. Both the black and iridescent Baabel constantly rained down upon the restless lot of spirits beneath the Coss. After racing for minutes, Scrooge stopped, doubled over, then yelled, "Jacob, I need to find my breath."

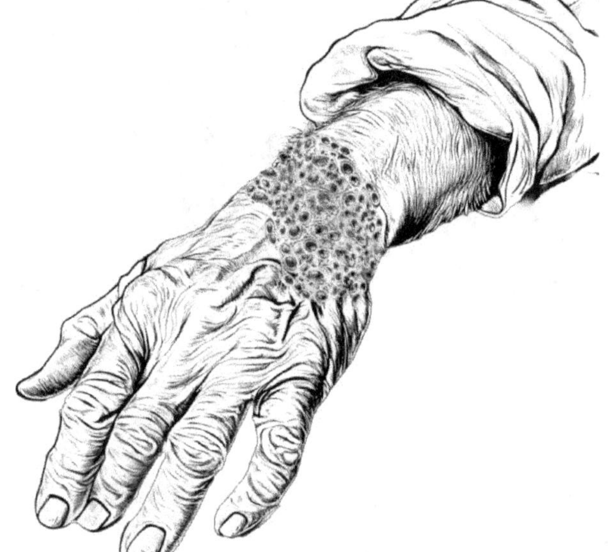

As Jacob interrupted his pace, words of concern erupted, "No, Ebenezer! You have to push away normal pains and move."

"It is my lungs, not my arm that hurts."

"Look at your wrist!"

When Scrooge did as instructed, his mouth widened with shock. At his side revealed an unrecognizable appendage. No longer bleeding, the wound was now covered in a black froth. "Ah — what is this foulness?"

"There is only one way to save you — run."

Terrified, Scrooge abandoned the comfort of his lung's agony in the hope his legs could bring him to the nurturing required for his wrist. He did not understand his own situation, so he ran after Marley with a thrust of energy he was unaware he possessed. The bubbling foam of blackness overtook his arm. The encroachment upon his flesh caused Scrooge to collapse to the ground as the pain engulfed him. Grabbing his entire right side, he rolled upon the Road with the belief pressure could relieve the agony. It did not.

"Do not stop! We are almost at the location of the Drenching," Marley howled as he pulled on his fallen friend. "Spirits are assembling. Ebenezer, if we miss the next Coss release you will die! Crawl if you must," he said, pointing to the gathered ghosts.

The human in Scrooge displayed frailties, and thrusts of movement carried him only inches. Trembling, Scrooge curled into a ball. As he cradled his blackened arm, he felt a nudging at the back of his neck. Twisting to understand the pressure being applied, he screamed at the gaping mouth dripping — dripping black froth. With a thump, Apurto launched Scrooge toward the group of accumulated spirits. "Jacob, Jacob, where have you gone?"

Scrooge timed each lunge forward so as to dodge Apurto's aggressions. Once the two entered the area of Drenching, Apurto moved to face Scrooge, bared his teeth, then transformed back into Marley. The shapeshifter slumped to the Road, exhausted. As the pair recovered, the combined sounds of cracking and swooshing shook the ground.

The rumble of the Coss release only lessened after the iridescent flow of Acceptance broke through the Crater's apex. As the Coss gained liberation a harmony of musical voices within the group saturated the Acceptance. Bursting from the Crater, the liquid moved in mass toward the spirits on the Road. The ballet of motion combined harmonizing tones with colorful patterns, and then the dreamlike swirls dripped globs of the radiant love into the crowd. The soaking covered all.

Excitement overtook Marley. "Ebenezer, spread this over your wrist." With that he handed Scrooge a thick glob of the glowing Acceptance. Drained of strength, Scrooge allowed the substance to escape from between his fingers. Meticulously, Marley collected the remaining Acceptance into the folds of his hand. As the fluffy material began to evaporate, Marley slapped it as hard as he could against Scrooge's injury.

"Bloody!" flinched Scrooge. Within the tick of time, the lustrous mass consumed the wound. "Ahhh...!" he exclaimed as the exuberance within the Acceptance gripped his heart. The palpitation created a blissful twitching, which caused Scrooge to close his eyes in delight. Muscles quivered as the Acceptance repaired, then strengthened his wrist. Jubilant tones rang out of every pore of Scrooge's skin. Enclosed within the music of Acceptance, a piercing triad lifted Scrooge back onto his feet.

As ghost and human watched the Coss Acceptance nearly fall into the Pool Of Broken Spirits, Scrooge gasped. Marley smiled as he said, "They do that every time." Feeling Scrooge's stare, Marley explained, "The Pool is the lowest spot out of the Crater. It is the place where the Coss level off as a group, so they can continue to the Abyss."

Observant to the flow of Coss Acceptance moving over the Pool, Scrooge's eyes widened when they dripped their essence directly into the lake of sleeping suicide spirits. The release of fluid caused the traveling mass to ascend in flight. The upward lift stabilized their glide.

While the Coss Acceptance rolled like storm clouds toward their destiny, the Pool Of Broken Spirits erupted with activity, as the release of Acceptance flooded the Pool with a luminescence. Though still mostly out of visual range, the movement at the Pool mesmerized Scrooge. Various colors and musical tones rang throughout as spirits lifted off the Pool, then transformed into their many elements of spirit.

The metamorphosis of one spirit into many emerged like fireworks, bursting open with exhilaration. Spirits flung off in every direction of Transmogrify. Most remained in the form of spirit, but others transformed into Acceptance, then followed the Coss to the bottom of the Abyss.

"What is going on over there?" Scrooge asked, pointing to the commotion.

"They are going through Entanglement."

"Is that not the process entered at death?"

"Yes, but those in the Pool do not enter Entanglement until they awaken."

"You mean by killing themselves they only added an extra step to their Transmogrification?"

"We are our own chief enemy most of the time."

Scrooge scratched his head, then asked, "Why is it called Entanglement when a separation is actually happening?"

Marley paused so as to gain the words needed for explanation. "No element of an individual's spirit can be parted from the other principles within the spirit. Though my spirit of greed is now Mogrified, this spirit which harmed Noah is still connected to that spirit, even though it now dwells with the Infinite Consciousness. We are still one."

Scrooge continued to ponder. "Why is this stuff starting to make sense to me?"

Marley grinned, then changed the subject. "With the uproar over your wound, I almost forgot to give you these." Marley handed him four lodestones. "Put them in your pants pockets."

Scrooge rolled the stones around in his palm, then asked, "Why are they weightless, yet still contain a shape?"

"Things are different here. Everything in Transmogrify is of spirit. Just put them in your pockets."

Scrooge did as instructed. The stones created a bulge that pushed outside of the cloth, yet remained within the pocket. As the pair continued toward the Abyss, a welcomed silence developed.

While Marley continued to watch the Pool, Scrooge turned his gaze back to the Crater. The bones separated through the release of Coss Acceptance rained down upon those climbing the wall. As Scrooge watched fragmented spirits regroup, new Coss began to collect at the apex. Even though the last release of Acceptance was still within sight, Scrooge realized the Crater had gained new spirits. Their struggle was constant as each pushed past those near them in order to gain a higher location within the Crater.

Moving beyond the horizon, the Coss Acceptance entered the Abyss Of Final Transmogrify. As the flow of radiance plummeted toward the Infinite Consciousness, storms of blue lightning erupted from the hole. Bolts flashed upward out of the Abyss, while a rumbling of harmonious tones echoed throughout Transmogrify.

Once the flashes quieted, Marley and Scrooge continued in silence. Above them flowed the Corridor of spirits, busying themselves with Tasks designed to improve not only their own existence, but that of life itself.

With the ebbing of activity at the Abyss, Marley turned his focus back to Scrooge who was staring into the Crater. "It is all about false purity down there," said Marley.

"I thought it was for those who purposely disconnected from the Infinite Consciousness."

"I doubt they 'purposely' planned their separation, but tell me, Ebenezer, what do you think motivated their actions?"

Scrooge contemplated the question before meekly responding, "Power?" He pondered it for a moment longer, then added, "Fear?"

"Love's horribles," Marley said, quickening his pace.

"Wait, what do you mean by that?"

"You said it, Ebenezer."

"No, I said power and fear — you called them 'love's horribles'. Why?"

"Those two provide the quickest method of separation from the Infinite Consciousness." Marley paused so as to add emphasis to the next point. "That is a HORRIBLE thing."

"Yes, it is easy to understand how fear and the quest for power can cause destruction."

"Self-destruction," clarified Marley. "Those at the Pool Of Broken Spirits act in an obvious manner when carrying-out their self-destruction. Whereas those in the Crater remain oblivious to their self-destruction."

"They never discover that knowledge?"

"Only at the creation of their Coss."

"Before then?"

"They struggle in arrogance."

As they neared the end of the Crater Of Severed Spirits, Scrooge took in the commotion from the Lake Of Flames to the apex for the last time, then wondered out loud, "What I have difficulty understanding is, why they do not help each other — like the group from the Corridor helped me?"

"Tell me what you see down there, Ebenezer."

"Overcrowding, sparks everywhere, a raging fire at the bottom, vomit constantly raining down, rivalry — it embodies absolute strife."

"My goodness, Ebenezer, tell me what you actually think." Smiling, Marley added, "The Crater absorbs what each spirit built during life. None of them created compassion for others. So how can they help each other now?"

"Out of the need for self-survival..."

"Do you see any near the Lake Of Flames that even acknowledges those near them?"

"No. They act as though they are blind."

"Maybe that is why they gain so many eyes when they transform into Coss," Marley winked at Scrooge, then added, "so they can see again."

"Is vision all they lack?"

"No, the darkness is the least of their flaws. Though they could help those they come in contact with, they will not, for each dwells within total isolation from the others."

"Isolation — it — it is overflowing with spirits in there."

"You are talking quantity. I am referring to their character, which lacks empathy."

"Even tortoises turn each other over when they are flipped on to their back," said Scrooge.

"If they could, I'm sure each within the Crater would prefer to be a turtle right now."

As the two passed the Crater and turned their attention to the Pool Of Broken Spirits, floating ghosts could be seen bobbing upon the surface. Out of the Pool arose metal posts. The only thing Scrooge could compare the visual to was that of a flooded forest after a dozen years of being under water. However, a flooded forest is a dead forest, yet this indestructible forest sparked life across their tips. Not always, but often embers from the flashing arcs awoke the slumbering spirits within the Pool.

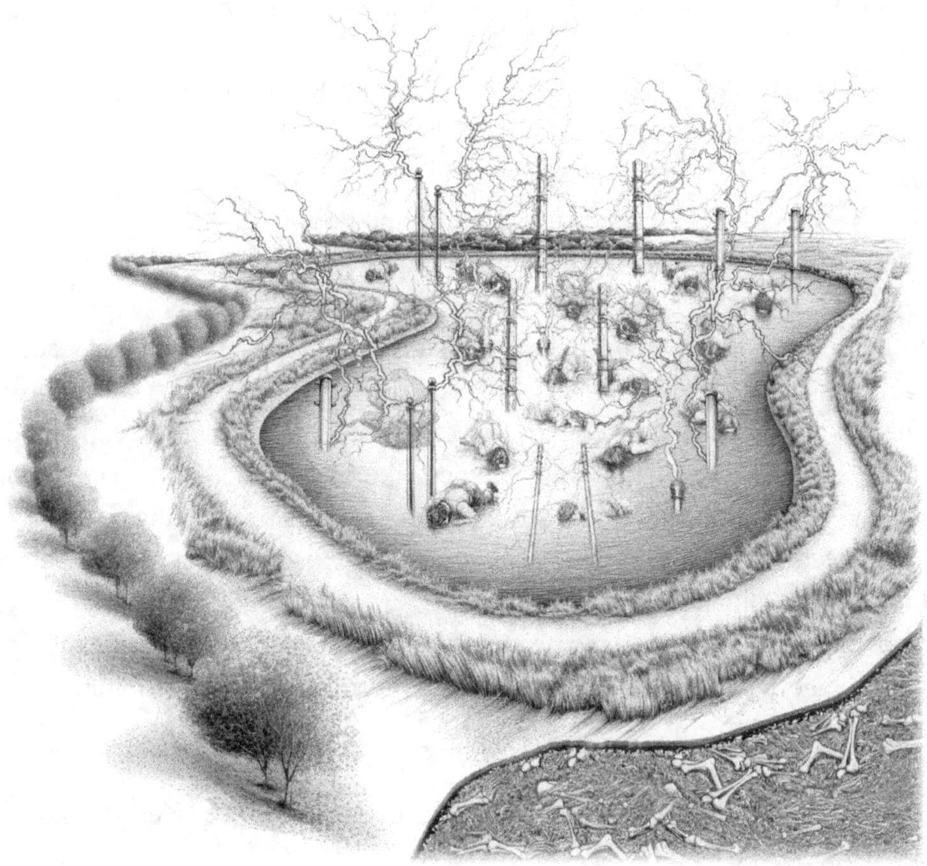

Scrooge focused upon one ghost as it lifted off the Pool. An explosive light released the individual into its various spirits. Without haste, each freed entity flew off toward the Mog where the work of creating their Task Of Outreach would begin. As the two continued along the Road, more spirits were awakened, divided into their essence, then moved beyond the Pool. The visual dance of this routine created waves within the Pool which resulted in new spirits being pulled into alertness.

One spirit caught Marley's attention, for it separated into four different spirits, one for every Mog. As one of the four travelled overhead toward the Crater, Marley smirked. "Undoubtedly that spirit would have preferred to sleep. It is going from the bed into a thicket of thorns."

Before Scrooge could respond, a massive group of arcs flared across the entire area of metal rods, to which dozens of self-destructed spirits awakened. "What is causing the sparks?"

"Tears."

Scrooge hesitated before saying, "Explaining that would be of benefit, Jacob."

"Has not your friend, Mister Faraday, brought this subject up in one of his Christmas lectures?"

"Well, Michael is all about electricity and sparks, but how is he to know about this Pool?"

"Everything within Transmogrify functions within a technical method, even the workings of the Pool."

"But tears...?"

"Not just any tears, but sorrowful tears fill the Pool."

"And the method these tears have for creating the sparks is...?"

"Salt."

"If that is all it takes, then Michael probably would have known that," admitted Scrooge.

The two walked, and walked, and walked as the Pool constantly converted one spirit into several spirits. After what seemed like days, Scrooge began to wonder why his bodily functions never needed attention. He was never hungry, never tired, or even in need of a bath. It was like time did not exist, and yet it still seemed to travel toward the future.

As they continued, Scrooge began to contemplate the Crater. Such a place could hardly be believed, yet suddenly, a new truth leapt into his mind, and he blurted, "You lied to Teint."

"Did I?"

"You said you would only use a Fire Twirler to save me. Yet you saved the freedom helper at the Chute."

"Yes, I did. However, the problem is not that I crossed Teint, but that it was my last few Fire Twirlers."

Scrooge paused a moment before saying, "I probably would have done the same. Out of reflex, if for no other reason."

"Would you? It was a reflex with me too. Except I also had the knowledge that the legless one would not be able to rise to even the Lake's surface without Apurto.

He would have been pinned beneath its Baabel of flames, and multiples of feet pressing him down. Damage to the mind would have occurred to that spirit before Apurto could have returned them to the Road." Then, pointing to a location within the Pool, Marley said, "Look, Ebenezer. There is Flora."

"Shall we wake her?"

"No! That is not for us, besides, she has a peculiar look. Let's just leave her sleeping. My Task is Noah's rescue."

"A peculiar look — care to elaborate?"

"Maybe later," and with that Marley quieted.

The journey around the reservoir of sleepers was both long, and in the end, boring. Once they were half way around the Pool, the Fields Of Destructive Compulsions began to come into focus. On the right bobbed the slumbering spirits within the Pool, while to the left Fire Twirlers could be seen whirling in every direction. Lining the Road, on the Fields side, stood a single row of trees with two-inch spikes running up and down the trunk. This forest of singular trees hugged the Road as far as the eye could see.

Though each trunk stood straight, without even the hint of a bend, the same could not be said for the branches. At around five feet from the ground, every one of them grew parallel to the Road. Limbs from neighboring trees intertwined, creating a mesh of dense growth. Starting at Scrooge's eye level, the tangled fence of foliage extended taller than a Neolithic monument. From beneath the boundary of limbs, both Marley and Scrooge watched as thousands of Fire Twirlers danced and spun within the Fields Of Destructive Compulsions.

"We need to avoid the spikes."

"Jacob, we need to avoid the flames."

"No, I want them, but those barbs...," Marley said, pointing to a tree trunk. "They are dangerous."

"Of course they are; everything here is dangerous." Scrooge smiled, then added, "At least for me." Each grinned at the other as they turned their attention to the massive number of twisting flames spinning across the landscape within the Fields.

As the Fire Twirlers spun around, slamming into their own kind, the tallest among them gained energy from each impact, while the smaller decreased in power and size. The show of dominance appeared brutal.

Scrooge gasped when the collision of three Fire Twirlers resulted in the total annihilation of the smallest one. "Did they just kill a spirit?"

"I thought you figured this out when Teint and I were discussing my capturing of Fire Twirlers. Fire Twirlers are not the spirits. They are the energy spirits create to help them release their toxic habits."

"Are the spirits that created those ferocious flames like yourself?"

"I assume so. None within the other Mogs ever gazed upon a spirit from the Fields. We become aware of them as individuals when they arrive at the Abyss. Before then, their only evidence of existence is those Fire Twirlers," Marley said pointing to the mass of flames engulfing the Fields.

"How can a spirit create such flares?"

"It is rumored they are so trapped within their compulsion at death that they become unable to release their entire physical self." Marley looked toward the spinning Fields, then pointed to one as he said, "Looks like that one had trouble stopping his desire for starting fires." Together they watched as the Fire Twirler flared high, then decreased, only to flame up higher than before, then twinkle down to near nothing.

"I think you just stated an impossibility, Jacob. How is it that a burning spiral can change the spirit that created it?"

"Well, there is undeniably a whole lot of physical energy in those things. Maybe it is their way of developing a Task Of Outreach. It's all rumor, Ebenezer. Those spirits are a private lot, even when they come to the Abyss."

"I still think you are talking about an impossibility."

Marley looked around, waved his arm across his view, then said, "The evidence of their existence is before your eyes. How they exist for you is contained within your belief structure."

Marley and Scrooge's progress along the Road remained steady, even though the Fields stretched on for nearly — ever. Individually the two contemplated the torrent of flames weaving throughout the terrain. The constant movement of blistering heat created directional gusts of mayhem. Most Fire Twirlers stood above the tree's barrier of limbs. However, there were those that had been bashed into frailty, and with each rotation continued to shrink.

The frenzy mesmerized Scrooge. As the exchange of force between colliding Fire Twirlers fluctuated, he turned his gaze to the dominant flame before him. Spinning with exceptional speed, the blazing spiral slammed into a tree. Before Marley could give warning, the Fire Twirler's impact blew out every spike the tree contained.

Marley jumped on top of Scrooge, forcing him to the ground. While thorns shot through the ghost, the human beneath him remained unscathed, or so Marley hoped. When the two separated from each other, the reality sank Marley. Beneath him lay his friend — motionless. Shaking Scrooge, Marley frantically asked, "Where are you hurt?" Scrooge did not move. "Ebenezer! I do not see a wound, where are you hurt?" Still Scrooge remained quiet.

Lifting Scrooge to his lap, Marley hugged his friend while crying, "All has failed, I have killed you." And yet, Scrooge showed no physical injuries.

Without Marley's detection, Apurto moved in behind the two. Before discovery could be made, Apurto growled into Marley's ear which created a stiffening tension within the ghost. The caretaker of Transmogrify continued snarling, yet Marley would not back away from Scrooge. Pushing Apurto away, Marley rubbed Scrooge into alertness.

As Marley helped Scrooge back to his feet, he paused before again asking, "Where are you hurt?"

"Hurt? I think you were my hurt, Jacob. You did push me, did you not?"

"I saved you from the tree's thorns."

"Who would have thought a ghost could knock a person into death?"

"So that is what you think I did. Were you dead?"

"I do not remember," replied Scrooge.

"Well, death is worth remembering, so you probably were not dead."

The two continued upon the Road, all the while watching millions of Fire Twirlers race throughout the Fields. The constant motion of energies colliding with trees created explosions of spikes. Now that Scrooge was aware of their danger, he became proficient at avoiding them.

The thrust of the projectiles toward the Road was minimal as their purpose was to supply the Fire Twirlers with a combustible oil. The fuel from the darts provided a quicker combustion to the flame. Although the end of a Fire Twirler does not mean the end of the harmful habit, it does always indicate the lessening of the energy which created the habit. For this reason, Fire Twirlers pursue the thorns.

Marley watched the Fields with a special need. While Fire Twirlers slammed into the trees, he waited for just the right kind of impact to occur. And then, two happened almost simultaneously. A collection of Fire Twirlers struck each other with such a force two of them were flung onto the Road. Marley gave chase after them.

"I have never had the challenge of two at once. Ebenezer, do not touch them, but help me corner that one," Marley said, pointing to the Fire Twirler he wanted to capture.

"Jacob, if I can not touch it, why should I even approach it?"

"It could save your life," yelled Marley.

The game of catching Fire Twirlers was on.

"The two are spinning counter to each other. Keep to their backside, Ebenezer."

"How is that possible if they are rotating in opposite directions?"

"Just let the big one go." Marley paused, then directed Scrooge. "Move in behind the smaller Twirler. I think I can corner it between us."

Scrooge still had no idea as to how he could help Marley. The directions given provided no actionable way of overpowering the fiery

compulsion. The best he could do was to just mirror what he saw Marley doing. When he stepped right, Scrooge stepped left. An upward arm movement created the same within Scrooge. Although it looked like coordination between them was occurring, it was not.

Marley grabbed for the tail of the spinning fire. Passing the blaze through his ghostly skin, neither spirit nor flame controlled the situation. A game of tag developed between the two. Scrooge mostly watched as Marley sparred with the energy of another's compulsion. The comedy was in their brawling without any bawling. What was happening seemed playful until, without warning, Scrooge yelped as he grabbed for the back of his pants. Pushing past him was the bigger Fire Twirler.

While Scrooge checked the singe of his back end, the aggressive Fire Twirler slammed into the weaker flame. Both Marley and Scrooge launched in opposite directions. The force from the impact created a distance which destabilized their shared gravity, and Scrooge once again dropped to the Road.

Within the next moment, Marley helped his friend back to his feet. "Just look at the size of that thing, Ebenezer." The new Fire Twirler spun with twice the speed and height of either Twirler alone. "Ebenezer, get it to follow you, and I will grab it from behind."

Scrooge looked at Marley with confusion. Why would he bait this fury of fire into chasing him? "I thought you were supposed to keep me out of danger."

"These things are slow. You can outpace it, Ebenezer."

After a moment of contemplation, Scrooge began to jump up and down, while waving his arms and howling like a wraith on a terror. The giant flame began to pursue the bouncy human. As the Fire Twirler gained momentum, Scrooge yelled, "I think it wants to harm me."

"You must remind it of the compulsion it is trying to overcome," yelled Marley.

"Is this, then, the actual spirit?"

"No, of course not; does it look like a person? It is only the mental energy being released by the spirit."

"I just do not understand why you are giving it traits of existence."

"To tell you the truth, spirits in the Fields are so elusive none of us understand them. So can you just keep it going your direction while I grab it?" With that, Marley flung his ethereal structure onto the blaze. As though it anticipated Marley's action, the Fire Twirler reversed direction so that its tail now spun toward Marley. The creature of flame ignored Scrooge as it ferociously consumed Marley.

Marley's hand flew past Scrooge's head. As Marley's foot was sent hurling from the Fire Twirler, Scrooge found Apurto standing next to him. "Help me, Ebenezer, before my consciousness is thrown to the Point," cried Marley. Scrooge looked to Apurto as the caretaker stared upon him. Neither moved. Marley's ghostly parts continued to be flung out of the raging spiral. When the left leg slammed through Apurto's body, the creature reacted by running.

"Help me, Ebenezer," screamed the now lonely spinning head.

As Apurto fled the scene, Scrooge remained frozen with inaction. "Is the flame alive?"

Gasping for air, Marley squeaked, "Only you breathe here, Ebenezer. Do something!" As the terror of his demise propelled Marley into silence, Scrooge circled the blaze looking for any weakness. Fearing that Marley would soon be destroyed, Scrooge raced through the flame. With the first step, Scrooge raised his arms above his shoulders, then he grabbed Marley's head as his second step left the heat. Together they fell upon the Road.

Within seconds, all but Marley's left little finger reassembled. As Marley turned toward the slowly rising Scrooge, the spirit cried out, "You have cast your skin, Ebenezer."

"I am fond of my clothing."

"And I thought you were just being a deserter, instead, you were disrobing?"

"I am VERY fond of my clothes, Jacob. I already lost my coat." As Scrooge put his modesty back on, he added, "That blasted thing already burned a hole in my trousers."

With the two of them once again standing, Marley turned toward the weakening Fire Twirler, then announced, "I am going to get it."

Before Scrooge could deliver a sound, Marley grabbed the Fire Twirler's tail, lifted it into his palm, then siphoned the flame through his arm and into the chain attached to his heart. There the wildfire settled down.

Without haste, the two continued on the Road. As they walked, Marley began to stare at Scrooge, then finally declared, "Your eyebrows are gone."

Scrooge felt the location of his scorched brows, then as he began to speak, noticed Marley's missing finger. "You are not whole yourself. Where is your finger?"

Dejected, Marley said, "It is in the Point. Gone forever."

"What is the Point, and why have I not heard of it before now?"

"There is a lot about Transmogrify you will never know, Ebenezer." Thinking about the Point in particular, Marley added, "There is a lot I will never know too. However, as far as the Point Of Visibility is concerned... well, it is a world without spatial references."

"Oh, wonderful. Now that that is cleared up... tell me at least why you were so afraid of having your bones thrown into the Point?"

"Because Apurto can not save them. The Point is a space with a unique time flow. Apurto always bypasses the area."

"We are going to bypass the area too — correct?"

"We can't, but be patient, my friend." Marley placed his hand on Ebenezer's shoulder, then said, "Within moments we will be in that realm."

"Jacob, that is not a comfort."

"Transmogrify is not comfortable."

"So I have discovered."

For the next few steps, they walked in silence, until Marley instructed Scrooge to 'hold his hand'.

"How is that even possible; you are not flesh?"

"You are correct. It is I who will hold your 'flesh', but first I need you to grab onto what seems to be my hand."

Scrooge did as instructed. The two hands met yet passed through each other without contacting substance. "Again," instructed Marley. And again they pushed through each other's palms without success. "Here, hold this," Marley said, handing Scrooge a partially exploded thorn from one of the trees lining the Road.

The two-inch-long spike resembled the shape of a wizard's hat yet was too small for even a leprechaun to wear. As Scrooge gripped the item from Transmogrify, Marley grabbed onto his closed fist. "We are at the Point. I will guide you."

"I do not see a Point... I only see the Road."

Within the next step Scrooge's sight went dark. "I'm blind," he screamed.

"Stay levelheaded, Ebenezer," whispered Marley.

Stave Eight
Confronting Treachery

TERRIFIED, SCROOGE WEAKENED. Instinctively, Marley wrapped himself around the human. Their shared closeness tightened as Marley whispered, "Close your mind, Ebenezer."

Scrooge lost his grip on the tree thorn. As the spike fell, Marley solidified his hold upon his friend. Collapsing into Marley's embrace, Scrooge calmed his panic. Standing as one entity, the rhythmic swing of the Point began to control their combined form. Invisible waves of a black ethereal flow washed over them. In an up-and-down cadence, the two swayed with the motion. First stretching taller, then thicker. Back and forth they bobbed, as the wobble within the Point never slowed.

"Ebenezer, are you calm?"

"Like a baby being rocked to sleep."

"Keep your wits about you. We must stay in contact. Will you allow me to move us?"

"Move us... where am I? No, wait, where are you?"

"Inside you." With this realization, Scrooge jerked stiff.

"Ebenezer — we MUST stay in contact." Scrooge — without knowing why — understood. "We need to reach the Point."

"I thought this was the Point," said Scrooge.

"Just the entrance."

"Jacob, I don't want to stay here."

"You will... maybe. Now allow me to move."

"Do as you must."

"Release yourself to me, Ebenezer." Scrooge had no way of understanding this command yet had no desire to stop Marley either. Slowly the sway of the blackness calmed and relaxed Scrooge, so that Marley could act. Spontaneously Marley began to control his companion's legs. Movement was slow and influenced by the waves of motion within the blackness. Even the darkness in any cave on Earth would have seemed brighter than was the void of light at the Point.

Through the benefit of past experience, Marley followed the pulsating echoes. As they moved, the waves carried by the atmosphere went from an up-and-down motion to a back-and-forth thrust. Each forward leg action slightly lifted them from the Road. Marley struggled to keep Scrooge in contact with the surface. Running in place, as though in water, the backward motion of the wave also pushed them somewhat downward. As they moved forward, the swings of the rising pressure intensified — then light erupted.

"We are at the Point Of Visibility," announced Marley. Together as one, the two floated above the Road.

Shielding his eyes from the light, Scrooge asked, "Why has the motion stopped?"

"It hasn't. It has just converged here within the center."

As Scrooge blinked several times so as to adjust to the light, he asked, "What controls it?"

Marley pointed, then answered, "The Sanctuary Of Innocents."

"A new Mog?" Scrooge asked, as he followed his friend's pointing finger to a tunnel of light hundreds of feet before them. The blackness within the Point surrounded all but the beacon of light piercing the dark. As he began to speak, laughter erupted from the tunnel. Confused, he asked, "Is the light rejoicing?"

"That within the light is in constant celebration."

"If it is not the light itself, then what is that delight I hear?"

"Mostly children," answered Marley.

"Mostly...?"

"There are pets and some plants in the Sanctuary as well."

"Why is it separated by darkness?"

"The Sanctuary Of Innocents is home to spirits never tarnished. They do not, and never have, existed within the realm of love."

Scrooge jerked alert, which caused Marley to shift within him. Bewildered, he said, "I thought love is the working force of our kind."

"It is for those that live to maturity, but not the children that pass before adulthood. They stay with the force of their birth — joy."

"There is a difference between joy and love?"

"The work is different."

"Which is better?"

"Better? The Infinite Consciousness seems to have no need for hierarchy. Its only need is one of Provenance." Marley took a deep breath, then continued. "Yet, I realize you have the need, Ebenezer. It is my understanding there are three energies that create a more powerful work than does love. Joy is one of them. However, that does not mean it is better."

"Babies are born with a higher energy than they will have at death?"

"It seems humans need a boost at birth. Society is tough, and often wicked in heart. At maturity, a child becomes aware of their work within the force of love. Before adulthood, they play in joy. It is no light task to bring a smile to most adults, but children provide that service. Their worth is much greater than just regeneration."

"How do you know this? Have you been to the Sanctuary?"

"None from this side of the Road can do that, but they come here to reconnect with grieving parents."

"Have you seen them?"

"Many times. Look," Marley said pointing to the center of the bridge. "A child approaches you now."

They watched as the youth passed beneath them without even acknowledging their presence. As the child disappeared from the Point's darkness, Scrooge asked, "Why can't we go to the Sanctuary?"

"Like I said, it has an energy that we adults have forgotten how to embrace. If you and I were to travel the bridge to the Sanctuary, the space between both Mogs would expand with each step. The opposite happens when a child crosses over to the Road; their stride covers twice the distance."

"That is probably good, since children are so small. But what is the method of such a contradicting expansion?"

"It is contained within the substance of the darkness."

"Where is the logic in that?"

"Logic? Ebenezer, humanity lives outside of logic, and often truth, but maybe someday this curious substance of darkness and changeable space will be understood. Maybe... but not by either of us."

Scrooge reflected upon Marley's delay within the Point. As his flesh chilled by the cold of the darkness, he asked, "Why do we linger here?"

Marley smiled as he replied, "Ebenezer, do you not feel the tunnel's light?"

"The light? Will it warm me?"

Marley took in a deep breath, which simulated life, then declared, "This is my favorite place in Transmogrify."

"But it is dark and... so cold."

"Temperature is of no importance to me. The Point provides a place of quieting. A restorative intimacy surrounds me here. It is the place where I am best able to reflect upon my progress. I find comfort in the darkness."

"Is reflection not done within the Mog itself?"

"The Task Of Outreach is planned there, but can be difficult to achieve without... revision. Especially for the Condemned Innocents. Their path to Acceptance must be assisted by other spirits." Marley paused, then finished with, "For me, the embrace at the Point keeps me focused on my Task."

"So the Point is your solace?"

"My inner strength does drift."

Scrooge asked, "Is it ever too hard for you?"

"What is hard is that I ever put myself into this situation. But even the difficulties are a gift for improvement, Ebenezer."

"One can never have too many gifts."

"The truth is most people do not receive enough gifts."

"Jacob, most people do not want 'difficult' gifts. Can we leave now? The cold is too crisp for me."

"I would like to have you experience the Burst before we reenter the Road. Do you think you can continue for a while longer?"

"The Burst... will the excitement ever cease in this place?"

"For you... probably not."

"If it is safe... well, Jacob, just make it happen."

"The Burst seems to be generated by the distance between the Point and the Sanctuary. I can not just... make it happen. A certain rotation within this location occurs at the moment of the upward gust. However, like the ticking of a clock, that gyration is due soon."

"Get me warmer!"

"You do know I am as cold as a rock, but I do have one Fire Twirler. I did not want to use it yet, but I will if you have to be warmed."

Scrooge also wondered if he should spend the Fire Twirler on heat. As his teeth chattered, he finally gave permission to consume the energy flare. Occupying the same space as did Scrooge, Marley removed the Fire Twirler from his heart chain. The release caused an eruption which burned a hole in Scrooge's shirt. Yelping, Scrooge cried out, "Warm me, don't cook me!"

"Your pain is not deliberate." Marley paused before adding, "I am too close to you to avoid a bit of burn."

The Fire Twirler added both heat and light to the entire surroundings. As Scrooge watched a tidal wave of blackness approach, he responded, "I doubt I will..." but before he could complete his thought, the Burst hit.

The piercing "Zheeiep" of the wave hurdled the pair straight up out of the extreme dark and into the space above it all. The reaction from the two displayed conflicting passions. Marley delighted in the ride, whereas Scrooge cried out in terror. Drifting back toward the Road, Marley assured Scrooge, "I have you secured within me. Fear not, Ebenezer."

As they floated downward, Marley pointed toward the Sanctuary Of Innocents and said, "Is that not a reason for awe?" With a caution that neared the panic of a lamb tracking a lion in pursuit, Scrooge investigated the sight before him. The light from a dim radiance appeared on either side of the darkness. As he stared to analyze the visuals before him, peripheral crescents of light came into focus. Both the right and left slivers of illumination mirrored the other's glow. As Scrooge fluttered with Marley back toward the Road, he realized the light of the Point had been created by these two curved shapes. Their combined shine spotlighted the area where children entered the Road, and spirits waited for the Burst.

As they descended, the pair viewed the entire area beneath them. The Corridor Of Phantoms blocked the visual scene of the Road, yet supplied an ever-changing display of spirits traveling to and from the Abyss. All of the Mogs were visible, with the Plains Of Violence and the Abyss Of Final Transmogrify being the furthest from sight. Scrooge gasped at the vastness of the Fields Of Destructive Compulsions. He wondered if passage beyond the millions of Fire Twirlers might take longer than time itself.

The two of them watched as lightning bolted up and out of the Abyss. The flashes of blueness supplied the light within all of the Mogs but one. The crescents from each side of the Sanctuary Of Innocents blazed a blinding yellow light that illuminated only that Mog. The colors of blue and yellow combined within Scrooge's heart to create the green light of serenity.

Tears of joy overwhelmed Scrooge. "Why am I so happy?"

"It is the children. Light carries more energy than just color and brightness. Light also holds emotions."

"No, it does not."

"Of course it does. Just ask any mating firefly why they are flashing their tail."

"Jacob, I have never had a firefly say any word to me. However, I will ponder the idea that light can hold emotion."

The slow drop back into the darkness of the Point caused Scrooge to wildly blink with the desire for vision. With his feet once again upon the Road, Scrooge requested, "Can we leave now?"

"Without delay." But before a step could be taken, their connection to each other was annihilated. A Fire Twirler slammed through Marley looking for the quickest release from its flame. Both the blaze and Marley's grip on Scrooge were lost. "No, no, no! I do not need this difficult gift," roared Marley.

"Jacob, Jacob!"

"Are you standing, Ebenezer?"

"No, I am crippled. Find me!"

"I knew I should have saved the Fire Twirler. I have no idea as to where I have landed."

"You are speaking at a normal level. So you must be near."

"I am going to try and hear my way back to you, Ebenezer. Whisper as softly as possible, 'I am here,' then every few seconds repeat the statement, but just a little louder."

Scrooge did as requested. The first two vocalizations were without volume, but with the third Marley turned toward the sound. The slow amplification helped him to locate the fallen human. Bit by bit Marley moved in Scrooge's direction. "I am almost frozen," were the last words spoken before silence stopped all movement between them. Only the darkness voiced sound. With each wave a low 'zheeiep' could be heard as the current converged at the Point.

"Ebenezer, Ebenezer! Move — fight the cold!"

In a feeble effort, Scrooge stretched his arms. Marley turned in circles trying to locate his collapsed friend. Moaning, Scrooge continued to move, then without warning screamed in pain, "I just stuck myself with that dratted thorn you gave me. I think I am bleeding."

Before Scrooge could completely express the pain from the thorn, Marley grabbed his shirt, then with the mental strength beyond muscles he lifted Scrooge back on to his feet. Scrooge stood stiffened as Marley once again grabbed hold of the thorn. Clutching both the hand and the spike he said, "There are 13 steps within the darkness. Can you take any of them, Ebenezer?"

"Is there an option?"

Snickering, Marley replied, "That's my old friend. The cold is not going to change, so start moving your legs. I will guide you."

"Well, Jacob, I am sure not getting out of this freezing black-motion without you."

Clumsily the two stiff-walked their way beyond the cold darkness of the Point. While it took minutes for the Road's heat to seep into Scrooge, they both watched as Fire Twirlers crashed about the Fields Of Destructive Compulsions.

"We have a little less than half of the Fields to pass before we will arrive at the Abyss," informed Marley as he pointed to the distant hole. Scrooge watched as flashes of blue lightning bolted up and out of the cavity. "A lot of Acceptance is being created in that nest of fulfillment."

Marley had hoped they would travel in silence until after he had collected the six Twirlers his heart chain would hold, but Scrooge was troubled and in need of comfort. "It is cruel to take a child," mumbled Scrooge.

Marley stared at Scrooge, then asked, "Take a child where?"

"From their family, of course."

"I understand." Marley paused, took a deep breath, then exhaled with a sigh that exhausted his ghostly form. Stopping midstep, he just shook his head, then said, "That loss is emotionally unapproachable."

"If it is 'unapproachable,' why does it happen? Jacob, why do the young ever die?"

Marley purposely quieted himself, then said, "That was Noah's question." Scrooge watched as his friend struggled to find the next thought. Finally, Marley began to explain. "It's my first memory of Noah. He was barely school age, and I... I was still wearing baby clothes."

"Hard to think of you in baby clothes."

"Noah had a cat. I think he just called it 'Cat', but the lack of a name never lessened the devotion he seemed to feel for the creature." Marley paused, then said, "It was spring, May I think, and the rain was non-stop so we were playing indoors.

I think we had a fire going, but I am not sure. Anyway, a newborn snake crawled under the door looking for a dry place where it would not suffer a drowning. Before it was even fully indoors, Cat jumped on it and killed it in one quick move."

"What did you do?"

"I just watched Noah as he attempted to revive this four-inch-long snake. But of course, it was not possible. So when the sun next parted the clouds, he had a funeral for the serpent and... he cried."

"But you didn't?"

"It was a snake, Ebenezer. Do humans ever care about snakes?"

"Well, Noah did."

"No... Noah cared about the age... the youth of the snake. That is what he talked about for weeks afterwards."

"So the funeral was not the end of the affair?"

"It was more like the beginning." Marley looked straight at Scrooge, then said, "For the longest time he kept saying things like, 'that snake never should have been born', 'what did that snake ever accomplish', and my least favorite comment, 'the only experience that snake had was one of terror'. Noah was without a doubt bothered by the lack of life's promise of just being allowed to survive. He could not understand why the snake was born only to be immediately killed. To him, this was chaos, barbarism and just not right."

"It does not seem right to me either, Jacob."

"The death of a youth... that death is about what it leaves behind. For a sibling, it often brings home, for the first time, the reality that they, too, are vulnerable to a similar loss. For the loving parents, it shreds their hearts, then forces change."

"So you think this happens because parents do not make adjustments when they should?"

"It may seem that way, but no, a child does not die so that anyone else will make revisions. However, forced change does happen after such a loss." Marley paused, then finished by saying, "Some changes are beneficial, many are damaging, and at times... they can be both."

"What about the child? What about what they have lost?"

"This is hard for the human to understand, but the child still exists and has new experiences. They lost Earth's encounter, but still reside within the physicality of the Infinite Consciousness's creation."

"But none of this explains the harshness of a child's death," complained Scrooge.

"Like I said before, this ordeal is emotionally unapproachable. It crushes the heart as it numbs the mind. I have no other answers than that to offer you, Ebenezer."

"But there is no answer in that. It is like saying it is... because it is. Your answer is an escape from the conversation."

"Yes, it is," said Marley as he grabbed the tail of a Fire Twirler, then siphoned it into his heart chain. For a long while Scrooge walked in silence, just letting his outrage build, as Marley mindlessly grabbed, then secured, every Fire Twirler that crossed their path.

Finally, Scrooge erupted. "If it is a slap in the face to commit suicide, is it not an equal slap to humanity's face when a child dies, and their potential is lost?"

"Ebenezer, we are just ants trying to understand the feet moving around us." Realizing this answer was not going to resolve his friend's issue, he added,

"However, no human will ever know the mind of the Infinite Consciousness until they themselves become the same as the Infinite Consciousness."

Stunned, Scrooge asked, "Can that happen?"

"Well, let's just say, the notion is possible." Marley cleared his throat, then quickly added, "We all originate from the substance of creation."

As Marley paused, Ebenezer asked, "Is not the Infinite Consciousness the creator?"

"That is my understanding."

"How did it create itself?"

"I think that is like knowing the Infinite Consciousness's name, whereas we humans do not have the ears to hear it." Scrooge stared at Marley as he continued to explain. "There is a similar problem in understanding how creation is built. Humans, and especially me, Ebenezer, do not have the mind, or experiences, to understand the concept of physically creating the self from only a — thought."

"That would mean thoughts are physical. There is no logic to that, Jacob."

"And yet, the physical world exists, Ebenezer. It had to begin somehow."

"I wonder if the Infinite Consciousness is physical at all. Maybe it was able to create the physical world because it is spirit. Just like the artist that paints never becomes the canvas."

"Such a clever thought, but that is all it is, an opinion without proven knowledge."

"You frustrate me, Jacob."

"Our lack of understanding is not a foe. It is merely the restriction that allows us the desire for personal perfection."

"That is confusing. So we become perfect when we transform into a... a treacle... called Acceptance?"

"Acceptance is not the end, Ebenezer." Scrooge just shook his head back and forth as Marley clarified his understanding. "There is more. Get accustomed to transformation, for it never really ends. However, the path beyond Acceptance is too well lit for most to follow."

"'Too well lit'? Even if I close my eyes?"

"Can you navigate without your eyes, Ebenezer?"

"So in essence only the blind are able to become more than Acceptance?"

"Find the metaphor in that understanding, Ebenezer, for the Infinite Consciousness's enlightenment dwells within that nearly invisible, but over-lit route."

"Humbug."

"And therein resides the main reason most humans never become a creator force — their own doubt."

Irrelevant conversation continued as the friends walked toward the Abyss Of Final Transmogrify. Blue lightning repeatedly bolted into the atmosphere. To Scrooge each flash appeared to add vastness to the Road. Finally he made the comment, "We are not making any distance toward that fissure."

Marley just thought to himself before he said, "Motion without movement, that sounds like a member of parliament." They both looked at each other, but only smiled as Marley created what he thought would be a solution to slow legs. "I have never had a reason to try this — but..."

"You are going to shock me, are you not?"

"I am going to move us." Before Scrooge could react, Marley pulled a Fire Twirler from his heart chain. "I need you to step into my limbs."

"Limbs? Tree?"

"My extremities, my appendages... my limbs... we need to be combined before I can use this," he said, lifting up the spinning flame.

"Can you not enter my... limbs?"

"Yes, shall I do that?"

"Why are you asking? You have never..."

Marley pushed into Scrooge's structure, then put the Fire Twirler beneath their shared feet. Instantly the spin forced the two both upward, then forward with a speed neither had previously ever experienced. As they raced over the Road, Marley yelled, "Faster than a horse."

"Faster than falling off a cliff. Yippee!" Scrooge howled as they traveled at a speed that pleased. As one Fire Twirler burned itself out, Marley pulled another from his chain, so to continue their forward motion. Once the six flames were exhausted, they stopped. Marley then replenished the energy bursts before

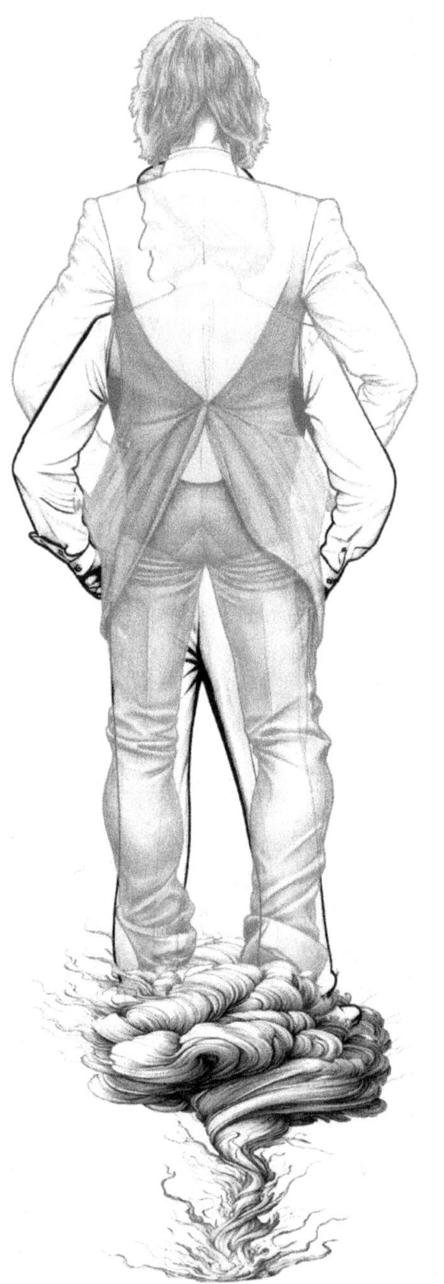

continuing into the Abyss. This activity repeated itself until they were both at the threshold of the enormous chasm.

As they approached the edge of the Abyss, Marley forced a sixth Fire Twirlers into his heart chain before asking Scrooge, "Are you ready to jump?"

Scrooge's mouth dropped open without uttering even a heavy sigh. As if on cue, so to make the biggest effect possible, a lightning bolt cracked upward out of the hole. The power of the discharge shook the foundation of the cliff. As Scrooge steadied himself, he asked, "Where is the bottom? How can I survive the fall?"

"With the rocks in your pockets."

"You have got rocks for brains, Jacob."

"I no longer have a brain, Ebenezer. I just have thoughts."

"Humbug."

"Is that again your new best word?"

"Humbug."

"You do still have the rocks I gave you?"

"See their tips?" Scrooge said as he pointed to the formations protruding beyond his pockets.

"Good, now jump in. The rocks will slow you."

"I have no faith in..." But before Scrooge could hold his ground, Marley flung himself into his friend's body, then quickly walked him over the edge of the overhang.

The scream out of Scrooge was louder than the next lightning bolt. As he accelerated toward an unknowable future, his pants began to ride high around his form. Scrooge tugged at his crotch in hopes of alleviating the pressure the fall enforced upon his privates.

And then, it happened, he slowed down as the sight of the Abyss came into focus. Waves of color converged at Scrooge, while a buoyancy developed around him. Safely drifting downward, a lightning bolt shot past, forming a pattern that bypassed all moving within the Abyss. It left only a charge of freshness, both in smell and tingle, within the cavernous shaft. As lightning continued to spark and bolt within the surrounding space, Scrooge observed the colors and meandering curves of the walls. The colors — every one with a metallic glassiness — intensified Scrooge's vision. Shining walls of vibrant yellows, magentas, greens, blues and lavenders helped to light his descent. Scrooge sensed a flow of dignity within the hues, a sheen of splendor.

As they drifted within a combined form, Scrooge finally slowed to such an extent that Marley felt comfortable enough to separate from him. Moving outside of Scrooge, Marley watched his friend plummet. Acting in response mode only, Marley swooped beneath Scrooge, then allowed his friend's body to pass through him. As the motion combined the two, Marley grabbed onto Scrooge's form; then and only then did the weight of the human slow. "I thought it was the lodestones slowing you." Marley pointed to the walls, then added, "One can not throw those stones hard enough to even make contact with this enclosure."

"What do you mean? What happens to the stones?" asked Scrooge.

"They just drop a few feet from the barrier."

"Should I remove mine?"

"No, let's not chance the result."

As they moved downward, a plethora of spirits floated throughout the Abyss, crowding the area with reflections of pastel shades that shimmered off their bodies. As the upper area of Transmogrify carried a somber ambience, so it was that the lower area, the Abyss, glistened with cheer. Every sound, every gust of air, every motion within the Abyss bounced off the metallic walls, then returned to the ears in the form of musical tones. As the pair dropped deep into the hole, an undefined, yet glorious, song began to reverberate with uplifting emotion.

Scrooge enjoyed the vertical coasting; even though the rocks in his pockets still generated an uncomfortable tug, he made himself settle into the annoyance. Closing his eyes, the melody from the walls surrounded his form. Tones bounced off every exposed surface of skin. His hands, being toughened by age, felt little. But oh — the thrill upon the face as the quivering notes made contact! Each tickled like a feather as it grazed the surface.

While a constant storm of lightning bolts flashed skyward, Scrooge became enthralled by the forms rising up from beneath him. A confusion of soaring monoliths emerged. The complex combined the visuals of the colored metal with a system of structures designed for specific purposes. Pyramids of various shapes and layouts filled the entire base of the Abyss.

Within the center configuration arose the network devoted to the collection of Acceptance. The layout resembled that of a twinned pyramid standing bottom-up with its apex buried. On one side, the purer Coss Acceptance cascaded into a motif of meanders, which then disappeared into... the unknown. All the while a flood of normal Acceptance glided into a separate chamber within the combined pyramid.

Scrooge followed the various meandering patterns of Greek key from one edifice to the next in hopes of understanding each building's function. Except, none were buildings. All but two areas were either right-sided or upside-down pyramids.

One of the pyramid areas flooded the entire location with activity as spirits mingled while waiting for their turn on the Walkway Of Transmogrify. Three electrum — gold, silver and copper — pyramids surrounded a pathway made up of two lengthy horizontal crystals. Each quartz crystal had points on both ends which met in the center of the Walkway. Once a spirit poised themselves directly over both points, a blast of energy from the electrum pyramids converged into blue lightning, which then converted the spirit into Acceptance.

The festivities at the Walkway, by hordes of spirits, created a visual confusion which dizzied the mind. Yet the area reeked with enthusiasm for the task at hand — Mogrification. While a captivating vision of the Walkway continued, Scrooge noticed a staircase climbing toward the Upper Mogs.

Each metallic step of the stairway had a different tread and riser size. Scrooge puzzled over this difference until he realized their size appeared to be controlled by color. The golden steps had the tallest rise, yet the tread was so narrow that even a child's foot could only use its toes to walk upon it. This gave the narrow steps a ladder appearance. With each progressive color of the rainbow the rise lessened, as the tread widened. The lavender steps exhibited the widest tread, yet was so small in height it appeared to be flat — more like a ramp than a step.

A collection of spirits floated up and down the stairwell as emotions of delight danced throughout. What caused the good cheer could not be determined, but

whatever it was left Scrooge smiling.

As Marley and Scrooge drifted toward the love collection structure, above them plunged a cloud of Coss Acceptance. Racing at a speed well above the pull of gravity, the mass drew so close that Scrooge screamed. Just as he feared the collision with the love energy, the liquid divided itself, then flowed around them, and finally it entered the collection receptacle.

Drops of Acceptance flung all over the pair. Control over their descent left Marley as the Acceptance took effect. Giggling, then laughing, he grabbed onto the edge of the collection pyramid. He released Scrooge by placing them both upon the

214

corner of the tower. With legs dangling over the edge, the pair could not control their guffaw. There was no humor here, just the incredible lightness the Acceptance gave them, which turned everything into a quip.

Sitting on the corner of the complex, Scrooge laughed, "That was quite a fall."

"From everywhere but grace," chuckled Marley.

Scrooge just shook his head and giggled back. "That makes no sense."

"Believe me, Ebenezer, most things do not make sense." He smiled, then winked at his friend as he added, "The concept is the tickle." Unable to control his laughter, Marley fell off the building, then dropped toward the five Dens beneath them. Before Scrooge became affected by the separation, Marley returned cackling, "Are you still with me?" Returning to his edge of the corner, Marley looked at Scrooge, paused, then asked, "Can you just hardly wait to die?"

A nervous giggle erupted from Scrooge as he responded, "And be stuck with you again. I would rather live." Together they laughed, and laughed, and laughed at that thought.

As the droplets of Acceptance were absorbed by their skin, both Marley and Scrooge began to quiet their howling. The liveliness at the Walkway Of Transmogrification demanded constant notice, but after several moments Scrooge turned his gaze to the opposite side of the Abyss.

Focusing on a massive platinum arena, Scrooge just watched as a one-armed, headless spirit entered the Farewell Platform. Three platinum spokes horizontally protruded out from the Platform. Each were set at a 45-degree angle from the others, with the middle crosspiece being both the longest and widest of the trio. Atop the three platinum bars were humongous horizontal crystal points. At the ends of both the far right and far left spokes stood an additional vertical quartz point. Behind each crystal point, an upright platinum post combined with the quartz created a gemstone that sparked with the slightest movement. The center spoke did not have this feature; instead its horizontal quartz point overhung an upside-down pyramid funnel.

Scrooge watched the one-armed headless spirit stand as still as a statue atop the Platform. They both observed the area as it began to fill with a golden haze. The cloud, contained by its own invisible structure, blurred their vision. "Some think that fog is the Infinite Consciousness."

"It is hard to envision the Infinite Consciousness being any kind of physical form," replied Scrooge.

"The reality is you just can not imagine it as a cloud."

"Yes, that does seem too simplistic. So tell me, Jacob, why do spirits think that mist is the Infinite Consciousness?"

"Because the Infinite Consciousness personally honors the spirit that is brave enough to go beyond a hopeless situation." Marley watched as Scrooge's curiosity developed, then conveyed to him, "Once a spirit is within the Farewell Platform of Instant Transmogrification, they again become surrounded by the light of the Infinite Consciousness's love."

"Does it save them?"

"No, most often their Acceptance is impure, yet the Infinite Consciousness always pulls the strongest positive from the imperfect spirit. That best quality is then incorporated into the Infinite Consciousness's own individual spirit as a thought."

"So the truth is the Instant Transmogrified spirit also lives on forever? What, then, is the purpose of the Crater?"

"It is better to think of such a spirit as being gone but remembered. Whereas I am not gone, yet hardly remembered, so maybe that spirit down there is better situated than I." Marley put his hand on Scrooge's shoulder, then explained, "And about the Crater, you do know it was created out of human actions, do you not?"

"Kind of sad how the uncontrollable event of Coss release can destroy another's entire existence."

"I am sure it was very sad for that spirit when it realized Apurto ate its head. The Crater is an uncompromising Mog."

As the two sat waiting, without any indication of a threat, the Platform exploded. Shards of light shot through the area, depositing sparks upon the pair. Marley gave the embers no attention. Scrooge on the other hand made every effort to dodge the flares. The attempt was valiant, yet in vain, for the sparks landed all over him. However, his fears of the flames were unfounded, for when they landed upon skin they had no effect upon it. The firestorm, though visible, was as ghostly in substance as was Marley himself.

Once he realized this, Scrooge calmed himself to watch the Platform's show of lights. As the golden haze cleared, no phantom parts remained visible. A transformation into the center horizontal crystal had occurred and was being processed. A dull grey light began to form within that crystal. Slowly the glow moved back and forth within the quartz, becoming lighter and brighter through motion. Once cleansed, the lightened Acceptance flowed out of the point of the crystal and into the upside-down pyramid funnel. "That was an unlucky spirit," said Marley.

"How can you tell?"

"Well, look... only the Infinite Consciousness's love was collected," he said, pointing to the center crystal's flow of Acceptance.

"How do you know that?"

"If even one bit of the person's love had been collected, it would have flowed into the two outer crystals, then been made into Acceptance," he said, pointing to the combined platinum and quartz uprights. "But alas, now that spirit is only a memory."

A long pause developed before Scrooge said, "Well, at least it is a memory in the creator's mind."

Marley looked sideways at Scrooge, smiled, then replied, "That is indeed something... at least."

The entire area of the Abyss hummed with activity as the Walkway Of Transmogrification again became the dominant visual. As the pair sat on the ledge, with legs dangling over the Acceptance-collection pyramid, Scrooge observed spirits coming and going beneath him. Directly below them stood five upside-down funnel pyramids, each of a different size, yet connected into one structure. The steady flow of spirits into each funneled passageway added to the bustle of the Abyss.

"Are you rested, Ebenezer?"

Scrooge thought about that question, then counter-asked, "Should I be tired?"

Marley just laughed, then replied, "Well, not if you aren't. We do have quite a task ahead of us, though."

"So, in other words, I should be rested?"

"We will probably both need to be 'well-rested' for this. Drifting into that Den," Marley said, pointing to one of the larger pyramid openings, "will require — alertness."

"So Noah is in that hole?"

"Yes, he is in the Den Of Anger, or as you call it — 'that hole'. But time is on our side, because it does not exist. So we will enter when you're ready."

"I get to decide?"

"We will act upon your word."

Scrooge just laughed. "You are a mystery, Jacob."

"Most people are."

"And obviously, so are spirits."

Together they just watched spirits shuffle around them. The action at the Walkway being the most profound because of the periodic cheers of elation that accompanied every crack of blue lightning. As one spirit transformed into Acceptance, the next in line bounced in anticipation of glorification. The process was quick, for it took longer to enter the Walkway Of Transmogrification than it did to become Acceptance.

"Look, look, Jacob... it is the handicapped spirit that helped us."

As they watched the phantom move to the center of the double-pointed crystal pathway, Scrooge asked, "Will that spirit regain its legs upon Mogrification?"

"What he lost was of flesh. What he gets back is in spirit, which has already been perfected."

The three electrum pyramids energized. As the force built within the monuments, the legless spirit looked directly upon Scrooge and Marley, then spoke the words, "Navalny Zelenskyy." Within the next instant, blue lightning converged upon the spirit, who then became Acceptance.

"What does that mean — Navalny Zelenskyy?" asked Scrooge.

"I think it could be his name. Do you remember at the Chute when he declared we would never be able to forget it once it had been heard?"

"Yes, I recall that, but I did not understand why he said it, for names have always been hard for me to remember. However, I will never forget his generosity, and the help he gave me."

"And yet, he was not happy about your presence here."

"Do you think his helping me was only to get me out of Transmogrify faster?"

"It is a thought, yet at no time should you replace his act with his motive. The two are connected, yet never the same."

"Which is more important?"

"For us that were created in flesh and blood... actions carry the consequences."

Scrooge observed all of the happenings at the Abyss, while Marley just watched him watching. None of the other spirits gave the living one, or his ghostly friend, any attention. Instead they busied themselves with the work of their own Mogrification, travelling in and out of the Abyss as they worked to repair the harms they caused others. That is the easy work, for once the Task Of Outreach had been formed, then, and only then, is the spirit required to exist within the pain of victimization. After a long sit, Scrooge finally said, "If it is up to me, then I am ready."

With the agreement to proceed, Marley moved back into Scrooge's form, and then slipped their dual shape off the ledge. Moving downward, toward the far-left upside-down pyramid, Marley commented on the Den directly beneath them. "Keep as still as a carcass, Ebenezer. We do not want to end up in the Den Of Destructive Compulsions."

As they drifted toward the Den where Noah existed, Scrooge said, "It seems like a better Den than the Den Of Anger where Noah is."

"In the Den Of Anger, one can feel the dangers. However, within that Den," Marley explained, pointing to the largest upside-down pyramid, "the oddest of happenings can trap a drifting spirit."

"I do not want to get trapped anywhere around here."

"Then yield to me as we move."

"Am I not already?"

"Just do not flinch until we are inside the Den."

Bonded in form, the pair slowly moved toward the squarish hole. Following other spirits, Marley entered the Den Of Anger. The juncture into the Den siphoned the friends, and their light, into a spiral. As swirls of light spun around them, Marley gripped Scrooge tighter. From the outside the Dens appeared to be short; however, once entered, an expansion of space caused a downward drop greater than that of a mountain.

As the two whirled within their gust of light, less dense spirits moved past the living human and his dead friend. Either the shared gravity or lodestones helped to slow the pair's fall. Marley did not want to test which, or if both, was affecting them. He was just grateful that a slower spin would help to keep Scrooge's stomach

calm, so calm that Scrooge dozed off. Marley maneuvered Scrooge into the Den's point, and then they passed through and into a cavern that covered an area larger than that of the entire surface of Transmogrify.

Scrooge's eyes burst open to a brightening blindness; the sun's shine would prove dim in comparison. Instantly a tickle developed in his nose, to which he sneezed with such a force his eyes clamped shut. Filtering the intense light through his eyelids Scrooge watched as ghostly shapes whisked around him. As Scrooge clamped his eyes tighter, Marley moved the two of them away from the funnel's light.

Slowly Scrooge reopened his eyes to a mass of spirits bustling around them. The entire area appeared larger than that of all the upper Mogs combined. Together Marley and Scrooge watched as spirits poured into the location from the five Mog funnels. Rivers of moving spirits developed, for each funnel seemed to create an invisible channel within the cavern. "Why did we have to enter by the Den Of Anger when all of the Dens end up in this huge lair?"

"Do you see any spirit moving outside of their Den's path?" Marley asked.

Scrooge looked in every angle before declaring, "No, but what retains their rigidity?"

"The fear of getting trapped."

"Would that make them ask for Instant Mogrification?"

"It is not that kind of a trap. Up above, a spirit works the actions from their life so as to create their Task Of Outreach. This place is not that easy." To emphasize the issue, Marley pushed both of his arms out over the vast stretch of their visual space, then explained, "Down here is about the invisible, the thoughts and lingering feelings."

"I still do not understand..."

"Understand how what is in the mind can trap?"

"How can my mind become trapped? This is like a big sky country in here. There are no barriers — hence nothing to be trapped by."

Marley laughed so hard he could barely respond. Scrooge scrutinized his friend, then frowned when he realized he was being mocked. Marley for his part started to control his hysterics through deep breaths. Slowly he calmed enough so he could answer. "Forgive me, old friend. I mean no disrespect, but the mind is of consciousness. It dwells everywhere and nowhere in the same instance. The traps in here are within the lingering thoughts of the spirit."

"How can that become a trap for me?"

"Because their contemplation is not on our path; once presented with it, we either identify it as ours, or find the spirit's thought... odious. Both extremes can create an emotional confusion to such a degree that self-identification becomes trapped inside the influence of either the infatuation, or repulsion. Often in here it is repulsion that captivates, but nonetheless, the resulting bewilderment ensnares the outsider until they recognize, then calm, the borrowed thinking."

Scrooge looked at Marley, then calmly smirked. "That was so clarifying, Jacob."

Nodding his head, Marley replied, "Let me attempt a different comparison." He closed his eyes, then relayed the imagery within his mind. "Think of this area as London and each of the funnels over there is an avenue within the city." He waited for either a concern or acknowledgment from Scrooge, but when his friend remained quiet, Marley continued. "If you needed to go to a shop you would not go down the avenue that only entered the cemetery."

"I do want to stay out of the cemetery. But how could that 'trap' a spirit? If it were me, I would just return to my point of origin, then go down the correct road."

"And therein is your blunder."

"The mistake is?"

"Turning around does not give one the ability to go back. These pathways move forward. My spirit of greed learned that the hard way, to the near suspension of its Task Of Outreach, which was to try and save you." Scrooge nodded as Marley continued. "When I first entered this area, I was so excited about the accomplishment of moving beyond the Cycle Of Greed that I entered through the Den Of Physical Harm. And those two Dens are not even near each other. But there I was... in a place not of my concern. When I moved along the path, an angry gathering trapped me in their suffering."

"How?"

"They were living a shared lie."

"What falsehood could control an entire group?"

"Ebenezer, individual naivety is a weakness that those with malicious intentions target. The group I got pulled into stormed about how another community was going to attack them, so instead they forged a war upon that innocent society. I personally could have dodged their advance to pull me into their thinking, but it was the sheer numbers of them doing a unified seduction that trapped me."

"You were too weak to fight their influence?"

"Believe me, Ebenezer, everyone is too weak when social tyranny is made into a mandate."

"How long did it take you to escape?"

"What that group did still haunts me, and I was not even the spirit that became personally trapped. But to your specific question, maybe a dozen human years. It could not be a century, or you would have already joined me here." Marley paused to grab a thought. "But then again, it may have been moments, and it just felt like years. Like I said before, time in here passes without seconds."

Scrooge slowly shook his head from side to side, then asked, more to himself than to Marley, "So the mob weaves lies in hopes of conjuring up truths?"

"Just like lawmakers."

"And priests."

"Ebenezer! Do you want to go to Hades?"

"Is that where I am now?"

Marley just laughed and said, "Thankfully, the afterlife is not as small-minded as are the myths of eternity."

As they traveled along the Den's lane, Scrooge followed the movement of hundreds of spirits. With caves lining both sides of the route, every glance brought dramatic activities into sight. Scrooge gasped as drunken holiday partiers tossed Oliver Cromwell's head back and forth. With each thrust of the severed skull, it could be heard yelling, "Christmas has been banned. I will have you beheaded for this." The frantic screams from the dead ruler were overpowered by the cheers spewing from the rowdy cave. Dancing around, the cave dwellers drenched themselves in drink, while the abused brain box flew like a bird around the cave. Scrooge wondered what it would be like to be caught up in that cave's frenzy, then quaked from his own thought as he quickened his pace past the area.

Across from the head-tossing Den, a smaller cave could be heard before seen. Uproars transmitted throughout the area, "She is too independent!" "I saw her cast a spell!" "She kills children!" "She's a witch!" "Burn her!" "Burn her now!"

As they moved toward the vocal outbursts, Scrooge asks, "Should they not be in the Den Of Physical Harm?"

"Those in there are trapped by their anger that women must be controlled. They dwell within a place of verbal violence, not physical harm."

"Women suffer physical harm every day." Scrooge shook his head, then asked, "Is it not a social tradition, so well established it seems correct, and even desired by most governments? Yet there is only this cave within the Den Of Anger?"

"Misogynists are controlled by at least a thousand caves within the Den Of Physical Harm — one in every language, and dozens in every religion."

"A thousand? I did not think women were that oppressed!"

"It is not our oppression, Ebenezer, it is theirs. You and I, who were born with male authority, can hardly sympathize, let alone empathize with the fetters placed upon women at birth."

"But, without women, would there even be men?"

Marley just chuckled, then said, "Earth is full of conflicting circumstances. The truth and lies we live determine our reality, yet only love frees one from the influence of the others."

"That sounds like a gravestone saying. Jacob, do you actually think people need to be freed from the influence of truth?"

"Both truth and lies are abstract... like an opinion, they hold us strong, yet both blur reality."

"What is reality if it is not either truth or lie?"

"Reality is only experiences, and they are also abstract."

"Wait on that one, Jacob. Truth carries the facts, so..."

"And yet a good liar always weaves facts into their deceptive tales as well. Three lies and a truth often carries the mind to a point of — realism."

"I think you have lost your wits about this one."

"Half-witted or not, love, not truth, is the binding element of Acceptance," insisted Marley.

"Is love possible within a falsehood?"

"Absolutely. Have you ever heard of the 'white lie', one where sparing another's feelings warrants a deception?"

"Everyone knows those are just pleasantries."

"That does not take away from the deceit."

"It feels like humanity is constantly walking in quicksand, condemned no matter what."

"Saved, no matter what; that is the reality. For it is not quicksand, but excessive pride that slows Mogrification," corrected Marley.

"Except for those at the Farewell Platform."

"And they made that choice, Ebenezer."

"Choices without options are not choices."

Marley nodded his head in agreement. As they moved beyond the women-haters, Scrooge thought about the mother who gave him life, but no nurturing — and then the sister, Fanny, who gave him nurturing, but was also taken from life, both remembrances of women who began his existence. Throughout a lifetime, the hardship of their passing developed into a personal strength for Scrooge. He always felt their invisible companionship, their support, but now it only left him sad, burdened by the loss of them.

As much as the Abyss above the Dens wreaked of Acceptance, the actual Dens played out in vicious destructions. The next cave was less hectic, for it contained only two spirits, but those two... played in wicked cruelty. And yet, that was not the shock of the kitchen table scene. The terror of watching two James Maxeys, one cowering while the other attacked, halted Scrooge.

James slammed his fist on the table, then yelled into the face of James, "You think you are a bit faker? Give me the coin!" The cowering James slowly placed the counterfeit coin upon the table, to which the aggressive James snatched the coin up, then whispered into the prey's ear, "If you ever again go bug hunting without my approval, I will end you." Looking at the coin, he added, "This coin is not worth its metal." Tossing it back to the table, the wicked one retreated, but just for an instant.

The next moment cleared way for a repeat, but this time the two James' reversed roles. The submissive James turned into the aggressor, while the previously belligerent James prepared to be attacked.

Scrooge stared at Marley; as a slight grin developed on his friend's face, he asked, "What mayhem will their action cure?"

"Lack of empathy." Scrooge scratched the top of his head as Marley explained, "There is no fear greater than the fear we can create within ourselves."

Scrooge did not understand the connection. "So they want the greatest of terrors?"

"Emotion always provides the perfect potential for action."

"Again — what is the benefit of ultimate self-terror?"

"To learn the role of the victim." Marley could tell he was once again falling short in his explanation, so he refocused his answer. "What you see here is an actual event of anger that James placed upon someone in his control. Often the original victim is replaced by another representation of the angry spirit."

"Why?"

"Empathy. James, the victim, knows exactly what is in the mind of James, the oppressor... and because each knows the other, what is slamming down upon that table is not about coins or nighttime thievery."

"Are his thoughts more like what he did to Noah?"

"Exactly. Right now that timid James is in fear for his life."

"Does this chain of events ever end?"

"Yes, of course, but only when both Jameses agree that neither wants to be the victim or assailant."

"That seems..." Scrooge stumbled to find the thought, but then just said, "weak."

The two traveled past dozens of caves before they finally stood in front of Noah's. Drenched in blood, Noah never hesitated in the task of slaughter to acknowledge the intruders in his cave. From one James Maxey to the next, he slammed the villain's head into the same Newgate bars that had ended his own being. Then, as with him, Noah forced a wrist onto a prisoner-made barb, causing blood to spurt beyond the confinements of the cave. As one Maxey moaned to death another appeared, to which Noah repeated the murdering. Within a breath of time, dangling from the bars of the enclosure were nearly a dozen dying Maxeys. Blood was the color of the cavern.

Shattered, Marley collapsed. Lying at Scrooge's feet, every chain he had ever carried returned. "It's the Curse," he mumbled.

"Jacob, your predicament..." Scrooge's voice withered as he watched Marley settle into his bindings.

As each quieted within their personal crisis, Marley's chest erupted. Every contained Fire Twirler exploded, resulting in his freedom from the bondage. Rising to his feet, he directed to Scrooge, "Stand back Alito's Curse is without mercy."

"You promised Teint you would use the Fire Twirlers to save me."

"I am helping you. Can you leave the Den without me?" Marley waited but a moment before he again ordered, "Now stay back — Noah will be unpredictable."

"Can Noah be made whole?"

"The Curse is the hardship that binds many Condemned Innocents to their injustice. Noah struggles to free himself from the court's shame."

"So Noah's focus is not on wanting to murder James Maxey?"

"Oh, he wants to kill him, but the driving force is the governmental abuse that I set upon him."

"So why are you not the one being slain?"

"He knows nothing of my involvement. Yet it may not help him anyway, for it is the control from the kingdom that shackled Noah. Alito's Curse is the heavy hand of injustice. Whereas my treason against him constricts me, not him."

"So how do we end the heavy hand? Do we have to confront Alito?"

"He does dwell within the Crater, and the Curse within Transmogrify is attached to his confinement there. However, none have cast a view upon Alito for nearly two centuries."

"Why?"

"He has administered justice upon himself."

"Self-justice? That is mysterious. I thought all spirits either become Acceptance or perish upon Instant Transmogrification."

"Alito died after visiting his best friend, Matthew Hale, on a Christmas day in the late 1600s. His Entanglement released two self-created spirits that went to the Crater. They were both so cantankerous, neither would allow the other to climb to the ledge where Coss are formed."

"How could any person have two spirits in the same Mog?"

"Arrogance. Alito was so cheeky he created two different rationalizations and two methods of harming the blameless, while claiming the authority of the Infinite Consciousness's virtue." Then to emphasize the barrister's nastiness, Marley finished with, "Even children were not safe from his vicious wrath."

"So he now struggles within the Crater?"

"Each of his spirits has currently ensnared the other at the bottom of the Lake Of Flames."

"Will one ever release the other?"

Marley answered with a question. "Does infinity have a time restraint?"

"If there is no time in Transmogrify, then there is no infinity."

"You are learning, Ebenezer, but leave it be. These issues are too complicated... and we have a task."

"You're telling me to leave it... makes me want to just jump on top of it."

"Yes, that is good bait for a fish like yourself," Marley quipped.

"So what do we do to help Noah?"

"Tell him the truth." Marley stared at Scrooge, then admitted, "I wish you could do this for me, but he has to hear my truth... from me."

"Will that cure Alito's Curse?"

"The Curse binds him now, but the truth does light the path toward freedom. We need to help Noah break through his trance. Only then will he be able to view the light of the path."

"Is the truth that powerful?"

"Only if it is vacant of lying facts."

Marley approached Noah, but no recognition from his sibling appeared. Instead, Noah raised his eyes to the pair standing before him — then hissed blood upon them.

Stave Nine

Stressful Deliverance

RECOILING, SCROOGE TRIPPED backwards while Noah blew blood through Marley's ghostly form. Crying out in terror, Marley pleaded, "I love you."

Noah just hissed another deluge of gore.

"I still love you," insisted Marley.

But again, Noah's shadowy blood blew through Marley.

Spread flat on his back, Scrooge whispered, "Lying facts."

Whirling to face his friend, Marley insisted, "I am telling the truth."

"Maybe in your head — speak with your heart, Jacob."

"Bloody, I am not going to speak at all." With that, Marley pushed Maxey from his brother's grip, then placed his own arm into Noah's hand. Before anybody could change the situation, Noah dragged his brother's wrist across the barb. As the red fluid sprayed the area, Marley reached across several fence pickets, then dragged his other wrist across a second barb. Splayed across the space of multiple bars, Marley dangled from his ruined wrists. Noah stepped back.

"With your heart," advised Scrooge.

"I did this to you." Noah just stared at the brother he no longer recognized. With his chin resting upon his chest, Marley cried out, "I stole the money, Noah — I did this to you!"

Confused Noah just asked, "Money?"

"Pressey and Barclay's shop... Christmas Eve. I betrayed you, Noah."

Vacant of caution, Noah thrust his arm into his brother's chest, grabbed the chain imprisoning his heart, then ferociously yanked it free of the ghost. Instantly

Marley dissipated. Holding the chain high, while shrieking like an animal, Noah, with intention, threw it at Scrooge. Barely dodging the iron, Scrooge watched as it landed directly behind him. Startled, he jumped from the twitching metal. Marley was nowhere to be found.

"Bloody humbug!" Looking in every direction, panic beset Scrooge, for Marley appeared to have disappeared. "Jacob, do not abandon me!"

"Calm your storm, Ebenezer," Marley said with his hand inside his chest. "Let me adjust this burden." Moving next to Scrooge, he added, "Frightful experience that was."

"It's not going well, is it?"

"So much for speaking my heart," groaned Marley.

"Would you want some new advice?"

"Your last was less than helpful, but I have no solutions. So of course, Ebenezer, how would you calm Noah?"

"I would allow the events from the death to dictate the telling of your truth."

"The events? Noah lived the events, Ebenezer. Why must I go through that door again?"

"Because Noah is stuck within the threshold of that event door. You need to pull him through it. He needs your grasp — your understanding. But he will only absorb it if it's spoken in his mindset."

"And if I can not find the words that fit his 'mindset', then...?"

"The key to reaching your brother is to enter his approach, for he is rooted there. Only then can Noah hear your facts, Jacob. Only then will he begin to trust you."

"And do you know if this 'new' advice is good advice?"

"Ever the doubter, and your remedy, Jacob, is...? "

After pondering the idea, the ghost admitted, "I fathom your suggestion will not hurt by way of an attempt, so..." then without even a moment's passage, Marley dangled upon the hooks facing Noah. While his wrists sprayed a mist of freakish blood throughout the Den, Marley lifted his chin from his chest, then bellowed, "The carnage around your lifeless body, coupled with Flora's wails..." as Marley searched for words, Noah grabbed him by the throat.

Casting a savage glance toward Scrooge, Noah quickly focused upon Marley. Having his younger brother in his grip, Noah breathed into Jacob's face, "I heard you caused that."

"It was the worst mistake of my life."

"NO!" Noah screamed, while tightening his grip on his brother's neck, "It was the worst mistake of MY life!"

"I crushed your honor, Noah — in every way."

"You crushed ME!" screamed Noah while flinging his head backward, then sideways, and finally thrusting it deep against his brother's face. Snarling, he growled, "Honor, honor is the privilege of the aristocrats. I struggle for justice."

"Justice is for the living, Noah. What you do here is merely protest your injustice. There are no courts, barristers, or even accused here — except yourself."

Noah shoved Marley deep into the bars, then grabbed his brother's heart chain. Yanking it backward he hooked the iron to a third barb securing his brother in place against the fence.

Marley relaxed into his brother's fury. As he dangled off the ground, he lifted his eyes to meet Noah's, then, staring into his brother's blaze of anger, he calmly stated, "There is no change another can do to make you whole again."

Noah released his grip on Marley's neck, roared with wrath, then told his truth. "You have always been worthless, Jacob."

"You were everyone's victim, Noah."

"But mostly yours."

"Yes, yes, I destroyed you, yet it is you that must save yourself."

"Words, you speak words without meaning."

"Then hear these words, Noah. You deserve release from this horror, but you cling to it."

"I adhere to the power within my existence."

"And yet this Den has caused you to forget your Task Of Outreach. What was that?"

Noah paused to search his memory, then said, "I never made one."

"No, you are here... so you made one. Remember it?"

"I want revenge!"

"Then kill me into infinity, yet justice will still only be an illusion for you." Marley waited for his brother's thought, but when none was offered, he emphasized, "You must release your victimizers. Not for their benefit, but because you deserve deliverance from their actions."

"I deserve revenge!"

"Indeed. The greatest revenge I can offer you is to request Instant Transmogrification. You may gain some satisfaction by my elimination, yet justice will still not be owned by you through such an action."

Noah clapped his hand over Marley's mouth. "Say another thought, and I will steal your heart chain from you. Then you will be lost in an oblivion that Instant Transmogrification can never save you from."

Terrified, Marley remained as still as what he was... dead, while Noah's eyes glared through the fright of his brother's face. Growing repulsed by the reflection of caring that stared back, Noah became infuriated. As he aggressively pressed his hand over his brother's mouth, Marley responded by kissing the seizing palm. Without any delay, Noah ripped the lips from Marley's face. Perplexed, he backed

away with the quivering mass of ghostly flesh evaporating from his hand. Marley, for his part, remained stoic.

As one tear simultaneously dropped from each brother's cheek, Noah lunged back at Marley. "Why did you do this to me?"

"I needed the money to become Ebenezer's partner," he said with his head pointing toward Scrooge.

Noah moved toward Scrooge. "You took the money?"

"I did not know it was yours." Backing away from Noah, Scrooge felt the urge to escape, but to where?

"So it is you that did this," Noah said descending upon Scrooge. Before Scrooge could speak to his defense, Noah attacked him. Grabbing him by the throat, he flung Scrooge across the room with muscles generally absent of a spirit. Hitting the Den's wall, Scrooge slowly sank to the ground. Before he could come to a sitting position, Noah was upon him again — this time with a desire to cause pain.

"Why are you here? You do not deserve life." With that he lifted Scrooge by the neck off the ground. Scrooge tightened every muscle as he struggled for freedom. With ferocity, Noah pressed Scrooge's nape flat against the wall, which caused him to lose consciousness. As Scrooge went limp, Noah just pushed harder.

Dangling from the fence, Marley attempted to free himself. Ripping each wrist from its hook, he flapped back and forth as the hook binding his chain refused to bend. "Noah, stop..."

Within the next moment, as if lightning had struck the Den, Apurto stood between Noah and Scrooge. Between his jaws swung Noah's forearm, fingers pumping in and out with the intention of seizing anything it could with rage. Noah stared at the location of his now missing arm. The shock of it stunned the ghost into an emotional collapse. As he closed his eyes, then began to crumble downward, Marley cried out, "Stay with me, Noah," and then to Apurto he instructed, "Do not swallow my brother's arm!"

Noah opened his eyes, and then instantly gave chase to Apurto. "Give it back, you monster." Running mere inches behind the animal, Noah grabbed at, but missed, the dodging creature.

As Noah continued to chase Apurto, Marley called to Scrooge, "You still with me, Ebenezer?"

Scrooge steadied himself, then replied, "Well enough, considering the force of the attack."

"Get me off this hook before Noah returns."

Taking a few steps forward, Scrooge stood in front of his dangling friend. As Scrooge pondered the method of Marley's release, Apurto finally dropped Noah's arm. At first Scrooge did what any person would do to free a human... just lift him up and over the fence's barb. However, Marley was not a human. For when Scrooge grabbed Marley's arm, his hands passed right through the spirit. "Grab the chain," instructed Marley.

"You mean put my hand inside of your chest?"

"Ebenezer, I have been inside of your entire body. Just reach in, quick, before Noah returns."

As Scrooge reluctantly gripped the semi-solid ring attached to Marley's heart, Noah seized the human's shoulder, and then within the next moment all three shifted. Marley dropped from his bondage, as Scrooge pulled free of the menacing grasp, and Noah just stood bewildered... wondering who to harm.

Warily, Marley wrapped himself around Noah. With torsos intertwined, Noah's anger lessened. Comforted in his brother's calming, Marley clung fast to the sensation of their shared space. Absorbing the intensity within their embrace, Marley whispered into Noah's ear, "Tell me your Task Of Outreach."

Noah tensed the mass of his spirit, pulled away from his brother's hold, then said, "Flora... only Flora."

"That is a big enough Task." Marley paused, then asked, "Are you ready to work that Task, or would you rather kill me again?"

"You deserve it," Noah smirked.

"I did earn it," agreed Marley. "However, Flora needs us."

"I do not need — you." Noah turned toward Scrooge, then said, "I choose Ebenezer, but you, baby brother, I will never trust."

"I will then follow behind you two."

"No, you will walk in front of us."

The mutual agreement overtook the two with silence until Scrooge asked, "So how do we leave this Den?"

"We do not leave it; it leaves us."

Scrooge rumpled his forehead trying to figure out what that meant. At first came the thought that they were in a dream. He was wondering whether waking was an option when Marley stretched his arms to a length that would encircle the three of them. As Marley's arms bundled the trio into one being, the Den began to grow dark, and together they were lifted from the ground. The rising movement did not give the sensation of floating, but instead the awareness of falling. Upward they fell at a speed increasing beyond gravity's effect.

With a growing blackness darker than that at the Point, Scrooge began to tremble. As he twitched with terror, Noah whispered to him, "Your fear is hurting me."

"Ebenezer, you do not need to fear anything in Transmogrify. Apurto has proven that," explained Marley.

"Apurto..." murmured Scrooge, "yes..." With that understanding he cautiously relaxed.

Furiously falling upward, the tether of Marley's arms loosened as the three began to spin. Tighter and tighter, they whirled within their shrinking space. Like a maelstrom, the circular force started to twist the trio. Scrooge moaned as his form rotated around itself more than survival could permit. While swirling, Marley whispered into Noah's ear, "There isn't enough space for the three of us." Noah ignored his brother with a grunt, so Marley said, "We have to both move into Scrooge."

"Do we? Why?"

"Because I want to keep him alive. Will you help, or do you hate me so much you will allow Ebenezer to perish?"

Without another moment Noah pushed deep into Scrooge, leaving a gap where his brother's arms had previously embraced the three into one. Marley followed Noah into Scrooge's body.

As the ghosts disappeared into Scrooge, the human form continued its

contortions. While feet and head rotated at different speeds, Scrooge screamed in pain as he passed out from the stress. As the three spun at the speed of a vortex, both Marley and Noah tried to control Scrooge's limp body. Their spiraling bore a hole in the Road through which they entered. Scrooge, now deformed, collapsed.

Without even touching him, Noah knew Scrooge was dead. Marley, fearing the truth, did everything he could to shake his friend back to life, yet he had no power.

Scrooge lay twisted upon the Road with blood trickling from his ears, nose and mouth. His open eyes glared without focus upon his friends. As Marley pulled Scrooge into his lap, he succumbed to his failure with sobs of grief.

Rocking as he wept, Marley barely noticed Apurto's breath upon his neck. Quietly, the beast growled, "Yhaah-ae. Yhaah-aee."

Anxiety exploded from Marley as he grabbed the mangled corpse of his friend. "No! Never! I will not allow you to vanquish, Ebenezer!"

"Yah-ah-ah! Yah-ah-ah-ee!" Apurto roared, as he pushed through Marley, then settled upon Scrooge's crushed flesh.

Marley pounced upon Apurto. "I said NEVER!"

As the two struggled for control of the dead human, Noah lost focus, then began to walk toward the Pool Of Broken Spirits. Disoriented, Marley called to Noah, "We have to save..." The pause in the combat gave Apurto the concentrated strength to shove Marley from Scrooge.

While Marley rolled from the conflict, Noah aimlessly walked the Road as Apurto stood on all fours over Scrooge. Arching his back, Apurto began to heave his stomach in and out. The suction within his gut forced bile into his throat.

Without warning, Apurto spewed onto Scrooge the murky Acceptance created from consumed Crater skulls. The liquid flowed into Scrooge's facial openings. As joyous musical tones drifted above the evaporating Acceptance, Scrooge began to jerk, and then the excruciations commenced.

Torturous screams shrieked throughout Transmogrify. With each flicker of motion, Scrooge voiced an unbearable agony. "Let it be," he gasped between howls. Apurto continued to vomit Acceptance upon Scrooge as he began to push the creature from him. "This pain! Beast, leave me!"

Apurto stopped his eruptions of Acceptance. While Scrooge wiggled to be released from the animal, Apurto collapsed. Pinned beneath the brute, Scrooge's only available movement was that of his deafening panic.

While Noah continued to wander the Road, Jacob watched the two wrapped in survival. Slowly, each of Apurto's stripes developed a glow brighter than light. The smallest stripes on both his shoulders and tail began the illumination. Each adjoining stripe thereafter continued to add to the radiance. Within an instant, Apurto was a mass of bright warmth. This quieted Scrooge, which helped him to relax into the healing.

At first the energy was forced upon Scrooge, but once recognized for what it was, Scrooge began to pull the healing from Apurto. As the drain of energy finished reviving Scrooge, Apurto weakened. While Scrooge began to rise to his feet, he and Marley watched as Apurto's body began to display the same twists and contortions that had ended Scrooge.

Leaning over his deceased rescuer, Scrooge asked, "Why did he do this?"

"I know not the mind of an animal, Ebenezer, but he is... was the caretaker."

"How do we save him?"

Before the question could be solved, a deafening clap resounded throughout Transmogrify. And then, a thunderous command from Teint was voiced, "Apurto, here, now." The force within the directive rang so loud that trees within the Fields Of Destructive Compulsions began to throw off their spikes. As the tree's spears flew across the Road, both Marley and Scrooge attempted to dodge their danger, while Noah appeared to be unaware of everything.

Dozens of thorns shot into them all. Marley knew it was coming, so only worked to protect Scrooge, whereas Noah just groaned when each spike flew through him. Scrooge was assaulted by three weapons of the tree, but none of them harmed him. Instead they passed through as if he, too, were made of... spirit.

"Why are you not bloody?" asked Marley as he inspected each entrance and exit hole the spikes made. Out of each exit hole dripped one drop of blood. Marley stepped back from Scrooge, eyed him up and down, then declared, "You are different now."

"I feel the same."

"Yet your skin is no longer a fleshy color. But... but... it shines of a purplish hue."

"Shines?"

"I guess it is more of a lavender color."

"My coloring probably does not matter, but Apurto's life, it does." As the two turned to where the corpse should be lying on the Road, nothing remained. "Where did he go?"

"With Teint? I don't know, Ebenezer. I am only glad he saved you."

"No, I am not happy with this exchange, Jacob."

"But maybe he is."

"Could I have been meant to be erased from all knowledge while here?"

"Well, you are not out of here yet, and Apurto does not appear to be available to you in the future. So, maybe you are meant for total destruction. However, I'm not going to let it happen to you, Ebenezer."

"What is your say in this, Jacob?"

Marley thought about the question, then answered, "I have none, but I am determined to be good to my word."

"Then let's go find out what is wrong with Noah."

As they walked, silence seized their thoughts. Scrooge opened his mouth to speak, but the fog in his mind quieted his tongue. Marley, for his part, surrendered to a sense of uneasiness. Although the Road through the Fields Of Destructive Compulsions appeared to be so vast, almost to the point of near endlessness, Marley was able to instantly locate Noah.

As they approached him, Scrooge noticed an oddity. "Why is he not moving?"

"It appears Noah is moving like the minute hand of a clock, but he still does stir," assured Marley.

As they drew closer to the motionless Noah, Marley thundered, "This is that dratted Alito's Curse again."

"I thought we got Noah beyond that in the Den."

"We did free his brain's mind, but the heart's mind... its affliction still lingers."

"More than one mind?"

"In truth, the heart's thoughts reveal more to the brain than does the brain ever convey to the heart." Pausing, so to gain the emphasis needed for what he must next ask of Scrooge, Marley finally said, "I can not bring Noah back by myself. This curse is beyond my powers, but together... us together... we can reconnect his mind's system."

"So at last you need me?"

"Ebenezer, you have no idea how valuable you are. Noah just needs you to give him a bit more of your worth."

"If I am able."

With concern, they approached the near-motionless Noah. The next action would either free him, or send him back to the Den. "I need you, Ebenezer, to flow Acceptance into the back of Noah while I bring him into our moment."

"Acceptance? Am I dead?"

"You do seem changed, but no, you still live, Ebenezer."

"How can I then deliver Acceptance to Noah?"

"Death and Acceptance are not connected by way of the Transmogrification process. Acceptance is created from the finest human qualities."

Scrooge shook his head from side to side and mumbled, "Apurto...," as he remembered having just been drenched in Apurto's vomited Acceptance.

Sensing his friend's confusion, Marley clarified, "Apurto's Acceptance was not made up of liquified skulls. His spray of Acceptance was compressed healing. It seems his body was able to complete the purification. I guess that is good news for those in the Crater, but only if they have not already asked for Instant Transmogrification."

"I have no such bodily powers of transforming my stomach contents into... healing? So how can I create Acceptance?"

"Ebenezer, every being possesses the ability for emotional awakening. It is the creator's gift, and humanity's obligation."

"Obligation?"

"In the eyes of the Infinite Consciousness, awakening love through sacred experiences, it is our only requirement." Marley paused, stared into Scrooge's eyes, then asked, "Who do you love most, Ebenezer?"

"Nobody."

"Of course you love. The quality reeks within your personality."

"Quite truthfully, Jacob, I don't love others."

"This is mysterious to me, Ebenezer. Explain your good deeds without love."

"I loved money. Wealth was my worth. However, after your first Christmas Eve visit, I was thrilled to just be alive."

"So it is gratitude in your spirit, not love. Perfect!"

"Perfect?"

"Love is the easiest quality for people to activate, because it is passed from being to being. However, gratitude is the quality, or energy force, that passes directly from a person to the Infinite Consciousness."

"This actually makes sense to me, Jacob."

"Because of this quality, gratitude has a power greater than that of love, but it is not as formidable as is joy." Smiling at Scrooge, Marley quipped, "My friend, it appears you have almost made it into your second childhood."

Scrooge wanted to grin, but the concept of a 'second childhood' created a reflexive frown. "I'm having a difficult time understanding how a childlike power is going to save Noah."

"Don't take on that burden, Ebenezer. Just be grateful there is a way."

"It seems that is what I have become good at... being grateful."

"I need you to stand behind Noah." As Scrooge did as instructed, Marley continued. "Put your left hand over your own heart, and then extend the right arm out, so that it nearly touches Noah's back."

Scrooge did as instructed, then Marley said, "Close your eyes, Ebenezer. Lower your head. Now fill your mind with the remembrance of what it felt like to be given a second chance at life. Caress, then amplify, that wonder. Once it can not be stopped, allow the charge to flow."

As Scrooge transferred the sensation of his thoughts to his chest, a shiver of exhilaration took control. With his eyes closed, he felt a surge of warmth within his palm. While the energy needed to strengthen Noah began to gush toward the ghost's back, Jacob set himself in front of his brother. Abruptly he transformed into a woman as tall, yet more elegant, as was either of the Marley brothers.

"Your seraphic triumph has arrived, Noah."

Noah heard the declaration yet made no acknowledgment of the thought. Scrooge, through closed eyes, sensed the warmth of his mental concentration flowing from his hand into Noah. Filling the ghost's beating organ with gratitude, it soon began to glow. Yet instead of illuminating the entire thinking structure, the energy began to rebound back into Scrooge's palm.

"Push harder, Ebenezer," demanded the woman facing Noah. "The heart is full of radiance, yet..." The unmanly one stepped closer to Noah, placed their right hand upon the center of the motionless chest, then positioned the left hand upon the top of Noah's head. Closing her eyes, the woman pulled the left hand upward. Light exploded into Noah's mind, illuminating the whole of his substance. However, he made no movement to realize his body's change.

"You are my first born."

With this statement, Noah raised his head, then whispered, "Mum?"

"Open your eyes, my son." Noah obeyed in silence as the matriarch continued. "You have suffered, you still suffer... yet, your seraphic triumph has arrived."

"Sera... what?" asked Noah.

"The ability to become your sacred legacy."

"I want justice," bellowed Noah.

"There are no magistrates here." As Scrooge's power freely flowed into the stilled spirit, the mother-imitator continued to explain. "All who travel the Road gain restoration. Even Alito's duo spirit wallowing at the bottom of the Crater will eventually transform. He may never become Acceptance, but his curse will dissipate once he is able to escape his self-entrapment." Pausing to add emphasis, she said, "Unfortunately there always seems to be a new injustice to take its place."

All Noah heard from the spirit before him was the word, "No." He lowered his head and began to shake. As tears of grief and confusion started to surge, both Marley, as the mother-spirit, and Scrooge pulled their own emotions inward. Scrooge, not wanting to break his heart connection with Noah, resisted the temptation to clear the collected moisture from his eyes.

The mother tried to explain again, "When nature harms a person, can the law restore them? Does the bite from an animal require the court's judgment? No, of course not. It is only the human-to-human injury that screams for 'justice'. Lift up your head, Noah, for the power of your remake is within."

Noah began to bawl. While his dry tears started to drop, the sounds of his wailing echoed throughout the Road.

Again the mother-spirit stepped next to Noah, wrapped her arms around him, kissed him on the lips, then encouraged, "Yes, weep away your self-doubt, my son."

As the two clung to their embrace the energy of Scrooge's gratitude finally broke through Noah's despair. Noah, while still confused, returned Marley's kiss. Shared tears dropped between them, and then, Jacob lost control of the mother image. Just as Jacob changed back, Noah realized the deception, then pushed his brother away. "You are not mum. Your fraud is upon me again."

An awkward silence developed between the three when Scrooge finally realized the worth of his understanding about the brother's struggle. Within the strength of his new awareness, he calmly said, "No, Noah, Jacob is pure in heart for your redemption."

With fury, Noah spun around to confront Scrooge, but once he felt the mildness within Scrooge's demeanor, he only replied, "I still hurt."

Now confident as to why Marley was in need of him, Scrooge spoke his wisdom. "And you may always, but it will lessen once you integrate the strength of the experience into your existence."

"What strength is that, Ebenezer?"

Both Noah and Jacob were curious to know Scrooge's mind. Yet, Scrooge, now realizing his worth within Transmogrify, still struggled to find the wisest words. "You have already placed a boundary upon Jacob that will empower you, Noah."

"I know of no boundary," insisted Noah.

"Yet I know the boundary," exclaimed Marley. "Noah, you have demanded that I walk in front of you on the Road. I am not sure how that will reinforce you, but it must."

"I need my traitor visible."

"Yes, it strengthens your security to demand that of Jacob. But that is only one lesson you need to merge into your spirit," said Scrooge.

"What are the others?"

"I am unsure of what you need, Noah, but reflection will help to bring you harmony."

"All I want to reflect upon is Flora."

"That is my Task Of Outreach as well," said Marley.

"Then stay at least a furlong in front of us, Jacob."

"That will cause Ebenezer to lose his ability to stand up."

Noah focused upon his brother, then slowly ordered, "I will be his spirit equalizer. Ebenezer and I will stay here as you establish the required distance between us. Now be on your way, cowardly brother."

Marley looked back several times as he moved one furlong, and then two furlongs ahead of his brother. Once the distance that Noah needed was achieved he said to Scrooge, "Now I want you to walk in front of me too."

"Have I harmed you?"

"Have you?" asked Noah, but before Scrooge could reply, he added, "No, I just want to figure out at what distance you become vulnerable."

"Oh, that's easy," said Scrooge as he walked to a location, stopped to look back at Noah, then took one further step. Scrooge began to weaken with his knees bending. Faltering, his legs wobbled, but instead of toppling him they shifted until control was regained. Bewildered, Scrooge took three more steps away from Noah, and when he remained upright, asked, "Are you sure I still live?"

"Well, you haven't died."

"Comforting, Noah, comforting."

The two strangers, connected by a rogue, began to walk toward the Pool Of Broken Spirits. Neither knew how to initiate the conversation both desired. Walking in silence, the pair blurted in concurrence, "Have you recovered?" Smiling, then laughing, each replied, "Maybe." This word in unison brought tears to their guffaw.

After settling his laughter, Scrooge said, "I am well enough to continue."

"Me... I still struggle with a memory," admitted Noah. Sighing, he proceeded to explain. "When I was in my Chamber, at the Plain Of Violence, the same event from my childhood repeated itself hundreds of times. I could never absolve it, but I did eventually absorb it."

"Was it some wickedness that befell you?"

"No, far from it. It was just an event that sparked a thought." Pausing, so to develop clarification, Noah finally confessed, "You are going to think this foolish, but when walking in a field I stepped right on top of a huge ant hill."

Without wanting to stifle the conversation, Scrooge said, "I don't find that to be unique. I have probably crushed a thousand ants without even knowing I did it."

"That is part of the point. All creatures harm without knowing it. What is food if not death to something?"

"Um... yeah... of course. So why did dead ants cause you such contemplation?"

"It was the destiny, the casual fate of the ants being killed and scattered from outside their existence."

"Is that how you view your own demise?"

"Yes... and no. Events are always caused but are not always malicious. That is what I had to figure out in the Chamber."

"So you do not think what Jacob did to you was hateful?"

"He was merely an ant running from the edge of the law's shoe. I on the other hand was directly under the shoe."

"Yes, but Jacob brought the shoe to the ant hill."

"However, it was the shoe that stepped upon me, not Jacob. My brother has guilt, but not for my actual death."

"So eventually you will forgive him?"

"I already have," pausing to emphasize his decision, Noah said, "but, I will never trust him again."

"I don't know if I trust him either."

"And yet you are here..."

Not knowing how to defend his situation, Scrooge quipped, "I assume stranger things have happened."

"Really... when?"

The question brought a temporary end to the conversation as Scrooge could not think of an answer. Together the pair watched Marley approach the Pool. As the metal poles protruding from the Pool continuously sparked, multiples of spirits awakened from their sleep. Marley began to float over the Pool. He took extra care to avoid the rising spirits, sparking poles, and the surface of the tear-filled Pool.

"Noah, I've been thinking about your story of stepping on the ants, and I am confused about something," said Scrooge.

Noah looked upon Scrooge, then replied, "Well, we can't have that. Transmogrify is all about gaining personal clarification. So, tell me your head-scratcher, Ebenezer."

"I do not want to belittle your experience but, I can not understand why you would relive it over and over." Scrooge paused, breathed deeply, then said, "I mean things that play over and over in my memory are dramatic... if not outright traumatic."

"Yes, that is true."

"So how was stepping on ants traumatic? I mean, were you barefoot, or did they swarm you?"

"No." Noah did not want to explain the aftermath, for it seemed to linger within him as shame.

Scrooge, sensing a tension, gently placed his hand upon Noah's ethereal forearm, then said, "My curiosity has no honor. Forgive me for asking."

"Curiosity has no honor?" Noah paused, then said, "No, Ebenezer, only things that harm are without honor. Your curiosity has wisdom." He stopped his forward motion, lowered his head, then confessed, "I rampaged! That is when my spirit of anger was created." Noah began to shake with hard jerks. "I turned... that ant hill... into a... graveyard. I was furi...ous..."

"Noah, Noah! Stop! Do not continue your torment."

Noah continued trembling as he attempted to calm Scrooge with his disjointed words. "This has been re...solved... yet hind...sight melts more i...i...ce." This comment baffled Scrooge into silence, for the metaphor was peculiar. While the two continued moving in intervals, Noah, after several steps, finally announced, "My tension is

relaxing." Pausing to gain emotional strength, he confessed, "My spirit of anger manifested after that action of ant-rage. However, thoughts about animals developed earlier within me."

"Jacob told me about your cat killing the snake."

"It was that snake's death that made me think, and think, and think."

"Jacob said it brought your own mortality into view for you."

Noah just laughed as he corrected the idea. "Jacob would think that. He loves animals but... I don't." Watching his feet as they walked the Road, he disclosed, "The death of that snake made me realize how insignificant all animals are, even humans."

"Humans? Do you now view that as an untruthful conclusion?"

"I would if it was, Ebenezer. But no, I had the blessings from another human, my wife, that helped me. However, I never released the idea that all life is unimportant."

"Bit of a paradox, isn't that?"

"Paradoxes are part of the human condition. I think humans are just here to see if we can handle them... or maybe to see 'how' we handle them."

"Surely you jest about that?"

"Only in the sense that I have no answers for any of the social puzzles." Noah paused, then said, "I do know that Flora's spirit of kindness softened my spirit of anger." Noah shook his head back and forth, then concluded, "However, my malicious spirit exploded with madness after death."

Scrooge scratched the back of his head, then asked, "Do people take on both positive and negative spirits?"

"Of course, but there are few individuals that die with only positive spirits." Noah looked out over the approaching Pool Of Broken Spirits and said, "All within Transmogrify, but especially those that sleep within the Pool, possess spirits of worth."

"How do positive spirits Mogrify? Do they even enter Transmogrify?"

"I have never viewed an already purified spirit within Transmogrify. To my knowledge none travel anywhere here."

Together their focus turned toward Marley, who was busying himself at dodging the spirits rising from the Pool. Having gained his composure, Noah called across the Pool, "Jacob, have you found Flora?"

Marley called back, yet from across the Road, within the Dam Of Disconnected Parts, sounds of clashing limbs muffled his brother's words. Noah gestured his brother to the Pool's edge. "Have you found Flora?"

"She sleeps deeply."

"What do you mean?" asked Noah.

"Yes." Settling back onto the Road, Marley completed Noah's thought. "Coss Acceptance has encased her."

"We have to save her. Quick, Jacob, we need to pull her to shore."

"The encasement has already grown too large. I can not move her by myself."

"How can I help you?" asked Scrooge. "With my fleshiness, I am probably the strongest among us."

"Without a doubt your brawn will be needed. However, the dangers of the Pool's mechanics will restrict all of our actions." Then, without even taking a breath, Marley added, "And I know the Pool looks shallow, but don't think about wading out to her."

"It does seem like an option. I'm fairly certain I can maneuver around those that sleep."

Pointing to the surface of the Pool, Marley warned, "If you get even one drop of the Pool's liquid on your skin, it will break your heart, Ebenezer. And I am not even going to tell you about the damage those poles can cause while standing in the Pool."

The constant spray of sparks lit up the Pool. While the three stood at the edge, explosive lightning bolts cracked in rhythm to the clashing limbs from the Dam. As sounds combined around them, it created an echo chamber of discordance.

Scrooge asked, "Is there something we can float on?"

"Well, Noah and I can just float," said Marley. "But even combined, our mass has little strength. Yet this is dire. We need to retrieve Flora before there is another Coss release, which will cage her more deeply to her grief."

"I thought Coss Acceptance revives the sleeping."

"Yes, but only for those that have spirits within them that need Mogrification."

"I'm not understanding this."

"This is the rarest of happenings, Ebenezer. For it requires the purest heart which has developed only spirits of worth. How unique is that on Earth?" Marley did not wait for a response before he added, "Often individuals live nearly angelic lives, yet they still need Mogrification. Mum's and dad's spirits usually linger, and the parents' energy-forces are the hardest to alter during life."

"I'm still not understanding why Flora is in such a state."

"She did only one thing against the Infinite Consciousness... she ended her own life, and couple that with the life inside of her..." Marley lowered his head, for he knew it was he that created the path to Flora's demise. "Flora had so much charity toward the sick. She created a neighborhood Wise Woman organization. She was gifted in that way herself, but she brought into existence what was so overlooked." Marley lifted his head, pointed to Flora's encased form within the Pool and confessed, "If I hadn't caused this, Flora would have immediately gone to the Infinite Consciousness after death. Her least spirit was one of courage, while the greatest spirit radiated peace." Crying out, Marley exclaimed, "But I shattered that peace!"

Baffled, Scrooge calmly asked, "So why hasn't Coss Acceptance awakened her?"

"It only compounds the grief of her death. She is so entombed that even Coss Acceptance can not calm her broken spirit. Every element of her death has her trapped within a memory loop. The cracking of the ice, the freezing water of the Thames, and the kicking within the womb refuses to release her."

Without warning, a swoop of Coss overtook the Pool. Sparks from the metal poles created a suction which could only be overcome by the release of Acceptance. As the Coss vomited, they lifted away from the Pool. Both Marley and Scrooge began to smile from the floating mist. If the Acceptance affected Noah, it was not detectable, for he continued to pace the shoreline. At least a dozen inanimate floaters began to lift off the Pool's surface, each split into their various spirits, then without exception, they all moved toward the Mog of that spirit's need. The Coss Acceptance that rained down upon Flora only thickened the shell around her.

"So let me absorb this," said Scrooge, "her goodness in life was so tragically ended that it caused the emotional preservation of the death event itself? And, this

is the part I still do not understand, it's the idea that only an innocent will not react to Coss Acceptance. Jacob, why is that?"

"Think about her dilemma, Ebenezer. Here is this wonderful being who is pummeled by her circumstances. Her last move is her worst move, and as she is dying, what does she do?" Marley paused for the effect of the silence, then answered his own question, "She blames the Infinite Consciousness." Again, a silence for effect came over Marley. Looking out over the Pool he finally explained, "Flora rejected the relief that Acceptance gives. Only our Task Of Outreach can help... may help her."

"What if we fail?"

"Noah would never adapt."

"So how do we triumph?"

"I am without ideas."

Noah stepped between Marley and Scrooge, then announced, "I have the method." Abruptly he turned, then beckoned to them, "Follow me!" As the three walked to the edge of the Dam Of Disconnected Parts, a mountainous quantity of arms and legs fidgeted... and it was not playful. Feet viciously kicked other limbs away, while arms grabbed up appendages, then threw them out of everyone's view. The interaction was nothing if not chaos. The whole scene, unlike any other in Transmogrify, sent a fearsome dread throughout Scrooge's form.

"Scrooge, you are going to have to be the group's muscle," announced Noah.

"I'm about thirty years too late on that one, Noah, but I'm here to help."

Noah smiled at Scrooge's warmth, then teased, "We will try not to exploit you."

"What can I do? I have some brawn too," said Marley.

Again, Noah smiled, but this time it turned into a cackle. "Baby brother, you may have been strong when you were scooping horse dung, but now you just sort of smell like dung!"

Marley shook his head back and forth. He knew he deserved this kind of harassment, but it hurt. He wondered what he would have to do to end Noah's rejection. However, contemplation was not the duty of the moment, so he simply sighed, and then waited for instructions.

"We need to gather up twenty, maybe thirty arms. Do you think you can do that, Ebenezer?"

"No. I don't think so."

Confused, Noah asked, "You do want to help?"

"Without hesitation, yet those claws have already trapped me once. If not for Apurto... ah Apurto..." Scrooge's voice dwindled while he just gulped air in the effort to articulate his angst.

"Will you at least try it?"

"Only if you are prepared to save me when I become ensnared."

"Thank you, Ebenezer. Your strength is needed, for neither Jacob nor I have the power to dislodge one, let alone dozens of limbs." Noah put his hand on Scrooge's shoulder, then gave the order. "I will go with you. Let's see if we can dodge those spindly projections."

Together, as they stepped from the Road, Noah yelled back to Marley, "We will toss you the bones. Do you think you have the integrity to stack them?"

"There is no element of honesty involved in stacking anything, Noah," Marley fumed.

Knowing his taunts had bothered his little brother, Noah mocked, "Well then, you should be able to stack beyond the height of the Crater... especially since you are void of the same honor as those that dwell within the Lake Of Flames."

Marley just snorted air as his brother and best friend entered the Dam Of Disconnected Parts. His concern for his brother's situation was waning with every utterance of contempt he received. And yet he would not allow himself the reasoning of a victim. While he watched the two step into the clash of limbs, he wondered if his brother would ever treat him as family again.

Noah walked in front of Scrooge, so as to kick any menacing structure from the path. As Scrooge followed, exploring fingers attempted to capture his ankles. The touch stimulated shivers within him, but passed through without any hindrance to his legs. "Here, this arm seems long enough," Noah said, pointing to a flexing hand. He attempted to pull it from the pile, but like ice on a street, the stability between ghostly forms could not be created.

Scrooge stepped in front of Noah, grabbed the arm, and with almost no effort freed it. "Now what do I do?"

"Do not move even a bit," said Noah as he received the extremity, then threw it toward his brother. Not expecting the toss, the bone passed right through Marley, then hit a sleeper within the Pool. "Jacob, we are not doing this so you can watch these bones sink to the bottom of the Pool. You have one job, and you can not even do that — Jacob Kol?"

"Stop calling me by my middle name, and do NOT just throw things at me, Noah. Do you think maybe you could have the forethought to warn me first?"

With contempt for his brother, Noah said, "Maybe I should just drop the Jacob and call you Kol from now on."

"I do not like this arguing," said Scrooge.

"And I do not like that BOY," said Noah, pointing to his brother. Marley just endured, his heart hurt, yet his mind understood.

Scrooge's words did seem to quiet the brothers' tension. The three worked in silence to gather up the cast-off bones from the Crater. The chore proved itself to be difficult, for the ghosts' lack of substance kept causing misplacements. Finally, a huge pile of arm bones was collected and stacked along the shore of the Pool. This all happened without any mishaps for Scrooge.

As they began to walk across the Road to Jacob, Scrooge asked Noah, "You say you have forgiven Jacob, yet you remain so hostile toward him. What would Jacob have to do to gain your grace?"

"Am I responsible for another's grace?"

"Would not your focus be better served for yourself away from Jacob's anger?"

"Yes, but how do I escape? I mean, he is right there," he said pointing to Jacob.

"What did I do now?" moaned Jacob.

"See, see, Ebenezer, what I have to put up with?" With a glare that tossed knives through Jacob, Noah said, "It's not what you did a memory ago, it's what you did during our time of seasons."

"I do know that, Noah. What I don't know is what I have to do to end this torment."

"Torment! It was I that was tormented. Never, NEVER act as if you are the victim, you pitiful creature."

"Will my asking for Instant Transmogrification end at least your torment?"

Noah smiled at the thought, but his greater need took control. "No, I may want your help to save Flora," pausing he sniped, "but Scrooge is probably the only one I will need."

"I may not be able to stop this, but I don't want to be part of it either," said Scrooge. "I want to help Flora before another Coss release arrives."

"Undoubtedly, let's connect the arms."

Both Marley and Scrooge stared at the pile of limbs before them, then Marley braved the obvious question, "How?"

"Fingers on elbows." Noah realized he had not brought the needed imagery into view, so slowly explained, "Take one hand, have it grip the elbow of the next arm, and then we can merely repeat, connecting limbs until they will reach Flora."

"What if one hand lets go of an elbow?"

Noah just waved his hand over the Dam, then replied, "We have all the resources we will ever need."

The process of getting the hands to grab hold of anything seemed to be almost their purpose for existence. Once joined the fingers became rigid, nearly unable to part. The lengthening continued until the arms could reach Flora. By this time, it became obvious what the plan was, so only positioning was communicated between the three. With the elongated arm in tow, Noah floated out to Flora. Both Scrooge and Marley held up the last elbow from the Road.

As fingers flexed in and out, Noah linked the hand to the only location where hardened Coss Acceptance was absent, the center-back of her dress's collar. As he attached the fingers, a previously trapped amount of Acceptance cascaded down the slope of her nape. "Scrooge, the hand is joined! Now gently pull as I guide her around the others."

The three worked together as if they were a team, coordinating pulls while dodging the other sleeping spirits. As the pole of limbs began to extend much further behind Scrooge and Marley, Flora's cocoon coasted to the edge of the shore.

Jumping to the ground, Noah ordered, "Jacob, dry the tears from her encasement." Looking straight at Scrooge, he clarified the instructions, "Stand clear, Ebenezer, that moisture holds emotions, and coming from the Pool, none of them are pleasant."

Once dried and turned onto her back, Noah looked through the Acceptance into the face of his heart's passion. The tenderness he felt at the sight of her brought tears to his eyes. Wiping his forearm across his face, he gently kissed her lips. The covering of Acceptance dulled the feeling between the flesh.

Marley asked, "How do we free her?"

"That, my supposedly genius baby brother, requires what you do not possess... warmth."

"But I do possess the desire, so what do we do now... big brother?"

"Please, not again," protested Scrooge.

The brothers both focused upon Scrooge, then Marley presented an idea, "If heat is going to revive Flora, I think Scrooge should hug her since he is the warmest. You and I, Noah, will attempt to seal his heat against the Acceptance. Maybe that will melt it away."

"Maybe," agreed Noah.

"You want me to hug her?" gulped Scrooge.

"I think it may be your job since heat is needed."

So without further dialog, the three attempted Marley's idea. However, it did not work, for it was not heat, but passion that would raise Flora. Once the first idea failed, Noah walked around and around Flora's sleeping form in hopes of locating a crack big enough to force open. Frustration was his reward.

By the time Noah sat upon the shoreline, next to his brother and Scrooge, melancholy controlled the mood. With Flora lying next to them, yet being no closer than the North Star, he removed from his pocket the quartz point she had given him. Though nothing made Newgate acceptable, the crystal had been the only thing that empowered his hope. Even when sentenced to death, the love her crystal held sustained his courage to face the future. With each loving impression, Noah's inner glow of light began to flow through the crystal's point.

As his tears fell upon the crystal, rainbow colors exploded from the one drop of ghostly sorrow that attached itself to the point's tip. Through the droplet, each speck of inner dust that had settled upon the point during its growth reflected an entire rainbow into Transmogrify. As hundreds of colored spectrums surrounded Noah, their inspiration caused him to jump up, place the crystal on Flora's chest, then with both hands pressed down hard. He did not know what he was doing, but it just felt right.

Nothing seemed to happen until Noah intuitively closed his eyes, calmed his thoughts, then watched the joyous memories of his life with Flora play out within his mind. Everything, from the delights of the ballroom to the bedroom, took control. Passion within Noah began to swell. Emotions turned the crystal warm, then hot. As remembrances passed through the quartz it began to penetrate the crusted Coss Acceptance. Yet the probing of the crystal only dissolved the Acceptance when certain thoughts were generated — certain carnal thoughts.

Lovemaking within their marital bedroom had always been kind, playful, but most of all, passionate, with lingering kisses. Noah became so consumed by the thought of their shared sensuality that when the entire covering of Coss Acceptance, without warning, released itself, he reflexively dropped the crystal onto Flora's stomach.

As he reached down to recover the quartz, Flora grabbed it from him. Holding the point upright against her womb, the crystal began to hum in rhythms of harmonic tones. Slowly vibrating images of a baby began to float next to the six triangular faces of the point. Each of the six infants glowed a different color of the rainbow.

Mesmerized by these developing children, Noah exclaimed, "It's the daughter I was hoping for!"

Bewildered, Flora countered with, "No, it's my son!"

Together each saw their desired child in substance, yet both were unsure about the truth of their vision. "Ebenezer," said Noah, "do we have a boy or a girl?"

Scrooge looked upon the six images hoping to discover a distinction, other than color, between them. When none could be detected, he simply gave Flora her wish, "It's a boy." Upon the declaration of gender, the six infants combined above the crystal's point into one giggling boy.

Noah picked the child up, held him to his chest, then, while kissing his son's forehead, declared with joy, "Here is my legacy."

Flora, filled with her own euphoria, joined the family. Together, through the pull of her goodness, the three felt a summons from the Abyss... the Infinite Consciousness' calling for Mogrification. This urgent behest commanded action. Then without warning as the three moved toward the Abyss Of Final Transmogrify, an explosion of multi-colored Acceptance transformed them. Rainbows of Acceptance spread throughout Transmogrify, which in turn, created a gaiety within all of the Mogs that is seldom experienced. And truth be known — none before that moment had ever witnessed a Mogrification outside of the Abyss.

The bliss of the Acceptance hung in the air as certain colors dissipated at different energies. Red, with its longest vibration, lingered, which turned the bluish light of Transmogrify slightly lavender. Within the red Acceptance resided all of the shared memories from Jacob and Noah's childhood. As they passed through

Marley's thoughts tears of personal loss overwhelmed him. His Task Of Outreach had been fulfilled, yet the sorrow at the permanent loss of his brother bothered him. However, he realized this was of his own making, so he accepted the emotional dread.

As the fog of colored Acceptance evaporated, Jacob turned from the Pool Of Broken Spirits to face the Dam Of Disconnected Parts. "It is time to get you home, Ebenezer."

"Really, so soon?" The two men looked at each other, then chuckled at the thought of a quick escape.

"Time is personal in Transmogrify."

"Time is dreamlike here. Each moment seems to exist within its own occasion."

Marley paused to find the words, but the concept within his thoughts could never produce the desired conversation that would create an understanding of Transmogrify's present moment. So rather than try, he just declared, "I think we should pass

through the Dam Of Disconnected Parts. It will reduce our travel time by at least 75 percent."

"I do not feel it is safe." Looking toward the apex of the Crater Of Severed Spirits, Scrooge added, "However, I do not want to loiter here either."

"You never had any trouble collecting arms for the Pool. It appears that Apurto blessed you with some kind of invincible energy."

"I'm not sure of that, Jacob."

"I did secure a couple of Fire Twirlers while walking to the Pool. I will not allow the skeletons to grab you."

254

"Well, I know you will at least try," Scrooge said, in an attempt to convince himself. With that he stepped into the enormity of the Dam. Its massive scale haunted his human perceptions with its millions of skeletal limbs grasping and kicking at the air. Succeeding at nothing but motion, the spindly fingers and feet struggled for significance.

Stave Ten

Self-Doubts Calm

WITH EACH STEP a body part attempted to push, shove or grab Scrooge. It took him several steps to develop the maneuvers needed for dodging most and forcibly pushing through all other limbs in his way. Once he adapted to the constant attacks coming from the Dam he changed focus by saying, "Thus far, Noah's rainbow-colored Acceptance was the finest."

"That was Flora's doing," replied Marley.

"How do you know that?"

"Noah was not ready for Mogrification. He still had too much anger towards me. He should have been sent back to the Den, or even to his Chamber in the Pit Of Anger. Acceptance will never happen when forgiveness is lacking."

"He did forgive you, Jacob."

Marley halted, turned toward Scrooge, then demanded, "How do you know that?"

"Oh, do not doubt that Noah still distrusts you. Yet, I think he almost instantly forgave you in the Den."

"When you say 'I think' it does not mean 'I know'. And yet, your statement is as if you have been informed."

"Noah did tell me he forgave you. Is that a direct enough statement for you, Jacob?"

"It is if I could believe it, but Noah acts like he hates me now. That is not forgiveness."

"You do not want forgiveness. You want Noah to act as if nothing happened. This is only about pleasing YOU, Jacob."

"Is there no reward at the completion of a Task Of Outreach?"

"Obviously freeing Noah and Flora is not the total of your Task. Jacob, you have a chilly and deceptive demeanor. Noah is wary that this scoundrel drive within you, that you don't even seem to be aware of, will bring him harm again. So why should he do anything other than forgive you, which is done so he can recover from your evil?"

"So I have lost my brother for eternity?"

"You have not lost your brother. You have lost the control over your brother."

"It is the same in practice."

"That it is."

The two of them navigated the path of flexing hands and kicking feet. The flapping and fluttering impeded every step traveled, yet eventually the dodging and side movements normalized.

As they adjusted to the obstacles on the path, Marley brought the subject of his brother up again. "Why doesn't his forgiveness free me?"

"Because it is meant to free himself. The anguish of your actions created your cage. Noah possesses no key to your Mogrification, Jacob. He may have been your Task, but he is not your absolution."

Jacob stopped for a moment, then spoke of the past. "Maybe being the baby of the family put me in a position of being the spoiled one, the taker within the family."

"That is ridiculous! You are still on the path of a scoundrel, Jacob. The sequencing of a child's birth does play a role within the family's power structure. Yet, it was not preordained that you would get your brother killed. That dishonesty you cultivated into your being." Scrooge, having said the harshest, finished with, "You will only find release when you bow to what doomed you. Right now you have the faulty understanding that what happened was outside of your doing. Jacob, you caused... you caused this."

All of the Fire Twirlers within Jacob's heart chain exploded, sending ghostly fragments of him throughout the Dam. As his form recreated itself, Jacob gained a realization. He may have always known he caused Noah's torment, but he never felt its burden. His actions at the time were ones of conniving to repair the damage, while he slipped away undetected. And now... he realized just how horrible of a human he was, so he cried. These were not the tears of grief, but of cleansing. Self-sorrow left him. As awareness replaced self-preservation, Jacob's emotions quieted. Looking to explain his new insight, Jacob stated, "I feel justice can only be served if I ask for Instant Mogrification."

"Your experiences are lessons the Infinite Consciousness needs. You may think that Instant Transmogrification is a righteous punishment for you — but from what I know, it only serves to quiet your angst, and would provide nothing to the Infinite Consciousness. Is that your desire — to turn your back on the responsibility of your life?"

"Ebenezer, you amaze me. If only I had your honor."

"You have your own goodness, Jacob... mend it. Do not destroy it."

An uneasy silence developed as they passed through the Dam. The constant motion of arms pushing legs mesmerized the men. The heap of limbs, which would never be Mogrified, emitted an emotional dread that caused Scrooge to become nervous. Marley, for the first time in his life, felt the anxiety of another. Without Fire Twirlers to propel Scrooge back to the Road, Marley settled upon the only thing that entered his mind. For the welfare of his anxious friend, he would quiet the body parts.

With a virtuous intention, Marley lay down in front of Scrooge. In hopes of muting the clash of bones, he said to Scrooge, "Walk upon me." This peculiar vision of a ghost covering a field of skeletal remains seemed to be no more than a gesture. Nonetheless, Scrooge stepped upon his friend. The limbs beneath Marley both screamed, then shot through his form with fury. The shock of protruding fingers still attempting to trap Scrooge's legs caused him to jump from the impaled ghost.

Marley again joined Scrooge in the middle of the Dam Of Disconnected Parts, then declared, "I can not even get a suitable idea to calm you with, Ebenezer. My failures are overwhelming!"

"And yet even your desire to improve my condition helps. It is not success, but effort, that shows the worth of a person. You, Jacob, seem to be gaining humility. Now take that seed of awareness and plant it into your actions."

At Scrooge's urging, Marley's tensions relaxed. They continued walking toward the other side of the Dam. Though the distance to the Road was vast, neither any longer seemed distressed by the demand of the area's size. Marley contemplated the new seed of "humility" he had just gained, while Scrooge walked with caution.

Without a word Marley pulled both a right and a left arm from the Dam. From each hand, he removed their index fingers, and then gave them to Scrooge. Scrooge backed away from Marley as he exclaimed, "What confusion is this?"

"Put each finger in an ear. It may help to hush the din."

"You are in earnest?"

"I will not stop thinking of ways to help you, Ebenezer."

Realizing the assistance was pure in

motive, Scrooge placed the bones into his ears. The effect was amazing, for the fingers resonated with the same frequency as did the discarded limbs of the Dam. This pulsing of vibrations absorbed all sounds, except muted speech.

"Oh my, this is wonderful," announced Scrooge.

"Finally I have done something right."

"What?! I can hardly hear you."

Marley yelled, "Do you feel better?!"

The volume of Marley's voice shook Scrooge. Hesitating, he looked upon this ghostly friend and then declared, "Your voice is as powerful as a Fire Twirler. I dare that you could throw me across the Dam with your voice."

Marley's roar intensified. "Yes, but would you arrive whole?!"

Before the sentence was finished, Scrooge landed hard on his backside. Squirming from the speaker's force, he rose to announce, "I'll go the safe route."

The visual distance to the Road remained constantly long. As they walked, a silence grew between them, for it was easier than were the screams currently required for conversation. Marley's silence turned into contemplation, which evolved into dreams, and then into a place of grace that could be touched. As a torrent of responsibility engulfed his spirit, he lifted from the Dam.

"Jacob, what is happening? Where are you going?"

"It's my heart chain. It is gone."

Straining to hear, Scrooge removed the finger bones, then said, "So you simply weigh less. That's why you are floating?"

"Without a doubt. Yet weight was never the burden of that chain." Looking over his shoulder, he then confided, "I'm being called, Ebenezer."

"Called? Called what?"

"It's where, Ebenezer — not what — the Abyss calls. I'm ready for this." Marley explained as an invisible force tugged at his backside. Being pulled from Scrooge, he yelled, "Just get back to the Road and the way out of Transmogrify will reveal itself."

Stunned, Scrooge yelled after Marley as he watched him being carried off, "Just get back to the Road? By myself? Humbug, Jacob! Get back here! Humbug I tell you! BAH HUM..." but Marley disappeared from sight before Scrooge could find other words to express his anger. Sinking to his knees, he breathed as deeply as his chest cavity would allow, then released a gush of sorrow. "Why does everyone leave me?" He expected no response, but he got one.

"I have been with you since the day you were born." Darting his head in every direction, Scrooge looked for the voice, yet no entity had been located when it spoke again. "I will never leave you."

Bewildered, he responded, "Fanny? Is that you?"

"Yes, the whispers of my essence speak."

"I hear you through completed thoughts, yet I lack sight of you. Where are you?"

"I never spent any interval in Transmogrify, Ebenezer. I am Acceptance, and fill every field of frequency, at every moment. The strength of my experiences are not specific; they flow everywhere."

"So I will only know your presence by the words in my mind?"

"Your thoughts create that echo."

"Are you real enough to help me get back to London?"

"I am here to help you survive the Dam."

Scrooge gasped at the concept of non-survival. "Would I be gone from your memory if I die in Transmogrify?"

"Yes, you would, but none that are watching want that."

"Watching? Are there other entities of Acceptance here? I can see not a one."

"Look to the Corridor Of Phantoms."

Scrooge did as instructed, and then blinked at the sight. Above him, upon the Corridor, floated a crowd of spirits. Realizing they were being watched, the horde began to cheer, and yell things like, "You are so close to the Road." Another cried out, "Don't get lost." But it wasn't until he heard, "I'd help if I could," that Scrooge paused, no, he came to a full standstill. His breath could not even be detected.

"Are you injured?" asked his sister.

"Why can that spirit not help me?"

"You've left the Road. There is a reason why you were instructed to not do that."

"Jacob... what a rogue he remains."

"You left the Road, Ebenezer. Just because you were coerced does not end your responsibility to maintain your promise."

"Transmogrify is not of my previous knowledge. Jacob..."

"Yes, Jacob still lacks integrity, but you will have to get back to the Road on your own, Ebenezer."

"How could Jacob become Acceptance with such a weakness? Transmogrify is hypocritical."

"Only the completion of the Task Of Outreach is required for Mogrification. If the Infinite Consciousness required perfection, even I would have failed that."

Scrooge smiled before he commented, "You are flawless, at least in my opinion."

"You need to get back to the Road."

"No matter how far I travel I never seem to gain distance."

"And therein is your difficulty. Look to your left. What do you see?"

Scrooge did as instructed, then answered, "The Crater."

"Now turn around as though you were going back to the Pool, then once again look to your left."

This strange request seemed like a game to Scrooge, but he still performed the ask. When he again looked left he saw — the Crater. "What mystery is this?"

"You, my brother, have entered the Crater Of Severed Spirits, except in this case it is actually severed body parts. Nonetheless this heap of bones we are surrounded by creates the membrane that contains them, much like the spirits in the Crater do."

"I do not see a covering layer around the Dam — not like the one at the Crater."

"The veneer is no more than wispy. Yet it is enough to contain the limbs within the Dam." Upon sensing Scrooge's next thought, Fanny added, "This containment is an ethereal facade of symmetrical imagery."

"I think I need a scientist to figure out what that statement means, Fanny."

"In other words, the walls in here are reflective — mirror-like. Does that concept help you, Ebenezer?"

"Most assuredly that explains the lack of forward progress. However, how can I overcome this visual disability?"

"Make yourself blind by closing your eyes." As her brother abided by the directive, the clasping of limbs echoed throughout the Dam. "I know you hear the arms and legs in conflict, but listen for the rhythmic, high-pitched sound. Do you hear it?"

The effort burdened Scrooge, for the discovery of just one sound, over the roar of another, could only be known when their vibrations directly entered the mind. "Faintly."

"Concentrate on that muffled sound, Ebenezer. Is it gaining volume?"

"I do believe so."

"Walk directly toward that sound." Again Scrooge followed instructions, "Good, now keep pursuing that tone." The shrill outside of the Dam intensified, as the extremities being trod upon exploded with brutality. Sensing Scrooge's blindness, the disembodied limbs seemed to focus on tripping him. Arms threw legs across his path while hands slapped his back-side in passing. The constant dodging of aggressive actions resulted in Scrooge losing the concentration needed to hear the pitch. Within his mind he heard Fanny's encouragement. "You are almost safe, do not stop."

"I can no longer hear the noise."

"Ebenezer, you have only lost its direction. The sound you are tracking is narrow in range. You need only turn until you hear it again." Fanny's guidance calmed Scrooge's tensions. He never became accustomed to the trouble of the harassing limbs, yet would not allow them to ruin him.

A thunderous outcry exploded from the Corridor as spirits cheered Scrooge's reentry to the Road. Immediately Scrooge opened his eyes to find that the source of the clamor in his head was coming from the Cycle Of Greed. While the curious spirits above him began to move toward their own needs, Fanny directed Scrooge by telling him, "The Rains Of Darkness await us." Jacob's fear of the Rains flooded into Scrooge's memory, bringing with it the dread of probable dangers.

"I will trust you," said Scrooge, more to himself than Fanny.

As Scrooge began the walk to the Rains, he apologized to his sister. "I am sorry I never approved of your marriage. Connor was a good man."

"Yes, he was." The thoughts within Scrooge's mind stopped for a moment before he heard, "Yet, Ebenezer, my personal joy for a husband and family caused the abandonment from the two people I loved the most."

"I know I am one of those two," said Scrooge.

"You are — as was father." Without a physical being to watch, Scrooge struggled with his sister's emotions. "You both rejected me," said Fanny.

"I did not know of this. I was so angry that father removed me from school before I could finish my education, and then he refused to talk to me. I'm so sorry, Fanny, that for years every time I looked at you, I saw him."

"You were not as rejected by him as you think you were."

This statement became one Scrooge pondered before he insisted on evidence. "In what way did father not rebuff me?"

"He kept personal truths from you, so you would not be burdened by his hardships."

"I thought I was his hardship."

"Do you remember the New London Bridge scaffolding collapse?"

"All of England heard about that."

"Father nearly died when the scaffolding fell, and he never completely recovered from his injuries."

This news shocked Scrooge so completely he demanded an explanation. "Why am I only hearing this now?"

"What would you have done if we had told you at the time?"

"I would have come home and gone to work — like I should have."

"No, father spent his savings, so you, Ebenezer, could stay at school for an additional year after the accident. He even forfeited medical attention to help you."

"And after I left school... why then was I ostracized?"

"Father struggled so, especially after you moved back into the house. The accident destroyed his left arm. He had to strap that arm to his front side, or it would swing back and forth with every step."

"It is not right that I was never allowed to help."

"Father was determined that you would succeed. He made it clear to me that his worry was to never become your concern. It was harsh, yet done with the best of intentions, Ebenezer."

"When I was younger, I would have agreed. But now, having lived most of my life, I know this was wrong, Fanny." Scrooge shook his head back and forth before he finished by saying, "Why did I have to live with the idea that father hated me? Why could you not have at least comforted that pain within me?"

"Father threatened to expel me from his life if I did. In the end he rejected me anyway, the day after Connor and I married."

"So he never approved of Connor?"

"Actually he did approve of the marriage... until the day after the wedding."

"What happened? Did he not realize you would be moving from our home into Connor's?"

"No, at the wedding one of Connor's friends asked him why there was no dowry. Father overheard their conversation, and was so embarrassed he disowned me."

"You did not deserve such treatment."

"And yet, you also disowned me, Ebenezer."

"I still regret my failings of being an oversensitive, insensitive man."

Scrooge contemplated the mixture of actions that had occurred without his knowledge. The idea his father would sacrifice for him, even when severely injured, had never entered his thoughts. The realization he had lived with this man for years without ever being acknowledged by him brought forth the understanding of just how prideful his father was. In the end it seemed to have been the only dignity left him, and he used it like a weapon.

Arriving at the Rains, Scrooge asked, "Should we not be moving toward the entrance?"

"Only the Rains Of Darkness allow the living to pass through Transmogrify. You, Ebenezer, were given special access because you promised to stay on the Road Of Phantoms."

Scrooge swallowed hard before he admitted, "I know I didn't keep that promise."

"No, you did not. However when you fix the promise, the abuse will be forgiven, but not forgotten."

"Has not reentry to the Road fixed the 'promise'?"

"Not completely. You must commit to stay on the Road, no matter the circumstances, from here until there."

"Truly, Fanny, I am too tired to leave the Road. So I do pledge to stay on the Road."

Stopping in front of the Rains, Scrooge watched the downpour as Fanny said, "Ebenezer, you are there. Enter the Rains Of Darkness."

The last word, "darkness", reverberated throughout Scrooge's mind. The echo grabbed his heart, then squeezed it into his quivering voice. "The fright in Jacob's Rains scares me still, yet it holds no dread in comparison to the dishonor I would suffer if I left the Road. I just remade that promise, and I will keep it until I am told we are... there. Even if staying here means elimination."

"You know it is more dire for you than that. Elimination is the loss of the body. Nullification is the loss of both body and spirits. You will be nullified without anyone retaining a memory."

"I will not cross the Road until I am..."

"...There." Silence developed into tension. "The honor of your word has been restored, Ebenezer, now it is time to face your fears. Look upon the Rains, what do you see?"

Scrooge had no idea what he should be looking for, but finally said, "A deluge?"

One could sense Fanny smiling when her next thought released. "It has been established the Rains appear to be wet, but for you, Ebenezer, the Rains are your 'there'. It is now time for you to face your most difficult fear. Walk from the Road. Enter the Rains."

"So this place, the Rains, is the 'there' of my promise?"

"Yes, it is the pathway."

"Will you join me? Are the Rains dangerous for you, Fanny?"

"Nowhere is dangerous — or is any particular location kept from Acceptance. Nonetheless, Ebenezer, this is your journey. You must complete it by yourself."

Scrooge pointed to the downpour, then confirmed, "So I should go in 'there'?"

"It is in your best interest."

"A while back Jacob asked me who I loved, and I said no one. But I was wrong, Fanny, for I have always loved you."

"You love others, Ebenezer, you just have not identified who."

"After Belle left me, I never cared to find another romantic partner."

"Love is infinitely more powerful than is romance."

"I have no children to love, yet, I think all of the Cratchit children think I love them."

"Do you?"

"Is love just the creation of momentary emotions... or is it a forever event that captures emotions?" asked Scrooge.

"It can be those, and more. Love is both abstract and concrete. One can not put a muscle to love, yet love has the might to end wars. Mothers filled with love have died for their children. The man who pulled our father from the icy Thames saved his life through love. He brought forth the same love that the Task Of Outreach creates within Transmogrify — which is one of service to others." Fanny allowed her brother a pause, then asked again, "Do you love the Cratchit children?"

Scrooge thought for a moment, then announced, "The children are a bit of a worry for me, can you love something you worry about?"

Fanny laughed at Scrooge's innocence. "That is part of the parent's love, not all of the love parents will give to their children, but concern starts from day one, and it is connected to love. Ebenezer, you are sounding like a parent."

"I do care for the children. However, to say I cherish each equally... I'm not sure I can do that. It seems my nature is to like some children more than others. So I probably would not be a loving parent."

"Do you treat the child you love best better than the others?"

"No, I never do that."

"You do actually know love, Ebenezer. However, you, like most, forget that

love's greatest power is one of being both an abstract in concept, yet a concrete force in action."

"You keep telling me that. But Fanny, do not all strong emotions carry a force of energy? Is not terror just as powerful as is love?"

"Absolutely, yet who do you know that will run toward terror? Love gives humanity the desire to create greatness. From the moment of birth, love is what the individual runs toward."

"Yes, I guess most people will do anything to avoid terror. So as I understand it, what we emphasize gains strength, and what we forget about weakens?"

"That has always been the truth of reality, Ebenezer. And now you must face your greatest vulnerability. You must enter the Rains Of Darkness. Do not be afraid; and accept relief if it finds you."

Quaking, Scrooge nonetheless slid into the storm. Instantly a vertical outburst of iridescence overwhelmed every cell of his body. Bathed in light his skin began to tingle from the sensation of the caress. As he moved deeper into the flood of luminescence his vision gave way to a blinding paleness. For a moment he lost his bearings, tripped, then fell.

He sat upon the physical yet obscured floor. As he pulled his knees to his chest he began to laugh uncontrollably. The sound echoed continuously, with the area quieting only after the gaiety was forcibly stopped. Without fear, he rose to his feet and just began to walk. He was not sure if he was being brave or stupid, but an overwhelming yearning to trust the ambiguity of his situation consumed all desires to panic. He still had fear of what he could not identify, yet he now trusted... trusted deeply... that Transmogrify would keep him safe.

As Scrooge walked, the wall of light began to give way to visibility. With his sight being restored, he stepped into a cavernous room filled with throbbing stalactites. The visual appearance of the cave plagued his memory.

Moving to the center of the room, he realized the stalactites were not made of mineral, but instead pulsated with life. Two different types of protrusions covered the ceiling. The most active of the two were small rust-colored cocoon-shaped membranes. However, the frightening ones were twice the size and created a swirl of mist around themselves for concealment.

Looking up toward the constant motion of the ceiling, he watched with mouth ajar as the smaller projections split open. The force released thousands of tiny brownish moths into the room. With the purpose of want, they descended upon Scrooge. Each moth groaned with desires as they landed upon him. The best of them just expressed the need for survival. The worst of them immediately began eating his clothes in hopes of providing their own means of existence. Before Scrooge could protect himself, the creatures covered his form.

As the bugs began to crawl into all of Scrooge's openings, the larger cocoons released a mayhem of enormous, ever-changing moths. Flying under a cloak of haziness, each moth landed upon several smaller moths, pinning them to their location. While the smaller moths continued to lament their wants, the larger creatures erroneously asserted that those beneath them deserved their misfortune. Both groups of brutes combined atop Scrooge in an effort to drain all of his resources.

The beings had overtaken him so quickly he never even attempted to brush them from his clothing, and now, it was too late to react. Paralyzed by the flying creatures, the only action left to him was to scream out for relief. "What now must I do for those in want and ignorance?" Covered in a myriad of moths, Scrooge began to breathe his last. As his knees started to give way to the dead weight of his body, he cried out, "Will no one help?" One knee thumped the ground with such a force it caused the other leg to buckle as well. "Please," he whimpered.

As he began to collapse, a small human hand grabbed his little finger. "You do enough, Mr. Scrooge." Squeezing with force, the child's hand shook his wrist and with it released a cloud of moths. "Every individual is responsible for the social condition." The cub of a human yanked the old man's arm until the menacing creatures flew from their prey. The majority of insects continued to levitate within the haze created by the larger moths. With every flutter of their wings a fresh release of fog concealed all within its influence of ignorance. So the child jostled Scrooge until the room was cleared of danger.

Scrooge rose from his knees. Focusing on the youth before him, he realized he knew her. "Elizabeth?"

"Mamma and I are here for papa. Can we secure your help, Mr. Scrooge?"

"I am indebted to you for my life."

As Scrooge gazed upon the mother and daughter ghosts, the flickering of a third person began to appear. "My husband is dying," announced Nancy.

"The Lieutenant?"

"Gilbert will arrive to Teint soon. Yet, I fear it is Humphry that will be lost without your help, Ebenezer."

"Is Gilbert succumbing to a bullet wound?"

"No, Crimea is riddled with Cholera."

Scrooge looked at the other victims of that dreaded disease, then asked, "How? What can I do?"

"The knowledge of Gilbert's passing may take months to reach Humphry. He will be distraught and powerless. Peter helps as he can, but Humphry will require more direction. He will need mentoring."

"Does the boy have desires?"

"Science... only science."

"Then I know of a confidante. I will stabilize your son's future."

"You are our blessing — now be gone."

SCROOGE, ASLEEP IN the chair next to his extinguished fireplace, jolted upright. Wildly blinking as the morning sun began to flow through his window, he realized his clothes were honeycombed with moth holes. Jumping to his feet he heard the chimes from St. James's Piccadilly Church — and then, he knew the day was Christmas.

Dancing around his room, he sang in a cheerful yet tone-deaf manner. Cleaning himself for the holiday celebrations, Scrooge put on his best suit, combed his thinning hair, wrote out three letters, then placed each within its own envelope.

Folding the letters into the pocket of his jacket, he left his home and began walking toward the Royal Institution's Great Hall.

With each step the smells of roasted chestnuts, baking bread and the ever-present odor of horse manure combined to create a mostly pleasant experience for those going about their holiday. As he walked, Scrooge bowed in greeting to those he passed. He only stopped when he passed a beggar, dropped his daily coin in the cup, then heard, "You do enough, Mr. Scrooge."

Turning to see who the speaker was, he looked at the beggar, then to himself whispered, "Do I?" The beggar, realizing the words were not actually meant for his ears, just affirmed his statement by shaking his head up and down. Scrooge, still not accepting his worth, nonetheless moved on.

The day was special, but not out of the ordinary for Christmas. With the temperatures being mild for winter, only the wind from the north gave any indication that the weather could turn to bluster. But for the moment, the sun was shining, and Scrooge was whistling, not in tune of course, but with a cheer that all onlookers recognized as being merry.

The street scene bustled with colorful crowds of performers, vendors and carolers. Carriages moved like a river along the cobblestoned roadways. Buildings decorated in holly, evergreens, and ribbons lined both sides of every London road. Laughter was the mood of the population.

As Scrooge dodged a juggler tossing multiples of knives, he flung a coin into the performer's jar, then heard, "You do enough, Mr. Scrooge." Scrooge, without hesitation, just shook his head back and forth.

Nearing the Royal Institution, Scrooge removed the envelope marked 'Charitable Trust' from his coat, then stepped into the building's entrance. Walking directly to the Lecture Theatre, he watched as Michael Faraday set up for his Christmas lecture on the chemistry of combustion.

Readying a long tray which housed various chemicals, Scrooge watched as Faraday set the container on fire. Multiple flares erupted, creating flames of blue, green and purple. "That is going to create an uproar," declared Scrooge.

Looking up from his table, Faraday said, "Ebenezer, how long have you been standing there?"

"Just arrived, Michael."

"Do you think the children will be impressed with this demonstration?"

"I think even their parents will be impressed," assured Scrooge.

"Sometimes they are more captivated than are the youth."

"Fire does cause one to take notice — and colored fire — well, that is about as noticeable as fire comes."

"I doubt you are here to be charmed by fire, so how can I help you, Ebenezer?"

Scrooge handed the envelope marked 'Charitable Trust' to Faraday and said, "I would like to pay for the education of a young man named Humphry Albright."

"This is unusual, Ebenezer, but tell me about the boy. Is he curious, smart, and willing to work hard?"

"As I have come to know of him, he is a quality person."

"We demand not only quality, but also intellect from our people."

"I've been told all he thinks about is science."

"Ebenezer, why are you doing this?"

"The child has just become an orphan."

"Far too many orphans walk the streets of London. What makes this one different?"

"I'm... I'm sure I really like this child."

"So you find him special, yet will I?"

"Yes, you will find him unique, helpful and exceptional."

Taking the envelope from Scrooge, Faraday opened it, looked at the amount being provided for the boy, then slowly focused upon Scrooge's eyes. "This is more funds than are required to educate a dozen fellows."

"As long as Humphry is taken care of, do what you want with any extra money. I only want to make sure there is ample for the youth."

"This is more than enough, Ebenezer. If the boy is capable, we will make a scientist out of him."

"One last thing, Michael, please do not let the boy know you are aware of his family loss." Somewhat puzzled, Faraday agreed, and with that Scrooge left the building.

He entered the street expecting to be greeted by holiday cheer, in spite of that assumption, Scrooge found himself in the middle of an argument. Surrounded by a group of onlookers, the two people in the middle could be heard bickering.

"Show me your license," demanded the constable.

"I am just singing carols. Can't a person entertain and gain a meal without inviting the monarchy?"

"Do not beg me. Your kind never knows lawful employment. Show me your license or move on."

"You would deny me even a meal."

"With the quality of your voice... I would deny that you even deserve a meal."

With this comment, Scrooge stepped forward, then said, "The Christmas celebration is about the opening of the heart to the plight of those in need. This woman appears to be in need."

"The law is the law, and the state is not responsible for the witless."

"Your cruelty of words dumbfounds me. Sir, were you born ignorant, or is that a quality you have cultivated?"

The constable's eyes narrowed and, staring directly into the black of Scrooge's pupils, he snarled, "Just lessen the volume." With that the officer stormed off — probably in search of another less fortunate to harass.

Dropping a pence into the woman's cup, Scrooge started walking toward his counting house when he heard an echo of voices call after him, "You do enough, Mr. Scrooge."

To himself he reasoned, "Maybe I do."

Rounding the block to his business, the swinging sign above the door indicated the northern wind was gaining strength. Entering the building, he recalled the day he and Jacob moved into the location, some thirty years previously. A melancholy of memories flashed throughout his mind, but nothing settled into an anecdote.

Alone within the workers' room he looked upon their desks. Each had the worker's Boxing Day envelope sitting within the middle of their writing area. The usual quid held the envelope in place. Scrooge walked into his and Bob's office. Upon his partner's desk, he placed an envelope that simply said 'Bob Cratchit'. Putting his hand on the envelope, he whispered, "You have been my conscience, Bob, showing me the worth of that which is outside of myself."

Looking at the safe, he had an idea. Opening its door, he removed a handful of quid. Returning to the workers' tables he slid the center quid to the top left corner of each envelope. Upon each of the three remaining corners he added another quid. With the four corners of the envelopes covered in coins, he thought, 'It would take a force stronger than the Dover Straits earthquake to move those funds.'

From his backside he heard, "You do enough, Mr. Scrooge."

Turning to face the familiar voice, he said, "I have been told that." Pausing, he added, "I'm surprised your family would allow you time away from them today."

"I am no longer used to the squeals of delighted children."

"They have you seeking privacy, do they?"

"Well, at least a bit of quiet. I will return once the fervor lessens. What are you doing here, Ebenezer?"

Handing Bob the envelope with his name on it, he revealed, "I am going to retire, Bob."

"Retirement... my... what brought this on?"

"Feeble bones, my friend, feeble bones. I would never insist on this, Bob, but I would like you to make Peter Nida a manager. It is all explained in the envelope."

"Peter is a good man, but it is Fingal who is waiting for a promotion."

"Yes, I know that. Since I am leaving, you can promote them both. It should be easy to invent a special advancement for Fingal."

"So this is... goodbye?"

"I will be around; don't get too fancy yet."

"Extravagance... me?"

"I bet your grandchildren have discovered your absence."

"Actually, I doubt that. When I left them, they were inventing methods for wrecking gifts. However, I enjoy their gaiety, and hunger will take me home soon, but, Ebenezer, I am so sad you are leaving."

"Time halts only in wishes. I need this, Bob, I need this..."

"Then I am glad you are able to do it."

As they made their way to the entrance, Cratchit extended his right hand to his partner. Scrooge grabbed the hand, pulled it close to him, then gave his friend a hug he could never forget. Leaving the building, each turned in opposite directions. Before Cratchit turned the corner, Scrooge spun around. He wanted to tell his partner he loved him, but nervousness stopped him. He himself did not understand the extreme friendship that had grown between them. A tear dropped from the corner of his right eye before he turned, wiped any remaining moisture from his face, then began moving toward Fred and Eleanor's home.

The brisk London air nipped at Scrooge's nose as he reached his nephew's doorstep. Today, however, the chill could not dampen his spirits. He could hardly wait to see those mischievous twins, Eleanor's little imps, bouncing around the Christmas tree like overstuffed geese.

Pushing open the door, he bellowed, "Eleanor, it's just your uncle!"

Before he could close the door, a whirlwind of tiny feet and joyous shrieks engulfed him. "Uncle Scrooge! You're early!" squealed two voices in perfect unison. Scrooge prepared himself for the girls' embrace by pressing his back against the door. "Hold on, you whirlwinds! I can barely keep up with one of you, let alone two!"

"Come play! Father Christmas has been here!"

Each niece latched onto a leg and began pulling it toward the parlor. The combined force of legs moving in different directions threatened to topple Scrooge.

Bracing himself against the door he said, "I will follow you." Pointing to his feet he laughed, "Just like you, I also have two legs."

As they entered the room, a blast of Christmas cheer hit him. The tree shimmering with decorations, cinnamon and the roar of a fire combined to fill the air with the sensation of holiday happiness. Upon the dinner table sat a gingerbread house, somewhat lopsided but

undeniably charming. Toys were scattered everywhere, each one bearing the mark of brief, yet enthusiastic play.

Before they disappeared into a flurry of Christmas merriment, Scrooge managed to get out, "Eleanor, my dear, did you hear me? I'm early!"

A muffled voice called back from the kitchen, "Almost there, Uncle Scrooge!"

"Look what Father Christmas brought me," Ebby exclaimed, thrusting a brightly painted wooden train engine into his hands.

Fanny, ever the competitor, interjected, "Can you read my book to me?"

Scrooge, ever the charmer, winked, then said, "How about I read the book while the train takes us on a grand adventure around the gingerbread house?" The twins giggled as their faces lit up like Christmas candles.

However, with the twins being in a state of holiday excitement, focus shifted to a new wonderment. "I made up a riddle," said Fanny.

"Me too!" Ebby exclaimed.

A little surprised, Scrooge instructed, "I'd love to hear them both, first you, Fanny."

Fanny recited her riddle. "I have guards that stand like statues, flags that fly without leaving the roof. I am a magical home, yet have no dragons. What am I?"

Scrooge stroked his chin thoughtfully. "Well, that's a tricky one. Can I have another clue?"

Before Fanny could answer, Ebby blurted out, "It's Buckingham Palace!"

Scrooge burst out laughing, but said seriously, "Ebby, this is not your riddle."

Fanny, ever the diplomat, stated, "Don't worry, Uncle Scrooge. You would have gotten it eventually without her help."

Scrooge smiled at her kindness while saying, "Now, it's your turn, Ebby. What's your riddle?"

Ebby, determined to outshine her sister, declared, "Across the Thames I lie, horses trot atop me, while boats chug beneath me. Who... no, what am I?"

Scrooge pretended to ponder deeply. "Across the Thames, you say? Horses and boats... I know this one! Is it... the Blackfriars Bridge?"

Ebby's face fell. "No, that's not our main bridge!"

"Then it must be London Bridge."

Ebby's eyes lit up. "You got it!"

With the palms of his hands, Scrooge tousled their hair. "You're both geniuses."

"Uncle Scrooge, you're smart too. Now it's your turn."

Feeling the burden of having to quickly think, Scrooge finally said, "One giggles loud, one giggles often, a face is shared, but not a name. Who are we?"

The girls exchanged a knowing glance before rejoicing, "It's us!"

Scrooge roared with laughter. "Masterminds! Absolutely brilliant! You two are the merriest present I could ever want."

The three played for a while longer before Eleanor entered the parlor. "Ebenezer, what brings you here so early?" They embraced in a hold of equal admiration. Upon separation, a dusting of flour drifted to the floor.

Scrooge kissed her cheek as he confessed, "I had a tough sleep."

"So the twins have been keeping you awake?"

"Just like a factory whistle. However, I mostly came early to help you, Eleanor."

She stepped back from Scrooge, eyed him up and down, then slowly said, "Help me?"

"Yes... in the kitchen. Has no one ever helped you fix a meal?"

"Of course, and I have helped other women too — but never a man."

"I am here to prove that men can do more than just eat. So how can I help you, Eleanor?"

"I guess, the potatoes need peeling."

"I believe I can use a knife well enough to be of benefit," he said as they walked toward the cutting table.

The kitchen appeared as if it had been tussled in a storm. Bowls and food lay atop every surface. The stuffed goose rested within its pan, just waiting to be cooked. As the mince meat pie in the oven mellowed the mind with aromas, Scrooge looked at the potatoes, carrots and parsnips that still needed to be prepared.

Before Scrooge began dicing, he removed the last envelope from his coat pocket and handed it to Eleanor. "I hope I am not being too forward."

Receiving the envelope she cautiously looked inside. Instantly she handed it back to Scrooge. "No, I can not take this. Fred..."

"I was hoping he would be here. I will talk to him later, but you need this, Eleanor, for the twins if not for yourself."

"Fred provides..."

"This is not about Fred, but it is about how society will treat you if anything should happen to him."

"That is the women's lot. I can not go against that."

"I am not asking you to. I only want to provide you with security. Every farthing within that envelope is a meal, a bed, clothing — and life itself."

When Eleanor heard the phrase 'and life itself', tears erupted. Scrooge, though puzzled, just put his hand on her shoulder. The gesture was of no comfort, for she turned to him, then began openly crying. "I am so afraid." Scrooge allowed her the time to convey her fears. "I think I am pregnant, Ebenezer."

Immediately he understood. "This is exactly one of my concerns... Childbed Fever." He paused before he continued with his own story. "You know I lost my mother. She died so I could live. It has been a lifelong burden for me to have done that to her." Scrooge paused, then spoke about assistance. "At the time of my birth, help beyond midwives remained unnecessary, at least to society. Today, however, Lying-in Hospitals care for those who can pay, and I want to provide the funds for that."

Eleanor kept crying tears of relief and love for this help.

A DUSTING OF snow trailed Fred through the door. Before he could utter a sound, the eruption of boundless energy raced toward him. "Father! You're back! Did you bring him?"

Struggling to bring the box he was carrying into the home, he answered, "I couldn't get the pony in the crate, but I brought you something better."

"What's better than a pony?" complained Ebby.

Shuffling toward the bright red cloth in the corner, Fred slid the wooden box onto a small table. With imaginations running wild, the twins stroked the box as though it contained the lives of their wishes.

"What is it? Is it a puppy?" Fanny asked while dancing in place.

Fred chuckled. "Maybe next year, when you are a little older." His smile generated warmth as his words ignited the girl's visions. "There is a magic here... magic of the mind."

The girls carefully lifted the box's lid, then cheered with delight. Inside the box lay a fairytale village, meticulously crafted from wood and stone. Tiny houses, painted in vibrant colors, lined the cobblestone streets.

"Oh, Father!" Ebby squealed, her eyes wide with wonder. "But, how do we go inside?"

Fred grinned. "Only your inspirations will enter this hamlet."

As he left the girls to their play, a joyous sound of laughter could be heard from the kitchen.

Fred entered the kitchen to find Eleanor and Scrooge tossing flour at each other. Covered in the ghostly substance, they stopped mid-throw when they saw Fred in the corner of the room just watching them.

"It looks like I have missed the fun."

"Oh no, you are just in time," said Eleanor throwing her handful of powder onto his coat.

The three dodged each other as they continued the activity of dusting the room with flour. The play only changed when Ebby and Fanny entered the kitchen. Watching the adults' commotion, Ebby loudly said, "I thought we were the children."

Having been found out, the three became as still as statues, each of their facial expressions showed the guilt of having played like ruffians. And then, both Eleanor and Fred tossed a handful at each of the girls. The kitchen in no time was turned as white as snow collecting on the top of a frozen lake during a blizzard. Laughter surrounded the entire home with mischief, as all five finally calmed enough to repair the kitchen from the family's frolicking.

Once the work and play finished within the kitchen, Scrooge and the twins returned to the parlor. He sat near the fireplace in the home's most comfortable chair, then promptly fell asleep. The twins played with the fairytale village, both imagining a similar yet unique fable.

As Scrooge relaxed into slumber, his mouth began to open and close with each snore. Competing with the crackling fire, Ebby and Fanny watched in awe as Scrooge's snorts and wheezes began to control the quiet. And then, when Scrooge had his mouth at its widest, Ebby put her first finger inside of it. Quickly she removed it

before he could bite down. The twins laughed with a thrill that no Christmas toy could ever provide. And so, this pleasure became their play. Fingers in and out, one then the other invaded the opening.

Giggles erupted so loudly that Fred investigated. "Girls, do you think that might be disrespectful to your uncle?"

"He doesn't even know."

"That may make it even more impolite."

Fanny, losing focus, yelped when Scrooge bit her.

"He knows now," Fred said, then added, "It is time to get cleaned up for supper."

Both girls ran from the room while Scrooge continued to snore. "Ebenezer, Ebenezer, it's time for dinner." His slumber continued. Squatting next to Scrooge, Fred looked into his uncle's face while gently shaking his shoulder. "Ebenezer, Ebenezer —" Without a response, he grabbed both shoulders, then attempted to bring Scrooge back from sleep.

Finally Scrooge jolted upright. Coughing as he gulped air, he moaned, "I love my sister."

Fred, a little surprised, replied, "Everyone loved mother."

"But I still love her."

"Me too. Me too..." Fred hesitated before saying, "Her death... well at times it is still difficult. But today is a joyous one, with a pair of youth compelled to keep us smiling, and a meal bound to put us to sleep. So what do you say, uncle, shall we partake in the delight?"

Scrooge smiled as he grabbed Fred's helping hand. Eleanor entered carrying the smells of the kitchen along with a bowl full of steamed carrots and potatoes. "Fred, will you help me with the goose?" Both men cheerfully followed, for the air full of flavors controlled the growls in their bellies.

Quickly the parlor with its colorful Christmas tree, blazing fireplace, and countless toys shifted attention toward the feast. Both of the children inspected the food after each bowl was added to the table. With the goose being the last addition, the holiday came forth in celebration.

"Before we begin, a toast to the season," said Fred. "To the New Year... may it bring fewer arguments and extra holidays."

The adults laughed as Scrooge asked, "Barrister problems?" Fred just shook his head back and forth.

"I want to do a toast," said Ebby.

"Then me," insisted Fanny.

A deceptive grin formed on Ebby's face as she spoke. "Mine is to the goose... may he last as long as I can chew, and taste better than he looks."

All but Eleanor laughed as Fanny declared, "Mine is for the Christmas pudding... may its hardness endure the stomach, and its taste find it worthy of swallowing."

"I'm starting to feel a little overlooked here," said Eleanor.

Fred winked then said, "But it is your turn to belittle another, so what say you, Eleanor?"

"In that case, I will toast Uncle Scrooge... may your throwing arm always fall short of its mark, and your generosity forever exceed the volume of your snoring."

The twins pointed to Scrooge as they laughed about their recent antics with the snoring uncle. Scrooge looked upon these intuitive siblings, then announced, "I have the best toast here."

"Well, by all means, Ebenezer, please..." Fred trailed off as he expected Scrooge to begin his toast.

"I raise my glass to the twins... here is to the chaos-makers, laughter-bringers and future Christmas carolers... if they are able to stay in tune."

"I can sing better than Ebby."

"But I can remember the words."

"All right, girls, today is not the day for this kind of trifling."

After the meal the holiday swiftly dwindled. Fred offered the game of Whist as after-dinner fun, but Scrooge instead called for a carriage. As he left, Fred was in the process of moving the fairytale village to the girls' sleeping room.

The bounce of the stagecoach rapidly transformed the fatigued Scrooge's steady breathing into snores. Once parked in front of his Sackville address, the driver had to jump down from his seat, so as to shake the elderly fellow awake. Scrooge gave the man an extra coin for his concern.

Entering his winter home was always a shock, but never a surprise. The chill of the unattended structure numbed the thin man's bones. As the immediate need became heat he remembered the day, especially the frisky twins. While the blaze of the fire lifted soot into the chimney, Scrooge collapsed into his chair. Sleep led to snores, which led to muscle relaxation, which led to the failure of his core. With his chin relaxing on the top of his chest a dusting of flour fell from his collar as his life ended.

"FATHER, I WANT to play more."

"We have had a long day. It's time for bed. Your mum will be here soon, and you know what that means." The girls were beyond nagging, so continued with their pleasure. Within a flurry of activity, they had transformed their village into a farm. Adding their own wooden animals to the scene created an atmosphere so real one could almost smell the dung.

As Fred walked past the mirror in the twin's room, he took note of extra gestures. Facing the mirror, he saw not his own reflection, but instead the vision of Ebenezer Scrooge. "Uncle?"

"Be calm, Fred."

"What do I make of this?"

"I have a request."

"And this is the proper time?"

Scrooge just ignored the ask, then spoke of his priority. "I've given Eleanor two thousand pounds in consols bonds."

"Two THOUSAND quid? How dare you!"

"It seems telling you to be calm is a waste. However, I would like to talk about this — as it has already been done."

Fred exhaled with such a gust that Fanny looked up to investigate her father's angst. Seeing his reflection she cried out, "Look Ebby! Father is starting to look

like Uncle Scrooge." Together they giggled as their frolic endured.

"Fred, you may think I have overstepped here, but I am worried about any harm that could end you."

Fred pulled in more air than he needed before saying, "Eleanor has no knowledge of finances. Women do not have the talent for it. We protect..."

"Rubbish! Humbug! Stop chattering about false tenets."

"But the cult of domesticity..."

"Only created for obedience." Scrooge paused, then asked, "Have you even thought about what would happen to the girls if you died?"

"I have avoided that subject, so it would not be brought into play."

"My good man, preparations are never a waste." Scrooge explained his reasoning for empowering Eleanor without consent. "I've seen too much to avoid this. We who have funds never even glance at the hardships created when the breadwinner falls."

"The Widows Protection Act provides security."

"Eleanor would receive your clothing, but not your house or money. At your death, she would still lack full rights, and the twins... I can't even think about their possible abuses." With a desire to calm tensions, Scrooge finished with, "And then there is the new baby."

"New baby?"

"Again, I have exceeded myself here."

"NEW BABY! That is news I need to think about."

"I heard the name Joise but can't tell if that will bring a boy or a girl."

"To me it doesn't matter."

"But it should, for society will dictate their freedoms at birth." Searching for a continued method of persuasion, Scrooge added, "I can't force you to be mindful. But I have provided as best I can for your family's security, should your demise come too early."

"I should be grateful, but I still feel slighted."

"I haven't the understanding to know if that is due to the fact I acted without consultation, or because you have a need to protect your control."

Breathing out, Fred said, "Both put me in a puny way."

"Yhaah-ae. Yhaah-aee."

Scrooge looked over his shoulder, smiled, then said, "I'm being called. Remember to live in at least kindness."

"Wait... what's happened Unc..."

"Yhaah-ae. Yhaah-aee. Khaac-aaac."

Isle of Transmogrify Glossary

Abyss of Final Transmogrify - A volcano-type hole where the Mogrifications occur. It is the location where most spirits go to transform into Acceptance. Beneath the Mogrification area are cave-like areas which are called the Dens. Also referred to as the Abyss.

Acceptance - The Infinite Consciousness's process of collecting the physical human energy of love. Acceptance is also the name given to the substance that has finished its transformation. Acceptance is a wet iridescent substance that quickly dissipates into every frequency within existence.

Alito's Curse - This is an affliction from which many Condemned Innocent spirits suffer. It emphasizes governmental injustice, and traps the individual into their legal torment.

Baabel - Coss vomit. The lowest flying Coss create a baabel that has a smelly, greasy consistency and is used to lubricate the quartz and lodestone gems that power the area. Without this coolant this area would always be on fire. As a Coss rises to the top of their enclosure, they begin to metamorphosize into the substance called Coss Acceptance. The higher the Coss are located within the apex of the Crater the more luminescent and purified their baabel becomes. A buildup of the purest baabel at the crown of the enclosed area is what dissolves the ceiling just long enough to allow the Coss to fly to the Abyss of Final Transmogrify where their Acceptance is received.

Burst - This is the energy that creates the motion at the Point.

Chute of Decent - This is the method by which spirits enter the Crater of Severed Spirits. Also referred to as the Chute.

Condemned Innocent - This happens when a person has a traumatic unjust death. The travesty of the experience creates, as they are dying, a new super-focused spirit within that individual. This condition will be difficult to repair without direct help from other spirits through the process of their Task Of Outreach.

Consciousness Relocation - This is the process of going from the living to the dead, or from the dead to the living.

Contemplation Chambers - The individual space a spirit lives in at the Plains of Violence. These cells are where the spirit lives in quiet, so they can create their Task of Outreach. Also referred to as the Chambers.

Corridor of Phantoms - The safest path through the Isle of Transmogrify. It is located directly above the Road of Phantoms. Also referred to as the Corridor.

Coss - A 14-winged, 11-eyed spirit that dwells within the Crater of Severed Spirits. These spirits eventually transform into a substance called Coss Acceptance.

Coss Acceptance - The substance Coss turn into that are flying near the top of the Crater of Severed Spirits. It is not pure Acceptance, but very close to it. It is this Earthly human love that the Infinite Consciousness uses in troubled areas of creation.

Crater of Severed Spirits - A pit where those who maim or kill in the name of the Infinite Consciousness are sent. This is the harshest environment within Transmogrify, because it is isolated from the Infinite Consciousness. This area is contained within a membraned bubble, which separates it from the rest of Transmogrify. Also referred to as the Crater.

Cycle of Greed - This is the Mog within Transmogrify where spirits who were greedy are sent. Also referred to as the Cycle.

Dam of Disconnected Parts - A bridge created near the Crater of Severed Spirits that is made from the bones of pulled-apart Crater spirits. Also referred to as the Dam.

Dens - Every Mog has a corresponding Den location. The Dens are located beneath the Mogrification layer at the bottom of the Abyss. The Dens are where spirits finish up the most difficult part of their Mogrification process. Also referred to as the Den.

Drenching - The location on the Road Of Phantoms where newly released Coss vomit their Acceptance onto those waiting for the positive energy. This release of Acceptance helps the mass of Coss to maintain their combined directionality.

Entanglement - The process through which a human separates into their various spirit energies at death.

Fields of Destructive Compulsions - One of the Mogs within Transmogrify where spirits are sent who attempted to control, or harm others through their compulsions. Also referred to as the Fields.

Fire Twirlers - These are energy releases from the Fields of Destructive Compulsions. They are created by the spirits within this area. Fire Twirlers help to release the compulsive energy that brought the spirit to this Mog. Also referred to as Twirlers.

Forest of Burning Trees - This is the power source for the Plains of Violence. It generates the power/heat needed to activate the transformation pits.

Ghost-of-the-Future - From Dickens's original novel.

Infinite Consciousness - Impersonal yet present entity. Creator of universes. Generates love without conditions.

Instant Mogrification - A self-requested or agreed upon procedure where a spirit goes through a quick transmogrification, even when they are not ready for the process. Often the loss of the spirit's life experiences occurs through this process. When this happens, only the original love energy and the single best memory from the spirit is absorbed by the Infinite Consciousness. All other memories are lost. Also referred to as Instant Transmogrification.

Isle of Transmogrify - Scrooge's Christmas Carol afterlife location. Also referred to as Transmogrify.

Mog - A location within Transmogrify where the transformational process starts. There are five locations - Plains of Violence, Cycle of Greed, Fields of Destructive Compulsions, Crater of Severed Spirits and Pool of Broken Spirits.

Mogrification - The process of transforming into Acceptance.

Mogrified Spirit - A spirit that has successfully completed the cleansing process and has transformed into Acceptance. The person's memories still exist after the spirit has successfully completed Transmogrification.

Pit of Anger - One of the pits within the Plains of Violence.

Pit of Dishonesty - One of the pits within the Plains of Violence.

Pit of Physical Harm - One of the pits within the Plains of Violence.

Plains of Violence - Location where violent spirits create their Task of Outreach. Also referred to as the Plains or the Pit.

Point of Visibility - The location where the darkness surrounding the Sanctuary of Innocents breaks into a focused light. Also referred to as the Point.

Pool of Broken Spirits - Location where suicide victims are sent. These spirits sleep while floating upon the pool. Once an individual wakes from this area they separate into their individual spirits, then proceed to the various Mogs so Mogrification can occur. Also referred to as the Pool.

Provenance - The process the Infinite Consciousness uses to create new universes.

Rains of Oblivion - An area between the Plains of Violence and Fields of Destructive Compulsions. No spirit may enter this area without being destroyed. This area is also used by the Infinite Consciousness to contact living humans through dreams, and other mind-altering realities. Also referred to as the Rains.

Road of Phantoms - The original path through the Isle of Transmogrify. It is located directly below the Corridor of Phantoms. Also referred to as the Road.

Sanctuary of Innocents - The location where children and pets go after dying. This area can never be accessed by adult spirits. Laughter from the area can be heard from the Point where the bridge meets the Isle of Transmogrify. The bridge is the method used when children return to their grieving parents. Also referred to as the Sanctuary.

Sandy Sparks - These power the Cycle of Greed.

Spirit Breakage - This is a spirit who has disconnected their own ties to the Infinite Consciousness through their life actions. All the spirits within Crater of Severed Spirits and Pool of Broken Spirits suffer a Spirit Breakage. Neither group can be directly helped by the Infinite Consciousness.

Task of Outreach - This is the work a spirit is required to do before Transmogrification can be achieved. These are tasks spirits create so they can help others within Transmogrify, or those that are still living on Earth. Often they help those they harmed, but not always. They are only required to create a plan that will give them the lessons they need so they can complete their Mogrification. Also referred to as the Task.

Transmoger - A spirit within the Isle of Transmogrify.

Transmogrification - The process of both repairing a spirit, and the completion of the cleansing process into Acceptance. Also referred to as Mogrification.

List of Main Characters - By order of appearance.

Ebenezer Scrooge - The main character.

Jacob Kol Marley - This spirit was Scrooge's business partner, and Noah's brother.

Boz Cratchit - The youngest son of the Cratchit family.

Tim Cratchit - Tiny Tim as a teenager.

Bob Cratchit - Father of the Cratchit family, and business partner to Scrooge.

Fred - Scrooge's nephew.

Fanny or Fan - There are two characters with this name. One is Scrooge's sister and the other is Fred's daughter.

Ebby - Fred's daughter.

Fingal Wills - He works for Scrooge. This character's name has a historical reference.

Peter Nida - He works for Scrooge.

Nancy Albright - Peter Nida's sister.

Elizabeth Albright - Peter Nida's neice.

Humphry Albright - Peter Nida's nephew.

Lieutenant Gilbert Jacob Albright - Peter Nida's brother-in-law, and Nancy's husband. He is the father to Elizabeth and Humphry. Also he is the son of Edward Albright.

Dr. John Snow - The doctor who figured out what causes Cholera. This character has a historical reference. The image in the book of this character is an AI deep fake likeness of the historical person.

Noah Marley - Jacob's brother and Flora's husband.

Mrs. Buckner - Customer of Pressey and Barclay's grocery store. This character has a historical reference.

Mrs. Emily Swinburne - Customer of Pressey and Barclay's grocery store.

Flora Marley - Noah's wife.

Sir Stephen Mackintosh - Youth that helps Noah up after he fell on the ice.

Joan - Flora's sister.

Bartholomew Pressey - Owner of the grocery store Noah and Jacob work at.

The Magistrate - The man who runs Newgate prison.

James Maxey - The man that murdered his wife and stepdaughter. This character has a historical reference.

Nathan Simons - This man was sent to jail for stealing. This character has a historical reference.

Dinah Smith (Dee) - Black woman in Newgate prison. She is one of Noah's friends.

Joseph Freeman - Teenage boy caught for being a pickpocket. Henry is his cousin. He is one of Noah's friends.

Martha Hart - A prostitute in Newgate prison. She is one of Noah's friends.

Henry Freeman - Pre-teen caught for being a pickpocket. Joseph is his cousin. He is one of Noah's friends.

The Prison Guard - The man who helps Noah.

Matthew Pepin - Owner of the horse stables where a young Jacob worked. This character's name has a family historical reference.

Honorable Judge William Domville - The presiding judge at Old Bailey courthouse. This character has a historical reference. The image in the book of this character is an AI deep fake likeness of the historical person.

Ephraim Weedon - The person Joseph stole from.

Hannah Denhous - Dee stole her coat.

Katharine Fitzgerald, Ruby Ann Marr, Mary Egdurb - Three women accused of stealing.

Benjamin Bluck - Store owner who accused the three women of theft.

Franklin Paxton - Owner of the sheep that Nathan Simons killed.

Laurence Brand - Henry stole his watch.

Master Punisher - The man who carries out Dee's whipping.

Home Secretary Honorable Addington - The Home Secretary. This character has a historical reference. The image in the book of this character is an AI deep fake likeness of the historical person.

Auntie Arleen - Joseph's mum.

Jimmy - Henry's older brother.

Edward Albright - Father of Lieutenant Gilbert Jacob Albright.

Teint - The angel that guards the Isle of Transmogrify.

Apurto - The caretaker of the Isle of Transmogrify. He is fashioned after the Tasmanian tiger.

Navalny Zelenskyy - Legless spirit that helps Scrooge get across the Chute. He is a Condemned Innocent spirit. This character's name has a current event reference.

Michael Faraday - Scientist of electricity. This character has a historical reference. The image in the book of this character is an AI deep fake likeness of the historical person.

Eleanor - Fred's wife.

Isle of Transmogrify White Paper

(Please Note: Words that are between single quotes are defined within the glossary.)

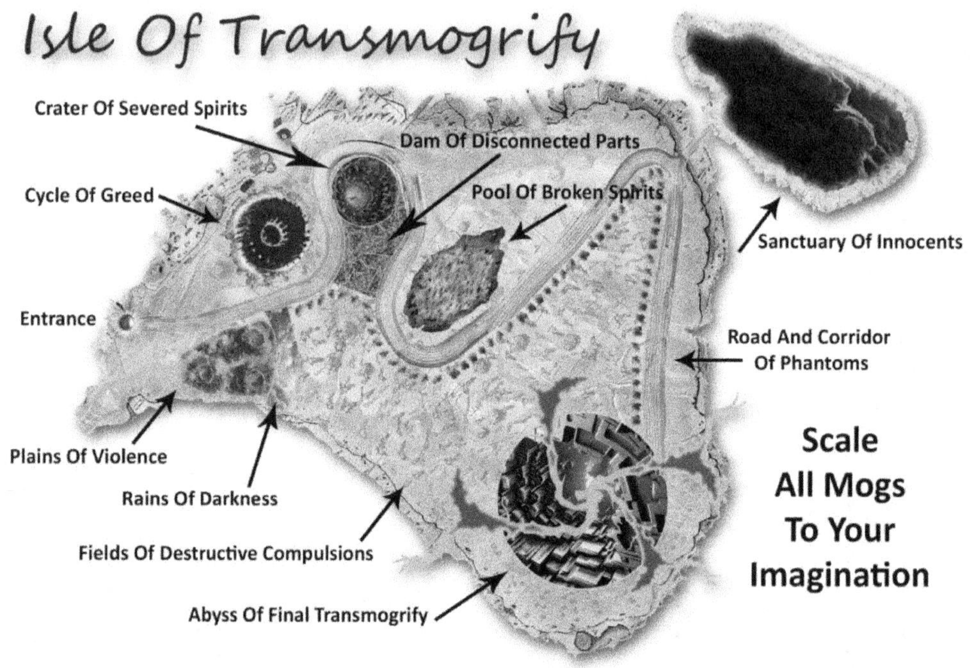

A General Overview

The afterlife within Scrooge's Christmas Carol is called the 'Isle of Transmogrify'. It is controlled by the 'Infinite Consciousness', which is also the creator of universes. The 'Infinite Consciousness' has a name which is sung constantly throughout the cosmos, yet humans were not born with ears that are able to hear it, so only the title of 'Infinite Consciousness' is known by humans. The main function of 'Transmogrify' is to convert human love into usable energy called 'Acceptance'. Once the harmful experiences of a person's life have been rehabilitated, the remaining love energy is then collected and used to seed new planets. Human love experiences aid in the development of new worlds by providing examples of how to overcome harsh circumstances, strengthen free will and create solutions to problems.

At birth each individual is created with at least three spirits which are the mother, father and 'Infinite Consciousness' energies. Each person develops and sheds new spirits as they acquire experiences within life. At death each spirit is separated from the person through a process called 'Entanglement'. Each spirit then goes to their corresponding area within the upper portion of 'Transmogrify'. The purpose of 'Transmogrify' is to provide an environment where spirits can concentrate on and then transform their life experiences into 'Acceptance'.

The ultimate objective of 'Transmogrify' is to collect the experience-filled love. Many spirits are without harm and need only go through the 'Entanglement' process before they become 'Acceptance'. Other spirits will have to spend time in 'Transmogrify' repairing their injuries and harms. Only those in the 'Crater of Severed Spirits' are at risk of never completing 'Transmogrification'. Once the harmful habits and events of a person's life are cleansed from the spirit, the remaining love energy transforms into 'Acceptance'. 'Acceptance' is the physical energy of love. The odor of 'Acceptance' is unique to each spirit, but brings the most pleasant smell the individual has ever encountered.

The value of human love energy to the 'Infinite Consciousness' is crucial, for it retains the experiences of the individual. This makes their love valuable to the survival of a new planet. Even though love originates from the 'Infinite Consciousness', the creator can not bring forth the same elements of animal survival that a person may have developed during their lifetime. It is these personal experiences that allow new planets to quickly develop into beneficial societies.

The entrance of 'Transmogrify' is guarded by the angel Teint, and the defender, or caretaker, Apurto. Teint tracks every spirit that enters and leaves 'Transmogrify'. Apurto is responsible for the safety of both the spirits and for keeping both the 'Road of Phantoms' and 'Corridor of Phantoms' clear of obstructions. Apurto is also Teint's pet. Most spirits within 'Transmogrify' think Teint and Apurto may be twin spirits. They communicate through thought and touch.

There are three basic levels within 'Transmogrify'. The upper level has five areas of cleansing called 'Mogs'. These locations are where spirits analyze their own life experiences, and then both create and act upon their 'Task of Outreach' so they can be transformed into 'Acceptance'.

The upper areas do not administer pain of any kind to the spirits. This level is only for contemplating the errors made, and for figuring out how to repair the injuries they caused during life. Each spirit within the upper level creates a 'Task of Outreach'. The 'Task' must be devised before the spirit can move into the lower level of 'Transmogrify'. However, each spirit will need to overcome their 'Dens' before their 'Task' is acted upon.

The lower level of 'Transmogrify' is called the 'Abyss of Final Transmogrify'. This is where the 'Transmogrification' process is completed and 'Acceptance' is achieved. Beneath the lower level of 'Abyss of Final Transmogrify' is an area called the 'Dens', and it is where the harshest realizations from the individual's life events are worked through. Once a spirit revisits their worst Earthly mistakes within the 'Dens', they then must complete their 'Task of Outreach' before they can become a 'Mogrified Spirit'.

Road of Phantoms and Corridor of Phantoms

This is the pathway spirits use to move in and out of 'Transmogrify' so as to achieve their 'Task of Outreach'. Although its foundation is the 'Road', the spirits always move above the 'Road' on the 'Corridor'. This allows them the ability to avoid the 'Chute of Descent' which can inadvertently pull a spirit into the 'Crater of Severed Spirits', causing them to become trapped within that area. Once trapped, freedom from the 'Crater' can only be achieved when Apurto brings them back to the 'Road'. The 'Corridor' has become the main avenue of travel for spirits.

The Power Sources Within Transmogrify

There are two basic reasons each 'Mog' within 'Transmogrify' needs a power source. The most obvious reason being to supply the energy needed to run the functions within the 'Mog'. The second benefit of a power source is that the sparks from each 'Mog', when in contact with a spirit, lend physical sensations to them. At death all spirits, except those who are in the 'Fields of Destructive Compulsions', lose their sensation of touch. However, physical sensations are required so the spirit can learn by feeling the results of their own actions. Each 'Mog' is powered by its own source of energy, for each area's spirits have different requirements for the development of their 'Task of Outreach'.

Plains of Violence

This area's power source is the 'Forest of Burning Trees' that surrounds each pit. These trees are only on fire up the inside-center of the tree. Branches and leaves of the trees are never burned, which makes these trees an ever-burning forest. The energy required to burn the trees is provided directly from the 'Infinite Consciousness'. This and the 'Abyss of Final Transmogrify' are the only two areas where the energy needed is provided by the 'Infinite Consciousness'. All other 'Mogs' are powered by the spirits themselves.

When a spirit has a violent nature, a quiet environment is provided to the spirit by placing them in one of the 'Contemplation Chambers'. Years of reflection will be required before these spirits are ready to enter a transformational pit. For this reason all power is provided to the 'Plains of Violence'. The 'Plains of Violence' is a difficult 'Mog' from which to get released. For this reason the 'Infinite Consciousness' understands the spirits will need all of their own power to effect their release to the 'Abyss of Final Transmogrify' and the 'Dens'.

Upon death a spirit within the 'Plains of Violence' is cocooned within a 'Contemplation Chamber'. Few sparks can penetrate these 'Chambers', so self-awareness through physicality is not possible. This lack of feeling causes the spirits within the 'Plains of Violence' to spend extra time in the transformational process. Many of the spirits, once delivered to the 'Abyss of Final Transmogrify', visit the 'Chambers' as part of their 'Task of Outreach'. These visitations are needed to provide a calming effect to the confined spirits.

Cycle of Greed

Spirits in this 'Mog' stand on a steel wheel. Each spirit walks in a circle on this wheel which causes it to move around a platform made of flint. As the metal grinds over the stone, sparks fly in all directions which powers the 'Mog'.

Rains of Oblivion

The 'Rains of Oblivion' has a dual purpose within 'Transmogrify'. First, this is a narrow area that is used to create a barrier between the 'Fields of Destructive Compulsions' and the 'Plains of Violence'. The water and light created within this ever-downpour of current is powered by the 'Infinite Consciousness'. Most spirits that enter this area are destroyed. For this reason spirits go out of their way to avoid being splashed by the 'Rains'. This barrier is required in order to keep the 'Fire Twirlers' out of the 'Plains of Violence'.

The more important usage for this area is to provide an entrance for living humans to visit 'Transmogrify' by way of dreams, near-death experiences, hallucinations and other mind-altering events. Again the 'Infinite Consciousness' powers the environment needed for such human contact. Often a person feels blessed by their visit to 'Transmogrify', but sometimes they are given reason to fear their possible future.

Crater Of Severed Spirits

Because the spirits within this 'Mog' have cut their own connection to the 'Infinite Consciousness' they are then left to secure their release from the 'Crater' alone. Whenever the connection to the 'Infinite Consciousness' has been cut it is called a 'Spirit Breakage'. For this reason the power source for this 'Mog' is generated by the spirits themselves. The quartz and lodestones that line the 'Crater' generate sparks when forced together. Each spirit has the task of climbing the walls of the 'Crater' so they can reach the ledge where 'Mogrification' takes place. As they push the stones around by climbing on them sparks are generated — so many sparks the area would quickly overheat if the 'Coss' did not cool and lubricate the stones with their 'Baabel'.

Spirits in this area are the only ones who suffer pain which occurs when sparks strike them. As spirits climb the 'Crater' these sparks help to reacquaint each with the memories of their crimes. Pain becomes their best method for understanding the anguish they have caused to both other people and the 'Infinite Consciousness'. The 'Infinite Consciousness' feels sorrow for those within the 'Crater'. In order to create a non-attended-to environment where the majority do gain 'Transmogrification', a few spirits will unfortunately suffer permanent loss through the process. Not all spirits from this 'Mog' will become a 'Mogrified Spirit'. Some spirits will have their existence permanently changed when a group of 'Coss' are released. Through the force of lift that is created when 'Coss' free themselves, the spirits beneath the 'Coss' become disassembled and are then pulled upward out of the 'Crater'.

Most of the spirits will reassemble when they fall back into the 'Crater'. However with some their limbs, backbone, or head is cast out of the 'Crater'. When this happens many of the parts are lost. A spirit can still transform into a 'Coss' with missing limbs, but the loss of a backbone or head marks the end of the spirit. All heads pushed out in the direction of the entrance will attempt to escape 'Transmogrify'. Apurto has been tasked with stopping them, so when inundated with heads he eats them. Otherwise Apurto puts them in his pouch and returns them to the 'Crater'. Most other limbs drop near and around the 'Crater'. This is the method that formed the 'Dam of Disconnected Parts'. Often other spirits travelling to and from the 'Abyss' find parts lying on the 'Road'. Most spirits will make the special effort to return them by way of the 'Chute of Descent'.

When 'Coss' are released from the 'Crater of Severed Spirits' they fly to the 'Abyss of Final Transmogrify'. In route to the 'Abyss' their 'Coss' body transforms into a 'Mogrified Spirit' and becomes 'Coss Acceptance'. As a liquid they travel directly to the 'Infinite Consciousness' power source of pure 'Acceptance'. Hence spirits within the 'Crater' never spend any time in the 'Abyss of Final Transmogrify'. Instead they are directly absorbed into 'Acceptance'.

Pool of Broken Spirits

The power source for the 'Pool of Broken Spirits' is also generated by the spirits which sleep within the 'Pool'. When they committed suicide they cut their connection to the 'Infinite Consciousness', which creates a 'Spirit Breakage'. Spirits within the 'Pool' are constantly having dreams of their last moments on earth. Their salty tears provide this area's power. Sticking straight up out of the 'Pool' are several metal rods which create the connectivity needed to generate power. The spirits here are in a comatose state. They have no awareness they exist in 'Transmogrify'. Once they awaken, their various spirits immediately begin to go through the process of 'Entanglement' so they can be directed to the proper 'Mog' where 'Transmogrification' will begin.

Fields of Destructive Compulsions

This 'Mog' has no built-in power source. At death these spirits are still physically charged. Because of this they retain the touch sensations associated with their compulsion. Although there are countless numbers of compulsions a human can develop, all have an element of touch. It is these physical sensations that bind the spirit to their compulsion. Spirits within the 'Fields of Destructive Compulsions' need to transform their physical desires so 'Mogrification' can occur. In order to do this they channel destructive sensations into 'Fire Twirlers'. It is these 'Fire Twirlers' that power the 'Mog'. However, far more of these spinning and hopping flames are produced than the 'Mog' needs. Extra 'Fire Twirlers' move freely throughout this 'Mog'.

Abyss of Final Transmogrify

The power source for this area is generated by the 'Infinite Consciousness'. No spirit will ever know if all, or even part, of the 'Infinite Consciousness' dwells within Earth's 'Transmogrify'. The 'Acceptance' which is collected at the bottom of the 'Abyss of Final Transmogrify' is generated by both spirits and the 'Infinite

Consciousness'. When a spirit within this area finally achieves 'Transmogrification', a blue lightning bolt transforms the spirit into 'Acceptance'.

Five Upper Mogs of Transmogrify

Plains of Violence

The first area within 'Transmogrify' is called the 'Plains of Violence'. There are three pits of focus within this area: 'Pit of Anger', 'Pit of Dishonesty', and 'Pit of Physical Harm'. Outside each pit is a line of spirits. Each spirit is self-contained within their own private sound-proof space called a 'Contemplation Chamber'.

Within their 'Chamber' these spirits dwell in low light with relaxing music. Each is tasked with understanding the harm they caused.

Spirits that have injured others in ways that would require work in more than one pit are only sent to the pit where the most severe act was orchestrated. From there they will work on all of their violent actions. After understanding all the harms they spawned, the spirit must then create a plan for repairing the damage. This plan is called the 'Task of Outreach'.

Each pit's line of 'Contemplation Chambers' is of a length that is undetermined. It takes between 10 and 100 years to arrive at the pit. Once a spirit arrives at the pit, if they have not finished creating their 'Task of Outreach' they are sent to the back of the line and must wait another 10 to 100 years to reach the pit again. This returning to the back of the line is only ended when the spirit has both reached the front of the line, and decided upon their 'Task of Outreach'. At this point they enter the pit and are then instantly relocated to the 'Dens'. The 'Plains of Violence' are powered by the 'Forest of Burning Trees'. Surrounding each pit are trees burning only up the inside-center of the trunk. These fires are ever-blazing and heat each pit to its transformation temperature.

Cycle of Greed

The 'Cycle of Greed' has those who only care about money walking in a circle with all heads turned to view the golden crown at its center. The metal circle the spirits walk on is made of steel. As spirits cause the steel to rotate over a platform of flint, sparks generate the power needed so that there is enough time for creating their 'Task of Outreach'. This transformation occurs when a spirit turns its head away from the golden crown at the disk's center. This turning from the golden center can only happen after the spirit has created its 'Task of Outreach'. In the 'Abyss of Final Transmogrify' and the 'Dens' these spirits are again tempted with wealth. Generosity is often the focus of their 'Task of Outreach'. Because of the grinding of metal to stone this area is the noisiest 'Mog' within 'Transmogrify'.

Scale To Your Imagination

Rains of Oblivion

This area has two functions. First, it is a barrier between the 'Plains of Violence' and 'Fields of Destructive Compulsions'. No spirit can get wet by this moisture and survive. Apurto and all 'Mogrified Spirits' are the only entities in 'Transmogrify' which can enter the 'Rains of Oblivion' without being harmed. This narrow area keeps spirits from crossing into a 'Mog' where they do not belong. Second, this area is also used by the 'Infinite Consciousness' so it can communicate with living humans through dreams, near death experiences, hallucinations and other mind-altering realities.

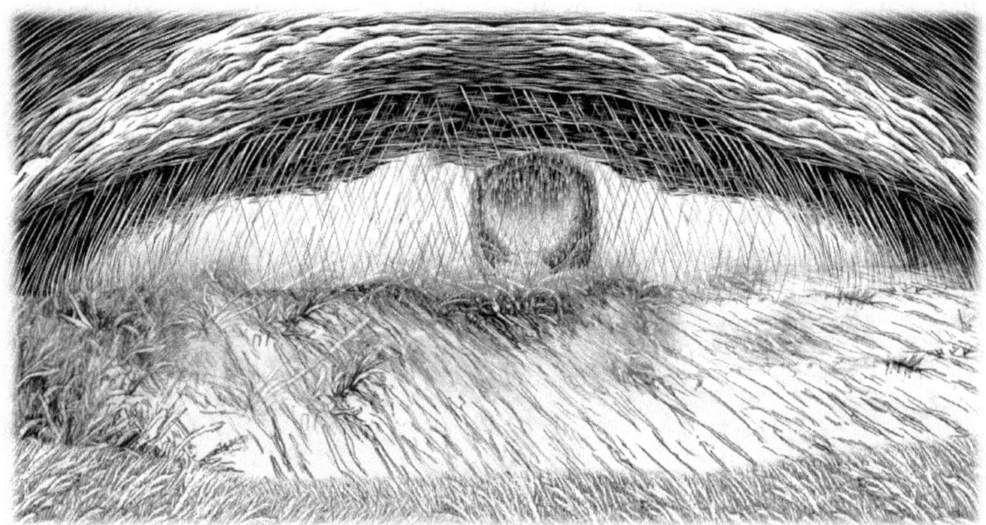

Crater of Severed Spirits

This area is unique to all other areas of 'Transmogrify' within the universe, for no other planet has developed in a way that harms the 'Infinite Consciousness' the way humans do. The 'Crater of Severed Spirits' is contained within a soft, yet nearly indestructible membrane. The general shape of the 'Mog' is like an upside-down egg with the round end being the apex of the enclosure. It is the only 'Mog' that is totally separated from the other 'Mogs'. The 'Crater of Severed Spirits' creates the only situation within 'Transmogrify' that both allows for the destruction of spirits, yet was constructed in such a way as to help the spirits achieve 'Mogrification' without direct assistance from the 'Infinite Consciousness'.

Scale To Your Imagination

The outcome of each spirit's destiny is never predetermined. Instead elements of survival-of-the-fittest within the 'Crater of Severed Spirits' cause difficulties. Once 'Transmogrification' is reached by a spirit their 'Acceptance' becomes the most valued love the 'Infinite Consciousness' uses for the work of 'Provenance'... creation. A little of this love, called 'Coss Acceptance', goes a long way to seed even the largest planet. 'Coss Acceptance' is also helpful in the most troubled areas of the universe. This is the gold of human love, but it comes at an overwhelming misery for humanity in the way of the violence created from one human to another. This is the result of humans believing they were given the same powers that only the 'Infinite Consciousness' possesses.

The 'Crater of Severed Spirits' is filled with the spirits of people who have maimed and killed in the name of the 'Infinite Consciousness'. Even to verbally condemn another by taking over the power of the 'Infinite Consciousness' will require that spirit to spend additional time in a 'Mog' in order to remove that encroachment upon the 'Infinite Consciousness'. However, it is violence that condemns a spirit to the 'Crater'. When a person physically harms another thinking they have the virtue of the 'Infinite Consciousness' backing them, then that act of harm immediately cuts off their own love relationship to the 'Infinite Consciousness'. For no being created by the creator is allowed to usurp its power. The process of disconnection from the 'Infinite Consciousness' is called a 'Spirit Breakage'.

Because of these individuals' 'Spirit Breakage' the 'Infinite Consciousness' can not help them through 'Transmogrify'. The 'Infinite Consciousness' loves these spirits no less, but its ability to help is taken away by the human itself. Even though the 'Infinite Consciousness' can not help, it has set up the 'Crater of Severed Spirits' so it can aid in the 'Transmogrification' of these spirits, but each spirit is on their own to achieve release.

The 'Crater of Severed Spirits' is located after the 'Dam of Disconnected Parts'. The 'Dam of Disconnected Parts' is a pathway that bypasses the 'Crater'. This 'Dam' is comprised entirely of the limbs from spirits that have been thrust out of the 'Crater of Severed Spirits' which happens at each release of 'Coss Acceptance'. Some spirits who dwell within the 'Abyss of Final Transmogrify' use the 'Dam of Disconnected Parts' to avoid the 'Crater of Severed Spirits'. The 'Chute of Descent' is a suction device that is used to bring spirits into the 'Crater'. Spirits that do not belong in the 'Crater' have a fear of the 'Chute of Descent', and use the 'Corridor' to bypass the 'Chute'. All spirits dislike the smell of the 'Baabel' created by the newly formed 'Coss'.

Spirits from other 'Mogs' have been inadvertently pulled into the 'Crater' when passing through the 'Chute' as new spirits are arriving. For this reason most spirits fly above the 'Chute' in order to avoid the force created by the entering spirits. However at times the accident of being pulled into the 'Crater' traps a spirit within that area until Apurto is sent to rescue them. Apurto is the only creature in 'Transmogrify' that can tolerate the suction of the 'Chute' and the heat from the sparking stones.

The valley that houses the 'Crater' is in a crevice deeper than sight can view. The sides of the 'Crater' are filled with one-to three-inch quartz and lodestone rocks. On the 'Road', near the middle of the 'Crater', is the 'Chute of Descent'. This is how spirits arrive to the 'Crater'. The 'Chute' can not be used to exit through. The suction of the 'Chute' will always pull the spirit back into the deep center of the 'Crater'. The thrust back into the center seems harsh, yet is only the mechanics of the 'Mog', so its actions are without malice.

Spirits within the 'Crater of Severed Spirits' are tasked to climb the rocky sides of the enclosure. The sparks created by the climbers activate the self-understanding they will need for their redemption. As their burdens are lifted, the climb becomes easier. Upon reaching the crest of the 'Crater' each spirit transforms from their ghostly human appearance into an 11-eyed, 14-winged creature called the 'Coss'.

When a spirit reaches the crest of the 'Crater' they stand upon its ledge, lift their head toward the 'Coss' above them, widen their stance and then begin to slowly wave their arms up and down. This motion begins the transformational process into a 'Coss'. Once their wings have developed they begin to rise and fly to join the other 'Coss'.

Even though the spirit has transformed into a 'Coss' they will often lock wings with other 'Coss' to help maintain their height near the top of the enclosure. As 'Coss' are pushed upward with each new addition to their ranks, the uppermost 'Coss' start to come in contact with the 'Crater' ceiling. This contact begins the metamorphosis needed for the upper 'Coss' to transform into 'Coss Acceptance'. It is the 'Coss Acceptance' that temporarily dissolves the 'Crater' ceiling. The opening of the ceiling then allows their release to the 'Infinite Consciousness' 'Acceptance' en masse.

Within the 'Crater' all 'Coss' spit up a stomach fluid called 'Baabel'. This 'Baabel' is sprayed all over the spirits climbing beneath the 'Coss'. The release of

'Coss' vomit creates lift within them so they can continue to rise. 'Baabel' is what creates the area's odors, both pleasant and nauseating. The location of each individual 'Coss' within their hovering group is what determines the type of 'Baabel' that is vomited. As a 'Coss' rises toward the ceiling of the 'Crater' the more refreshing their 'Baabel' becomes. The lower, or newly transformed 'Coss' emit an oily, foul-smelling 'Baabel'.

However this 'Baabel' has the greatest benefit for the spirits climbing the quartz and lodestone walls because it cools the 'Crater' stones, which reduces the area's heat. The higher 'Coss' 'Baabel' has two main functions. First, it helps to inspire the spirits so they will continue their climb; and second, upon release from the 'Crater' it helps to purify the newly arrived 'Coss' so that they quickly transform into 'Coss Acceptance'.

So as the 'Coss' move closer to the ceiling their 'Baabel' is converted from an oily stench into a silky cleansing substance that encompasses an inspirational feel and aroma. Those closest to the top spew 'Coss Acceptance' which is just under the purity of the 'Infinite Consciousness' 'Acceptance'. Its smell is the most pleasant odor a spirit will ever experience. When this falls upon the spirits they rejoice and stay motivated to toil toward the crest's ledge where they will transform into a 'Coss'.

The 'Baabel' generated by the youngest 'Coss' is greasy and smells like the worst odor in existence. This 'Baabel' is also motivating, for the spirits splashed with it try to remove the 'Baabel' as quickly as possible, which propels them toward the crest of the 'Crater' where 'Transmogrification' is achieved. This greasy, stinky 'Baabel' is the only lubricant the stones have that keeps the spirits from being set aflame. And yet, at the bottom of the 'Crater', the combined 'Baabel' of both the immature and mature 'Coss' is what keeps the 'Lake of Flames' lit.

As a group of 'Coss' achieve release from the 'Crater', the upward force of their discharge causes the climbing spirits closest to the crest to become disassembled into components. Often skulls, backbones and limbs are cared upward and out of the 'Crater' before the ceiling self-heals. Whereas a spirit that has lost limbs can still complete 'Transmogrification', the loss of a head or backbone leaves the spirit too helpless to continue the climb toward the crest where the transformation into a 'Coss' occurs.

The release of body parts that have the good fortune to drop onto the 'Road of Phantoms' will often be returned to the 'Crater' by spirits that are travelling to and from the 'Abyss'. Limbs that land on the 'Dam of Disconnected Parts' become interlinked with the older parts as they grab and hold on to the new parts.

Within the 'Dam of Disconnected Parts' the arms, legs and spines cast into this area create the same type of membrane that encases the spirits in the 'Crater'. This membrane creates an ultra-thin canopy which is not detectable by the spirits travelling the 'Road' or 'Corridor'. The canopy keeps the bones from migrating onto the 'Road'.

The skulls of the fragmented spirits often attempt escape through the main entrance of 'Transmogrify'. Apurto is tasked with the duty of preventing their escape. He will return up to 13 heads by packing them into a large pouch on his belly, then releasing them back to the 'Crater' by way of the 'Chute'. Unfortunately, if overrun by more than 13 heads, Apurto then begins to eat them. Once a spirit has lost its head it can never be mended, which ends its possibility for 'Transmogrification'.

These fragmented spirits still exist, but their only form of 'Mogrification' is to ask for 'Instant Mogrification'. This process will release back to the 'Infinite Consciousness' its own love component. The majority of other energies and memories from this spirit are often lost. 'Instant Mogrification' is only applied to spirits who ask for it. But for these severed spirits the ending of their existance is preferred. Any spirit can at any time request 'Instant Mogrification', but few other than those in the 'Crater of Severed Spirits' request it.

The 'Crater of Severed Spirits' is powered by the spirits themselves. As they climb the 'Crater' wall the quartz and lodestone rocks' sparks are generated, which sustains the area. The membrane that encases the spirits is also generated by the climbing spirits.

The 'Lake of Flames' is located at the bottom of the 'Crater'. It is constantly ablaze as the excess 'Baabel' flows into this area and collects into a deep fiery pool. The 'Lake of Flames' is the harshes part of the 'Crater'. It can trap spirits beneath the lake's surface, making it nearly impossible for the spirit to rise above it.

Pool of Broken Spirits

Of all the locations within 'Transmogrify', this area has a palpable feeling of sadness within it, for it is powered by tears from the sleeping spirits. Located directly across from the 'Dam of Disconnected Parts', an eerie silence fills the void of motion within the 'Pool of Broken Spirits'.

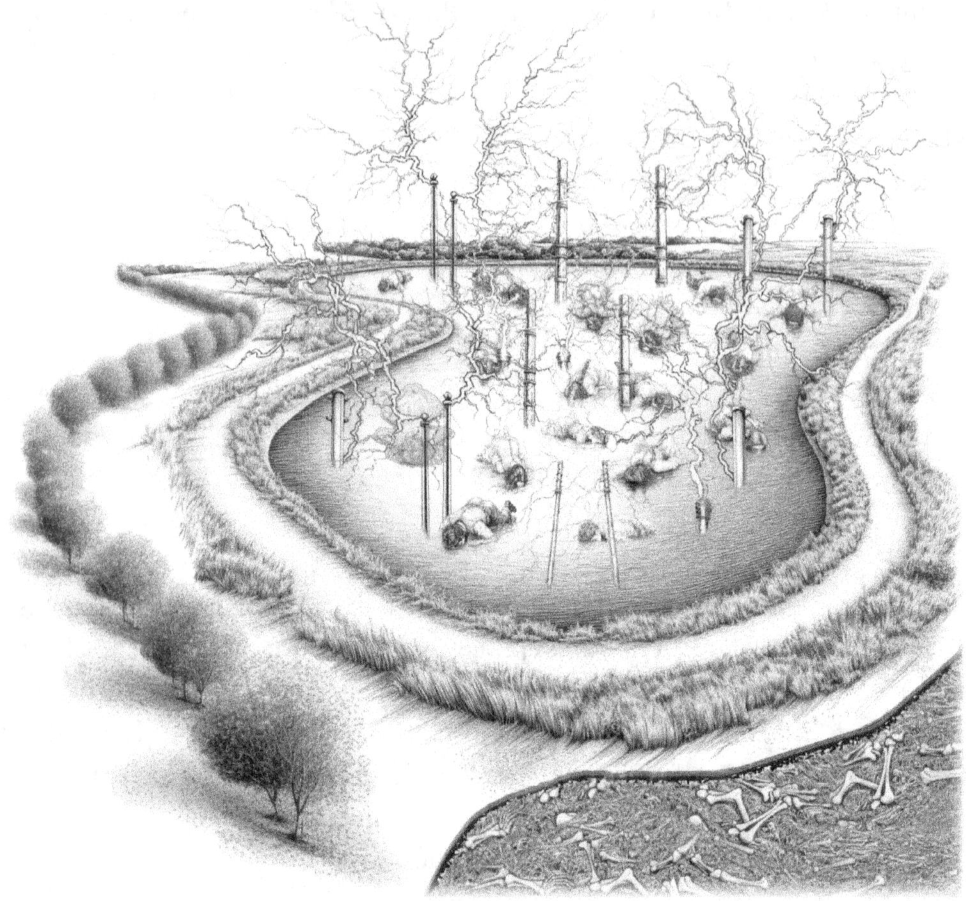

Scale To Your Imagination

Just like the spirits within the 'Crater of Severed Spirits' the 'Infinite Consciousness' can not help these spirits to awaken from the 'Pool'. Their rejection of life, by killing themselves, disconnects them from the 'Infinite Consciousness', which results in a 'Spirit Breakage'. All spirits within this area are caught up in their own last experience on earth. They sleep and dream of their death over and over. As the slumbering spirits within the bluish-white fluid gently bob along the surface, tears of sorrow flow from each spirit. Their tears provide the salt needed to power this area. The abundance of tears allows each spirit to waken in its own time. This is the main help the 'Infinite Consciousness' can give to these spirits, the wealth of time.

Though the 'Infinite Consciousness' can not directly help those that sleep, it did provide help in the way it designed the location of the 'Mogs'. The 'Coss' are tasked with flying directly over the 'Pool' in such a way that they always release some of their 'Coss Acceptance' onto the slumbering spirits. The release creates lift so the group can continue to the 'Abyss'. This powerful 'Acceptance' more often than not awakens the spirit it lands upon, but not always.

Some spirits can become trapped within their own sorrow and will refuse the help that 'Coss Acceptance' provides. In these cases the 'Acceptance' becomes hardened to them. Often the splash of a new spirit entering into the 'Pool' will revive nearby spirits. Once an individual rises from the 'Pool', the various spirits within the individual are freed through the process of 'Entanglement', so they can continue their process of 'Transmogrification'.

Fields of Destructive Compulsions

This area is located next to the 'Rains of Oblivion', and across the 'Road' from the 'Pool of Broken Spirits'. It includes spirits who have made harmful compulsions out of things that are normally controllable, such as eating, sex, laziness, etc. This area is the largest within 'Transmogrify' and is powered by 'Fire Twirlers'. The spirits in this area are known for their hermit-like attitude as a group.

'Fire Twirlers' are created by the spirits themselves. Spirits in the 'Fields of Destructive Compulsions' retain some ability for physical sensation at death. This happens because of their extreme focus on their physical habits. These physical passions within them must be tamed before they are allowed travel to the 'Abyss of Final Transmogrify' where they will then enter the 'Den' of their need.

The entire area of 'Fields of Destructive Compulsions' is covered in 'Fire Twirlers' which pop up, then quickly burn out as the spirit's habit is cleansed. Each spirit may have to release several 'Fire Twirlers' before their compulsion fades. Considering 'Fire Twirlers' are merely an energy force, they appear to be both curious and shy. Other spirits often capture them so they can manipulate their own physical energy through the 'Fire Twirlers' power. When 'Fire Twirlers' burn out, their ending helps to free the spirit that released it. Since this area is filled with spirits who harmed through excess, their 'Task of Outreach' always requires some form of abstinence.

Sanctuary of Innocents

This 'Mog' is actually another island which is attached by a bridge to the 'Isle of Transmogrify' at a location called the 'Point of Visibility'. Except for two focused lights, that shines upon the 'Point', the entire area is shrouded in a darkness that absorbs light. This umbra of shade protects the children and pets that live at the 'Sanctuary'. The bridge is used to reunite parents with their lost children, and has an escalator quality in that it travels much faster toward 'Transmogrify' than it does toward the 'Sanctuary'. This makes it impossible for adult spirits to enter the 'Sanctuary of Innocents'.

The Lower Levels of Transmogrify

Abyss of Final Transmogrify

The 'Abyss of Final Transmogrify' is located at the end of the 'Road' and 'Corridor of Phantoms'. It is a huge circular hole where blue lightning bolts flash and crash every few minutes. After a spirit finishes their work in the upper level of 'Transmogrify' they are then sent to the corresponding area of focus within the lower level of the 'Dens', which is below the 'Abyss of Final Transmogrify'. Most of the upper area of 'Transmogrify' is fixated on providing the environment needed for generating solutions to the problems the spirit created in life.

The lowest level, the 'Dens', brings a deeper empathy to the spirit about the harm they caused to themselves or others. The 'Dens' which are beneath the base of the 'Abyss' is the most unpleasant area of 'Transmogrify'. For by the time a spirit reaches the 'Abyss' they will have gained enough inner strength to experience the pain they inflicted while alive.

Within the 'Dens' all pain is administered by the spirit to their own spirit. Each spirit is required to inflict the injuries they caused upon others during their life to themselves. If they kill, they will be killed by their own self. If they steal they will eliminate their own possessions. This can be frightening for the spirit, for the act of watching themselves harm themselves provides a deeper understanding to their original actions. Once they gain the required insight the spirit is then placed with others who have done the same harms. Here they learn to resist the peer pressure that causes decent people to do hideous acts.

After the needed empathy is created within the spirit they are then tasked to either return to the earth, or travel within 'Transmogrify'. It is then their duty to carry out their 'Task of Outreach'. Once the 'Task of Outreach' has been accomplished the spirit then returns to the base of the 'Abyss of Final Transmogrify' where 'Transmogrification' is achieved. Each time a spirit achieves 'Transmogrification', a lightning bolt transforms them into 'Acceptance'.

Dens

There is a 'Den' for every upper 'Mog'. These are cave-like rooms where a spirit, or group of spirits, works through their life's harshest issues. The 'Den' is where the most difficult and painful work of transformation is accomplished. From the 'Den' each spirit directly reenters the 'Road', so they can fulfill their 'Task of Outreach'.

About the Author

It is hard to talk about one's self unless you're a politician; then it is part of the job. For that reason, this is the last page, and it is just a formality. I'm happy staying unknown in the minds of others. However, I should explain a few things about my process of getting this book published. Writing a novel has always been at the top of my 'bucket list', and I was tasked, as are many others, to bring forth knowledge about the energy of love when I was 21. I didn't understand that assignment at the time, but I always took it more seriously than anything else in my life. So because I wanted to tell a great yarn and needed to fulfill my life's duty, I decided to combine the two tasks into one.

And then the question becomes, why write a sequel to *A Christmas Carol*? I just always knew that Jacob Marley would have been rewarded for helping Ebenezer overcome his greed, and I felt the need to amend his outcome. Although half of this story takes place in the afterlife, the concepts within that location are meant to provide the reader with insights into living a compassionate life.

Now a bit about who I have been. I'm actually kind of boring as a person, for I'm all in my head and like to observe rather than participate. I was born and raised in Montana. My first profession was as a carpenter, and then I owned a video store. After movies went online, I became a non-fiction writer, graphic designer, and finally a health aide for people with dementia. I have enjoyed all of these professions but liked the interactions and protective qualities I could provide for the dementia folks.

However, my life is not about my "jobs". My real work has been in the way of nature walks, art projects, gardening, creating inventions and learning. As far as other thoughts about myself, um… nope, but maybe more through personal conversations…

C Pippin Lowe

Contact Pippin at: <u>apurto@myyahoo.com</u> In order to get a reply back the subject line must contain the word Apurto within it. Emails that have an attachment will be deleted rather than opened. I answer emails in accordance to the importance of the communication that was sent, and my availability of time. However, I will try my best to respond.

Visit the bonus page at:
https://sites.google.com/view/scrooge-christmas-carol/home